MARTIN WEITZ

The ELENA TEXT

Book One in THE MOSES FRANK TRILOGY

A FREEWHEEL BOOKS PUBLICATION

THE ELENA TEXT

Book One in The Moses Frank Trilogy

www.theelenatext.net

www.freewheelbooks.com

Originally published in the UK by Freewheel Books in 2016.

Cover Design by James Willis, Spiffing Covers

For details of the publication dates of Books 2 and 3 in The Moses Frank Trilogy and to sign up to The Elena Text newsletter please visit the Freewheel Books website.
www.freewheelbooks.com

For LHM
With my love

'It's time the world knew what was really discovered at Delphi.'

Dr Moses Frank,
Director of World Antiquities Research, Vienna

PART ONE

Isabella

1

Delphi, Greece

The nightmare was over. Her body sank into the embrace of the bucket seat, she turned the ignition key and swung out of the driveway.

The villa quickly disappeared behind her with the finality of a guillotine as she roared into the first curve at a hundred and ten.

With the empty road ahead, she saw her chance. Switching to high beam, she drenched the hills in white light and stamped on the gas.

When she reached a hundred and forty she took one hand off the wheel and brought herself to an easy climax – her body tingling as the illuminated rocks flew past in a grey-green blur.

As the highway straightened out, she felt she could go further, pushing the pedal hard until she reached one eighty.

She juddered in her leather seat, glancing upwards at the aubergine sky as she came again.

Both hands back on the wheel the rush of adrenaline quickly faded from her body, but her lips began to move as if in silent prayer. The agnostic young woman had re-discovered her God.

'Thank you, Holy Father, for the brief moment of pleasure, after all ...' she paused to find the right words. 'All the bad things that happened earlier in the night,' she mumbled as she took a blind corner at one sixty.

Coming out of the sharp curve on the wrong side of the road she looked up again – a shooting star was exploding over the Aegean, rewarding her with a final swell of pleasure as it pierced the night sky.

It always worked for her on the empty highway but she knew it could be a fatal game on the twisting tarmac out of Delphi. She'd been lucky this time.

Slowing down to a meandering one twenty, she began talking to her saviour again.

'Forgive me, Holy Father. I didn't mean to do it, I needed the extra comfort tonight. I promise not to take these risks again. Everything will be better now, I promise you,' she whispered, adding a, 'please, God,' half in prayer, half in self-affirmation.

Her face was burning and she opened the window. The warm night breeze rushed past, cooling her cheeks with honeysuckle and sea salt-perfumed air.

She was driving out of the village of Galaxidi when she first noticed it sitting in a layby, shiny and dark, its sleek body reflecting the moonlight like a slug.

It sprang to life as she drove past, accelerating into position behind her as if it had been waiting for her to arrive.

She stamped on the gas and it soon fell into the distance, disappearing out of sight as fast as it had arrived.

In two hours she'd be boarding the ferry, catching up on lost sleep, lying on soft white sheets inside a first-class cabin, enjoying a long, undisturbed rest, free to play behind a bolted door.

Releasing her seat, she stroked the soft leather before pushing it back to stretch out her legs. She switched on the radio, and the mellow sounds of Leonard Cohen filled the car.

It was some friendly company at last.

2

It was leaning down on her again, so close it was sitting inside her slipstream, its cold white xenon headlights only a few metres off her bumper. It was a large Mercedes by the look of it, a heavy lumbering saloon with reserves of power, maybe a 4.2 litre.

She tried accelerating away but it made little difference.

A sign for Klovinos came and passed in a blur. It might have said 5 km, she wasn't certain. She'd stop for a coffee and it would disappear out of her life.

There was a fork in the road for Lidoriki. She stopped at the junction and began to pray again.

'Holy Father, make the Mercedes fuck off to Lidoriki – or in any direction away from me.'

God must have been busy elsewhere in Greece at that moment. The car stayed glued to her bumper. She'd have to ignore it if she wanted to catch the first ferry.

She felt a stream of sweat, warm as olive oil, slide down her spine, and a hollow banging inside her chest cavity. Something was thumping against her rib cage.

Driving into the village of Klovinos, she circled twice around the main square, and stopped by the only café. The shutters were down, the whole village asleep.

The Merc was lingering fifty metres up the street. She looked around and, deciding it was a good time to break away, released the handbrake and began accelerating.

The village was not dead after all.

A few old women, dressed in black, emerged from behind doorways, their faces rigid.

For a brief moment Isabella felt guilty for waking them

with her imitation of the Grand Prix. Then she told herself, 'it's rural Greece – they've probably been awake since the first cockerel.'

She emerged quickly into open countryside, and Klovinos became a few flickering lights in the distance. Apart from a boarded-up Shell garage, the road ahead was empty.

Five minutes later, alone and unfollowed, she saw the amber lights of a vast milking shed. A farmer appeared on the road, glowing in his hi-vis jacket. He waved her on wearily before letting his cows spill back onto the highway.

Behind her, a shiny steel tanker was reversing out of the farm, its coiled pipework still dripping with milk.

It stopped dead in the middle of the highway. The driver jumped out and wandered nonchalantly back to the farm.

She allowed herself a hint of a smile as she saw the Mercedes approaching. Holding her naked arm out of the window, she gave her four-wheeled stalker a one-fingered farewell. Her long black hair was flowing easily behind her in the breeze, and she was in mid-prayer again.

'Thank you, Holy Father, for sending the dairy truck into the middle of the road and stopping the Mercedes,' she murmured softly, embarrassed by her intermittent belief.

A sign told her that Patras was only 54 km away. The port felt reassuringly close. On a good day it was less than an hour's drive, and she would easily catch the first ferry.

The towers of Efpalio came into view, the swaying leaves of eucalyptus trees camouflaging its thousand-year-old monastery. Slowing down to admire the weathered stones of the Byzantine church, she saw it approaching once again, speeding towards her, dark grey or silver – she wasn't sure in the half-light of early morning.

'They must be catching the same ferry out of Patras,' she

reassured herself. 'Where are you Father, now I *really* need you?' she cried, crashing through fourth into third.

She took one hand off the wheel again and made the sign of the cross.

3

From the upper deck she watched as the last vehicle drove onto the ferry.

Against the peeling white paint, the name of the ship was clearly discernible in the crisp morning light – she was on board the *MS Apollonia*, the twice-weekly service from Patras to Brindisi.

A member of the Greek crew tapped the bonnet of the late arrival. The driver squeezed the handbrake, switched off the engine, and slumped over the wheel.

There was a deep blast from the funnel and a cloud of black smoke blew into the sky as the ferry began to sail out to sea, slicing through the ink-blue water.

Isabella was about to go down to her cabin when she saw someone getting out from the last vehicle – it might have been a silver grey Mercedes, but the dazzling sunlight was playing tricks with her vision and she couldn't tell for certain.

A tall man with dark brown hair, talking on his mobile phone, opened the back passenger door and stepped into the bright sunshine. As he glanced upwards to the upper deck their eyes met for a moment and Isabella drew breath.

She'd seen his face before.

His posture was familiar as he walked towards the restaurant on the main deck. The face lingered in her thoughts, as if she knew it from her childhood.

Exhausted and needing a rest before the next leg to Milan, she dragged herself to her cabin. Lying on the starched cotton sheets, she felt a familiar trickle from under her arms.

She shut her eyes and imagined the gentle rippling waves at Paros beach. Despite the sunny imagery, she couldn't help worrying about the antiquities in the boot of her Audi. She reassured herself that she had a set of authentic-looking, near-perfect export certificates, and lay down on the metre-wide bed.

The throbbing of the engines made her feel aroused again. It was all due to her levels of anxiety, she told herself. She was feeling too exhausted to move, but her tired fingers found their way downwards and she brought herself to a half-hearted orgasm.

The stress of the moment dissolved and her body loosened up. It felt safer than taking her hand off the wheel whilst driving at 180, but it was a less memorable rush. Her body shook one more time and she was away, in another place.

She woke up seven hours later as the ship swayed gently from side to side and the engines hummed away. After a shower she got dressed and wandered around the ship, but discovered there was little to do – the cinema was full, the duty free was chocolate, booze, and tourist junk. There was nothing left but to go and eat.

There was a sprawling buffet, heaving with every kind of fried food. You could eat as much as you wanted, but drinks were extra. Tepid lamb, once-warm chicken in tomato sauce, and dry-baked fish filled a series of unappetising stainless-steel trays. Red watermelon, creamy cakes, and strawberry meringues made up a table of deserts.

Isabella bought a small bottle of New Zealand Sauvignon

Blanc and chose a smoked salmon salad. She looked around for a corner seat near an exit where she could sit down without being seen.

As she finished her meal she saw him enter the restaurant and approach the food.

She didn't want to take any chances. With her bottle of wine in one hand she hurried to the bar next door, ordered a black coffee with a brandy, and took her drinks to the privacy of her cabin.

The rolling of the ship, the drone of the engines, and the alcohol made her feel drowsy again, and she collapsed, fully clothed, onto the bed.

When she opened her eyes the ship was already in port. As she ran down the stairway onto the empty car deck, the crew were laughing. Her car sat alone, deserted by every other vehicle.

'Don't worry. It's OK for a pretty woman to be late, we are not laughing at *you*,' said a smiling deckhand.

She accelerated off the ship and the Audi's suspension took a heavy battering as the wheels bounced over the metal ramps. If she'd been less distracted she would have noticed the huge yellow arrows warning her to drive slowly, but she was too preoccupied with looking out for the sign to Bari.

A fleet of dazzling cruise ships were lined up against the harbour walls, the mirror images of their white hulls shimmering on the clear blue water. Air-conditioned buses hummed alongside them, waiting for passengers to disembark for daytrips to Naples and Pompeii.

Sliding her fingers over the touch screen on the dashboard she chose Mozart's Piano Concerto No. 23, and accelerated onto the Viale Albert Einstein.

'For Christ's sake,' shouted Isabella as she shot off in the direction of Pescara. It was there again, in the middle lane, crawling up behind her.

A massive road sign flashed past announcing *Cafe and Servizzio* – 1 km. At the last moment, fifty metres before the exit, she saw a gap between a Porsche and a slow-moving truck. Without thinking, she wrenched the steering wheel to the right and slid up the ramp. A truck behind her blew its horn.

She gazed down from the bridge that hung over the autostrada and watched the Mercedes disappear in the direction of Bari, unable to turn around for another 55 km.

Isabella turned the key in the ignition. The engine came to life and the Audi juddered as if glued to the tarmac.

She revved the engine, checked she was in gear, but it still wouldn't move.

'Holy Father,' said Isabella, 'Why are you punishing me like this?'

4

The aroma of maple syrup and fresh coffee filled the air as Isabella walked into the cafeteria. She bought a large Americano, two *cannoli* pastries, and a blueberry pie – she needed sugar, she told herself – and waited.

The mechanic in blue overalls was suddenly walking towards her, peeling off a pair of white latex gloves blackened with grease. He threw the gloves into a nearby bin, sat down opposite her, and held up a small plastic box. There was a faint tremble in his lips as he started to speak to her.

'You have a new tyre, Signorina, but what shall I do with this?' he said, rolling the box between his thumb and forefinger. 'Do you want me to put it back?' he asked.

Isabella looked at him with a confused smile. 'Put what back?' she asked.

'You don't know what it is?' he said, surprised by her reaction. She hesitated before replying and leaned forward to study the black plastic box.

'I've no idea,' she said.

'Oh, I see.' He paused and sniffed as he looked across at her. 'This is an electronic tracker. It was attached to the wheel hub of your car.'

After a few seconds it dawned on Isabella what he meant.

'You mean something for following my car?' She paused and took a breath. 'As if I was a kind of fugitive on the run?'

'Exactly,' the mechanic said.

Isabella put her hands to her face and stared into the dusty sediment in her empty coffee cup. Everything started to fall into place. The noises at the villa. The headlights in the hills. The Mercedes waiting for her to join the road. But how did this device end up on her car?

Her lips quivered as a feeling of vulnerability swept over her body. 'I think I know how it might have got there. When I was packing to leave my house this morning I heard a vehicle outside. Someone must have entered the garage,' she said, recovering her composure.

'Perhaps, Signora. It would only have taken a minute. From then onwards, it will have followed your every turn.'

Isabella moved closer to the mechanic and whispered, 'so does someone know that I'm here now, at this service station?'

'Yes, probably. But why do you think it was put there?' he said, smiling.

She saw him look at her body, and instinctively threw her head back. His eyes followed her long hair as it fell over her shoulders.

'Are you trying to avoid your husband? Sorry, it's none of my business,' he added, and leaned forward to touch her shoulder to apologise.

She saw his nostrils twitch as they reacted to her scent, and she pulled in her jacket.

'Sometimes jealous husbands put them in their wives' cars,' he said, turning the small box around in his fingers.

'But I'm not married,' she said, and then wondered why she'd told him that. The mechanic smiled and she looked embarrassed, her cheeks blushing light pink.

'I'd throw it away,' he said. 'Whoever it is, he'll never find you.'

'Won't they be suspicious if it stops moving?' Isabella asked.

The mechanic seemed uncertain. 'They'll probably think it's a technical fault.'

She paid the repair bill with a Bank of Greece credit card and walked towards the exit. Her hand hovered over a waste bin, but she reconsidered, squeezing the box into the back pocket of her jeans.

5

Isabella made her way back onto the autostrada. Once in the flow of traffic, she remained alert but only half-conscious of the other cars.

Her mind drifted like a kite cut loose in the wind, wandering in every direction. She began to remember the day she travelled along this same road with her father at the age of nine.

They'd been on holiday in Rome. She was licking an ice cream by the Colosseum, wearing an 'I Love Roma' T-shirt. He was filling her hand with almost worthless drachmas to throw into the Trevi Fountain later.

When they got back home to Delphi, her mother had already left for good.

The next morning, her father came to wake her very early. An important visitor was arriving at the museum – an antiquities dealer was coming all the way from Vienna.

'No one must know about his visit. It will be a secret, only between us,' he said.

From the first-floor window, she saw him arrive. A giant of man, he was big in every way, with a wide smile and a booming voice, accompanied by his long-legged girlfriend who dressed like a hippy in cut-off jeans. She had a blonde Mohican haircut with a bright green stripe across the top of her head.

Isabella looked up at the highway.

A blur of roof tiles flew by as she drove past the town of Canosa di Puglia. She slowed from a hundred and ten to eighty and cruised over a wide red bridge. Below, the sun was sparkling on the River Ofanto.

Her neck tingled. Although she could feel her hands holding the steering wheel and was conscious of the cars streaming past her on the autostrada, she was in another place, in an earlier time.

The early morning visitor, so eagerly awaited by her father all those years ago, seemed so familiar now. Her recollections began to merge with the events of the day.

The man from Vienna and the man on the ferry became one. The white almond blossom, masking the church spire of

Chiesa del Carmine in Cerignola, flashed past in a snowy blur. Isabella slowed to glance at the elegant bell tower. Its classical baroque splendour could not distract her from her one unlikely thought.

A faint echo of the visitor's name buzzed around her head, but she couldn't grasp it. It kept moving away, out of reach. She had a sense it sounded like a ram's horn. There was a biblical flavour to his name. She saw a bunch of roses. The face of Anne Frank, the tragic teenage girl who wrote the diary, floated by. The name hovered too briefly before it dissolved into thin air. She saw the roses growing on the wall.

It was Moses.

But Moses who? She almost had him in her grasp. Frank – of course. It was Moses Frank. It made sense now. He was the antiquities dealer from Vienna, and his hippy girlfriend was … Anya, or Anna. She wasn't sure.

Isabella caught a momentary glimpse of the crumbling stucco towers of Foggia as she drove onwards to Pescara. But her mind had travelled on.

She was looking up at the turquoise sky over Delphi on a late spring day in Greece. The morning sun was beating down on her face.

From her first-floor window she saw everything unfold that morning at the archaeological site.

It was a day that changed her life.

Moses Frank was the man of the moment, and her father, Dr Andreas Green, director of the Delphi Archaeological Museum, couldn't do enough to make him welcome.

PART TWO

Moses

1

A cloud of dust rose from the tyres as the half-ton silver Mercedes rolled to a halt on the warm gravel. Three hundred feet below, white flecks of foam jostled on the Ionian sea.

The thousand-mile overnight journey from Vienna to Southern Greece was complete.

In the back, two semi-naked people turned over. On the front seat was a well-thumbed copy of *Die Presse*, purchased the previous morning, on the front page a picture of Nelson Mandela, recently released from prison, shaking hands with President Bush on the lawn of the White House.

Sam opened the front window for some fresh air and scrambled for his shades. Greek coffee and purple bougainvillea smells drifted towards him.

Early morning Delphi smelt a lot sweeter than rush-hour Vienna.

It was 6.55 am, five minutes before the rendezvous, and Sam gently woke his passengers by tapping on the glass separating them.

'Thanks Sam, I'm awake … and well done for getting us here on time,' said Moses, who'd been awake for ten minutes observing everything from the double bed in the converted Mercedes. Next to him, Anna was still asleep.

Through the glass doors of the museum building, Moses saw a short man tapping an unopened cigarette packet. His blue eyes squinted in the sunlight as he watched him take a Marlboro from the soft red pack in his breast pocket and flick open his lighter. Grey smoke wafted over his head as he waved a greeting to the chauffeur.

Anna, a tall Czech woman with a Day-glo green Mohican

haircut, stirred and felt around for Moses as he placed the silk sheet back over her shoulders.

It was a futile move, and she began to twist and turn, the sheet slipping away again, revealing her breasts.

Her possessions had fallen out of her backpack and lay on the floor of the car – pink luminescent socks, lace underwear, a flower press, a bottle of musky perfume, and a nineteenth-century copy of the *Materia Medica*, written by the Greek physician Dioscorides.

Moses twisted the top from a small bottle of Menthos sparkling spring water, leaned backwards, poured the bubbling liquid over his face and shook his head from side to side like a wet dog.

Sam handed his boss a white towel and tried to avoid looking at Anna as her half-naked body came into view.

Moses was watching her face, mesmerised by the sight of her eyes darting delicately left and right under her closed lids.

He looked and acted as if he was in his late twenties but he was now aged 39. He was six foot two and a former Hungarian refugee, but had transformed himself into a multi-millionaire by dealing in rare antiquities in a way no one else had done before.

He was beating the international auction houses at their own game.

The son of a Catholic mother and a Jewish father, he conveniently appealed to clients across the religious divide, and travelled fully equipped to attend a church or synagogue at short notice. In the boot of the Mercedes he always carried two wooden boxes with religious paraphernalia. The first box contained a sixteenth-century set of amber rosary beads, the second a pair of phylacteries or *tefillin*, a skull cap and a prayer shawl, rescued from the Krakow ghetto before it was burnt down. Moses treasured both symbols of his heritage with equal pride.

He decided to wake Anna, he looked at her mouth, moved over her and became slightly aroused as he kissed her on the lips. They still tasted moist and luscious - despite the overnight journey from his flat, a lavish penthouse perched on the 52nd floor of the Leopold Tower in Johannestrasse, in downtown Vienna. It had been a long, tiring drive, via Budapest and across Croatia, with six hours of frequently broken sleep.

Moses opened the car door and stepped onto the gravel. As he darted into the shade of a huge blue oleander bush, he heard the car's back window sliding down.

'Hey there, Moses, I'm up,' a sleepy Anna said in her honey-soaked Eastern European accent.

She leant out of the window and blew him a kiss, but Moses missed it. He was distracted by the clanking sound of the museum's glass doors and saw Dr Andreas Green, the director of the museum, checking his watch, before emerging from the marble entrance at precisely 7.00 am.

He looked relaxed in shorts, trainers and baseball cap placed tightly over his head of curly black hair.

Green waved at Moses and lit up. The smouldering cigarette hung precariously from his dry lips, bobbing up and down, as he loped forward to greet him. The diminutive five foot six inch Dr Green, an expert in ancient Greek manuscripts, shook his visitor by the hand, glancing over his shoulder at Anna, still leaning out of the car window.

'Thank you so much for making the long trip all the way from Vienna. I know you won't be disappointed, Moses. It will be worth all this trouble,' Dr Green assured his guest, clasping Moses' hands with his own sweaty palms.

'And your lovely friend?' said Green, looking again towards Anna.

'Sorry, it's been an early start and such a long journey, I wasn't sure if Anna was … ready yet,' said Moses, bowing down to Green with an awkward smile. He walked over to the car window and peered at Anna's state of undress – she was wearing a loose top – and little else below, apart from a fine wisp of pubic hair. 'It'll be fine, if you stay low,' he whispered.

'Let me introduce Anna Nemcova, from Prague,' said Moses, standing in front of the window. Anna rewarded Green with a large smile and a perfect set of teeth as Moses did the talking.

'Delighted to meet you, Anna, and what do you do?' said Green, revealing his own nicotine-stained row of teeth. Anna looked at Moses and signalled that he should explain everything.

'Anna has joined me on this trip take a look at the flora, to compare it with what grew here in ancient times,' said Moses, adding, 'she's looking for possible herbal medicines.'

'I'm an archaeo-botanist,' she said proudly, leaning further out of the car window. Green's face became wildly animated, and Moses tried to turn him away from her. He could see Green was distracted by the sight of her partially uncovered breasts.

Aged 27, born in Prague, Anna had told Moses she was a roving botanist who travelled in search of plants used in Roman and Greek times for their medical properties. They had met at a dinner party only one week earlier in Vienna. It had all happened by complete chance. She told Moses she knew all about the plants that grew in Delphi in ancient times. Moses was enchanted by her rare and unlikely knowledge.

'Poisons make great drugs. Think Belladonna,' she told him, her green hair almost unnoticeable in the candlelight. He smiled and said he was looking at a true *bella donna* at that moment. Moses was attracted to the unconventional woman. She was bright, pretty in an exotic way, tall, and unpredictable.

After several glasses of wine, Anna told him she was desperate to go to Greece to look for a plant once used as a poison in Delphi against a nearby village – the *Helleborus niger*, the Black Hellebore, otherwise known as the Christmas rose.

She stayed at his flat that night. Moses thought he'd never see her again but she re-appeared, two days later, on his doorstep with a small backpack.

'She's so tired,' said Moses, putting his arm on Green's shoulder to steer him towards the archaeological site.

'Seems you've already cleared up all the damage,' Moses said, casting his eyes around the dusty site for signs of destruction caused by the recent earthquake.

'Don't believe what you read in the papers,' Green murmured in a low voice.

Moses looked at him in surprise. 'What do you mean?' he asked. Green came within inches of his face and whispered into his ear.

'I must tell you a secret, my friend. The government has exaggerated the extent of the earthquake so they can milk the disaster funds,' he said, his tobacco-scented breath floating up to Moses' nose.

Moses pulled back a couple of feet.

'You know, Moses …' he paused for emphasis and took the opportunity to inhale deeply on his cigarette. 'People pray for earthquakes like this. To be honest, my friend, the earthquake destroyed nothing. Absolutely nothing.' Green broke into a grin and winked. 'On the contrary, it had a very helpful, I would say miraculous, effect.'

'A miracle, that's nice. We can all do with the occasional miracle, especially my saint-making friends in the Vatican,' Moses said, trying to step sideways to avoid Green.

'You see, my friend, the earthquake has opened a tunnel into a chamber which had been sealed off for nearly two thousand years—' Green was interrupted by the sound of a car backfiring.

Moses looked towards the main road and saw a Fiat Tempra, and tried to make out the number plate.

'That must be a rare sight. A Vatican-registered vehicle, out here in Delphi,' said Moses, who counted the Vatican as one of his biggest clients.

'We need to get going,' said Green, ignoring the comment.

'Is it far?' asked Moses.

'We have to make a short hike up the mountain to reach the chamber, my friend, then walk underground for a few minutes. It's nothing really,' said Green.

Moses took off his cotton jacket and tossed it towards Anna in the car. She hung it carefully, then crawled into the front seat, and re-appeared with a chilled bottle of spring water. Moses drank a few sips, pushed it into his trouser pocket and realised he'd forgotten his favourite toy.

'Can you pass my M3? The Leica,' he said.

As Anna handed him the camera through the window, Green put his hand in front of the lens and shook his head.

'Sorry Moses. I would prefer if you didn't take any shots today. I promise to give you some excellent photographs in a few days.'

'Tzzst,' said Moses, pushing his tongue against his front teeth and sucking in air. 'Look, I'm not going to publish them in *The New York Times*,' he protested.

Green shook his head. 'I have to think about the security problem.'

2

Moses handed the camera back to Anna and reached into the back seat for his Italian leather briefcase. From a zipped section he pulled out a special khaki shirt with double-breasted pockets and a pre-fitted button lens. Waiting until Green turned away, Moses stripped off, put on the crumpled shirt, and fed the black cable from the left-hand breast pocket under his belt and into his trouser pocket.

'It'll take 15 to 20 minutes to walk up the hill, a distance of around 1,200 metres,' Green said, pointing towards the winding path up Mount Parnassus.

'Let's go – it'll get too hot if we leave it too long,' said Moses, looking at his watch and starting to walk. Green did not move. He was looking at Anna.

'What about the lovely Anna? I'd like her to see it too,' said Green.

Moses laughed. 'My apologies, Dr Green – may I call you Andreas?' asked Moses. Green beamed with pleasure at the idea.

'Look, I'd love her to come, but we must let her catch up on sleep, we didn't get much rest overnight. There will be other times,' said Moses.

Green's smile sagged down to his chin. 'Such a delightful young creature you have there, my friend.'

Moses had other reasons for keeping Anna away from the relic. As he started to walk up the hill, Green came staggering after him, panting and out of breath.

'Such a shame, I think she'd really enjoy the experience.'

Moses decided he needed to change the subject of the conversation. 'Andreas, you speak such excellent English,' he told his host.

Green gurgled with pride and explained his mixed parentage. 'I am the result of an American father who fell in love with a beautiful Greek woman.'

After two hundred metres of strenuous climbing, Green stopped to wipe the flood of perspiration from his face.

Moses could see he was shattered but elated. 'The discovery must have been a great moment for you?'

'Sure, but it's taken a lot out of me,' he said, fanning his face with his baseball hat. 'When I first found the relic, I thought it was a fake.'

Moses began to feel that the all-night drive from Vienna might have been a waste of time.

'You'll see why, my friend. It looks too perfect.' Green paused again, almost overcome with emotion, tears welling in his eyes. 'We are talking about a missing relic from biblical times.'

He started to wheeze like a broken water pump – looking down at the pencil pines growing on the foothills gave him a few moments to regain his breath. 'These ruined pillars – unreal aren't they?' he said in a high-pitched voice. 'They're like film props … we could be in a Hollywood movie, eh Moses?' he continued, trying to laugh, his voice virtually a falsetto.

Dr Green's anxiety level was increasing with every step up the mountain.

The two men reached a small workman's hut covered in a red canvas and bearing a sign in both Greek and English:

Στάση!
κλειστός δρόμος
συντήρησης

STOP!
PATH CLOSED
DANGER – WALL REPAIRS

'Tzzst,' Moses uttered, and was about to make a comment but held back.

'Don't worry, my friend. Ignore it. It's one of my signs. I put it there to keep out unwanted visitors.'

Moses laughed. Green spat a lump of white phlegm onto the ground, shuffled into the hut, and beckoned Moses to follow.

At the far end he saw two heavy cast iron plates covering the ground, loosely padlocked to a piece of scaffolding.

A continuous trickle of water was running down onto the metal plates from further up the mountain.

Green took a bunch of keys from his pocket and unlocked the metal plates, and with an almighty heave pushed them aside, his face turning purple.

A large black hole opened up at their feet and Moses stepped back from the edge. He peered into the darkness below.

'Are we going down there?' said Moses.

'It's the only way to go,' said Green, laughing. 'But it's one-hundred percent safe, my friend, believe me.' Green's laugh echoed in the tunnel. He produced two head torches and gave one to Moses, who fixed the elastic band around his forehead and switched on.

'You may also want to wear this over your mouth, unless you really like the smell of ripe bananas,' Green said, handing Moses a white cotton mask. 'It's to hold back the sickly sweet odours of ethylene gas, bubbling up through the rock.'

Moses began to descend the sixty-five steps, his leather shoes sliding sideways on the wet limestone as he gripped the rope at the side.

Before them lay an alien landscape of undulating flowstones.

Stalactites growing out of the ceiling were dripping slowly into pools of water on the stone floor.

'Beautiful aren't they, worn smooth over thousands of years

by the minerals in the spring water,' said Green. The cave ahead began to narrow and soon turned into a low tunnel.

'You'll need to crawl along on your knees, for a short distance,' said Green. 'It may be a little wet – there are ancient underground springs here. It means there can sometimes be water running down on both sides.'

The cave widened into a room-sized chamber, and they stood upright in the darkness.

'OK. We're here. Look over there, towards the stone shelf at the far end,' Green said. 'It will soon appear, out of the void.'

Moses couldn't see anything and tapped his head torch in an effort to make the beam brighter. It went dead and then came to life again. 'Greek batteries,' he cursed.

'They die early, just like the Greeks,' said Green.

After three minutes, a shapeless blur appeared out of the blackness. Moses held out his hand falteringly and tried to touch it. He was expecting to feel solid rock but his fingers touched something soft and damp.

'What's this?' Moses shouted, as if he'd touched a poisonous snake.

'It's nothing. Just an old blanket, Moses, don't worry. I put it there myself,' Green said.

Moses' heart started to pound and his entire frame shuddered. He tried to play down his reactions, but deep down he sensed he was about to witness something momentous. Using the sleeve of his shirt, he wiped the sweat off his face and from the back of his neck.

'I must tell you, over the years I've seen quite a few ancient relics that no one believed existed.'

'This will be one of those occasions – but even more so, my friend. Don't move an inch,' said Green solemnly in the darkness.

'Are you ready, Moses? This will be a little shocking for you.'

Green aimed the beam of his torch directly at the shape. Moses became aware of the outline of some kind of tall object. He had a feeling that Green was shamelessly milking every ounce of drama before the final reveal.

'For God's sake, Andreas, get on with it. I can't stay much longer in this dripping mausoleum.'

3

Green lifted his arms and the blanket slowly fell away.

Nothing could have prepared Moses for the sight in front of his eyes. Seven arms of solid gold appeared in front of him, like the branches of a palm tree. Moses immediately recognised what it was.

A fistful of Hungarian expletives flew out of his mouth, the memories of a language from another time in his life. '*Istenem, istenem,*' he said, again and again, shaking his head.

'I don't understand you, Moses, but I know what you mean,' said Green.

'What's it doing *here*?' Moses spluttered. 'I'd always thought that this relic was hidden in the bowels of the Vatican museum.'

Then he saw why it was not in a museum. It was trapped in stone. A constant drip for two-thousand years had encased the antiquity in a stone jacket. It was half-treasure, half-geological formation, partially buried under the grey limestone rock.

It lay on its side, and had probably done so for all that time.

Stood upright it would have been as high as a man – just under six feet high and four feet across, tapering down to a base of about three feet in diameter. Nearly one third of the relic remained buried under the speckled limestone, but enough was visible to allow its identification.

Seeing it made Moses tingle like a small child. It was a feeling he'd never experienced with any other antiquity before.

It was pure gold, but the precious metal had oxidised, giving it a dirty orange hue. At the top of each arm was a cup, to hold olive oil. In its full ceremonial glory, each of the seven arms would have carried a burning flame.

Moses circled the relic. It made him think back to his father's family. His uncles, aunts, and cousins who had not survived Auschwitz. How would they have felt to see this ancient symbol of their heritage?

But with the sense of elation came a disturbing feeling of confusion.

Was it really what he thought it was?

Moses couldn't understand the presence of this relic in an underground chamber in Greece, so far from its historic home.

'I can see you're desperate, Moses. Touch it, if you want,' Green said, sensing Moses' desire to feel the relic with his hands.

'You realise that could corrode the gold? Sweat is acidic,' said Moses.

'It has survived worse things than some drops of sweat from your fingers,' said Green. Moses caressed it like the body of a woman, applying his fingers gently to its curved surface, checking for marks or letters scratched into the gold.

Green, who'd gone without a cigarette for half an hour, pulled off his mask, took out a Marlboro from the soft pack, and stuck it between his lips. He flicked open his lighter and its yellow flame illuminated the ground for a few seconds.

During the short burst of flickering light Moses saw something glinting near his feet. As Green looked up to exhale his first drag of smoke, Moses bent down and scooped up something solid and metallic in his fingers, along with a handful of dust.

He could feel a thin round object about half an inch across, possibly a coin. Pressing his fingers against the grit he realised there was also a sliver of paper, slippery to the touch, nestling in his palm.

'It feels as if I am touching human history,' Moses said, as he dropped his haul into his breast pocket. 'It's a sensational discovery, Andreas. Congratulations.' He clapped his hands with praise. Green purred with satisfaction.

'But what puzzles me is that the location of this relic doesn't make any sense,' Moses said, and saw Green's smile dissolving. 'I don't understand what it's doing here.'

Green shuffled back and forth on his feet. 'Your eyes do not deceive you, Moses,' he said, nodding calmly as if he'd been expecting this response. He moved his head torch so he could look Moses in the eye without making him squint. 'You have to accept it. Touch it again, it is real, my friend.'

Moses took a deep breath. 'There's something strange about this,' he said.

'The fact is … this is an anomaly,' said Green, opening his hands. 'It's the *Delphic* Anomaly.'

There was a sound of rushing water beneath his feet.

Moses' eyes flickered, and for a few moments everything went black. He could see nothing at all in front of him.

4

Moses sat back in his chair.

'When I saw it for the first time, I had a most profound realisation. It was almost a religious feeling. I'd been dealing in antiquities and selling them on the black market for over twenty years. It'd turned me into a young millionaire. I liked the lifestyle, it gave me everything, if I can put it that way.' He lowered his voice.

'I was screwing the rich and lots of beautiful women at the same time, I had it all – power, wealth, and a certain status within the private world of collectors. But I always detached myself. You can't get too emotionally involved, otherwise you'd never sell anything, you'd hang onto everything, wouldn't you?'

Sat opposite him, a woman in her fifties was writing notes as he spoke. She looked up at Moses and raised her hand.

'But was something different for you on that day?'

'This was the first time in my life that I realised I'd been living a vacuous dream, devoid of any tangible value. At that singular moment in the chamber, standing next to Green, I was face to face with my own cultural identity. My heritage looked me in the eye and was shouting at me – screaming at me to do something.'

Moses fell silent. He got up from his chair, went to the window, and looked into the rose garden.

'For a brief moment I felt I had a chance to transform my rather pleasant but empty life into – I know it sounds like a stupid cliché, into one that had some meaning. The possibility stalked me, circling above me like a bird of prey,' he said, punching his fist into the palm of his other hand as he turned around and went back to sit in the chair.

'But I couldn't do it. It went against my instincts – all the rules of survival I'd learnt in the refugee camp. One small weakness and you were dead.'

'So what did you do about your realisation?'

'Nothing. I drank a large glass of whisky and drowned my thoughts, hoping they would wither and die.'

'And did you succeed?'

'I'm good at self-delusion. I pushed those feelings out of the way and carried on as before. It's easier to do that than change your life, isn't it? What was I going to do anyway? Give my wealth away? Become a schoolteacher or a postman? It wasn't going to happen. I loved my life. I wasn't going to swap all that.'

He got up again and stood at the window, and after a few moments of silence let out a quiet cry.

'I'm sorry. You see, I knew it would gnaw at my conscience. I knew it wouldn't go away.'

'But something *did* change in your life, didn't it? Otherwise you wouldn't be here.'

Moses rolled his head back and shut his eyes. A succession of female faces filled his head. One stayed in his mind, and came to life before him.

He saw the face of Helena Delacroix. Helena was coming towards him, and he was mesmerised by her touch, her sensuous mouth hovering over his lips.

She kissed him. He melted.

'Yes, you're right. Something happened to me,' he said, and hesitated for a moment. 'I met this crazy young woman, Helena. She changed all the rules in my life. Actually, she wasn't crazy, she was brilliant in most ways. Beautiful, excruciatingly so. Screwed up, irritating and maddening, all at once.'

'You haven't mentioned Helena before.'

'I find it difficult to think about her. Sometimes I feel she's too strong. I've deliberately tried to push her out of my thoughts – she can be too provocative and challenging. But I'm obsessively drawn to her.'

'What's so tantalising about her?'

'She's a very determined woman, she likes to dominate ... let me be frank – in a highly sexual way. She told me how frigid and repressed the French were – and set out to prove she was the exception to the rule.

'The most challenging fact about Helena is that she has an over-riding desire to shock people out of their boring, predictable lives.

'And within my own little universe, I suppose it's true, yes – I was getting boring and predictable. And so she was intent on shocking me, by whatever means available to her.'

'With Helena that meant exhibiting her body, and using it as an hors d'oeuvre for sex. You have to understand that nothing embarrasses her. And, I should add, she also came to me for a special favour, so maybe she thought she needed to offer herself to me, in return ... I don't know.'

'What kind of favour?'

'She'd heard I supported artistic endeavours and such like, so she wanted help with her rather unconventional archaeological research project.' Moses took a long, deep breath. The therapist looked up and shrugged her shoulders.

'OK look, it was somewhat risqué, shocking perhaps, even for those times.' He paused for a few seconds. 'Do you really need to hear all this stuff?'

The therapist nodded. 'You must tell me the details, otherwise how can I help you?'

'I remember the first time we met. My God, she was always so determined to be provocative. I had to hide my feelings, to remain professional in my dealings with her – she never made that easy. She always liked to tease. It was a game for her. She liked to play with you, in every sense of the word.'

'And what was her research project?'

'You have to remember it was the late '80s, early '90s, the "anything goes" era. And Helena took great pleasure in winding up all the dull, boring and inhibited people all around her.

'She'd told me about the day it all began. It was the day she went to look for a copy of an ancient manuscript discovered by her grandfather at Delphi, the so-called Elena Text, at the National Library in Paris.'

His eyes lost focus as he stared towards the window.

'And she was right, of course. Nothing changes if you worry what people might think.'

PART THREE

Helena

1

With her fraying blue jeans wrapped tightly around her thighs, her unzipped leather jacket falling off her shoulders and her ample breasts squeezed inside a low-cut bra, Helena was scoring high that morning.

Her crimson hair bounced off her shoulders as she emerged from the Palais Royal metro onto rue St Honore. She always liked to make the heads turn as she went around the centre of Paris.

The marble faces of Voltaire, Pascal, and De Maupassant gazed out, as ever, towards the silver birch trees off rue Richelieu. They were probably the only male eyes not following her as she snaked her way through the rush-hour crowd, towards the steps of the French National Library.

She handed her leather bag to the elderly cloakroom attendant, but her appearance seemed to mean little to him as she leaned over his desk, and he soon returned to reading *Le Figaro*.

Stripped of her usual possessions, Helena entered the archaeology library through the tall oak doors, carrying only her notebook.

She looked around in surprise at the lack of seats. It was only 9.30 am but every work desk was taken. Unable to find a seat she joined the queue at the information desk.

She could feel the perspiration running down her neck. After five minutes her turn came. As she arrived at the front of the queue, she fanned her face with her fingers and undid the top two buttons of her blouse.

'It's hot in here today,' she said as the young librarian glanced down at her exposed cleavage.

'You can look and enjoy the view, it's OK, really, but I need you to find a volume for me as well,' she said, smiling.

He went bright red and looked up at her face. 'Are you a student, Mlle?' he asked.

Helena flashed her Sorbonne University membership card in his face, but she knew there would be a problem.

She took a deep breath and made her request.

'I would like to see the reading copy of the Elena Text, please,' she said. He nodded, clicking the retractable top of his ballpoint pen repeatedly before dropping it on the floor.

'What's the name of the volume again?' he asked, lifting his head from his screen.

'The Elena Text. I know you keep a copy for researchers to read,' she said, with a hint of irritation.

She watched him as he tapped the name into his keyboard. He looked up with a tired frown. She could see he'd found it, but there was an access issue.

'I'm sorry, but it's not permitted for the general public to see it. It's not available on the open shelves. It's only available to scholars with written authorisation.'

Helena glared at him. The librarian stepped back as her face went the same scarlet red as her hair. She had no qualms about venting her anger in the presence of a library full of people.

'Why is it still banned in the major library of France, fifty years after it was discovered? Why is this country still full of such hypocrisy?' she asked, not expecting any answers. The librarian's face turned pale as her voice echoed through the great reading room. Students who'd been sitting at their desks looked up to see what was happening.

She lowered her voice but she hadn't finished.

'Do you realise that just across town, in Pigalle, people can pay money to see men and women simulating sex, yet I'm forbidden from reading an ancient manuscript because it openly describes pagan sex rituals in Greece from two-and-a-half thousand years ago.'

'It's not my fault, Mlle, it's the rules,' he said, shrugging his shoulders.

'You should be ashamed of such a policy,' she continued to shout at him, knowing full well it wasn't his decision.

'I'm sorry, I do not make the regulations,' he said quietly, shaking his head and looking down at his computer.

'I understand. But look, Monsieur,' she began very softly, moving towards him. Helena decided to try another approach. 'It's important for me personally that I see this manuscript. It was discovered by my grandfather. It's part of my past, it's my personal history.'

She put a hand on his shoulder. 'I hope it will also be my future,' she said, tears welling in her eyes.

'I understand, Mlle, I will try to help you,' he began. 'Maybe … if you can obtain a letter from your professor, I think you may be able to see it.'

Helena reached into the back pocket of her jeans and removed an envelope – it was concave, warm, and slightly damp as she pulled it out and handed it to the librarian. He held the edge of the envelope with the tips of his fingers to extract the letter. He skimmed it and handed it to an older female colleague.

After five minutes of discussion and two telephone calls, he called over to Helena, a nervous smile on his lips.

'I'm sorry Mlle Delacroix, but the Elena Text is not actually kept here.' He paused for a moment. 'It is in another building, at the National Archive Collection, near Parc de Saint-Cloud, on the other side of Paris. I can check if they can find it for you,' he said.

'Tell them I must have it today,' she said, tapping her fingers on the desk.

Twenty minutes later Helena was issued with a reader's pass in the form of a typed letter. She could now use the National Archives for one month and the Elena Text would be made available to her for research purposes.

'Just one more thing. Come here please,' Helena said, as she stood at the reception desk. The librarian turned and walked back towards her slowly. She grabbed his shoulders, pulled him to her, and planted a moist kiss on his left cheek.

Helena walked briskly out of the library. Before she exited through the oak doors, she turned around and looked back at the librarian. He was standing there, puzzled and dazed, rubbing his forefinger over the waxy imprint of her red lips on his cheek.

Armed with her permit, Helena hurried out of the library onto rue Richelieu.

As she waited for the traffic lights to change, she took a tobacco pouch from her shoulder bag and rolled a wire-thin cigarette between her fingers. Ahead she could see someone waving at her enthusiastically. It was an old university friend, who came towards her, his arms held out for an embrace.

But Helena was in a hurry. She had a low capacity for any small talk today.

'Really nice to see you again,' she began, stepping to one side. 'But I'm late for a meeting on the other side of Paris. No time to talk now – another time, eh?' she said, swinging around and touching her lips, throwing an empty kiss into the air with a flick of her fingers.

For a few brief seconds she wondered why she'd been so unkind towards an old friend. As she entered the subway she extinguished the roll-up, ground it into the pavement, and wandered onto the platform.

She boarded an empty train to Opéra. Thumbed copies of that morning's *Le Jour* littered the deserted carriage, but Helena left them unopened on the seats.

The train clattered noisily over the steel tracks as she stared at the reflections in the window. The old family photos of her grandfather Niko Delacroix filled her thoughts.

In her mind she was in Delphi, under a blue sky, walking barefoot on warm marble steps, towards the Temple of Apollo.

2

The exit from St Cloud station pointed Helena towards an underpass. It smelt of urine and was daubed with graffiti sprayed from aerosol cans. Two drunk men were living down there, sitting on the concrete floor, surrounded by dirty nylon sleeping bags and empty cans of lager. One was holding an emaciated dog. It pulled on its string leash as Helena ran past.

Emerging from the tunnel, she inhaled a few lungfuls of the traffic fumes pouring from the Paris ring road.

In the distance she could see the archives building, a large modern warehouse on the edge of the Parc de Saint-Cloud.

Inside was quiet and civilised, and a welcoming scent of expensive perfume floated in the air, worn by the elegant, older woman who sat with a smile at a reception desk.

She already knew all about Helena and had been expecting her arrival. They exchanged pleasant small talk as Helena handed her the typed letter she'd been given by the central reference library. In return, Helena received an official reader's card and a piece of paper with a desk number for the eighth-floor reading room.

She was directed towards an industrial grey metal elevator. It took her to the top of the building, as its fluorescent light buzzed loudly on the ceiling.

The reading room was almost empty – only two elderly men who looked like retired professors occupied the desks.

She sat and waited at seat number 35.

From the corner of her eye she saw two silver-haired male workers enter the reading room wearing lab coats and white cotton gloves, one holding a plain manila folder.

As she realised they were walking towards her, she felt her heart accelerate. Her mouth trembled slightly as she confirmed with a small smile that she was indeed Mlle Helena Delacroix.

The Elena Text was finally in her hands.

Bound in a black leather book, it was a high-quality colour facsimile, not the original two-thousand-year-old manuscript itself. It was written in ancient Greek, but attached to it was a plastic folder with a typewritten translation.

As she opened the pages, a pneumatic drill started up in the courtyard below. A few moments later a cleaner entered the reading room and handed her two sheets of toilet paper, and indicated that she should mould them into temporary ear plugs.

Her ears filled with the paper, Helena started to read the manuscript, writing notes in her exercise book.

She used the symbol > as shorthand for *greater*, and after an hour had only written down four words on an otherwise bare page.

> ECSTASY > AWARENESS
EXPMNT @ DELPHI

The idea for the experiment had come to her in a flash of inspiration.

It was simple but extraordinary, and she knew immediately

that she wanted to perform it at the temple site in Delphi. The plan was clear in her mind, and it was obvious to her exactly what she had to do – and how she would go about it.

In the courtyard below, the drilling ceased as the workmen downed their tools and walked away for coffee. Helena removed the tissue plugs and began a second reading of the Text.

She closed the manuscript with a sense of accomplishment and walked down to the basement. To avoid the buzzing elevator she took the emergency staircase and found a coffee machine. Next to it was a fizzy drinks machine and a payphone. It was occupied by a middle-aged woman who seemed to have taken root, with several shopping bags, inside the booth.

Helena stood outside and waited, making it clear that she was anxious to use the phone. The conversation ended and the woman left the basement looking pale and tired as she struggled to carry all her shopping.

The receiver was still warm as Helena dialled an 11-digit number. It was the direct line to Dr Antoine Palousey, the head of Archaeology at the Sorbonne.

She spoke quickly – she couldn't get the words out of her mouth fast enough to catch up with her thoughts.

'Hello Antoine, I must speak to you about my idea for my PhD thesis. Something important has developed out of my research into the Text—'

'Where are you? You sound a little drunk,' he said, interrupting her. 'I'm not sure if you're euphoric or close to hysteria, my darling. And where the hell are you?'

'At the archives in Parc de Saint-Cloud. It's a really shit area, just off the Périphérique, but a nice building once you get inside.'

'Have you been drinking?' he asked.

'I'm only drunk with happiness. I think I've found the perfect research experiment for my thesis.'

'I'll cancel my next tutorial so you can tell me all about it. Let's meet at Rive Gauche in an hour,' he said.

Helena put down the phone and walked in a daze up a flight of grey stone steps from the basement into the foyer. The receptionist smiled at her as she left but Helena drifted past without saying goodbye. A moment later, as she reached the door, she turned round, having remembered where she was and belatedly called out, 'goodbye. Thank you so much for your kindness and help today.'

'Any success?' the receptionist asked Helena.

'Oh yes, great success. It was a revelation,' Helena said.

Taking a breath, she pushed the revolving door and stepped into the humid air. A flock of feral pigeons swooped onto the ground in front of her. The birds seemed to know the weather was about to change.

3

Helena arrived at the Rive Gauche bar at 5.00 pm looking pale, her hair still wet from the rain. Antoine Palousey smiled at her from a distance. She walked to his table and collapsed into his arms.

'So how did it go at the National Library?' he asked, pouring her a glass of wine.

'It was like Moscow – they ban books, they think a two thousand year old sex ritual will corrupt the morals of the country. Your letter helped, though.' Palousey nodded appreciatively.

'It's everyone's right to read about the origins of our culture,' Helena said, taking another sip of wine and kissing him on his mouth. 'Don't you think so, Antoine?' He leaned back and enjoyed the fading smell of her perfume.

'I have to do this, it's in my blood,' said Helena.

'Because Niko Delacroix was your grandfather?' Palousey asked.

She nodded.

'But do you really need to test the erotic rituals described in the old manuscript he discovered?' he asked, and swallowed another gulp of wine.

Helena could hear in his voice that he was appalled by her plan.

'Are you serious, Helena? Have you thought it all through? I fear you'll be ridiculed. It may not look good for the department, either.'

'That's a typical male reaction. It's the right time to do it. Women can now do this kind of research without any shame.'

'Let me get this straight – you want to perform an experiment to see if the Delphic oracles really improved their prophecies by having an orgasm? Is that right?'

'You've summed it up perfectly, Antoine. And isn't it a brilliant idea?' Palousey's eyes narrowed as he looked back at her. She'd thought he was unshockable, but he was not as broadminded as he'd led her to believe.

'Are you completely crazy, Helena?' he said, placing his hand on her shoulder.

'Don't patronise me, Antoine, I'm not a child. I'm a grown woman who makes her own choices. Whom you choose to fuck, actually,' she said, raising her head and letting her hair fall over her shoulders.

'Of course you're an adult. But Helena, please tell me this is some kind of bad joke. Do you realise how many people you will offend with a sex experiment at the Temple of Apollo?' he said, rolling his eyes.

'Counting the number of people who are embarrassed could be part of my research. The university has a moral duty to shock people out of their narrow-mindedness. It will be good for them. It will expand their consciousness. We must elevate people beyond watching game shows on TV,' Helena said with a smile. 'There are more exciting things to do in life.'

'But what about the science? How can you do it scientifically? The Sorbonne is a distinguished university, not some hippy outfit.'

'No problem. I'll put it to the test rigorously, one-hundred percent scientifically. I will use statistical methods,' she said, leaning forward, her glass in her hand. 'Look Antoine, this is nothing new. We know from Masters and Johnson that the orgasm actually relaxes the entire body, not just the sex organs. It puts the mind in a more receptive mood for any sensory engagement, so it's all perfectly plausible. Ancient people knew things we've forgotten,' she said, and drank her glass of wine.

'Oh really?' Palousey said, sounding amused. Helena took no notice and carried on talking.

'It's well known from EEG recordings that an orgasm causes an increased blood flow to the brain, bringing about greater awareness, better neuronal interaction, more alpha waves – you name it. The human body benefits in every way.' She paused for breath.

'And, this is the crunch – there is evidence that it also puts women into the optimum brain state for receiving weak signals associated with extra-sensory perception. Do you want the references for this? I have them too, Antoine.'

He looked uncomfortable and began moving around in his

chair.

'And another thing. It's also been shown that any physical activity, like sex, improves all kinds of intellectual ability even at an *unconscious* level. Antoine. Are you getting my drift?'

He shrugged his shoulders.

'Ask any school teacher, they'll tell you how their children improve at doing maths *after* they've been running around in the playground,' Helena said, and clapped her hands together.

'OK, OK. I get the picture, Helena, you can stop now. I agree, exercise is good for the brain.'

'Let me finish. I'm coming to my big conclusion. So it follows that there should be heightened awareness after sex as well. Agreed, Antoine?' He nodded repeatedly and sank into his chair. She knew she'd said enough to silence any initial criticism.

'Look, Helena. You know me, I'm an archaeologist, I'm not a psychologist. You're straying into territories beyond my area.'

'Yes Antoine, this is a whole new branch of science. It's the boundary between archaeology and biology,' she said, leaning forward and whispering into his ear. 'Another glass, please. And in case you're worried, I'll be totally discrete in everything I do.'

He turned so their mouths met, and then whispered, 'that's a very sensible thought, I don't want you to have a problem with your husband. But look, I don't understand how you'll actually do the research.'

Helena stood up, unpeeled her leather jacket, and sat down again. 'And another thing I want to say – I must tell you Antoine, I know we have become lovers, but I want this research to have academic integrity and not be waved through on account of our relationship. Do you have a cigarette?' she said, and he looked at her in surprise.

He lit a Gauloises and handed it to her. She inhaled, forgetting it was far stronger tobacco than her roll-ups. She held the cigarette awkwardly and coughed on her words as the smoke streamed from her nostrils.

'OK, Helena. I have to bow to your vastly superior knowledge on this subject, but please tell me how you'll do your experiment.'

'Alright, this is the situation,' she said, bathed in a cloud of blue smoke. She began to describe how she intended to validate the Text, but stopped herself. 'No – I can't do this here in the bar. It's too public. Can we go to your apartment?'

He looked up at her and lowered his eyes again.

'Please Antoine? I need to show you what I'm going to do, You asked me to.'

4

Two glasses of red wine had affected her balance and Helena stumbled on the gravel path several times as they walked through the small park, en route back to Palousey's flat.

'Perfect, that's a laurel bush. I'll need some of those,' she said to Palousey, who looked puzzled as she tore off a handful of the leaves. When they reached the apartment. Helena ran through the front door into the kitchen, grabbed one of the bar stools, dragged it into the bedroom, and shut the door.

'But you're stopping me from going into my own bedroom,' Palousey called out.

'Go away. I need to change out of my clothes. Stay in the lounge and read a book for ten minutes,' she said.

As she undressed she saw a man staring from the first floor

window in the opposite building. She switched off the main ceiling light, lit a candle and went to pull down the blind, but when she had the cords in her fingers, she changed her mind and left it open, so he could watch her. In the flickering shadows she looked at herself in the full-length mirror, sitting astride the bar stool, her legs crossed. She tilted her head back, her hair falling onto the wooden floor.

Apart from a thin silver chain hanging loosely around her waist she was naked. For Helena, the chain was a physical separation between her mind and body, but she was well aware it added a touch of eroticism.

She sat admiring herself in the mirror and called out to Palousey. 'I'm ready for you. Come in,' she said in a slurred voice.

She tightened all her muscles and pushed her breasts into the air as he walked towards her. She was pleased to see he was unable to stop himself from running his fingers down the length of her body.

'Quite sexy,' he said, and began to laugh at the strange spectacle before him.

She glared at him with wide eyes.

'Stop laughing. I am PhD-serious,' she said angrily. 'This is my doctorate proposal in the form of a human sculpture.' His smile disappeared and he listened patiently to her explanation.

'I am the priestess who foretells the future.' She looked towards Palousey's bed. 'Let your bed be the temple sanctuary. I am the Oracle, the mistress of Apollo. This stool represents the ancient Greek tripod where the Oracle once sat, directly above the chasm in the ground.'

He stood watching her with his mouth half open. 'What do you want me to do, Helena?' he said with a faint smile.

'You will be my High Priest,' she said solemnly.

'What do I have to do?'

She listed his tasks, with no emotion, as if she were running through the instructions on how to operate a drill. 'Firstly, you have to fuck me, really hard. Secondly, you must give me a five-star orgasm, and thirdly, you must ask me some difficult questions, just as if you were seeking the advice of the Oracle on a major problem.'

Palousey nodded patiently, trying hard to keep a straight face. 'OK, that sounds acceptable. Just tell me when you're ready,' he said, restraining the muscles in his face.

'I am not sure you're taking this seriously, Antoine,' Helena said, looking straight at him.

'Absolutely not, this is … er,' he began to stumble over his words, 'just like any other PhD proposal.'

Helena took up her pose on the kitchen stool again.

'From my tripod, I will enter into an ecstatic trance state to help me answer the most difficult questions,' she said, placing a single laurel leaf in her mouth and chewing it. Palousey watched her with concern as she swallowed and bit into another leaf.

'You're not really going to eat any more of those leaves? They're poisonous,' he said, trying to grab them from her hand. Before he could reach them, she pulled them tightly against her breasts.

'Look, Antoine, they're only mild hallucinogens, that's all. They're not at all toxic in small doses. It's what the Oracles would have dosed up on in Delphi,' she said, munching slowly on her third leaf.

Palousey shook his head in disbelief.

'You don't understand, Antoine, they're safe. Believe me, I've read the Text very thoroughly. It's the combination of the hallucinogenic leaves and the orgasm which makes all the difference.' Palousey went into the kitchen and returned with a packet of table salt.

'Why the salt?' she snapped at him.

'Oh nothing, really, just in case you poison yourself,' he said drily.

'What total crap you come up with, Antoine. Do you think I don't know the safe dose of laurel leaf? I've been doing research on this for some time. Stop treating me like a child, I'm a responsible adult.'

'Adult – yes. Responsible – I'm not sure.'

Helena climbed down from the tripod and began to dance around him, She grabbed her silk scarf and pulled it around her waist, accentuating her hips. It covered little of her, but she felt it added another layer of sensuality.

'We will now test the theory for the first time in two-thousand years,' she said, unbuttoning his shirt from behind him.

'That feels good, Helena,' he said, as she pressed her breasts against his back. He turned to face her and ran his fingers down her spine. She shivered and pulled him closer to her body.

'More like that please,' she cried. She pulled him towards the bed and lowered herself onto the ruffled sheets. 'Take everything off, I want you to come into my sanctuary,' she whispered.

A breathless Palousey untied the scarf from around her waist and slowly eased himself between her lips.

'I like it slow, tease me like that again,' she said, unable to stop herself from pulling him deeper inside her.

'This will send you into a higher orbit,' he said, pressing down into her.

'Push me into the next state of ecstasy, along the path of the orgasm – as it is written in the Text,' she said breathlessly.

Helena imagined that she was making love at Delphi, on the floor of the Temple of Apollo – the marble ground, her bed, a stone step, leading up to the temple, her pillow.

They made love until their bodies were soaked in perspiration, kissing, gnawing and scratching each other towards a climax.

As he pumped his load into her, their bodies slammed tightly together, twisting to get closer, leaving no hollow, no gap between their skins, bound together by their own sweat.

It was over for him. He wanted a cigarette and began to pull himself out of her.

'No, don't go yet, I want you to stay inside me,' she said, as he tried to go.

She clenched her legs around him, so they became locked together. He couldn't move an inch.

Grabbing him around the neck, inter-weaving her fingers, so he was pinned against her, she began to push her legs up and down against his, increasing in speed and sinking her claws into his back as she came.

After a few moments of uncontrollable nail-digging frenzy, her body collapsed under him.

Whilst she lay there, suddenly still and calm, he gently pulled himself out of her and lay back on the bed, exhausted but relaxed. He looked around the room for his packet of Gauloises.

Helena was revitalised and sat bolt upright, her skin glowing with the pink flush of orgasm.

Palousey lit a cigarette and blew the blue smoke across the room towards the window.

'That was very nice, Antoine, thank you,' she said, ruby-faced, her head bubbling over with enthusiasm about the first trial of her experiment. 'So do you think the faculty will agree to my doctorate proposal?'

He shrugged as smoke streamed from his mouth.

'Oh, no!' she screamed, putting her hand over her mouth. 'I forgot the question. I was so carried away by the ritual that I forgot to remind you.'

'Remind me of what?' he said, with a sigh.

'You must now ask me some questions so I can make a prophecy, like the Oracle at Delphi.'

Palousey said nothing and went into the kitchen, returning with a bottle of chilled Sauvignon Blanc. She jumped from the bed and sat again on the kitchen stool.

'I'm here, waiting for your question,' she said, a wail of panic in her voice. 'Antoine, please, please ask me something now, anything, please.' she begged. He mumbled an OK as he pulled the cork from the bottle and poured out two tall glasses. He tried to give Helena her wine, but she shooed him away.

'Ask me now, I beg you. It's important not to linger, Antoine. My elevated state of ecstasy will soon fade, I fear.' Watching him slowly sip his wine, she began to pull at her hair. 'You're too relaxed. I'm waiting for you,' she cried.

'OK, OK, Helena, I'll ask you something,' he said, as she grabbed her watch to check the minutes ticking by. He began to speak, but from the smile forming on his face she had a feeling it would not be a question she wanted to hear.

'OK, my darling Helena, here is my question for you.'

'Yes?' she said loudly.

'Tell me, Helena, how many men will you need to test your hypothesis?' he asked, grinning at her.

'You mean, how many men will I have sex with? I'm a scientist, this has to be statistically significant. It will be at least twenty, maybe thirty, I'm not sure, I haven't done the stats yet.' He threw a pillow gently at her. She threw it back with greater force.

'Why do you have to mock me? Is my research too embarrassing for the department?' she said, pausing to catch her breath. 'Or is it that it doesn't fit into its misogynistic, out-of-touch, nineteenth-century agenda?'

Antoine tried to answer, but she was still in full flow. 'Ritual eroticism is culturally significant, you know,' she said, 'it's part of the Greco-Roman tradition. Christianity reeks of eroticism, but it's never admitted. Just take a look at the paintings of all those orgasmic Madonnas.'

She paused for breath and Palousey shook his head. 'Come on Helena, this is crazy. How could anyone take it seriously?'

He said nothing more and sat there holding his chin. Helena looked at him with a frozen expression. He was fumbling for cigarettes again. She found his Gauloises and threw the pack in his direction.

She was sure he was going to say how sexy she looked when she was angry, but she didn't want to give him the pleasure. Walking out of the bedroom, she gathered her clothes from the floor and slammed the front door of his apartment.

Outside it was raining as Helena ran through the park to the warmth of Rive Gauche.

On reaching the bar she heard footsteps behind her. She turned and saw Palousey standing there looking guilty, his head down.

'You left your keys and some of your stuff.'

'Stuff? What kind of stuff?' she said.

He put his hands into his pockets and she watched as a small triangle of silky black lace fell onto the wet pavement.

5

The rising water swirled gently around Green's shoes. He took off his mask to whisper into Moses' ear. 'It's nothing at all Moses,' he said in a hushed voice. 'I promise you. It happens every day at this time. Just a trickle of spring water and then it's gone. Finished.'

Moses shuffled uncertainly, but when he looked down he saw that the water level was indeed receding. He watched it disappear under his feet, into the same cracks that had produced the gas that smelled of ripe bananas.

'Well done Andreas, you were right, it's a great relief to see,' Moses said and Green purred with satisfaction.

'Listen, my friend, I want to talk business with you,' said Green, rubbing his hands. 'I need you to sell this relic soon. I want you to put it on the market, quickly and quietly,' he said. 'You can do this easily Moses, can't you? It's why people with archaeological discoveries keep knocking on your door, isn't it?'

Moses said nothing but allowed himself a slight nod of his head.

'My wife is ruining me, she's demanding the house. She wants everything. I'm going to be bankrupt, but she doesn't know about the Anomaly. It would be a disaster if she ever found out. You understand my need for confidentiality, my friend?'

'I understand, Andreas, this happens all the time,' Moses said, nodding in sympathy, but his cheek muscles revealed a tremor of disapproval. This was the moment Moses found most difficult. He was a man with a conscience, but he knew he couldn't allow his doubts to threaten a profitable deal. He had to make a living. It was always a tricky balancing act for Moses. Moral doubts were luxury goods he could live without, but after a few moments, he decided he should push Green for a few answers.

He turned to him and put an arm around his shoulders.

'Tell me, Andreas, do you feel that the Delphic Anomaly is *yours* to sell?'

Green was flustered by the question. Beads of sweat appeared on his cheeks, accompanied by an expression that made his face droop on one side. Moses looked at him and felt that Green must have practised this expression over the course of a lifetime to induce a feeling of pity.

There was a long pause whilst Moses waited for an answer.

'Look, Moses. Despite all the superficial trappings of wealth, I'm just a poor museum director.' Moses watched as Green forced a few small tears down his cheeks.

'I have toiled like a poor serf all my life in a modest backwater in southern Greece, away from the bright city lights. And now this shit happens. My wife is suing me for every drachma I have. You've got to help me, Moses,' Green said, with a mournful expression.

Moses said nothing and stood there listening, nodding in sympathy.

'I have my faults, Moses, I must confess. No one is perfect,' he said, his lower lip curling down as he coughed.

'People like us, my dear friend Moses, are acting in the *very finest tradition*' – he emphasised the words – 'of the great nineteenth-century archaeologists.'

Moses smiled. 'It's just good, old-fashioned business, isn't it? What tradition are you thinking of anyway?' he said, tightening his nostrils.

'You know what I mean, Moses,' Green said, looking at him in disbelief.

'I'm sorry, I don't. Spell it out, Andreas.'

'It's *mine* to sell because *I* found it. I do not need any more justification. You can't have forgotten that Lord Elgin took our Greek marble treasures back to England. He claimed them as his own. So, I will take my Delphic Anomaly.'

'Don't you think—' said Moses, but before he could finish Green interrupted.

'I'm in very good company with the English Lord Elgin, not to mention the Great Belzoni, Lord Pitt Rivers, and all the rest of those British explorers. They helped themselves to our treasures, they had no qualms about it.'

Moses laughed. 'All aristocratic thieves, but protected by their governments. They all deserved to be locked up, don't you think Andreas? But not you – of course not!'

Green ignored the comment and held out a limp hand to Moses. 'Let's agree on a deal, Moses. Here and now.'

Moses hesitated for a moment. 'Look, I'm doing this because I'm a businessman at heart, not because of some bullshit about a "fine tradition".'

Moses shook Green's hand with a firm, cool motion, restraining the temptation to clench his fingers.

'I'm shaking hands on the condition that you, Dr Andreas Green, were the first and only man to discover the Delphic Anomaly, and you can assure me that it's definitely yours to sell. Agreed?'

'Of course, my friend. Agreed. There is no doubt at all about it. And what difference would it make to our agreement anyway?'

'It would make it null and void,' said Moses.

'Don't worry, Moses, my friend,' said Green. 'It will all be fine.' He pushed his hand into Moses' palm for the second time. As their fingers locked together, Moses noticed water seeping across the floor of the chamber.

'This is looking higher than before. I don't like it.'

'Moses. Don't you trust me?' asked Green.

'I don't know yet. Let's get out of here,' he said, grabbing hold of Green's arm and dragging him towards the tunnel.

'I don't want to drown in a flooded cave.'

PART FOUR

Anna

1

Anna slid out of the Mercedes by the Delphi museum and ran behind a pink oleander bush. Hidden by the large blossoms, she changed into a pair of tight shorts and leather sandals. It was easier in the open air than struggling in the car.

Lighter clad, she returned to the Merc and positioned herself squarely behind Sam in the back seat. She took a map of southern Greece from her backpack and found the village of Itea, six km south.

'Can you do me a big favour Sam? I need to visit an ancient village, named in early Greek texts as Kirra. It's only a few km from here, marked as Itea, that's the modern name.'

Sam took out his own map and measured the distance as 17 km. 'It's a 20-25 minute drive at least. I'm sorry, I can't go,' he said.

Anna put her hand on his neck and massaged it. The muscles on his face tightened, soon becoming wet from perspiration. 'If you're worried what your paymaster Moses will say, you've nothing to fear,' she said.

'I'm under instructions to always wait. I'd feel uncomfortable about driving you on your own. I'm not used to leaving Moses without his Merc.'

Anna knew she needed eye contact with Sam if she was going to get to Kirra. She got out of the car, went to the front door, opened it wide and stood with one arm resting on it, the other on the roof. She leaned down and looked into his eyes.

'PLEASE Sam. Just for me. Please,' she said, pushing her chest slightly forwards. He looked away in embarrassment and stared through the windscreen, saying nothing.

'Hey, Sam. Please,' she said, cupping the palms of her hands together into the prayer position and waving them pleadingly. 'You'd be back within a few minutes, I promise. Long before Moses returns.' She ran her fingers along the green stripe in her hair. 'Is it because you think I'm a little crazy with this green stripe?' she asked.

Sam sat with his arms locked together. Anna didn't feel confident this was going anywhere.

'This is just normal hair, like anyone else's. I've simply dyed it green to look a little different. Feel it,' she said, grabbing his hand and putting it on her hair. 'Stroke it. It's soft, isn't it?'

She got closer to his ear and whispered. 'Actually, it's just as soft as my pussy hair.' She grinned at him. Sam stopped abruptly and withdrew his hand.

'Sorry, I only said that to see how you'd react. OK – how about visiting the beach at Itea for a dip in the sea?' Sam looked at her uncertainly and bit his lower lip.

'I've things I must investigate there, it's not just about going swimming,' Anna said. She stretched over to the backseat to grab a well-fingered book from her backpack – her battered copy of the *Materia Medica*. She opened it on the page marked with a postcard from Prague. It was the page for the *Helleborus niger*.

'I'm trying to find this,' she said, showing him a hand-painted drawing of a white bloom with shiny dark green leaves.

'What is it?' he asked.

'It's a plant that used to grow around there.'

'I know nothing about …' said Sam, before stopping and looking down in embarrassment.

Anna put her hand on his shoulder and finished the sentence for him. 'About SEX?'

'No Anna! Please. I was going to say I know nothing about PLANTS. I left school at 17.'

'So tell me, Sam, how did you get such a cool job driving

around as an assistant to Moses?'

'I trained as a mechanic. I became a driver, ending up as a chauffeur to the chairman of a large company in Vienna. Then Moses offered me a job.'

'So he poached you?'

'I suppose so. It was a promotion. More money and responsibilities,' he said, looking more closely at the plant. 'It looks like a rose. Maybe a wild rose?' he said uncertainly.

'Yes, but it's poisonous. People call it the Christmas Rose, but the scientific name is Black Hellebore.'

'How poisonous?'

'Pretty bad. Listen to this.' Anna moved in closer until her face was a few inches from his, opened the page, and started reading aloud.

'It purges the intestines from above, driving out phlegm and bile. It is also boiled with lentils and broths that are taken for purging. It is good for epilepsy, depression, delirium, arthritis and paralysis. Given in a pessary it expels the menstrual flow, is an abortifacient, and cleans fistulas. In the first half an hour to hour it swells your tongue and throat. You will feel thirsty ...'

Anna put her forefinger into her mouth to wet it, drew a line in saliva across Sam's lips, down his chin and over his Adam's apple. She could feel his pulse throbbing through his skin.

'And then it will suffocate you, finally making your heart stop.' She laughed. Sam started to breathe again and tried to smile.

'Are you alright?' Anna said.

'No. I never know what you'll do, or where you'll touch me.'

'Sorry Sam, I just like touching, I'm a tactile person. I can see the world of Anna Nemcova must seem an alien place to you, but it's warm and friendly, I can assure you. Just relax. Maybe we can enjoy our bodies together one day.'

'I am not sure that would be acceptable to Moses.'

'Don't worry, Moses will never find out.'

Sam bit his lip again and changed the subject. 'So how much of this poison will kill a man?'

'I don't know – want to try it, Sam?'

He didn't answer but cracked his knuckles.

'D'you have a girlfriend?' Anna asked.

'Does that make any difference?'

'Not at all. It's just fun seeing your reaction,' she laughed.

Sam hid his face with his hands. 'You mustn't say things like that. And about having a girlfriend – I'd like one really, but it's hard to have a relationship when I'm away much of the time.'

'So you're a free man, then?' Sam looked quizzically at Anna. 'You don't have to worry about being loyal to anyone,' she explained, and moved to slide into the front seat of the Merc.

'Look, if it's easier for you just drop me off at the beach. I'll make my own way back.' She found a Rolling Stones cassette on the dashboard and slid it into the tape deck, turning up the volume. The oleander leaves on the bush next to the museum started to shake from the bass.

Sam lowered the music and switched on the engine. 'OK, I give in, you've worn me down. I'll take you, but you'll have to be fast.'

Anna was surprised by his abrupt change of heart. She gave him a kiss on the cheek and sat next to him in the front seat like a child on best behaviour. As he released the brake and the car slid out of the museum entrance, she put her hand on his shoulder.

'Please don't touch me as I drive, Anna,' Sam said calmly.

'OK, I'll be good.'

2

A blast of cool air blew from the air-conditioning as Sam drove down the mountain road.

Each time he approached a steep bend Anna tried to stroke the back of his neck. As she touched him, Sam leaned forwards to avoid her touch and the Merc lurched to the edge of the road.

'Please don't touch me Anna, it's not safe on this road'

'Fine. I'll leave it until later then,' she said with a grin.

The unkempt beach at Itea appeared through the car window. Two small fishing boats rocked in the sea breeze about fifteen-hundred metres out, but otherwise it was deserted.

Sam parked on a tarmac strip above the sand dunes and checked his watch. It was 10.45 am.

'I'm prepared to stay for half an hour, but no longer.'

'Perfect,' said Anna, taking off her T-shirt and revealing a black bikini top covering her small breasts. She made a pile of clothes and ran down to the sea.

'I'll come with you,' Sam shouted, jumping out of the Merc and kicking off his shoes. He found her at the water's edge, hopping from one foot to the other. As soon as he arrived she removed her top and looped the straps into her briefs before jumping in the water, swimming out a few yards. She stood up and walked back to Sam, small drops of seawater running down her breasts as she came towards him.

'Come in, it's not too cold,' she said, but Sam looked away in embarrassment as she played in the crystal-clear water. She swam a few yards, turned around and stood up, arms above her head.

'It's exhilarating, Sam, the water will do you good after the long drive from Vienna.' He looked back at Anna uncertainly.

She could see he was wavering.

'Come in, it's so refreshing,' she said once more, and he finally pulled off his shirt.

'And you must take off those trousers,' she said. 'You're on the beach now, not the autobahn.'

'Moses likes me to stay presentable,' he said. Anna grabbed his hand and pulled him down into the water. He lost his balance and fell into the surf as it trickled over the sand.

'That's more like it,' she said, combing his wet hair out of his eyes with her fingers.

'Anyway, how do you know that the Black Hellebore grows around here?' he asked, walking up the beach.

They walked back to the beach and she pulled him down onto the sand where they sat cross-legged, facing each other.

'Three-thousand years ago, when visitors came to Delphi, they landed here, on this beach,' she said, scooping up a handful of sand and letting the grains run through her fingers. 'We know this happened, it's described in ancient Greek manuscripts. They often came with valuables, expensive and precious gifts for the Oracle.'

'What's this to do with the Black Hellebore?' Sam asked.

'Remember this plant is a powerful poison? Can you guess what happened?' she said, putting her arms around him. 'Any ideas?'

Sam looked around to see if they were being watched. 'It's obvious. The people down here in Kirra stole the gifts meant for the Oracle. The poison was retribution, I imagine.'

'You're cleverer than you let on, I can see why Moses hired you,' Anna said, sliding her fingers down his spine. Sam bristled and tried to check his watch.

'But the question is, Sam, how did they do it?'

'I must get back to the museum,' he said, pulling himself

away from her body. She took no notice and was squinting at an object at the end of the beach.

'Look, it's over there,' she shouted, pointing across the fine sand.

'What's over there?'

'The pipe to Delphi. I have a feeling it's what they used to poison the Kirra water supply.'

'But how can you say that's the *actual* pipe?'

'I can't see any other water pipe around here. Why not? Roman aqueducts still exist from over two-thousand years ago, let's be open minded to the possibility,' she said.

'Maybe,' said Sam with a smile.

They walked back to the Mercedes and jumped inside. Anna kissed Sam on his lips as he inserted the key. His face went purple.

'Thank you for bringing me here. I won't forget it.'

3

As he released the hand brake Sam glanced uncertainly at Anna. 'I think you should get dressed now.' He watched as she strapped her bikini top.

'Can you help me out here?' she said, turning her back so he could tie up the flimsy cord.

'A double knot?' he asked.

'Not necessary. As you can see, I have quite small breasts – also it will be hard to take it off later,' she said.

'And who do you work for, Anna?' Sam said, as he tied the knot over her naked back.

'Ah, that's not easy to answer,' she said, turning to face him as he started to drive along the mountain road.

'Don't you work for a drug company, looking for medical herbs?'

'I dabble in a few other things too,' she said, placing her hand on his leg.

'So in what else do you dabble?' Sam asked, ignoring her fingernails on his thigh.

'It's a little complicated. I'll tell you the whole story when we know each other more.

'As long as I'm working for Moses, that won't be possible,' he said. 'And please – I'd rather you didn't touch me as I drive.'

Anna folded her arms. 'I love your loyalty, but remember what I said earlier.'

'What did you say, Anna?'

'Moses does not need to know everything you do. You can be loyal and still have fun.'

Sam drove on in silence, as if he was deep in thought.

When they returned to the museum there was still no sign of Moses. Sam reversed the Merc into the shade, reclined the driver's seat, and shut his eyes. Within moments Anna had placed her hands on his shoulders.

'What is it, now Anna?' he shouted angrily, lurching forward. 'I'm still tired from the drive from Vienna. Can you let me rest – please?'

'Don't shout at me Sam,' she said.

'I'm sorry, I'm tired,' he said, looking down.

'I've one more small favour to ask you. Can you just take me up the hill? It's too hot to walk. You don't have to wait for me. I'll walk down myself.'

Sam looked at Anna with sealed lips and nodded his head. Without warning he pulled up the seat, switched on the engine, and set off at high speed. The car shot up the narrow mountain road without any warning.

'Stop it Sam. Stop this craziness. I don't feel safe.'

'Is this the way, Anna?' he asked coldly, accelerating close to the edge.

'HEY! STOP now, please,' Anna screamed. He slammed the breaks and she fell forwards.

'I can see you're angry with me, but it's dangerous to drive like that.'

'OK, I'm sorry. I haven't slept much. Maybe it got to me.'

She opened the door and stepped onto the stony ground. Without saying goodbye, she set off on a goat track. After a few steps she span round and gave Sam an unsmiling look.

'I'll be back in an hour. Don't wait. I'll walk down myself.' The green stripe in her hair caught the sun as she disappeared into the gorse.

Sam looked at her tight shorts and almost naked back. 'Anna, cover yourself up. Stay away from the local shepherds. Anna, can you hear me?' There was no reply, and she kept walking without looking back.

As she came to the summit of the first hill, she took her field glasses from her backpack and trained them on Sam as he drove down the mountain, following him until she saw him reach the museum. She scanned the archaeological site and saw clusters of tourists making their way to the exit from the Temple of Apollo, into the shade of the gum trees. There was no sign of Moses and Green.

It was midday and an unforgiving sun shone through the five remaining pillars of the Temple of Apollo.

She turned up the path and began to sweat heavily from the

heat. Convinced she was now completely alone and would not meet anyone up in the hills, she removed her top, tied it around her waist, applied tanning oil to her breasts, and continued walking between the gorse.

The warm mountain breeze was beginning to cool her down, at last.

4

'We have to leave – I want to get to the surface now,' Moses said, looking at a stream of water running down the wall of the chamber.

'There isn't any danger, Moses, I promise you, it's the same every day. I'm a true coward, I assure you, I wouldn't take any risks. Listen, my friend, the water cascades down from the Parnassus stream two miles away. It's a daily pattern. It never rises higher than this.' said Green, lighting a new cigarette.

Moses juddered as he heard the sound of water crashing down. 'What's that noise?'

'It's just an underground waterfall in another chamber, totally separate from this chamber, it also comes and goes twice a day. Don't worry, it's tidal. I hear it every time I come down here.'

Moses shook his head, unconvinced, and began to walk towards the tunnel entrance. Green tapped him on the shoulder.

'But what about the sale of my relic? Tell me about the sale, Moses.'

Moses ignored him. He was determined to leave the chamber,

but Green was persistent and jabbed him in the back again.

'What about the sale?'

'We'll go into that later. In essence though, the problem is you'll have to remove the anomaly from the hard limestone that's formed around it.'

The two men walked around the rock feeling it with their hands. Green stopped, and Moses watched him lick it.

'Are you hungry, Andreas?'

'It's not salt, that's a shame. Salt would be easy to hack away, but this is tasteless, a somewhat harder rock to deal with. It will be limestone.'

Moses thought for a moment. 'I've an idea. Ordinary cola or any kind of lemonade will dissolve it.'

'Are you serious, Moses?'

'Sure. Any fizzy drink will dissolve limestone. Didn't you know that? It's because fizzy drinks are acids.'

'Aha, that explains why they are so bad for my teeth,' Green said with a cavernous smile that exposed a cluster of gold fillings.

'And another thing, Andreas. Who else knows about the existence of the Delphic Anomaly?'

'Only Isabella, I promise you.'

'Isabella?'

Moses conjured up an image of Green's girlfriend, a young, sexy Spanish archaeology student who'd come to Delphi to join a summer dig and Green had persuaded to stay on. She was the reason why Green's wife was suing him for a divorce. Moses had the impression that Green was the kind of man who couldn't resist showing off his archaeological prowess to women.

'I'm sure she's quite something,' he said.

'Yes, she is. I've a picture here,' said Green, as he opened his wallet and flourished a photo of his nine-year-old daughter.

Moses trained his torch beam on the picture. 'Sorry Andreas, for some reason, I thought Isabella was a young woman, your partner,' said Moses. Green shook his head disapprovingly.

'Apart from my daughter, there is only you, Moses. You are the *only* person who also knows about the Delphic Anomaly.'

Moses stroked his chin. He knew someone else must have seen it. He was playing with the evidence in his pocket. He ran his fingers over the silver medallion and asked Green again.

'Are you sure about that, Andreas? Don't you think the Vatican may have sent someone here to take a look at it?'

'The Vatican? Are you crazy? What for? Anyway, the chamber only became visible a few weeks ago,' Green spluttered, 'when we had the lucky earthquake.'

'The church is full of strange miracles that defy common sense,' said Moses.

Green said nothing. His facial expression said it all. He looked like a man who'd flushed a bag of diamonds down a toilet.

'Look, I know the Catholic church are thieves,' said Green, beginning to get worked up, spitting on the ground. 'It's not beyond them to steal religious treasures. They have form. Eight hundred years ago they stole our relics from Constantinople. They've never returned what they took from us in 1204.' He made a wailing sound, and came back to the present. 'But I've fixed a good padlock, so no one can break into the chamber.'

Moses rolled his eyes. He knew that any half-trained burglar could pick the lock in minutes. He felt sorry for the man, and didn't want to tell him the truth. 'Trust no one. Take nothing for granted, Andreas, that's all I'm saying.'

'OK Moses. We'll go back now,' Andreas said, and Moses raised both thumbs in approval.

Green stumbled as he climbed the steps, and had to put his arm on Moses' shoulder to steady himself.

When they came out into the fresh air the midday sun was

ablaze. Six miles above them, a lone jet was painting a vapour trail across the turquoise sky. There was a rustling of leaves, which could have been a large bird, but Moses was sure he'd heard human footsteps as they emerged from the chamber.

He could also hear a child crying. Twenty metres below them, on the path down to the site, he saw a young girl sitting precariously on a stone boulder. Floods of tears were rolling down her cheeks. He recognised her face from the photo. It was Isabella.

Green rushed up to her and held her against his chest. 'Where's your mother?' he asked, as the stubble on his chin rubbed against her face. '*She's* supposed to be looking after you today.'

'She left you a note. She said she's gone to Athens, so I came up here to look for you,' cried Isabella between the sobs.

'But you know this place is out of bounds …' Green paused to calculate what to say. 'And, er, a dangerous place for children. It's not safe for you to come on your own.'

'What *else* could I DO?' Isabella screamed at her father.

'Don't worry my darling, Papa's here now.'

The two men dragged the metal plates back over the access hole to the chamber and Green padlocked them to the scaffolding. Moses looked down at the vegetation by the path and scanned the hilly landscape for any moving shadows. If there had been any people around they would have merged seamlessly into the thick undergrowth by now, and Isabella may have seen them.

'Did you see anyone else come up here whilst you were waiting for your Papa?' he asked her. She looked up at Moses and shook her head without speaking.

Gripping her father's hand, she walked down the hill towards the museum. When they reached the entrance Isabella shot off towards the museum offices, weaving through a group of Japanese tourists, scattering them like lambs.

The pink and white oleanders growing around the entrance came into view. Moses was relieved to see the Mercedes parked under the shade of a spreading gum tree. Sam was asleep at the wheel, but there was no sign of Anna.

They entered the air-conditioned museum building, walked past the reception area and Green ushered them into his office. He produced a jug of iced-lemon water from his fridge and poured three cold drinks.

He gave one to Isabella and told her to run off and play in her special room. Green had converted a museum room, once used for storing pottery, into a play area. She could watch TV and do her homework. It even had two bunk beds. It was convenient for Green when he had to work late, but for Isabella it meant she was left alone for long periods of time.

'Look, I need to get going in 20 minutes,' said Moses, as Green disappeared to look for a packet of cigarettes. He came back empty-handed looking agitated, biting his lower lip, his shirt damp with fresh sweat. He pulled out some padded envelopes from the drawer beneath his desk and found an old pack. He was about to throw the ancient packet away but instead took one out and lit up. He inhaled deeply, filling the room with a heavy blue smoke.

Moses' nose twitched as the stale tobacco smouldered, producing the acrid smell of burning rope. He stood up. It was his last opportunity to ask a question that had been troubling him all day. He walked over to Green shaking his head.

'What is it Moses? What are you saying to me?' said Green, stubbing out his half-smoked cigarette. He began to look for his worry beads and, finding them in a drawer, looped them around his fingers. After a moment he dropped them on his desk and lit another cigarette.

'OK, Andreas. I'll tell you what's on my mind. I just don't understand how the Delphic Anomaly just appeared before you in the underground chamber, it's like a scene from a Hollywood film. How did you know it was there?'

Green twitched and covered his mouth with his hand whilst remaining silent.

'Is that really what happened, Andreas?' said Moses.

Green was about to open his mouth when a piercing scream echoed through the museum.

5

Palousey held the door open for Helena.

The comforting aroma of wine-soaked floors and fresh perfume, mellowed by warm skin, filled the air.

Rive Gauche was always crowded after work. With people talking loudly and shouting, it was a good place to have an argument.

Helena marched towards an empty table at the back of the bar. She had a defiant, rose-tinted glow on her cheeks, the vibrant, full-bodied complexion of a woman who'd recently had an orgasm.

She turned to check if Palousey was there, and saw him trailing behind her, his shoulders sagging. He went straight to the bar and ordered two glasses of Pinot Noir and two double espressos as Dave Brubeck's 'Take Five' played in the background.

Helena sat looking relaxed. She'd been his best student, winning respect and prizes inside the Sorbonne archaeology department for her rigorous intellect. Palousey, a married man with two young kids, had broken the cardinal rule of not sleeping with his students. But Helena was more than a one-essay shag. Now he remained utterly committed to her as his preferred mistress. She was sexually supercharged and always exhausted him, making his balls ache contentedly.

But she was never an easy proposition. How could he square her intellectual ability with her dubious research project? Her spiritual side was over-developed and needed to be held down. How could he prevent Helena and his department from being ridiculed by such a laughable project?

Sex and psi were an explosive combination. He lit up, exhaled a tunnel of smoke towards the ceiling, and moved forward.

'Look, my gorgeous,' he began. 'You may think we live in liberal and tolerant times, but those adjectives do not apply to the archaeology department.'

Helena licked the wine from her lips with the tip of her acrobatic tongue. Her eyes grew larger as she tried to speak to him above the noise.

'I want to show you something,' she said, still looking flushed by the outing to Palousey's flat. She stubbed out his cigarette and gazed around the bar. He watched as she walked over to an empty table and collected several beer mats. Once she'd gathered six mats she returned to Palousey.

'I'll show you what you can tell all those old misogynists in your department.'

Helena ruffled through her bag and produced a black felt-tip pen and began to draw some cryptic shapes on the back of the beer mats. On the first she drew a wavy diagonal line with a head and feet. She held it up to him.

'This is an aleph,' she said.

'OK,' he said slowly.

On the second mat she sketched out a mouse-tail, labelling it 'Yud.'

﬩

On the third she carefully made the shape of a three-fingered hand and wrote 'Shin' underneath.

Finally, she drew a door-shaped letter and called it 'Hey.'

ה

Palousey watched and put his hand over his mouth. He was mesmerised by Helena's newly acquired calligraphic skills.

'Do you know what I am writing?' she asked.

'Of course I do,' he said nonchalantly. 'It's Hebrew, the language of the old Testament.' As an archaeologist he'd often come across it in biblical texts. He could read ancient Greek but had never learnt to master Hebrew as he didn't do any Middle Eastern work. He'd seen it written outside the Parisian synagogues when he cycled past them in the Marais and when he'd attended an archaeological conference held in Jerusalem, but he'd no idea what the letters were called or what sounds they made. All he knew was that, unlike French or English, the Hebrew alphabet, like Arabic, was written back to front, from right to left, which made it confusing to read.

Helena pointed at the letters she'd drawn. 'This is the *first* letter of the Hebrew alphabet,' she told him. 'It's the aleph and sounds almost like the first Greek letter alpha, or our letter "A," or sometimes like an "E".'

Helena showed Palousey the mouse-tail.

'This is the letter Yud. It sounds like our letter "Y".'

'OK,' he said slowly. Palousey's eyes rolled upwards as he tried to comprehend where this was all heading. Helena said nothing. He could see that she'd no intention of making it easy. He knew from past experience that she liked to remain in total control, both intellectually and otherwise.

'You may have heard the three-fingered letter used in foreign news reports. This is a Shin,' she told Palousey. 'Does Shin ring any bells?'

He thought about it for a moment and repeated the sound to himself. 'Yes, I think I've heard of it. It must be the *Shin Bet*, the Israeli secret service,' he said, surprised by his own knowledge.

'And what about Mossad?' said Helena.

'No, I think that's the intelligence service. Oh look, who cares anyway? This is all madness. I'm grateful for the fascinating tutorial in the Hebrew lexicon, but tell me something – what are you going to do with all these biblical beer mats?' he said, shaking his head.

'You're going to help me make some words using these letters,' she said with a triumphant look in her green eyes. Helena took three of the mats and placed them next to each other.

אִישׁ

'I've made the word for a man,' she said. 'Can you read it?'

Palousey looked at the three letters and tried to read them from right to left. He struggled to remember their sounds and gave up. 'Of course I can't *read* it!'

'OK, maybe that was a little difficult. I'll help you out – it's pronounced *Eesh*.'

He said the word. Helena helped him get it right. He repeated it again – he hated to admit it but he was beginning to enjoy her stupid game.

'OK, so *Eesh* is the word for a man,' he said. He looked up at her after the final repetition. 'And so what, Helena? *Why* do I need to know all this? Are they rebuilding the Tower of Babel in Paris?'

'You need more patience, Antoine. I shall now make the word for *woman*,' she said, taking three new beer mats and writing on them.

אשה

'This is pronounced *Eesh-uh*. OK, now let's see what magic takes place when the man and woman lie together and,' she paused, 'shall we say, make love?' She smiled at him.

'In the missionary position?' he asked.

'Yes, that's perfect, the missionary position would be excellent,' she said, 'with the man on top of the woman. Can you do it please, Antoine? I know you can, you've had quite a bit of practise.' She smiled at him. 'Place the *Eesh* over the *Eesh-uh*!'

Palousey arranged the words above each other and looked at his arrangement on the table. He also wrote out the English words to help him remember.

MAN – איש

WOMAN – אשה

'Excellent. Very good work, Antoine. Now, I want you to remove the letters which are *common* to both words. Do you understand me?' she asked.

'Sure, that's easy enough' he said, nodding at her.

Palousey looked at the shapes carefully. First he removed the aleph from each word.

Then he took away two shins.

'Brilliant, Antoine. Now we only have two letters left on the table. The Yud and the Hey.'

'Now what?' he said.

'I want you to place these letters next to each other. This is the most exciting part of this game, Antoine! Do you know which new word you've just created?' she asked, bubbling with excitement.

Palousey had no idea what he'd created. He looked perplexed, and began searching for a clue, but there was nothing obvious.

'I've no idea, how on earth am I meant to know this, Helena?'

'Think about the Elena Text, think what happens. You will be truly *amazed* Antoine!' she said, moving her fingers through the air. 'The Yud and the hey, put together make the word for …God! Actually, this is an abbreviated version of the word Jehovah.'

'I can see what you're getting at,' he said, swallowing the last drops of his wine.

She moved round to be closer to him to explain the whole point of the exercise.

'When a man and woman have sex, and reach orgasm, they experience God. God is an orgasm. God is pure ecstasy. In other words, a couple experience God when they fuck, and this is at the heart of all religions.'

'Wow, I don't believe this, what are you saying now, Helena?' Palousey asked with a look of exasperation.

She glared at him as if he was being deliberately stupid. 'When they make love they not only experience ecstasy, they experience the intense power of God.'

'Really? When I make love to you I don't see God, it's just highly pleasurable.'

'It's only true for people who are devout believers, of course. This is why people scream at the moment of ecstasy – it's so powerful,' she said, clicking the fingers of both hands to make her point. She drank down her wine whilst Palousey shook his head.

'So what's the connection with the Text?' he said.

'This is exactly what's being claimed in the Elena Text. The god Apollo reveals himself and the future of the world at the moment of pure ecstasy. Do you understand, Antoine?'

'Maybe. Are you really saying God and ecstasy are experienced together at the moment of orgasm?'

'Exactly. God is an orgasm. God is revealed when we come!' Helena shouted in triumph.

Palousey shrugged his shoulders. 'This is weird stuff, Helena.'

'You know, Antoine, cultures have been trying to explain the meaning of sexual ecstasy ever since time began. The quest for it may have even been the origin of all religious belief.'

'I can see your theory puts religion in a biological context, which is interesting,' Palousey said, holding his empty wine glass against the light to see the patterns it produced. 'It's not an area I have studied at all, but I suppose it seems plausible.'

He lit a cigarette. As he exhaled he couldn't help wondering if the letter game was just an alphabetical accident, a party trick, but decided to stay quiet. He could see that Helena was looking pleased with herself and was touching him again.

'Listen to me, Antoine. I've shown you that the Text is not alone. It's not a one-off cultural anomaly. It's not unique. It's actually part of a pattern across different cultures and religions.' She stood up, swung her red hair away from her left shoulder and turned to face him.

'And this is why my research could be so groundbreaking. If you start looking, Antoine, you'll quickly discover that every culture has its own way of explaining the experience of ecstasy. For the ancient Greeks it was via the god Apollo, for Hindus it was the goddess Shiva, for the Hebrews it was with Yahweh or Jehovah. So the concept of God as pure ecstasy has a universal cultural basis. It's something the Sorbonne should be proud to support, not ashamed.'

'OK Helena, I'll try my best.'

'So you will be considering my PhD proposal?' she asked, running her fingers up and down the stem of her wine glass.

Palousey moved his shoulders like a man who could say no more without going to his research committee. 'It's not *me* Helena. I have a whole faculty of quite conservative—'

'—miserable old farts.' She finished the sentence for him. 'I want you to talk to Bertrand.' Helena zipped up her leather jacket and got up to leave.

'It's good Helena, very good indeed. I can't deny the cleverness of what you've just shown me.'

'OK, Antoine. But what will you *do* now?'

'I'll try to find a way, I promise you. Maybe if you can make it sound more scientific, perhaps find some studies that show an increased psychic transference in a state of ecstasy.'

'There is evidence at an unconscious level. I'll look up the references,' she said, and drained her last mouthful of wine. As she walked away she span around with a final thought. 'Surely it's your decision anyway?'

'Not *only* my decision, I'm afraid.'

'But they'll follow your recommendation, surely? Won't they? That's how it works? They haven't got time to read through every proposal.'

Palousey's face hung low over his glass.

'What's your problem Antoine? Don't look so fucking miserable. Just do it. It will be a piece of piss for you,' she said, standing over him.

'The problem is how do I pursue this without creating a scandal in the press?'

'It's only sex, the very stuff that makes us survive as a species. What is there to be ashamed of? Just use the intellectual skills for which you are paid so handsomely.'

He looked at her with a blank expression.

'Do it Antoine, or just fuck off out of my life,' she snapped, and walked off without turning around.

She disappeared through the door of Rive Gauche, her long red hair waving an unintended farewell. Several pairs of prurient eyes followed her as she swung through the exit.

She dissolved into the evening traffic and headed into the dingy bowels of Châtelet metro station.

6

Blood covered Isabella's face. The source of the bleeding was a small cut on her finger, and she'd rubbed it all over her face, and now she wouldn't stop screaming. Green tried to comfort her, but she continued for ten minutes.

'I tried to cut some cardboard with the knife and it slipped,' she said eventually, through her sobs.

Green looked at the bloodstained knife on the floor. 'That's a breadknife my darling, you must always use a pair of scissors,' he said slowly.

He cleaned Isabella's face with a tissue. She ran off and Green and Moses returned to his office.

'I'm sorry Moses, it's my ex-wife's fault,' said Green quietly, through his teeth. 'As you can see, my daughter is angry with the world at the moment. All that blood on her face was a cry for attention, after her mother,' he lowered his voice again, 'fucked off to Athens. Excuse my English, my friend.'

Green gazed at a framed picture of his young wife in a revealing bikini on his desk. Then he turned it face down. 'It was too good to be true, I suppose.'

Moses nodded in sympathy. 'Would love that drink,' he said.

'It was *her* day to look after Isabella,' Green said, opening the fridge. He filled two whisky glasses from a dusty bottle of Ouzo, took an ice tray from the freezer and slammed it against his desk. Four powdery cubes fell onto the stone floor. He picked them up, dusted them down against his shirt and quickly dropped them into the drinks. The ice cracked like shattered glass as Moses swirled the liquid around, watching it turn cloudy white. He held the drink at arm's length, concerned that a colony of E. coli had taken up residence in the ice. He would have preferred a cognac and quickly swallowed the whole glass in one massive gulp, releasing a quiet belch. For a few moments the aniseed and fennel flavours lingered playfully on his tongue and reminded him of childhood medicines.

Green found a jar of kalamata olives in the bottom drawer of his desk, twisted open the lid, and pushed it towards his guest.

'Tell me, Andreas,' Moses said, as he shook the ice in his glass. 'How did you actually find the Delphic Anomaly? It's such a big site you have here.'

'I want to show you something rather interesting,' Green said, dodging the question. He jumped from his chair and began to build a stack with the hardbound volumes of the *Annals of Ancient Greece* which littered the floor. He climbed onto this precarious DIY step and reached for something at the back of the bookcase. Stepping down again, he presented Moses with a dusty marble statue.

'Ever seen anything like this? A French archaeologist discovered this little plaything,' said Green, trying to rub away several years of dust and a crusty lump of dead flies with his shirtsleeve. He blew at the cobwebs knitted around the sculpture and sent more dust flying towards Moses. 'Of course, it's never been exhibited in the museum,'

'Why not?'

'It's really not suitable for young children. Take a look, you'll see what I mean.'

Moses held the sculpture in his hands and studied it with interest. A brutish-looking man and a young woman – not unlike a three-thousand-year-old Barbie doll, with long hair and an hour glass figure – were shown with their bodies clasped together.

Moses laughed. 'Nothing changes, eh Andreas?'

'They're in the canine position,' said Green,

'You mean the "doggy" position, Andreas. I think they must have read that ancient bestseller *The Joy of Sex*.' Moses laughed at his own joke. He turned the sculpture upside down and noticed there was a postage stamp-sized label, written in French, on the base. He read it out. '*Decouverte 1932 par Niko Delacroix (accompagne par le Texte d'Elene)*. So who was Niko Delacroix?' Moses asked.

'Oh, him,' said Green, pursing his lips, as if he'd completely forgotten about the identification label.

'And what is the *texte d'Elene*?'

Green mumbled into his moustache.

Moses asked him again. 'Who was Delacroix? Anyone I should know about?'

'You really don't want to know about Delacroix, my friend. An awkward bastard, a troublesome archaeologist, a big pile of trouble,' said Green, fidgeting with his worry beads.

'Now you've said all that, I want to know all about him,' said Moses.

Green put his hands together, interweaving his fingers. Stretching them away from his chest, he broke them apart again. 'In the mid-1930s – 1937 actually – Niko Delacroix was a famous archaeologist working around here. He was a member of the second group of French researchers who unearthed the great secrets of Delphi, from the French School of Archaeology. They took over the whole place. It was like Paris for a few years. It became a world-famous dig. Pictures appeared all over the world, in *Life Magazine*, *The Times of London*, everywhere, as they slowly uncovered the hidden Delphi. It was a sensation.

'What is interesting is that during one of his unauthorised, private digs, Delacroix found a highly controversial manuscript. It became known as the Elena Text,' said Green, walking over to a picture frame hanging on his wall. It contained a full-sized facsimile of the opening sheet.

'This is it,' he said, staring at the disintegrating handwritten document, held against a thin piece of glass.

Moses walked across the room. 'It must be important to you Andreas, to have a copy on your wall?'

'Yes. It was a sensational find, in more ways than one. No one believed it was genuine until it was carbon-dated. It is actually 3,400 years old.'

'And why was it sensational?'

'It described sex rituals performed by the Delphic Oracle and the High Priests,' said Green, pointing at the wooden frame. Moses pulled out a small magnifying lens from his pocket and held it over a line drawing of a couple. It closely resembled the explicit drawings he'd found on some early Greek ceramic vases.

'And there is a historical tradition for these sex rituals,' Green added.

'So what else do you know about the text, Andreas?' asked Moses.

'It describes the lurid antics of one particular Greek god, Dionysius, the son of Apollo, who enjoyed putting women into a kind of sexual frenzy. The priests who ran the whole prophecy show here in Delphi were clearly inspired by him. They chose the prettiest girls in town to be their Oracles, and dreamt up a cunning excuse to have ritualised sex with them. Delphi became so rich from this, you wouldn't believe it. It was literally dripping with gold. The treasuries were overflowing.'

'But how did the priests justify using these young women for sex?'

'They came up with the crazy idea that the so-called sacred semen of the god Apollo would enhance the power of the Oracles, to help them make prophecies,' said Green, shaking his head.

'I love it, that is so brilliant. The Ancients knew how to enjoy themselves.'

'As you can imagine, this sacred semen had to be delivered by the High Priests to the Oracles,' Green said. 'The idea was to drive the Oracles into a state of ecstasy and frenzy, and in this way make their prophecies look and sound even more dramatic for the visitors.'

'So you're saying that the Oracles screamed louder when they came to orgasm to impress the visitors from overseas? Is that what you're really saying?' asked Moses.

'Almost, but not exactly,' said Green, explaining that the sexual rites were performed *before* the prophecies were made, in private. 'The trick was that the Oracles *never* made any specific prophecies. They'd come out with gibberish, incoherent sounds and screams.'

'So it was a con trick?'

'Absolutely, but of the highest order. It was the oldest trick in the book. The high priests merely interpreted all the bullshit utterances and translated them into the prophecies.'

'Amazing they got away with such a scam for centuries. You know something, Andreas, I know only too well from my line of business that people will believe anything they choose to believe.'

'And just to add to the effect, the Oracles were forced to dose themselves up with laurel leaves to help send them into a trance state. This had the effect of awakening their minds, fine-tuning their perception,' said Green. 'Or, you could say, simply making them hallucinate as if they were on LSD.'

Moses walked round to Green's desk and took another olive. It was salty and he tried to wash it down with the last drops of melted ice in his glass.

'Actually, I saw a few laurel bushes as we walked up earlier,'

Moses said.

Green laughed. 'It's very convenient that these plants grow on the side of Mount Parnassus, given only a few leaves can make you hallucinate.'

'So tell me, what kind of trouble did the Elena Text cause when it was discovered?'

'OK Moses, I'll give you the uncensored truth. Obviously, it was quite sexually explicit. It was an account of a young woman, an Oracle of Delphi, named Elena, describing the lurid rituals she practised at the Temple of Apollo here in Delphi.' Moses twitched with interest and took another look at the picture frame.

'Do you mind telling me what this text actually said?' asked Moses

'Suffice it to say that the basic instincts were totally fulfilled, Moses, let me assure you. It states that the beautiful young Oracles had full sex, in the open air, with the High Priests before making their prophecies.'

'What was the official story put out to the world?'

'They claimed that if the Oracles achieved the heights of sexual ecstasy, they would, for a few minutes following orgasm, be able to see directly into the mind of the god Apollo.'

'So the sex made for much higher quality predictions. Improved psychic power? Is that what they believed?'

'Exactly, Moses. You have it. And you know something, for the first time there was a plausible explanation for Delphi's success – you know it became the most successful Oracle in the whole of the Mediterranean world?'

Moses laughed out loud. 'I suppose it's one kind of explanation. So crazy and wonderful.'

'At the time Niko Delacroix discovered the Text, it was thought to be a complete forgery. None of his archaeologist colleagues believed it was genuine. It was just too much for many of them. When the French National Archaeological Museum carbon dated it in the sixties they found it to be 3,400 years old. But it was too late for him.'

'Why?'

'Delacroix had always resented the fact that he'd received no credit for his findings. So he decided to announce the discovery of the Elena Text to the world's press.' Green paused. 'And that was a big mistake.'

'What happened?'

'They abandoned him to the wolves. Most of his colleagues turned their backs on him.'

'Did he find other things as well?'

'It's rumoured he made other discoveries at Delphi that were never publicised, but he didn't recover from the fall from grace. He'd go off on his own, he was very secretive. He used to go digging without authorisation from the leader. It was not very pleasant. There was a civil war going on between them, not helped by the fact that Delacroix was having an affair with the leader's wife.'

'OK, so what's new?' said Moses, dismissing the scandal with a swipe of his hands.

Green walked over to his filing cabinet and pulled out an old brown folder, fraying at the edges. He opened it carefully, removing a faded newspaper cutting.

'Take a look at this, Moses,' said Green.

Moses held the fragile news clipping in his fingers. It was an article from *Le Figaro* dated June 26th 1937. It announced to the world that Delacroix had found a manuscript thought to be over three-thousand years old, describing ancient sex rituals carried out by the Delphic Oracle.

'He must have made a few enemies announcing this without

the agreement of Dr Henri Mollet, the expedition leader,' Green said, and walked to the other side of his office. He opened the middle drawer of his filing cabinet and took out a large, transparent plastic folder. Inside was a well-preserved edition of *Paris Match*, dated September 14th 1937.

Moses pored over the six-page article and the pictures of Delacroix surrounded by various archaeologists. He was drawn to the smiling face of the young-looking Delacroix, standing next to an admiring young woman. She was captioned as Dr Sylvie Mollet, 'the first French woman to obtain a doctorate in archaeology,' and wife of the leader.

'Attractive woman, isn't she? You can see why Delacroix was tempted,' said Moses, as he looked at her picture. 'She has a striking resemblance to Catherine Deneuve, don't you think?' Moses could identify with the charismatic man attracted to young women.

'He craved publicity and attention, as you can see,' said Green, looking out of the window. 'I can remember Delacroix myself. I was only a young man then but I used to see him around in the village. He was a friendly guy – maybe a little ruthless and direct if he wanted to be, but a much nicer fellow than the smug expedition leader, Mollet. I could see why Delacroix hated Mollet so much, and why Mollet's wife strayed from him, into bed with Delacroix,' said Green, sucking on a new cigarette.

'So what happened to Delacroix in the end?' Moses asked, feeling there was not going to be a happy ending.

'He was found dead one morning at the bottom of the mountain,' Green said.

Moses lost his balance, almost falling over, but caught himself on Green's desk.

'Are you OK, Moses?'

'No problem, I'm OK now. I was just a little surprised by

what you said.'

'They called it an accident,' said Green, 'but Mollet would have been extremely happy to have him out of the way. It was all hushed up.'

'Of course,' Moses said, feeling his cheek muscles twitch. 'You do realise, Andreas,' said Moses, holding his face to hide the spasms, 'that other people may also have wanted him out of the way.'

'What do you mean?' asked Green, threading his worry beads from finger to finger with ever-increasing speed.

Moses made the sign of the cross.

'What do you mean?' said Green again, looking around the room anxiously.

'The Church would certainly have liked to see the end of Delacroix, especially if he'd also just discovered the Delphic Anomaly.'

'But why Moses? I don't understand you,' said a white-faced Green.

'Do you *really* think the Vatican would have been happy with the world seeing the Anomaly, such a potent symbol of God's covenant, with the old enemy?' Green screwed up his mouth.

'The old enemy?'

'The Israelites, the Jews, my friend,' said Moses, nodding gently.

'I see what you're getting at,' said Green, and stopped swinging his worry beads.

'Imagine the dramatic pictures in the world's newspapers. It's just another slap in the face for the Catholic church. They don't really like any competition from other major religions, no matter what they say, believe me, Andreas.'

Green sat back in his leather chair and stroked his lips. 'And what would they do if they discover I've found it again?' he whimpered.

'Who knows? We know they can be ruthless,' Moses said, drawing a finger across his throat. He watched as large beads of sweat formed on Green's face.

'The church isn't all loving kindness, my friend,' he said.

7

There was a loud knock on the door of Green's office. Sam was standing outside, his whole body shaking.

He gestured that he needed to discuss a problem privately. Moses grunted in disapproval and followed Sam into the museum lobby.

'What's wrong? I've never seen you look like this.'

Sam bit his lip and looked down at the floor. 'It's Anna. I don't know what's happened to her.'

'What do you mean?' said Moses, his mouth hanging open.

'She's over three hours late. I drove her up the mountain. She promised she'd be one hour. I feel responsible because I took her.'

'What's all this about a trip up the mountain?' Moses said. For a moment he recalled his doubts about bringing her to Delphi. He realised he knew so little about her.

'I wish I'd …' Sam didn't finish the thought.

'Was she in search of that bloody plant, Sam? She's obsessed with the, what's it called, the helle thing …'

'The Hellebore.'

'Tzzt.' Moses shook his head, and put a hand on Sam's shoulder. 'Look, she's an adult. Admittedly a wild, free spirit, I'm afraid, but I've a gut instinct she knows what she's doing. She'll be back soon.'

'But you didn't see how she was dressed,' said Sam.

'I can imagine, you don't need to tell me.' Moses clicked his fingers to signal an end to discussing Anna's state of undress. 'She always wears tight shorts, don't worry. It's her style, she can defend herself, and she's a big strong girl.' He remembered this from the last time they had sex.

Moses walked back into the office, but Green was no longer there so he followed Sam back to the Mercedes and climbed into the passenger seat.

'Let's go and look for her,' he said.

'What about your meeting with Green?'

'Forget about him. Our slippery friend seems to have slithered down one of his wormholes,' said Moses, taking from his pocket the small metal coin he'd found on the floor of the cave. It was the first time he'd had a chance to study it in daylight. As he moved it around in his fingers the silver medallion caught the light, making him blink.

'Where shall we look?' Sam asked.

Moses didn't answer. He was too distracted by the medallion in the palm of his hand.

8

Long fingers of white cloud hovered over Paris in the late afternoon heat.

Maria Delacroix opened a new bottle of Rémy Martin, and poured a double measure into the crystal brandy glasses on the antique coffee table.

Dressed in semi-transparent silk, her daughter sat opposite her, reading a photocopy of the Elena Text, newly arrived from the National Archive that morning.

Helena's neck glistened with a few beads of sweat mingled with perfume. She had plenty of her delicately perspiring body on view – it was her own special way of marking her Catholic heritage. Being a Friday, she made a point of displaying liberal quantities of her own bare flesh.

She enjoyed the irony that the family name Delacroix meant 'of the cross.' It may have implied a high degree of religious observance, long ago, in medieval times when the family was bound up with the church, but the only thing Helena was bound up with these days was tight leather.

Marie Delacroix was a well-known art dealer. She'd met many famous twentieth-century artists, including Marc Chagall, Salvador Dali, and Pablo Picasso. Now in her middle sixties, she lived in an elegant apartment building in the exclusive 16th arrondissement in the centre of Paris, on rue Raynouard.

Helena had always hoped that, having a mother with a bohemian background, she'd be able to cope with her nudity, drugs, and sex. But Maria was a puritan.

Her seventh-floor penthouse, overlooking the Paris skyline, was furnished with traditional antiques interlaced with tasteful modern art. But she had an eye for budding young artists and had been lucky with some purchases. Highlights of her collection included a Matisse pencil drawing of woman undressing and an early Dali watercolour of a peregrine, but she hated his melting clocks, the lurid landscapes, and his naked women hidden inside his paintings. They were all gimmicks, in her view.

She was proud of her brilliant daughter, but didn't understand her. They disagreed on most things. She'd given birth to Helena at the age of 42 after having artificial insemination, from an unknown donor, at a private clinic in town, following a string of unsuitable male partners who were more interested in her collection than her mind and body.

Helena was her only child, and they had a volatile relationship. For months all would stay calm until there were wild explosions for a week or so, followed by periods of calm, much like Mount Etna in Sicily.

Helena leaned forward, tossed her tangled red hair backwards, and took out a plastic tobacco pouch. A few strands of marijuana and tobacco fell onto the two-hundred-year-old Chinese rug.

'Haven't you grown out of that yet?' Maria said.

Helena shook her head as she licked the edge of the cigarette paper with a clean swipe of her tongue. She placed the sharper end between her lips and with a snap of her Zippo lit up her joint, drawing deeply on it.

'It gives me an expanded consciousness. You should try it,' she said, trails of smoke streaming from her nose as she enunciated each word.

'I prefer this poison,' Maria said, lifting her brandy glass in the air before taking another sip, swirling the alcohol around her mouth. 'What's new?' she asked.

'Some good news. I've put in my PhD proposal now. I'm hoping to get approval from the university to research Niko's Elena Text,' she announced. 'But look, I must warn you, it's not yet confirmed, it has to go before the faculty committee first.'

'I suppose I should say congratulations. It could give some belated recognition for your grandfather's work at Delphi.' Maria said, turning towards the sepia photograph of her father on the wall. She focussed on it for several seconds and smiled.

'I'm so pleased, Helena, that's such good news. His work may finally have a life beyond the grave. His reputation can only grow if you do the PhD.'

Helena held her breath.

'I also have a little problem, *maman*.'

9

Moses' face quivered as he held the silver medallion in his hand. He was disturbed by the intricate filigree work on the back and front. It was simply too good.

As he tilted the shining coin, he put his hand into his pocket and felt for the slip of paper he'd scooped up with it. He rolled it out on his knee. It was a shop till receipt for two espressos and panettone from *La Valetta*, a café on Via Aurelia in Rome. The date showed that the transaction had taken place two days earlier.

Moses looked up as he heard the museum door closing.

'He's back.'

Sam looked back at him and shrugged. Moses moved closer to so he could speak without being overheard.

'I'm afraid I can't believe everything Green's been telling me,

Sam,' he whispered.

Green appeared as if from nowhere, climbing up the steps from the museum basement and walking hurriedly past the Mercedes. They watched him re-enter the museum, weaving between clusters of heat-dazed tourists.

'Look, I'm sorry, I can't come with you now,' said Moses. Sam looked at him in disbelief.

'But Anna's been missing for hours …'

'I know, I know – just go and look for her on your own. Come back and get me in forty minutes if you still haven't found her.'

'Where shall I …?' Sam started to say with a soft wail.

'I'm sure you'll find her coming down the mountain very soon.' Moses paused and raised his hand. 'And one more thing – and this may or may not be important – there was a grey Fiat Tempra with Vatican plates driving around the village this morning. Can you see if it's still around?'

He opened the palm of his hand and swung the silver medallion from his fingers. 'See this shining beauty? I've a feeling the Fiat driver will be after this. Good luck Sam,' said Moses, stepping out of the Merc. He slammed the door and walked briskly back into the museum, making his way to Green's office.

He knocked on the heavy oak door and discovered a dishevelled Green on his knees, scrabbling under the desk, an unlit cigarette drooping from his lips.

'Excuse me, Moses. I can't find my lighter. I had it a moment ago.'

'No, no, no, the apologies are all mine. I'm sorry I had to leave you earlier, Andreas.'

'I have it!' he shouted. A smiling Green rose from the floor, sat down behind his desk and tried to make the lighter come to life. He rolled his thumb over the wheel, but it refused to ignite.

'It's empty. It's an old one I threw away months ago.' He

threw it onto the floor and placed his hands on his face like a man who'd lost the will to live.

'Can you talk now?'

'Whatever pleases you, Moses. I'm at your disposal.'

Green offered him the leather easy chair, but Moses chose to stand. The proud museum director was looking jittery. His shirt was falling out from his waistband and his jacket was dusty as he looked up at Moses.

'I've been thinking about what I said earlier and I've a confession,' he said, rocking from side to side in his creaky leather chair.

Moses could see he was perspiring heavily as sweat leaked through his shirt. He thought of all the other things he might have done over the last eight hours instead of wasting his time with Green. *Not* driving through the night from Vienna to Delphi. *Not* dragging himself up a mountain under the hot morning sun. *Not* risking his life in a flooded cave.

'I must tell you something, Moses,' he began falteringly.

'Spit it out, my friend.' There was a long silence. 'What's the problem?' said Moses, trying to restrain a smile.

Green noticed it. 'Don't laugh at me Moses. It's not easy to say this, but, on reflection, I believe the Delphic Anomaly MAY' – he shouted the word – 'MAY have been first discovered by Delacroix. I think it's possible. But if it happened, it was over half a century ago, and it definitely became lost again until I found it.' Green stood up and tried to make himself taller.

'And were it not for ME' – he raised his voice again – 'I must tell you, Moses, the Delphic Anomaly would still be lying undiscovered, hidden from the world, for ever more.'

Moses smacked his fist against the palm of his hand and looked straight at Green. 'I'm sorry Andreas, but do you know what this means?'

'No, please tell me, my friend.'

'It means the family of Niko Delacroix, wherever they are living these days, will also have a claim on the Anomaly.'

'Moses, I cannot believe what you're saying. I've been one hundred – no, two hundred percent honest in telling you this, and now you sell me down the Ganges. That's not right. It goes against the spirit of our understanding.'

'I'm a fair man, Andreas. You'll have to trust me,' Moses said. 'And I must leave it there. I need to go and find Anna. We must be on our way soon.'

'Ah yes, Anna! What an attractive and interesting young woman. You're a very lucky man,' said Green, clearly relieved to think about something else for a few moments.

They walked out of the shaded office, and stepped out into the bright sunshine.

'Andreas, what can I say? Thank you for a truly momentous day,' Moses said, putting his arm on Green's shoulder. 'You need to call me as soon as you've freed the Delphic Anomaly from its limestone handcuffs. I'd start stocking up with cans of cola or lemonade, if I were you,' said Moses, with a smile. 'It should dissolve the rock quite easily, and then we can arrange for shipment to Vienna. After that, and once I can see it in all its beauty, we can talk through the terms of our deal.'

'I'll drive it to Vienna myself,' said Green, lurching towards Moses.

'That's a good idea, but you'll need to pay off the customs guys at the borders. It may be easier to use a private jet. I always use one for transporting large relics made of solid gold, otherwise they tend to create a bit of a stir at the frontiers.'

'I like the sound of that Moses.' Green smiled and held out his hand. 'I feel we've established a real bond of trust.'

Moses pressed Green's hand and the two men shook. Green

walked slowly back into the museum, his shoulders hunched like a man in deep thought. Moses stayed outside, waiting for the Merc to reappear.

Ten minutes later he saw it speeding towards him. It stopped abruptly, a few inches in front of his feet. Sam jumped out and ran around to open the back door, and Moses slipped inside.

'No sign of her ?' he asked quietly.

'I'm so sorry Moses,' Sam said, covering his eyes.

'It's not your fault, Sam, she's a pretty wild woman. You can't keep her in a cage, she needs to roam free.'

'But I shouldn't have left her alone on the mountain, dressed like she was.'

10

The road climbed gently until they were one-thousand feet above the Temple of Apollo.

Moses looked down at the archaeological site through his lenses. He didn't know which way to turn.

There were two paths going in opposite directions. He put the binoculars up to his eyes again and re-focussed – some wild jasmine bushes came sharply into view.

'She has to be in there somewhere, it's full of interesting-looking plants she'd go for,' Moses said to a subdued Sam.

They walked another two-hundred metres towards the valley. In the distance they could see a boulder in the grass.

'Try over there,' Moses said, stamping noisily on the dry

ground. Thirty metres ahead of them they could see a body shape, and Moses felt his throat draining of saliva. The image of Anna's battered corpse wouldn't go away. He looked again and saw a figure lying on the ground, partially hidden in the vegetation.

It could be Anna. He could feel his pulse racing. Why hadn't he listened to Sam instead of having another meeting with Green?

He could feel himself getting carried away. Anna was a strong, capable woman – perhaps she was lying very still for a reason. He held the binoculars steady.

'ANNA,' he shouted with all the force in his lungs. His voice echoed across the hills. 'She'd hear that,' he paused for a moment. 'If she's conscious.'

'I think so,' said Sam.

'Fucking move woman. Anna!' he shouted. He took a deep breath and tried again. 'Move that arse, for God's sake, Anna!' he screamed. For a moment he imagined the she'd twitched. He was beginning to doubt his own senses and looked at Sam.

'Did you see her move? Or am I deluding myself?'

'I'm not sure,' Sam said, wiping the sweat off his face.

'Anna! ANNA! Can you hear me?' He shouted so loud that Sam put his hands to his ears.

The shape sprang to life, sitting bolt upright. It was Anna, looking startled and confused.

'For Christ's sake Sam, look at that girl,' Moses said, laughing out loud and shaking his head. 'I don't believe it – and clutching that damned book as well.'

They watched Anna look left and right, the *Materia Medica* in her left hand, a bunch of plant specimens in her right. She stood up and tried to run down the goat track towards them. She was nothing but long legs and a brief pair of shorts, rolled up tightly to her crotch.

'You can't go around like that, Anna. You're in the Greek countryside, not a beach in Marbella,' Moses said.

'It's been very hot on the mountain. I needed to cool down,' she said.

'Don't look at her Sam, she's no idea what's acceptable here in Greece.'

Anna shot into Moses' arms and locked onto him like a lost child.

'So Anna, what were you up to? Apart from worrying us sick?'

'I've been looking for the Black Hellebore. Look,' she said, untying her backpack. 'They're still growing here after four-thousand years.'

'That's great. I'm glad you found them,' said Moses, drily. Her look of smiling innocence irritated him. 'But where were you all this time? Sam told me you were over three hours late. We thought you'd been raped and murdered by a Greek shepherd.'

'Actually, I was watching a snake. I couldn't move or it might have disappeared.'

'For three hours? For fuck's sake, Anna.'

'You didn't need to come looking for me. I was on my way back to the museum.'

'My powers of telepathy are not that great, Anna. But listen – all's well that ends well, eh?' Moses held onto her tightly. He knew there was nothing to be gained by making her feel worse.

Anna let go and sorted out her plant specimens. Moses pointed out that some looked more like laurel leaves than Hellebore.

'Yes, Moses, you're right. They *are* laurel leaves. Actually, I wanted to tell you – I've uncovered another secret about them. Laurel leaves grew on the hills above Delphi and were eaten by the Oracles before they made their prophecies,' she told him. 'To put the young prophetesses into a state of delirious ecstasy.'

'So it wasn't just the sex?' Moses said quietly.

'*What* did you say?'

'I'll tell you about the sex later. And you can tell me about the laurel leaves.'

'It's a deal.'

Sam swung the back door of the Merc open and Moses stepped into the luxury of the cool air conditioning. Anna reached into the front seat, removed the bottles of spring water from the cooler, and deposited her plant specimens. The car glided silently down the mountain road with Moses slumped on the back seat. He was exhausted. Anna put her arms around his waist and shut her eyes.

'But you were away with Dr Green such a long time. I missed you,' she said in a little girl voice.

'I was, that's true. But you are joking now, aren't you?'

Moses lay in silence for a minute.

'I need to talk to you, Anna. I have to go to Paris. You might enjoy coming along too. I know it wasn't part of the original plan, but things have moved on quickly.'

'I've never been there before,' she said.

'On the way, I also need to stop briefly in Rome. I need to check something out. Actually, I'd like to test something out with you.'

'Are you still road-testing me? What does that involve? A new position …' she stopped herself and used her fingers instead, but Moses did not need the extra piece of mime.

'And that as well,' he said, smiling as she spread her hands over his chest.

'As well as what?' she asked.

'You'll see when we get there. I can't say now. Too many questions. Take it easy for now.'

'Is there anything else?' she said.

'Oh yes,' he said, taking the medallion from his pocket and swinging it in front of her eyes. 'I need to find out where this little dazzler came from.'

Moses leaned forward and asked Sam how long it would take to drive to Rome. Without warning, Sam stopped in a layby, opened the glove compartment, took out a Michelin map of Europe and spread it across the front seat.

'About eighteen hours with the ferry crossing.'

Anna started kissing Moses. He pulled the privacy blind over the window as Sam pulled away. They were soundproofed, and could be neither heard nor seen as they drove slowly down the mountain.

'Aren't you hungry?' Moses whispered softly into Anna's ear.

'I'm hungry for everything, Moses,' she said, placing her hand under his shirt and clawing at his chest.

'Me too,' he said.

Anna untied his belt and climbed on top of him, lowering herself slowly and slipping her tongue inside his mouth. 'We are a perfect union of biology and machine,' she said, as she wrapped her long legs around him and leaned backwards.

They made love as the harsh, grey Neolithic rocks flew by in a blur, interrupted by occasional clusters of gnarled olive trees. He stayed inside her for the next 10 km, pushing and braking in harmony with the progress of their descent, the gentle movements of the car's suspension heightening their pleasure.

When the Merc reached one eighty they came within seconds of one another. As it slowed to seventy, Anna lifted herself off Moses and lay next to him, gazing dreamily through the smoked glass windows.

She pulled the silk sheet over their bodies and curled up, attaching herself to Moses. They didn't fall asleep – they were still too hungry.

Moses said nothing. He was thinking about the Anomaly.

His eyes scanned the floor of the vehicle, searching for his khaki shirt. It was still there, crumpled but safe. He removed the buttonhole camera from the breast pocket, took out the tiny spool of film, placed it inside a plastic canister, and pulled open the privacy window.

'Sam, can you get this film developed when we reach Rome, 12 x 10 inch colour gloss? Take it to Pellici's, they'll be open.'

Sam knew the photography routine well. He'd often take Moses' microfilms for developing during the course of a journey. Moses had a worldwide account with Pellici's – he liked to use them because they could deliver large colour prints within hours, in every major capital.

'Tell them to force it by 4 stops. It'll be grainy – there was hardly any light in the chamber,' said Moses.

Sam took the roll of film and in return he handed Moses a slip of folded paper.

When Anna's eyes were firmly shut and her breathing had changed, Moses opened it. He was wondering why Sam had resorted to sending him messages written on small pieces of paper. He realised the answer as he read the contents.

'Grey Fiat Tempra, VC 21 53 99 42.' Moses read it out to himself, trying to commit it to memory as he stared blankly through the front windscreen.

'For Christ's sake, Sam! There's a grey Fiat right in front of us!' he shouted, unable to contain himself. 'Get closer so I can check the number.'

'You don't need to. That's the car. I checked it a few moments ago,' Sam replied.

'The gods must be on our side. Keep following Sam, wherever it goes – but I've a feeling all roads will lead to Rome.'

Moses sat back in the leather seat and stretched out his arms triumphantly – in the corner of his eye he saw that Anna's eyes were flickering.

'Are you awake Anna? I want to tell you something exciting,' he said as he turned to her.

'Exciting?' she asked, dreamily, looking surprised, her mouth slightly open. 'I thought I'd had enough excitement for today.'

'This is different.'

'OK, tell me Moses,' she said in a sleepy voice.

'I believe that our oily friend, Dr Green, has stumbled across the world's greatest missing antiquity.'

'But what do you mean exactly? The Ark of the Covenant? No, is it Noah's Ark?' she said and laughed. 'Isn't that supposed to be the most sought-after relic?'

'No, not that. But wait a minute,' Moses said with a slight smile. 'I think you already know, don't you?'

'What are you saying?' she asked, screwing up her face.

'You'll have to wait,' he said, kissing her fingers. 'Go back to sleep and dream about it.'

11

Helena went to the window and watched as a Citroen diesel sprayed a fine powder of soot into the air from its dirty exhaust pipe.

Accelerating away from the lights at the junction with avenue de Lamballe, it was followed by a cleaner petrol-engined Renault 16 and a noisy 50cc motovelo, spewing a cloud of blue smoke.

For Maria they were all racing too fast down her beloved street. 'It was never like this when I first came to rue Raynouard,' she sighed.

One floor above her, the international concert pianist Eleanor Bellecoeur was playing Schubert's piano sonata in A minor to an audience of Siamese cats and a tank of angel fish.

Despite the wails of the police sirens and the hum of traffic, the sonata could still be heard as gentle background music inside Maria's apartment.

'Why did you say you have a problem?' she said.

Helena returned to the white leather sofa and sat knees crossed, her short dress three quarters of the way up her thighs.

'There are no more scholarships available. I will have to fund the research myself, if it is approved by the archaeology faculty.'

'That's ridiculous. After getting the highest marks ever for an archaeology degree they won't fund you? Who *are* they funding for a PhD? I suppose you'd have to sleep with the professor these days.'

'If only that were possible, *maman*.'

Helena rolled a cigarette and went back over to the window to blow the smoke outside. 'It's too controversial,' she said. Her mother looked puzzled. 'The problem is, I've had some negative feedback. They're saying the content of the Elena Text is too risqué.' She was standing by the window, playing with strands of her long red hair, blowing out smoke in short, rapid bursts.

'I think some funding *might* get approved at a later stage, but it's not happening right now. I just wondered – would you be willing to underwrite the cost of the research?'

'Possibly,' Maria smiled at her. 'How much do you need?'

'I need enough to support me for about six weeks of research in Delphi. Enough to cover my hotel and air travel, living costs – about six-thousand francs altogether. That's all,' Helena said, looking over the Paris skyline towards the Tuileries Garden. Maria was staring at the ceiling as if in deep thought. She glanced at Helena and a smile crept over her face.

'You know I really want Niko to be remembered in a positive way. Your PhD would help restore his reputation, help bring his name back into the international journals. It's time his pioneering work was given recognition. But tell me – what will your research actually involve?' Maria asked enthusiastically.

'It will be,' Helena chose her words with care, 'a truly scientific experiment. But it's … very unusual, and … how can I say? A little daring.' Helena had decided that her mother didn't need to know every detail.

'Is it controversial?' Maria asked, knowing her daughter had a passion for the provocative.

'Let me put it this way, it's no more controversial than Niko's original discovery,' said Helena, trying to exploit Maria's devotion to her father.

She'd been calculating exactly what to say for several days. It would have to be a delicate balancing act. She would be honest, but not say so much that she frightened her mother away.

'Tell me about it, Helena, I'm pretty broadminded.'

Helena's mouth fell open as she heard her mother claim she was broadminded. 'Look, it's a scientific study of the Elena Text, designed to test its central hypothesis—'

'It was so long ago since I last read it, I can't really remember any central hypothesis, as you put it.'

Helena sat down and smiled at her mother. 'Let's consider the bigger picture. Every religion has tried to explain the feeling of ecstasy as a way of directly experiencing the power of God. We can try and attain ecstasy in different ways, through prayer, devotion and,' she paused and coughed, 'with the help of another human being. That is, during the act of love,' she said, rushing the last five words so they were nearly inaudible. 'As you will remember, the Text makes the interesting observation that there is a positive correlation between levels of ecstasy and the accuracy of the prophecies made by the Oracle.'

Maria nodded and walked over to the window, pulling the secondary glazing down over the older art deco frame to keep out the traffic noise. She came back to the glass table for another sip of brandy, draining the whole glass in one large gulp.

'That sounds fairly spiritual, from a modern viewpoint. But I suppose the Ancient Greeks believed in supernatural powers from the gods …' Maria's words trailed off.

'I am not going to pre-judge anything, *maman*. I'll let the results speak for themselves. It's the nature of scientific inquiry. You take a hypothesis, no matter how far-fetched it may be, and you test it against the reality of the world. You do it again and again. That's how science makes progress, isn't it?' Helena decided not to push it too far at this stage. Her main objective was simply to get Maria to act as a sponsor, not to initiate an argument.

'So how will you get your results?' Maria asked uncertainly. Helena felt her pulse shoot through her body.

'It's complicated to explain,' Helena mumbled, whilst she looked around the room. She started rolling another cigarette. 'It's really straightforward and intellectually sound, don't worry about it. To be honest, I will get someone else to do the statistics.'

'Just give me the basic outline,' Maria said. Helena got up and walked around the room, searching for the right words.

'OK, *maman*. As you know, the Oracles were young and attractive women. They were probably chosen for their sex appeal. Let's say they were the Brigitte Bardots of Ancient Greece.'

Her mother smiled at Helena, nodding her head. 'They were

like you, Helena, they were beautiful and no doubt practised the erotic arts,' said Maria, still smiling.

'So far, so good,' Helena whispered under her breath, and braced herself.

'So the Oracles chewed hallucinogenic plants, laurel leaves, to induce a feeling of ecstasy. They believed it would give them the power to make better prophecies by boosting their unconscious sensitivity.'

Helena flourished her colour photocopy of the Elena Text.

'It's beautiful,' said Helena, running her manicured fingers over the page, 'one of the great treasures of our cultural heritage.'

'I've always thought Niko had discovered something of historic value,' Maria said.

'I totally agree, *maman*,' said Helena, nodding vigorously.

'And tell me, Helena, how will you be investigating it?'

Helena coughed. 'I don't want to bore you with all the technical minutiae.'

'Look, this means a great deal to me, Helena. If I'm going to sponsor you, I want to know everything about your project. You'll only have one chance at this. As a family, we can't afford to have Niko's reputation blackened again.'

Helena took a deep breath, looked straight into her mother's watery grey eyes, and began. 'Well, according to the Text there is another, more effective way to reach a state of ecstasy than chewing laurel leaves,' she said calmly.

Maria forced half a smile as it began to dawn on her what might be involved. Helena's lips quivered and she laughed nervously. She brought both hands together and made a tunnel with the tips of her fingers.

'If you are talking about *sexual* ecstasy, I realise it can be achieved in two ways: with a partner, or without,' said Maria, pointedly. It was a knowing comment from a woman who'd spent much of her life without any sexual partners.

'From the little you've revealed so far I can only presume that you will be having sex with your husband to authenticate the Text? Have I got that right?' Helena was surprised that her mother had openly come out with it – with one small error. She decided she had to correct her notion of the experiment.

'Roughly, that's about it. But it would be too exhausting for one man, and not scientific either,' Helena pointed out. Maria laughed nervously, which was followed by a short, tense silence.

'Michel has to be in Brussels and Geneva every other week,' Helena said, leaning backwards so her crimson hair fell all the way down her back. 'And he totally supports what I'm planning to do. We have a strong relationship. This research will not affect it at all. I can separate my professional work from my private life. As it's a scientific inquiry, which has to be statistically significant, I'll need a larger sample of subjects.'

Maria looked at Helena with a fixed expression, her cheeks rigid and taut.

'So are you saying that you will be the *only* female subject, and you will have sex until you reach orgasm with a long line of different men?'

'But *maman*, as you can appreciate, it would not be valid otherwise, and it would also be difficult to recruit volunteers, and quite expensive, too.'

Maria's face reddened with anger. 'Let me get this straight, Helena – you'll be lying in the Temple of Apollo, offering yourself to a succession of different men for sex, to bring you to orgasm?'

'It won't be like that, *maman*. They will be highly selected, fully briefed, and psychologically assessed beforehand. They'll understand the serious and scientific nature of the experiment,' she said, surprised by her own ability to invent plausible procedures as she talked.

'Do you really think I will sponsor you to be a prostitute?' Maria shrieked.

Helena could feel herself trying to undo what she'd said, but it was too late to backtrack. She recoiled as her mother rose up and pushed her towards the door. Helena ducked sideways as Maria threw her bag of belongings at her, tears rolling down her cheeks. She was out of control.

The flying bag missed Helena but knocked over a valuable Italian glass vase, a Murano sculpted in green and blue glass. A chunky bottle of Chanel fell out of the bag along with tobacco and cigarette papers. Helena expected to see a shower of glass, but only a few drops of perfume seeped out.

'Leave my home. I don't want you here anymore. You're disgusting and you don't even know it.'

Helena scrambled for her belongings as she left the penthouse. She tried to slam the four-inch thick door behind her but it was too heavy, and the slam was reduced to a quiet thud. The elevator doors opened and she sat on the floor whilst it took her to ground level. Louis, the hall porter, found her sitting in a huddle against the wall as it arrived in the lobby. He ran up to her but she shooed him away. She pulled herself up, lit a cigarette, and blew smoke as she staggered from the elevator.

'Helena, what's happened this time?' Louis asked, but she didn't want to speak.

'Don't worry, forget about it,' she said, and walked off into the empty street.

He tried calling after her. 'Helena, can I get you a taxi?'

'I don't need one,' she called back, as she walked towards the traffic lights on the corner of avenue de Lamballe.

In her short white skirt, a cigarette dangling from her mouth, and her long hair flying in the wind, Helena quickly attracted attention.

A silver Ferrari screeched to a halt in front of her – the bass of its sound system made her ribs vibrate as it cruised along next to her.

The driver, chewing gum viorously, was wearing mirrored sunglasses and an open-necked shirt showing a large expanse of tanned bare chest. He smiled at her, leaned over and opened the passenger door. The music of the Rolling Stones blasted out across the pavement. Mick Jagger drawled about a little red rooster on the prowl. Helena found herself heading uncontrollably in the direction of the leather bucket seat.

12

The smell of pasta, petrol fumes and pizza filled the evening air as Sam steered the Mercedes into the chaos of rush-hour Rome.

He was trying to follow the Fiat Tempra into the Vatican City through the Angelica gate, but as it passed under two archways flanked by sprawling pizzerias it disappeared from view. He looked around at Moses anxiously.

'Where to now?'

'Try that first small turning on the right, we just passed,' Moses said calmly, unfazed by the sudden loss of the Fiat.

Sam slammed the brakes, reversed a few feet, and made a sharp right turn into the deserted-looking Via della Posta.

It was a street with few pretensions, full of 1930s' granite office buildings built in the heavy armoured tank style of Mussolini.

A hundred metres down the street a vehicle was turning into an underground car park.

Moses grabbed his binoculars, threw open the door and sprang onto the pavement.

'It's the Fiat, for sure' he shouted, and clapped his hands.

'Just wait here,' said Moses. He looked around at the metal shutters lining the length of the street, his eyes resting on the car park entrance.

The driver was repeatedly pressing a key fob. There was a problem with the electronic door. An unshaven face, grey with exhaustion, loomed larger than life in the magnifying lens. Moses moved the binoculars slightly to the left.

Black-coated steel shutters, built into the wall, started to move, shimmying from side to side. A dark rectangular black hole appeared as the shutters ended their dance. The entrance to the underground garage was now fully open.

A blue alarm light flickered on the wall above. He watched the driver return to the car and grab the steering wheel. The Fiat quickly sank into the basement, completely disappearing from view. Moses counted to sixty, put on his white straw hat, and walked down the street to find the number of the building. He stopped outside 98 Via Della Posta and pushed gently against the steel shutters. They clanged quietly, and he looked upwards at the blue light on the wall. It was the same colour and shape he'd seen through the binoculars.

He returned to the Merc and found Anna hanging out of the window.

'Moses, can I get out of here soon please? I've been crammed in this metal box all night.'

'But this is the most comfortable four-wheeled metal box in the world, with the softest of sheepskin seats, and a double bed. What more could you want, my darling?'

'I believe you, Moses, but we've been travelling for eight hours and I'm getting desperate.'

'OK. Sam – let's go.'

As they drove to the hotel the city played like a looped film in front of their eyes. Moses enjoyed the chaotic visual feast. His eyes followed a pretty dark-haired *bellezza* in her short tight dress, weaving precariously between two old women in black on her Lambretta.

He loved the crumbling ruins on every street corner, the animated priests in black-rimmed hats darting through gothic courtyards. The overflowing gutters, brimming with cigarette packets, the old lottery tickets and pizza wrappers floating down the sides of the streets – for Moses they were all part of the colourful mosaic of an ancient city, vibrantly flowing with the dirt and grime of twentieth-century life.

He loved Rome – it was relaxed, messy, and alive. It was totally unlike Vienna.

Sam turned into Via Della Minerva and Moses remembered that the hotel was located only fifty metres from the Pantheon. The Roman place of worship should have been shut at this late hour, but there was a photo shoot going on.

'I want to show this place to Anna,' Moses said to Sam. 'This may be our only chance. Can you check us into the hotel? I'll catch up later.' The Merc stopped outside the Grand Hotel Minerva and they slipped across the street towards the Pantheon.

Moses took Anna past a roped-off entrance. They found themselves in the main hall. It echoed with the whispered voices of a camera crew, thin, long-legged models, make-up artists, and lighting technicians. No one seemed to take any notice of Anna and Moses as they wandered around.

'You'd think the Romans would have removed the pagan gods before they took up Christianity,' said Moses, looking at a statue of Apollo.

'The church was too clever to do that,' said Anna, looking up at the hole in the ceiling, She was mesmerised by the huge orifice above her.

'You like the oculus? A brilliant example of Roman design, providing worshippers with a direct link to the heavens so they could see how the gods entered the building,' said Moses.

'I love it. How do you say it? The oculus? But what happens when it rains?'

'Another example of advanced Roman engineering. It drains away without any problem,' said Moses kneeling down on the floor. 'Look at these narrow grooves. They chiselled these into the marble floor to carry away all the excess water. They're almost invisible, but they worked and they still do, two-thousand years later.

'And there, look at that statue of Venus next to Christ. You know, Anna, they were such clever psychologists, allowing the citizens of Rome to keep their old pagan gods whilst brainwashing them to follow the new Christian cult.'

'But the church did some good as well,' said Anna, as the Pantheon was bathed in bright light. The shoot was beginning. An assistant cleared the floor area, and the models took their positions and disrobed, revealing a new range of designer swimwear.

Moses took Anna's hand and they crept out, making their way to the Minerva. It was only a few steps around the corner, and they entered the palatial hotel and took the elevator up to a roof garden overlooking the whole city.

They ate gemelli pasta with fresh salmon cooked in white wine and Moses began to talk about his plans.

As they drank espresso, he dug into his pocket and produced the silver medallion, holding it in front of Anna's face. It glowed brightly against her delicate skin.

She cowered and pushed it away.

'What's the problem, Anna?' he said, holding the medallion midway between their faces. She placed her fingers on her lips and began to hyperventilate.

'Why does this coin disturb you so much?' he said, still turning it over in his fingers.

'No … it doesn't really, I'm just tired, Moses,' she said, pursing her lips and trying to breathe more slowly.

13

Her breathing returned to normal.

'I'm fine, now – maybe it was the wine that set me off,' Anna said, trying to make light of her reaction.

Her cheek muscles softened as she smiled and leaned over the table to take a closer look at the medallion.

'I can see it's very delicate, and so beautifully engraved.'

'Yes – in contrast to the organisation it probably represents,' said Moses. He could see she was trying to be enthusiastic.

'But where did you get it?' she asked.

'I found it in the sealed chamber under Delphi,' he said. 'Here, feel it, if you like.'

Anna pressed her fingers hesitantly against the edge of the medallion to feel the ridges of the engraving.

'It looks so new. What was it doing in a two-thousand-year-old chamber?'

'I've a pretty good idea – dropped on the ground by someone who broke in.'

'How do you know it happened recently?' Anna asked anxiously.

'Lying by it was a receipt from a café in Rome, a place just outside the walls of the Vatican City.'

'From when?'

'Four days ago.'

'Oh. How strange,' Anna said after a long pause.

Moses blinked at Anna. She smiled back at him and took a deep breath. Her breasts swelled slightly and their outline became visible through her top, and she breathed out. Moses looked across at her and smiled. He was reminded of the first night they met, when she'd lain on the sofa in his Vienna apartment.

'Who do you think left it there?' she said, wetting the top of her lip with her tongue.

'I don't know. Some Italian agent who likes espresso and has a sweet tooth. The bill included a panettone,' he laughed. 'What do you think?'

'That's ninety percent of the Italian population. I need some more wine.'

He filled her glass with Frascati but poured himself sparkling water.

'The point, my angel Anna, is that I found this medallion in Delphi.' He paused and gestured downwards. 'It was deep underground, inside a sealed chamber. It's very odd, don't you think?'

'Maybe. I don't know much about this,' said Anna.

'The problem is that poor old Dr Green is convinced that he'd sealed off the chamber from all prying eyes. It's barricaded with a huge metal drain cover, kept in place by two mighty padlocks.

It would have been very difficult to enter the chamber. He swore I was the only other person to have ever been there.'

'And what do you think?'

'I think he's a little naïve. He doesn't realise he's probably being watched.'

'Does it matter?'

'Yes, of course. We may have a fight against the Church on our hands. And if it's them, I know they won't give up.'

'Really?' Anna's face went salsa red. 'But why should the Vatican be interested in a biblical relic found in Greece? It's not a Christian antiquity. I don't understand why they'd bother.'

The waiter arrived with one thousand lira change and two dark-chocolate mints on a plate. Moses sat back in his seat and smiled at Anna as she ate hers.

'Can I have yours too, Moses?' she said, grinning at him.

He pushed the chocolate towards her. 'I have a feeling the Church want to have the Anomaly back here in Rome,' Moses said, as he threw a few notes on the table. They stood up and walked over to the edge of the roof garden and looked across the city against the reddening sky. It was dominated by the vast cupola over St Peter's Basilica.

'What do you mean they want it *back*?' Anna asked.

'Tomorrow, it will all be clearer,' he said as they entered the hotel elevator.

On reaching their suite, Anna fell asleep the instant she put her head on the pillow of the king-sized bed. Moses looked at her soft pink lips and remained awake, his head rattling with thoughts.

At 1.30 am he heard an envelope being pushed under the bedroom door. Moses opened the door to find Sam walking away along the corridor.

'I need to speak to you. Have you got a moment?' They walked to Sam's room and he unlocked it, switching on the lights.

'Can I sit down?' Moses asked, making his way to the panoramic window where there were two small armchairs.

Sam looked anxiously across at Moses, chewing his thumbnail. 'If this is to do with Anna … look, I'm sorry Moses, but she's very hard to … how can I put it? To control – no, sorry, I don't mean that exactly. It's just hard to predict what she'll do next,' Sam said. There was a sustained silence in the room whilst Moses tried to absorb what his young chauffeur was saying. Then he laughed out loud.

'No, no, don't worry at all about Anna, she's a crazy woman. Sometimes I'm sure she needs some gentle persuasion, maybe even a little taming. I need to talk to you about the building we drove to earlier this evening.'

'98 Via Della Posta.'

'Exactly, that's the place. I'd like you to check it out, first call tomorrow. Try to find out what goes on there, discretely. If you can, take a look around from a higher vantage point. It would be helpful to know exactly where our Fiat driver ended up today. I'd like to know who's employing him.'

'No problem, boss,' said Sam, looking relieved, the creases on his face dissolving away to release a gentle smile.

'It's very late, I must get to bed. Goodnight, Sam,' Moses said, walking to the door and making his way down the corridor.

To avoid waking Anna, Moses crept into the en suite bathroom with the envelope Sam had given him to scan through the photographs.

He flicked through the shots, one at a time. In a highly magnified close-up of the base of the Anomaly he noticed three small Roman letters scratched onto the metal.

'NFD.' He repeated them under his breath until they were set in his memory, re-sealed the envelope and placed it in Anna's canvas backpack.

Crawling into the kingsized bed he found himself pressing his body against Anna's. He'd woken her from a dream. She was not fully awake, but she pulled Moses on top of her and tightly against her body. She parted her legs allowing him to enter her, and she began thrusting wildly, legs in the air, pulling him deeper inside her for several minutes until she came. Moses came shortly afterwards.

'That was nice,' she mumbled, half asleep, and began to kiss him, but soon she was gone again, straight back into the world of the unconscious.

As Anna's muted gasps died away and turned into the quiet breathing of sleep, Moses heard the sound of pigeons cooing outside the window. He wanted to join her but couldn't sleep, no matter which way he turned in the sprawling bed.

As he drifted in and out of asleep, the letters 'NFD' kept reverberating in his head.

14

Moses sniffed the air – the sharp smell of espresso was balanced by the vanilla bouquet of sweet biscotti.

The city was already sweltering when they set out along the Via dei Fori Imperiali, at 7.30 in the morning.

They soon found a small huddle of people standing in front of an open-air kiosk selling hot coffee, right next to the House of the Vestal Virgins.

Moses couldn't resist his morning shot of caffeine, and holding their cardboard cups of espresso they headed on towards the Arch of Titus.

'It'll be time for your test soon,' said Moses, as they made their way down the two-thousand-year-old marble path.

'I'm not at all sure about this,' Anna said, rubbing the back of her neck. 'I don't want to do it, Moses.'

'But I want to see if you can find the Anomaly,' he said.

'You're crazy. It's in Delphi, we're in Rome.'

'It's in Delphi, yes. But it's also here.'

'Moses, you're speaking in riddles.' He fixed his eyes on her without saying anything. They wove their way between groups of tourists and disappeared into the labyrinth of ruins and paths of the Forum. Moses wandered in the direction of the Via Sacra, keeping the vast silhouette of the Colosseum on the horizon.

A weather-beaten Italian tourist guide, in her sixties, brushed past him, a flock of dutiful Swedes trailing behind her as they arrived at the Arch of Titus. She held up a stick with the blue and yellow cross of the Swedish flag above her head and, in perfect English, described the massive structure that rose up in front of them. The tourists listened and clicked away with their automatic cameras. Moses stood still, mesmerised by the words of the guide.

'Built to honour Emperor Titus eighty years after the birth of Christ in the years between AD 81–85, it celebrates the victory of Titus and his father Vespasian over the Jews. And you can see, carved onto the side of the arch, images of the temple treasures, captured from Jerusalem and brought here to Rome.'

The guide herded her group closer to the arch so they stood directly underneath it. Moses followed discretely. As the guide pointed upwards, the Swedes produced a collective gasp.

It sent a shiver down Moses' back.

'The battle for Jerusalem lasted many months. Thousands of Jewish fighters were killed defending their temple which was reduced to ruins by the mightier forces of the Roman legions. Only one wall was left standing after the victory. The remains of this wall, the "Wailing Wall," stands today in Jerusalem, bearing witness to this epic struggle.'

Moses stood there, gripped by the account, unaware of where Anna had wandered to. The guide led the Swedes around to the other side of the arch.

'When the army returned to Rome, Emperor Titus erected this arch to celebrate his victory,' she began, and pointed upwards. 'You can see how the treasures, looted from the Jerusalem temple, were carried by the Roman slaves in a victory parade, shown here. Any questions?'

A young man in his twenties, wearing a T-shirt bearing a peace symbol, spoke up.

'What happened to all the looted treasure? Where did it go? Can we see it?' he asked. Moses' ears pricked up. He turned towards the guide and listened carefully to her answer, putting on his sunglasses to avoid the glare of the early morning sun.

'That's a very interesting question,' the guide said, smiling at him. 'There is evidence that at first the treasures were put on display in a building in the middle of Rome, so that Roman citizens could admire the sensational golden relics captured from the Temple. They stayed there on display for several years. And then they … well, they simply disappeared. It's thought they became lost in the desert somewhere. No one really knows after that. It remains a mystery.'

Moses was convinced the guide would end it there, but then she dropped a bombshell.

'There are rumours that they still lie hidden in a secret vault under the Vatican. But maybe that's a myth, it's never been confirmed. I don't think we will ever know where they ended up.'

Moses' pulse quickened as the stunning image of the Delphic Anomaly flashed into his head. His thoughts were interrupted as Anna ran towards him, grabbing his hand and pulling him towards the front of the arch. The Swedes slipped out of sight, disappearing down a path leading towards the Colosseum.

'I hate tourist guides, they can be so boring,' said Anna.

'Actually she was good, quite passionate for someone that has to tell the same story every day of the year.'

Anna sat on a wooden bench and removed her backpack.

'I'm feeling uncomfortable. I think it's the backpack, it's making me feel sweaty all over my back,' she said, taking it off her shoulders. Then she saw the large brown envelope and began to pull it out of the bag. 'What's this?' she said, sliding her fingers under the seal.

'No, Anna. Don't open it!'

15

'What's going on with you, Moses?' Anna said, looking hurt.

'Sorry for over-reacting. You can take it out, but don't open it yet,' he said. 'Do you have any ideas about the contents?'

'I've no idea what's inside Moses, but is that arch connected to it?' she asked, pointing up at the Arch of Titus.

'Maybe. Tell me what you see,' he said.

'Soldiers ... maybe slaves, I don't know what they look like. They're holding some kind of tree, perhaps.'

'Describe it.'

She looked again but was unsure of what she saw.

'An ancient lamp? With many uprights? I don't know what you'd call it.'

'Hand me the envelope.' Moses looked around to check they were still alone. The Swedes had walked away but a new group of Japanese tourists were heading towards them, still some 150 metres away.

Moses pushed his thumb under the seal and pulled out seven glossy photos. They were as grainy as snowstorms, but there was no mistaking the contents.

Anna put her hands to her face in disbelief. 'But how ...' Her words petered out as she realised what she was seeing. 'It's the same relic as the carving up there,' she said.

Moses grinned.

'But how did you get these pictures?'

'With the buttonhole camera. Do you remember when I changed shirts outside the Delphi Museum?'

'This is freaking me out, Moses. How could I know that? I've never seen this picture before. I had no idea what you saw down the chamber in Delphi'

'Anyone could've done that. Let's not call it intuition – you worked it out. You must have picked up a few things and put them together, unconsciously.'

'I suppose I can take that on board, sure, why not?'

'Tell me something Anna – how did you know where to look?'

'I didn't know,' she shouted. '*You* led me here, Moses, didn't you?'

'No, I thought you led me, Anna.'

Her eyes remained locked on the photographs. Moses held his Leica up to his eye.

'One frame left!' he told her. He was lying, but it was a trick that always worked. 'Over there, Anna.' He took a shot of her in front of the arch. He was enjoying her long legs through the lens.

'So what does all this say about the relic found in the chamber at Delphi? she asked.

'It probably means the world's greatest missing treasure has been found,' said Moses, looking at Anna with a tortured expression.

His mood had changed. He was satisfied that Anna possessed a high degree of empathy, if not a good measure of intuition. He knew this already from their interactions over the last seven days, but it was good to see it confirmed, out here, in the Roman Forum.

He moved close to her and pushed his hand under her skirt. He was surprised to feel her bare skin.

'It's too public here,' she said, as a group of fast-walking nuns sped towards them. Locked tightly together, Moses and Anna watched as the nuns, dressed in their black-and-white habits, huddled together like a group of penguins sheltering from an Arctic wind.

Moses separated himself from Anna and walked round the nineteen-hundred-year-old frieze. He took two more shots and ran out of film. Sitting down on the grass under the shade of a rowan tree, he found another roll of Ektachrome in his pocket, loaded it into the Leica, rotated the split-screen viewfinder and pointed it up towards the arch. He had few doubts now about the authenticity of the Delphic Anomaly.

He was still finding it hard to grapple with the fact, that two days earlier, he'd touched the same relic captured by the Romans whilst he was under the Temple of Apollo in Delphi. It still made little sense to him.

They returned to the hotel room and Moses placed the 'Do not Disturb' sign on the door handle.

'We have unfinished business, Moses,' Anna said with a smile, and threw herself onto the enormous bed.

'It was quite daring of you to walk around in public this morning with nothing under your short skirt.'

'Did you like me almost naked, in public, surrounded by flocks of tourists?'

'Sure, it was a big turn on.'

'Me too. But you know, Moses, I had no choice. After seven days of running around with you I've run out of clothes. I can't keep wearing the same things.'

Anna bounced on the bed, and her skirt flew up. She pulled Moses towards her. She was ready for him.

The phone started to ring. Anna ignored it and went to work on Moses as he calmly picked up the receiver.

'Fine, I'll be down in about thirty minutes,' he said, and hung up.

16

Sam was waiting for them at the front entrance of the Minerva hotel when they emerged. In his hands were a large white envelope and a bouquet of fresh looking roses.

'Where'd you get these lovely flowers?' Anna said, the blush on her face matching the pink roses.

'Around the corner, in the Campo dei Fiori.' He paused in embarassment. 'I thought you'd like to have the scent of some fresh roses as we travel,' he said, handing Moses the envelope. Moses tore it open and scanned the list of names, nodding his head appreciatively.

'Twenty-three Parisian phone numbers. That's much better than I would have expected. I can't wait to start,' he said, looking at Sam's face.

'Hey Sam, I think you're looking a little pale and shaky today, are you alright to drive?' said Moses.

'I'm OK, Moses,' Sam stuttered. 'But I need to talk to you about Via Della Posta. Something happened over there whilst I was checking out the building this morning.'

'Can we sit in the car?'

Moses went into the front seat with Sam whilst Anna got into the back. 'OK Sam, it's OK. Just tell me slowly what happened.' Sam looked across at Anna uncertainly.

'Come on, it's fine to talk with Anna here, so long as she doesn't mind us talking business.'

Sam leaned his head back and shut his eyes, as if he was sifting through his thoughts. 'OK, this is what happened. I climbed up to the sixth floor of the Vatican Museum to get a view of the building from a higher vantage point. From the emergency exit I was able to get onto the roof and look across to 98 Via Della Posta.

'It's quite a communications hub. There were about a dozen high-frequency antennae and three microwave dishes aimed in different directions, and a large satellite dish, four or five metres across. They must be in touch with centres around the world with all that equipment.'

'How far away were you?'

'I was about a hundred metres away looking straight across at it all.'

'But wouldn't they have seen you?'

'No, I was hidden behind an air conditioning unit, watching through the fan blades.'

'And what happened?'

'A hatch opened onto the roof and two men climbed out, and walked towards the edge. One was a large well-built man aged about 45 or so with a wide face, black curly hair, slightly balding, nice tan, a bit overweight. Looked like he enjoyed his food and wine.'

'Sounds just like Guillini. He likes to live *La Dolce Vita*. And how was he dressed?' asked Moses.

'A well-cut blue suit, a jacket with a white open-necked shirt, Cuban heels. He looked smart.'

'That's him. Guillini wears Cuban heels,' said Moses. Anna coughed and cleared her throat as she listened in the back of the car.

'How about the younger man? What did he look like?'

'Thin and wiry, aged about 30. They walked together to the edge of the roof and lit up. I had a feeling the thinner younger guy was the driver of the Fiat we followed from Delphi, but I only saw the back of his head.'

'Then what?'

'They were talking, normally at first, moving around a

bit, gesticulating with their hands. It was clear they disagreed on something and their conversation soon turned into an argument. The younger man held up his hands as if he was pleading with the older guy, who became angry, throwing his cigarette down and pushing the younger one close to the edge.'

Sam stopped speaking and shook his head, staying silent for several seconds.

'He grabbed his arm and twisted it, so the other man fell onto the ground. He tried to get up but was punched in the face and fell backwards, his head hanging over the side of the building. It was awful.'

'Did he throw him off the building?'

'He did it, he disappeared in front of my eyes.' Sam's voice dropped to a whisper.

'And?'

'He must have fallen about two hundred feet. I heard a scream and then nothing. Just cold silence. It was unreal watching someone being ... killed, through a lens, as if it was not really happening.'

'What did Guillini do next?' said Moses.

'Hey Moses, how do you know it was actually Guillini?' Anna asked from the back of the car.

'He wears those Cuban heels and he has black curly hair. I know he can be a ruthless bastard. What more proof is needed, for Christ's sake?'

'Half the men in Rome probably have black curly hair!' said Anna. Moses noticed her rosy glow had turned pale.

'What did you see next?' asked Moses, turning back to Sam.

'The guy in the suit knelt down at the edge of the building. I could see him shaking his head and leaning back. He lit another cigarette and made the sign of the cross. Afterwards, he walked back to the hatch and disappeared into the building.

It was all over.'

Anna started to cry in the back. Moses reached over the front seat and placed his arm over her shoulder.

'Did you go down to the street?' Moses asked Sam.

'No, I didn't.' He paused to gather his strength. 'Sorry Moses, I suppose I should have. I couldn't think straight after what I'd seen. About five minutes later I could hear the sirens wailing – an ambulance must have arrived, I suppose, so maybe he was taken to hospital,' he said, biting his lip.

'Probably straight to a morgue. I have a feeling he's a dead man,' said Moses.

PART FIVE

Botelli

1

'OK, stop here, this is it,' said Moses.

Sam dropped them off on the corner of Via Lorenzo, from where they walked down to Via del Sandria, a pencil-thin street in the heart of Rome's antiques area.

Halfway down they saw *Antiqua Botelli*.

A display of Etruscan pottery filled the window.

'That's him, there he is,' said Moses, peering through the glass.

In the back of the gallery, he could see that the silver-haired Paolo Botelli was examining something under a large lens.

'Let's go inside,' said Moses looking at a nervous Anna.

'Don't worry, he's a lovely guy, you'll like him.'

Botelli sprang out of his seat as he saw Moses enter and opened his arms to greet him.

It was the warm hug of an old and trusted friend. Botelli looked up and down suspiciously at Anna several times as Moses held her tightly around the waist.

'This is Anna Nemcova, a close friend of mine from Prague. She's a highly expert and most passionate botanist,' said Moses.

Botelli rewarded Anna with a smile and they shook hands.

'Any friend of Moses is a friend of mine. Delighted to meet you.'

He turned to Moses. 'Well, what a surprise, I wasn't expecting you at all. When was it last?'

'September was the last auction in Vienna.'

Botelli was in his mid-fifties, an elegantly dressed man wearing a starched white shirt and check trousers with a crease sharp enough to cut sirloin steak. Moses could sense immediately that Botelli was concerned about talking in front of Anna.

'Don't worry. You can speak openly, my friend. Anna is one-hundred percent.'

'May I offer the young botanist a herbal tea. Perhaps fresh hibiscus or mint?' said Botelli. Anna looked overwhelmed and chose hibiscus. Moses stayed silent, fingering the silver medallion in his pocket.

'Maybe something stronger for you, Moses. How about an espresso with a shot of Vecchia Romagna?'

'Too early for me, Paolo.' Moses paused and shifted in his chair. 'Look, my friend. I've come to pick your highly knowledgeable brain.' Moses produced the silver medallion from his pocket and placed it in the palm of his hand.

Botelli froze as if he'd seen a corpse. His warm smile transformed into a thin narrow slit across his face, and his pupils shrank to small black dots.

'I sense this means something to you?' Moses asked hesitantly.

Small beads of sweat formed on Botelli's forehead. He took the medallion from Moses' hand and dangled it from his outstretched arm, some distance from his body.

'Where did you get this, Moses ?

'Why? What's the problem, Paolo?'

'Normally, Moses, these would never be seen by anyone. They are very private items of jewellery.' He twisted his hands through the air. 'What can I say to you? Put it like this – they are personal medals of honour received for acts of great bravery.'

'But what is it? Why did you react like that?' asked Moses. There was no immediate answer from Botelli.

'Come on Paolo, you can trust me. Anna is perfectly reliable. Tell us the truth.'

Botelli swallowed and his lips started to tremble. 'OK Moses, this is only between us and the four walls. This medallion is a personal trophy, only given to the members of a secretive order.

It's called the Rosamund Order. Whoever lost it will be missing it badly. Their life may even depend on it. It's not something you allow yourself to lose, unless you want to give up living.'

'I'm not sure he will care anymore, if he's the man who fell off a Vatican building yesterday.'

'I see, the penalty has been executed at great speed.'

'But tell me, Paolo – how are these medallions awarded to members of the Rosamund Order in the first place?'

'For an act of brutal—'

He stopped himself from saying 'brutality' and replaced it with a more diplomatic phrase.

'For an act of bravery. But look, Moses, I'm very curious to know how you came across it.'

'Well, I'm not sure I'm at liberty to say,' Moses stalled.

'Sorry Moses. I shouldn't have asked, I know that's unprofessional. None of my business, I realise. I've never seen one before today, but I've heard all about them, there are engravings in the old Vatican history books.'

'So what is the Rosamund Order exactly?'

'Come over here. I'll show you something you may not have realised,' said Botelli. Moses and Anna moved over to his desk. Botelli put the medallion under an illuminated magnifying glass.

A silver horse loomed before their eyes. Behind it, an ornate double cross was delicately etched onto the silver surface.

'Can you see a cross and a knight on a horse?'

'Yes, yes, and what do they signify?' said Moses, losing his patience.

'It's a classic icon used for the Rosamund Crucifixes. I'm afraid that members of this order have a notorious reputation.'

'Notorious?'

'Have it back. I'd rather you held onto it now, Moses.' Botelli seemed agitated by the presence of the medallion in his studio.

'What's the problem, Paolo?'

'It stresses me out to hold it.' He began to choke on his words. 'I'm not superstitious, but these medallions are associated with – how can I say? Bad things happening. Bad luck. They have a certain negative reputation.'

Moses and Anna looked at Botelli.

'Look Moses, there's no need to take any risks. But in case something happens, you should know that it may not be a good idea to hang on to this medallion for too long. Take my advice – get rid of it. As soon as you can.'

'I'm sorry I brought it to you, I didn't mean to cause any trouble. I'd just like to know a little more about the background of the Rosamund Order.'

'OK, alright, this is only for you, Moses. I'll tell you what I know. I suppose I owe you quite a lot of favours, after all the things you've done for me. It's the least I can do.'

Moses slapped him on the back. 'Good man, Paolo, that espresso and Italian brandy sound like a nice idea now.'

Botelli went to make coffee and find brandy glasses. 'Please leave it over there on the table, we can sit at the other end of the studio.' Botelli mopped his brow and walked over to a leather sofa with the drinks.

'What do you know about this Rosamund Order?' Moses asked as the hot coffee warmed his throat.

'It was an elite group of papal soldiers who guarded the Pope back in the sixteenth century.' He went to a bookshelf and pulled out a dusty old volume entitled *Canoni Sacri Helveticae* and began searching for the reference. 'Traditionally, these medallions were given as awards for exemplary service, for protecting the Holy Father beyond the call of duty. It's in here somewhere.'

'Are you talking about the Pontifical Swiss Guard?' asked Moses.

'Not exactly. Those are the guys in medieval costume who pose for the tourists. The Rosamund Order was an ultra-secret group of soldiers, actually taken from the ranks the Swiss Guard, but with their own agenda.'

'And what do you know about them nowadays?'

'You know something, Moses?' Botelli said, covering his mouth as he spoke. 'I really don't think they exist anymore, no one talks about them.' Moses could see he was lying.

'But that doesn't make any sense, Paolo. Are you sure?' said Moses. 'Look at the medallion, it seems brand new.'

'Maybe, I don't really know. There are always rumours about these things,' said Botelli, shaking his head and looking embarrassed. 'More tea, Anna?'

Moses felt sure Botelli had more information. 'What else do you know about this?'

'Nothing, really. I'd heard some rumours, through the Vatican grapevine, about the order being resurrected. That's all,' he said. Moses' nostrils twitched.

'Rumours?' asked Moses.

'There's no point repeating rumours, is there?'

'Yes there *is*, my friend. Rumours mostly start with a grain of truth,' said Moses. Botelli wore a pained expression. Moses could see his upper lip was trembling.

'It's OK, my friend we'll leave you in peace, soon. By the way, Paolo, do you want to stay on the Jupiter invitation list?' asked Moses.

Botelli felt his throat. 'Of course, Moses. My life depends on it. If it weren't for your auctions my whole world here in Rome would collapse,' said Botelli, his arms outstretched like a beggar.

'I understand, Paolo, and I'd really like to keep you. You're an important contact.' Moses paused and placed his hand on his chest. He knew he didn't have to say any more.

Botelli took off his gold-framed glasses, wiped his eyes with his handkerchief, and began to blink.

'Moses, I beg you. I *need* to stay on the Jupiter list,' he said, shaking his head. 'Please don't take that away from me. Everything depends on your auctions. My family – everything.'

2

Anna was looking uncomfortable.

Moses felt embarrassed but forced a smile – he felt reassured Botelli would now talk.

He felt guilty for making him beg like a prisoner pleading for his life, but it was all for the greater good, he told himself.

'I'll do my best to keep you, just tell me a little more about the Rosamund Order,' said Moses, knocking back the brandy.

'There are personal risks involved. I don't want my sources compromised,' said a shaking Botelli.

'You have my word,' said Moses. Botelli glanced again uncertainly at Anna, as if he still wasn't sure about trusting her. Moses placed his hand on Botelli's shoulder.

'Anna is a good person, you have my word. You can trust her with anything, I can vouch for her,' he told him.

Botelli nodded gently. 'OK. Here's what I know,' he said, turning to face Moses. 'I've heard from a Vatican insider that there is a Cardinal Guillini who runs Vatican security internationally. He's resurrected the Rosamund Order as part of a new and more aggressive way to strengthen the church and its international reputation.

'As you know, the church has suffered from a few scandals in recent years. He now has a handpicked team of agents working personally for him. They are the new Rosamund Order.'

'Anything else?'

'That's everything. Please don't put me under any more pressure, Moses, it's not good for me. I already have a heart condition.'

Botelli collapsed into the chair and poured a glass of sparkling Pellegrino to revive himself. Anna sat down next to him and mopped his brow with a tissue. He managed a modest smile as he looked at her face.

'And why are they called Rosamund Crucifixes?' she asked him, pressing her fingers between his shoulder blades.

'I'm glad you asked me that, Anna. It's an interesting question. In the early days, the medallions were given to knights on horseback. Nowadays they probably go around in Alfas or Lamborghinis.'

'Fiat Tempras, actually,' said Moses.

'Oh really?' said Botelli, smiling and looking back at Anna.

'Sprichst Du auch Deutsch? The name has a German origin. The German for horse is *hros*, and *mund* means protection or guarding, so you have the whole word *Rosamund* by combining those two words – *Horse Guards*. So, the Rosamund Order refers to 'The Order of the Guardian Knights.'

'Are you sure? Anna said.

'You're not convinced?' Botelli asked.

'As a botanist, I would say that Rosamund has a more straightforward interpretation. Rosa and Monde from the Latin would translate as 'Rose of the World.' Don't you think that makes more sense, for a secret order, here in Italy?'

Botelli looked at her with an amused smile and laughed. 'A charming thought, my dear, but I don't feel that the Papal guards would ever name themselves after a flower! No way, these people are not angels. It's kill or be killed. I'm not sure they'd be happy carrying a medallion called the Rose of the World.'

Anna shook her head. 'With respect, Signor Botelli, the rose is not such an innocent flower. You forget it's surrounded by dangerous thorns.'

'To protect the perfection within,' added Moses, a smile forming on his face.

'Quite poetic. I must say, I like your idea,' said Botelli, looking more relaxed. Moses pushed up his sleeve to check his watch.

'One last question, Paolo. When people have mislaid a Rosamund Medallion in the past, what have been the consequences?

'Listen Moses, this is the badge awarded to a papal agent who has been given authority to do whatever is necessary to protect the Pope. *Anything at all.* These guys believe they have God's blessing to dispose of anyone in the way of the Church. Lose it and you lose your cover. You're a marked man.'

'I see, Paolo. That all makes sense.'

'There have been a couple of incidents I've heard about, but best not to go any further. Let's leave it at that, Moses, please. And you won't forget your assurance to keep me on the Jupiter list?'

'I never break a promise, Paolo,' said Moses. The two men hugged and Botelli gave Anna a kiss on the cheek.

Moses and Anna left *Antiqua Botelli* and stepped into the sunshine that lit up Via del Sandria.

'I don't like the idea of carrying the medallion around with us. It might bring us bad luck,' Anna said, holding tightly onto

Moses' arm.

'You don't believe in superstitious nonsense, do you Anna?' Moses said, as they walked along the cobbled street to find the Mercedes.

'What was that?' Anna shouted suddenly. 'Someone touched my back!' She turned around and there was no one there, but her backpack fell off her shoulder onto the pavement. It had been opened.

'Must be a pickpocket,' said Moses, as Anna's precious copy of the *Materia Medica* fell out. A loose page flew up in the air into the path of oncoming traffic. Anna ran across the road, and as she knelt down to pick up the page she looked up at Moses standing over her.

'Please, Moses, get rid of it soon? I don't want to sleep in the same room as that medallion.'

'Don't worry Anna, my darling,' said Moses, stretching his hand out. 'You won't have to be near the medallion anymore.'

'What do you mean? Have you got rid of it *already*?' said Anna, checking the loose pages.

'Not yet, but we're about to return it to its proper owner.'

'How can you do that?' she asked. 'That's not possible any longer.'

'I have a way to do it,' said Moses, picking her up from the pavement.

'But how?' asked Anna, shaking slightly.

PART SIX

Guillini

1

'He likes blondes. Do it for me.' said Moses, squeezing inside the changing room of *Parrucchiere Gina*, a hair salon, one hundred metres down the street from the Hotel Minerva.

She nodded her agreement with a tilt of her head and Moses wrapped his arms around her waist.

'You even taste different,' he said, kissing her lips.

She shook her hair and gently pushed her fingers into her scalp. The blonde wig came off and her whole personality seemed to be transformed in a split second. Her green Mohican spikes had been flattened and she revived them with her fingernails.

Moses went to the sales counter, opened his wallet and signed away forty-thousand lire for the wig, the matching shoes and a short red dress.

They returned to the hotel and Moses waited downstairs whilst she changed. When she appeared twenty minutes later, Moses dropped his paper and applauded her new look.

She had slid into the tight mini-skirt. It was so short it was more of a belt.

'I'm only dressing up like a prostitute so you'll get rid of the fucking medallion,' she said.

'He'll be eating out of our hands, like a helpless baby,' said Moses, almost dwarfed by Anna in her six-inch heels. 'You know, Anna, if you weren't a botanist you could easily earn a living …' He didn't finish the sentence.

They fell into the back of the Mercedes and Sam drove them to Via Della Posta. It was quiet outside the granite office block, with no one around but a priest walking by on the opposite side of the street. Outside, a sign declaring *Libretto di Preghiere Edizioni Roma* showed it was the office for a publisher of

Catholic prayer books. But Moses had a feeling that this wasn't the only activity conducted here.

He'd known Cardinal Giovanni Guillini for nine years. Guillini was a regular and enthusiastic visitor to his private auction rooms in Vienna where he bought antiquities on behalf of the Vatican museum. He was a loud and effervescent character who fully enjoyed the nightlife of Vienna – a special service laid on for some energetic clients.

Although he was a full Cardinal, appointed by Pope John Paul II, he had no parish and reported directly to the Holy Father. When he was away from Rome he abandoned his religious duties, dressed in normal clothes, and was not averse to partying in the company of Czech and Polish hostesses, who knew him as 'GG.' No one knew he was a Vatican Cardinal.

Moses checked the number of the house and pressed the electronic buzzer. A video camera fixed to the wall jerked to life. Moses could hear the zoom motor focussing on their faces, sending its pictures through an armoured cable into the nerve centre of the Vatican's security building.

'One of Guillini's minions is probably watching us at the end of that lens,'

'Shall I wave?' she asked.

'Why not?' said Moses. Anna stood on her toes and blew two kisses at the camera.

'OK, that's enough,' said Moses.

After a long wait the door opened. An elderly nun in her seventies stood there holding a Motorola walkie-talkie that crackled with short, sharp bursts of sound. She looked up at Moses and across to Anna with a blank expression, totally unfazed by her sluttish appearance. It was as if she was totally used to seeing half-naked women come and go through the back entrance.

'I've something important to return to the Rosamund Order,' Moses announced in perfect Italian. The nun pursed her lips in disapproval.

'Che cosa?' she said after a few moments thought, staring at him as she fidgeted with the walkie-talkie glued to her left hand.

Moses repeated himself, put his hand in his pocket, and waved the medallion in front of her pale blue eyes. She squinted as it caught the sunlight and the double cross appeared on her cheeks as a flash of white light. He heard the zoom lens inside the CCTV security camera whirring as it tried to focus on the medallion, but it was too slow for a full close up. Moses snapped it out of shot and slipped it back in his pocket. 'Attendere qui,' the nun squawked, and disappeared through the narrow gap in the doorway. They waited and listened as she gabbled at high speed down a phone line. After a few moments she opened the door and, with a flap of her habit, beckoned them to follow.

They were guided through a labyrinth of corridors decorated with Renaissance paintings of the Madonna and baby Jesus. After two minutes, they found themselves squeezing through a heavy doorway into a typing pool full of younger-looking nuns sat at word processors, listening through headphones. They all looked up without smiling for a brief moment as Moses and Anna walked through their office towards another door at the far end.

The architecture changed dramatically from modern to Renaissance as they followed the elderly nun down a staircase into the basement of a small cloistered hall.

Elaborate gilt-framed oil portraits of popes from the sixteenth century lined the walls – Pius III, Julius II, Leo X, going as far back as Marcellus II. Every few metres there were modern thermostats and humidistats to maintain the best air temperature and moisture levels for the well-being of the paintings.

They continued along windowless corridors across uneven, sloping wooden floorboards, passing under two medieval Gothic archways, until they came to a hallway with a modern Schindler elevator at the far end. It stood open, as if waiting for them. Moses was impressed by the sight of this modern metal box encased in medieval stonework.

The nun shooed them inside the elevator and pressed the button labelled 'Minus 3' before stepping aside and speaking into her walkie-talkie. The doors shut and the elevator began to descend at some speed into the depths of the Vatican vaults.

'Where are we now?' Anna whispered into Moses' ear.

'We must be going down to GG's underground bunker, his master control room, somewhere underneath St Peter's. He once told me, after he'd had a few brandies, that the Vatican has an underground office complex and a subterranean museum, built during the Cold War era to withstand nuclear attack, to continue God's work after the apocalypse.'

The air became cooler as they travelled deeper underground.

'Do you think this is safe, will anyone ever hear from us again?' said Anna.

'I think we're quite privileged to be going down here. Very few people have ever been allowed inside the Vatican's underground city.'

The elevator decelerated and came to a stop. The doors slid open and another nun, this one orange in complexion, was waiting for them, clutching her walkie-talkie. She announced their arrival into her transmitter and ushered them into a modern hallway with numbered doors. The air felt dry and air-conditioned.

'It feels like the inside of a nuclear submarine,' said Anna.

Moses nodded. 'It's the whirring of electric pumps. You can hear them carrying air into the underground rooms.'

The nun knocked on door No. 1. There was no reply at first, but Moses caught the muffled voice of a young woman saying she would leave now.

The nun pushed open the door and peered through the narrow gap.

'Uno momento,' said the nun, turning to them.

She walked back to the waiting elevator and the doors closed, leaving them on their own.

Moses gazed up at the camera pointing at them from the ceiling.

He began to wonder how, from the innocent doorway outside 98 Via Della Posta, they had arrived at the deepest vaults of the Vatican.

2

From nowhere, a curly haired, slightly balding and shoe-less figure appeared beside them.

It was Guillini – he'd emerged from a secret panel, hidden inside the wall, next to the door where they'd been standing.

Dressed in shirt sleeves and black silk socks, he looked relaxed and was smiling, as if he'd enjoyed making his unexpected entrance.

'Hello Moses, what a wonderful surprise. I didn't expect to see you here in Rome.'

Guillini's eyes were focussed on Anna, looking her up and down several times and then back to Moses with a puzzled, 'who the hell is *she?*' expression on his face.

'You keep yourself too well-hidden down here,' said Moses. 'Let me introduce my trusted friend Anna Nemcova, a very gifted botanist who's now working for me.'

'I didn't realise you'd expanded into the world of plants, Moses,' said Guillini, kissing Anna's hand repeatedly, whilst simultaneously ogling her body.

'You know me, GG, I like to keep growing my business,' Moses said with a wry smile.

Guillini led them into his vast and opulently decorated office where sixteenth-century gilt-framed paintings were offset by the latest Apple Macintosh computers.

The walls were filled with works by Renaissance artists that Moses had never seen hanging anywhere before. He recognised paintings by Donatello, Tintoretto, and Bellini, but his eye was drawn to several nudes by Raphael.

Moses felt something under his feet as he stepped forwards to sit down. He noticed a small item of woman's underwear lying on the floor.

Guillini saw Moses hesitate as he stepped over the lace item and discretely kicked it out of sight, under the table.

They all sat down around one corner of an eighteenth-century mahogany banqueting table which served as Guillini's desk, Anna sitting between the men. Moses began to study the expert marquetry in the table, feeling the intricate floral inlays made of slivers of pearl, maple and walnut.

'Nice desk, GG,' Moses said.

'Yes, it's a Borsani, but I need a larger desk nowadays,' he said, fixing his eyes on Moses. 'That's enough of the pleasantries, my friend. Let's not beat about the bush. I gather you've come across something which belonged to one of my staff?' He pointed a finger at Moses and waited for him to respond.

'Yes. I had a feeling you'd like it returned,' Moses said, pulling the silver medallion from his pocket and holding it up to Guillini.

'How kind of you to return this personally. May I ask how you came across it?' Guillini asked, pulling it out of Moses' hand whilst taking a magnifying lens from his pocket. The cheek muscles on his pockmarked face tightened as he copied down the tiny identification letters engraved on its face.

'Tell me honestly, my friend, how did you find this?' he asked again, pressing his fingers together until they went white.

'It's rather difficult to explain,' said Moses. Guillini squeezed his lips together, as if he was irritated.

'The fact is that it was found inside a totally sealed chamber in Delphi, underneath the Temple of Apollo. Maybe you know the place I'm talking about?' said Moses, his voice rising, clearly agitated.

Guillini opened his arms wide and shrugged his shoulders. 'I really don't know how it got to Delphi, but I can confirm it belonged to one of our best—' he stopped abruptly. There was an awkward silence.

'One of your best … priests? Or agents? Which one was it, GG?' Moses said, but there was no response from the cardinal.

'May God rest his soul,' Guillini said without further elaboration, moving his head from side to side as if he felt some sadness. Moses bit his lip, while Anna quietly took an inward breath. He could see that she was carefully avoiding all eye contact with Guillini.

'I gather the owner of this medallion died tragically. It was a shocking, highly unfortunate accident,' said Guillini. He got up from the table to remove several leather-bound volumes from a bookshelf behind him, pressed open the door of a small safe recessed into the wall, and placed the medallion inside, closing it quickly.

'The family are from Sicily. They will be very proud of their son. I will do my best to return it to them,' he said, turning to them. He smiled at Anna. 'Did you enjoy your visit to Greece, Anna?' he asked. 'You can't beat a good souvlaki – and I can't resist baklavas with a Greek coffee.'

Moses threw his hands up in the air. 'Wait a minute, GG,' he said. He wasn't going to let Guillini get away without explaining himself. 'Let's not get distracted by how you stuff yourself with Greek food. You still need to explain to me how this medallion, belonging to a member of your staff, was found in a sealed chamber under the temple at Delphi.'

'Moses, I sense you're in a hurry. A lot of sightseeing to do in Rome, eh?' said Guillini laughing. 'Relax, the shops never close in the eternal city. Can I offer you a drink? I've some very fine Chianti from the Holy wine cellars.'

'No thanks, let's stick to business. We'll keep the wine tasting for another visit.'

'How about you, my darling Anna? You're looking a little dry and thirsty.'

'Some sparkling water please, if you have some,' Anna replied meekly.

'Look, my old friend,' he said, turning to Moses. 'I haven't had anyone working for the Holy Father in Delphi, is that clear?' Guillini said, nodding at Moses long after he'd finished speaking. 'As far as I know.'

Moses laughed. 'You've always enjoyed having it both ways, haven't you GG?'

Guillini walked over to a drinks cooler and took out a bottle of San Pellegrino, poured it into two crystal glasses, and gave one to Anna.

'Are you sure, Moses? A small Napoleon is very good for the

digestion, especially before lunch.'

'No, no, no,' said Moses, shaking his head. 'Please don't bullshit me. We've known each other long enough, GG. You *did* have someone working there until very recently, didn't you? Be honest with me. I know what you've been up to,' Moses said, and walked over to inspect the Raphael of the Madonna and Child hanging on the wall opposite.

'This operative of yours who's just died – I have proof that he was in the chamber in Delphi. You must know what he was doing there.'

'We'll never know what actually happened, Moses. Maybe it was stolen from him, or he was visiting family, or perhaps he had a private passion for Greek archaeology – how can I possibly know everything? Even *my* desk isn't large enough. I'm sorry to disappoint you,' he said, smiling at him with a set of perfect, capped white teeth.

'Let's be straight with each other, GG. We both know what he was doing there,' said Moses.

Guillini smiled back at him and then stared at Anna's cleavage as she leaned forward to take a sip of her water.

'OK then, let *me* tell *you* something, GG.'

'That will be most interesting to hear. I know you're always well-informed about new finds in the antiquities market,' said Guillini.

'A major biblical relic has just been discovered in that chamber at Delphi.'

'How extraordinary.'

'I think you know all about this,' said Moses. Guillini said nothing.

'It's been called the Delphic Anomaly, because it seems to be the long-lost temple treasure from Jerusalem.'

Guillini shrugged, but Moses noticed beads of sweat forming

on his face. 'Look, everyone in Rome has heard rumours like this for years. If it really exists, it's the greatest antiquity discovery of the century, but I have doubts it's the real thing.'

He leaned over the desk and looked directly into Moses' eyes. 'Can I still trust you, Moses?'

'That's my business GG. Trust is the core.'

'You know I wouldn't want this to become known beyond these walls if it turned out to be true. I think you understand the position of the Church on such matters, don't you my good friend?'

3

Guillini put his feet on his desk and began to pick away at his fingernails with the pointed end of his letter opener.

'You understand that the church would have to take appropriate action – if this were a reality?'

'Look GG, the Delphic Anomaly is real. I've seen it myself. It was discovered by a Greek professor and he believes he has the right to sell it,' said Moses.

'Why ruin a great friendship, Moses?' Guillini said, as he stroked Anna's bare arm.

Moses shook his head at him disapprovingly. Guillini removed his hand.

'I have to tell you that the people in Tel Aviv and Jerusalem will also be interested. They will see it as a matter of recovering their stolen property after two-thousand years,' said Moses.

Guillini laughed. His calm expression changed and he looked sternly at Moses.

'You don't really want to do this to us, do you?' said Guillini.

Tired of exchanging banter with Guillini, Moses got up from his chair and went to stand in front of a portrait of Raphael's mistress, *La Fornarina*. Anna's eyes followed him as he moved along to the next masterpiece – a sketch of a bare-breasted Lucretia.

'Such fabulous unseen works of art by Raphael you have down here. I've never seen the like of them anywhere before, GG,' said Moses. 'How is it you have these down here in your own office?' he asked, enjoying himself as he compared the portraits.

'It's sixteenth-century soft porn. We couldn't hang them in St Peter's Gallery. They're too provocative for religious visitors. So the Holy Father said I could keep them down here. He's very good like that.'

'One of the perks of the job,' said Moses.

'Look, my old friend, go and tell your Greek professor not to waste his time. Tell him he shouldn't bother to dig up his Anomaly. If it's the real thing it will cause too many problems, though it would be nice to bring it back home to Rome.'

'Home? What do you mean?' said Moses bristling.

'*Certo*! Rome is the natural home for the relic you're talking about,' said Guillini. 'After all the Roman blood that was spilt, it has to come back here. Of course it should, we paid dearly for it.'

'That was nearly two-thousand years ago. Surely you don't really think that anymore?' Moses said, returning to his chair.

'For believers, two-thousand years is like yesterday, Moses. Just look around the world and you'll see I'm right.'

He could tell Guillini was getting bored and was struggling to keep his hands off Anna. She was proving to be too much of a distraction, and Moses was beginning to regret asking her to go blonde.

As he stood up to leave, Guillini leaned across his desk and pointed his finger at Moses.

'Go back to Delphi and tell your Greek fortune hunter it's not in his interests to pursue this.'

'I can tell him, but he has already set serious plans in motion.'

'So you must stop him. NOW! It's your responsibility, Moses,' shouted Guillini, and banged on his desk. Anna's glass of water spilled on the priceless marquetry. She dried the water with a tissue as Guillini threw his hands in the air.

'I'm sorry, it doesn't matter, don't worry about it. There are many more like it,' Guillini said, standing up and taking Moses' arm in his hand. 'If you force my hand, Moses, we can easily stop him. It's not a problem. We have the manpower.'

Anna, who'd kept silent during the exchange, tried to make a peaceful overture. 'Surely the whole world deserves to see the Anomaly? Don't you have a moral duty to put such a famous symbol of the world's heritage on public display, for everyone to see it freely?'

Guillini began to laugh. 'Oh, she's such a sweet girl, isn't she? She likes to share her sweets with everyone,' Guillini said to Moses in a rasping monotone, and then turned towards Anna.

'My dear girl, sadly the real world is not like this. You cannot rewrite religious history. Ancient rivalries will always exist.'

Moses was tiring of Guillini's lectures and held his hand out to him.

'It's been a pleasure to look around your bunker, GG. I've enjoyed seeing all the forbidden art on the walls and it's useful to know how you feel about the Anomaly,' he said, looking at his watch. 'Can you please let us out of the building, now?'

Guillini picked up his phone and rang through to his assistant. As they waited, Moses watched Guillini scribbling a quick note onto a small pad.

'I'll ask Angela to show you out – the quick way. It'll be easier than going through all the corridors, past the prayer book department.'

Guillini put his hand under his desk and pressed a hidden button, making a bookshelf in the wall opposite split into two sections. A doorway opened in the middle of the shelf, from behind which an attractive high-heeled secretary appeared.

Guillini sailed up to Anna, took hold of both of her hands, and gave her a kiss on the cheek. Moses couldn't see the whole manoeuvre but had a feeling he'd pushed something into Anna's palm.

'It's been good to have a frank exchange, GG,' said Moses, and the two men hugged as if they were still best friends.

'*Viva Roma!*' said Guillini, as they turned to leave. 'Angela, please show my guests out through the VISI building.'

Angela led them through her office and directed them into a new elevator.

Eight floors later, they found themselves entering a sun-drenched glass building. They had arrived at the ultra-modern VISI offices in the main lobby overlooking St Peter's square.

'I need to visit the bathroom,' said Anna, anxiously, her fingers firmly locked together.

'I'll wait for you in the main square, just outside. I won't go far,' Moses said.

He walked on through a set of glass doors and discovered he was in the southwest corner of St Peter's Square.

The sun was shining through a scattering of white clouds while coachloads of the faithful were amassing for the Pope's weekly blessing.

4

Anna closed the bolt on the door of the cubicle and checked it was firmly locked.

She sat down and slowly unfolded the square of crushed paper stuffed into her hand by Guillini.

The handwritten message was almost illegible.

She read it several times and decided it said 'Call me Roma 750 4531. GG.' She stared at the number, memorised it, and screwed it into a tight ball. Not convinced she'd remembered it correctly, she re-opened it and looked at Guillini's scrawl once again, before tearing it into small pieces and flushing them away. It didn't all disappear first time, and a few shreds floated on the surface while she waited for the cistern to refill.

Moses was leaning against the wall of the Chiesa San Dominico checking his watch when Anna emerged from the VISI building. She put on her sunglasses as she walked towards him. A party of priests walked out of the church and crossed her path as she fell into his arms. 'Are you feeling alright? I can see you're still recovering from the encounter with Guillini?' Moses said with a sympathetic smile. She was not a practised liar and could feel her face blush as she looked back at him, stumbling over her words.

'He's a hard man to like,' she said, covering her face. 'Oh look, I hope you don't mind, Moses, but I feel so exhausted after the meeting, I need to go and lie down, recharge my batteries.' Moses nodded. She stared at St Peter's Church half in a daze, repeating the numbers to herself under her breath like a woman in prayer.

'I need to go to the docks anyway,' Moses said, 'and check through a consignment of antiquities with Italian customs.' He raised his arm and a taxi slammed to a halt in front of them. He gave the driver a five hundred lire note. 'Hotel Minerva, by the Pantheon, please,' he told the driver, holding the door open for Anna. 'I'll see you back there in about three hours,' Moses said, blowing her a kiss.

The taxi dropped Anna off at the hotel ten minutes later. As she ran through the hotel lobby in the blonde wig and short skirt, the receptionist jumped out of her seat and called after her. Anna smiled and held up her key. 'It's OK, I'm a resident, here, I'm Mrs Frank, Room 406.'

Alone in the bedroom, Anna locked the door, undressed, and lay on the bed, trying to relax before trying Guillini's number.

She dialled the seven digits. It rang slowly and interminably until, a minute and a half later, it was answered by a deep male voice which simply said '*Si*.' Guillini never had time for common courtesies.

'I thought it wasn't meant to happen like this,' she said, stroking her legs as she spoke.

'I broke the rules,' Guillini said. 'But I got away with it. Moses didn't see a thing.' He paused and took a deep breath. 'Look, I have to see you today.' His words burst down the phone like rapid gunfire. 'Anyway, it's your own fault for driving me wild, dressing up like a whore, for God's sake. Whose idea was that?'

'I'm sorry about the wig, but he insisted on it at the last minute. There was no time to—'

'It was strange,' said Guillini. 'I didn't recognise you at first. I thought Moses had dropped you and acquired a new girlfriend. That would have been a waste of all your training. Is it safe to meet you now?' he asked.

Anna hesitated. She was tired.

'You have to, there's no question Anna, it's an order. For security reasons. I'm under strict orders, the Holy Father insists—'

'OK I get it, I get it GG. You want to perform a security check on me,' Anna said, turning over on the hotel bed.

'It's essential. I must see you before you leave Rome. For operational reasons.'

'OK. I don't have much time. Moses is coming back in less than three hours.'

'Walk over to the Vatican Gardens. I'll meet you in the courtyard of Villa Pia. Tell the guards at the gate you are meeting Cardinal Guillini on church affairs. I'll be there waiting for you.' He paused. 'And Anna, for God's sake dress down a little. Normal clothes, eh?'

'I need to wash.'

'No, don't do that. And …' he thought for a second, 'and bring the hellebores.'

'I'll see if I can find them,' she said, slowly replacing the phone.

5

Guillini was sitting on an acacia bench sipping a Peroni.

A small fountain was dribbling slowly into a pool of lilies as Anna wandered into the courtyard. She brushed past bunches of grapes hanging from an ancient, gnarled vine as she approached him. He made the sign of the Rosamund Order, twisting his hands together, three times back and forth, with his fingers overlapping, before kissing her on the lips.

Anna didn't bother to respond in kind, it was still quite new to her.

'Now at last I have you to myself.' He paused for a moment. 'You know something? I'm surprised to hear myself say this, but I don't like sharing you with Moses,' said Guillini, holding a large iron key in his hand.

He led Anna down a stone staircase and unlocked an oak door to reveal a two-bedroomed apartment inside the shell of a fifteenth-century cellar.

He took Anna into the bedroom, lifted her into his arms and threw her to the bed.

'So what have you discovered?' Guillini asked, taking off his shirt. Anna unhooked her bra and let it drop onto the floor.

'So many things. It's all going well, but he can be unpredictable. Do I need to tell you now? I'll be sending you a report when I get back to base in a few days,' she said, kicking her silk briefs into the air.

Anna was actually a shy woman, but she'd been brought up to regard sex as a normal, day-to-day activity. No barriers. It was an extended greeting for her. Most of the time it didn't have any meaning. It was just an occasionally pleasant physical activity that happened as part of her work, or helped to keep a relationship ticking over.

'Have you found out what he's planning to do about the Delphic Anomaly?' Guillini asked.

'I haven't forgotten the aim of my mission. I'm developing a relationship. It takes time, you have to build trust slowly. It doesn't happen overnight,' said Anna as she straddled Guillini and pressed herself onto him.

Anna started to move on top of Guillini. With every downward movement her eyes followed him, as if she was imprinted on him. But she was sure she didn't feel any emotional connection with the man. She sometimes enjoyed the short-lived physical high of the moment. She believed she could simply walk away – back into the arms of Moses, or whoever the Church had decided was important. A work colleague. Or a friend in need. She was willing and sexy.

'Where d'you get all your energy GG?' she asked.

'From the praying the Holy Father expects us to do,' he said, gripping her shoulders. 'And do you think Moses suspects anything about our working relationship?'

She said nothing. Anna was unable to speak and simply nodded. Her fingers made their way into his mouth, and this made him erupt inside her. His body shook and she followed him within a few seconds. She lay still for several minutes, her eyes darting around the room, until she sat up abruptly to check her watch. She was worried about getting back to the hotel after Moses.

'Some wine? asked Guillini.

'No wine, but a coffee,' she said, as she put on her clothes. They went into the kitchen area.

'You do understand this could be a long-term mission? I want you to stay on this until the problem has been taken care of,' Guillini said as he loaded an espresso machine with ground coffee. 'It could take months, possibly years. You must be prepared for that eventuality. You know that Anna, don't you?' he said as he poured a glass of red wine from a bottle of Vatican Estate Pio Cesare Barbaresco.

'And we have to stop this Greek academic, the museum director, from trying to dig up the Anomaly.'

Anna was climbing back into her clothes, and nodded in agreement. 'I've seen the photographs. It's a stunning antiquity, in perfect condition, apart from all the stone around the bottom half,' she said enthusiastically, spraying some perfume across her breasts. 'If it was ever excavated it would cause a sensation.'

Guillini brought over the coffees and a spray can. 'Just lie down on the bed again, for a minute,' he said.

She did so, and did not speak or move as Guillini lifted her skirt, pulled aside her briefs, and squirted a few inches of cream onto her fuzzy mound.

'Hey, wait a minute, GG, what are you doing?' she said, realising this was not the kind of cream to go in coffee.

'I'd like to trim your sweet little bush into a beautiful heart shape,' he said, rubbing in the cream. 'And you can tell him you did it yourself.'

'OK, that sounds cool, I think he'll like it,' she said.

Guillini pressed down on her skin with one hand and started to shave her with another. He did one side and rinsed the blade in a small mug of water on the tray.

'Let me finish this off, I think I can do this a little neater than you,' Anna said, taking the razor in her fingers.

'Anna, you have to do whatever Moses asks of you, you know that. It's part of your contract.'

'That's fine by me. I quite like him, actually,' she said, feeling her new heart-shaped crotch. 'I'll do anything you ask because of our special agreement. You won't let me down, will you GG?' He said nothing.

She smiled uncertainly at him and walked into the bathroom holding up her dress to check her new shape in the mirror.

'Don't worry, my flower,' Guillini said, following her. 'You'll get your free pass into the Vatican Herbarium. But I have one small question,' he said, grabbing her wrist and pushing her down onto the bare wooden floor.

6

'I want the truth, Anna. How did Moses know?' Guillini said, pressing the whole weight of his body down on top of her as she lay pinned to the floor.

'Know what, for Christ's sake?' Anna said, sobbing.

'That the medallion was owned by a member of the Rosamund Order,' he said, twisting her arm a little further.

'Hey, stop that GG.'

'Answer me, Anna, and I'll let you go.'

'Moses has a huge knowledge of antiquities and history,' she said, trying to wriggle free.

'Don't bullshit me, There must have been an informer. Someone told him. Who was it?' Guillini pushed her onto her side and dug his knee into her naked back, pressing her breasts down onto the wooden floor.

'Remember, you're working for the Holy Father, not for Moses.'

'Don't do this to me, GG. Let me go now, I beg of you,' she cried, tears flowing down her face.

'Tell me his name, Anna, and you will be a free woman.'

'If you promise not to hurt him,' she said quietly, her large eyes watering, imploring Guillini to release her. He nodded. 'Sure, I just need to know for my records, no other reason at all,' he mumbled, his words almost inaudible.

'It was an old guy in the antiques area. He has a shop with Etruscan stuff in the front window.'

'And his name?'

'I really can't remember,' she wailed. Guillini twisted her arm once more and again jabbed his knee into her back.

'Something like Botelli,' Anna said, gasping for breath.

Guillini released his grip. She scrambled free and stretched out her bruised arm.

'Paolo Botelli, I know that name. Forgive me, Anna, I have to do this. As you can appreciate I need to know who is leaking Vatican secrets, it's my job. Otherwise, I'd end up in the gutter, a knife in my back. You do understand, don't you, my little flower?'

'Don't hurt him. He's a kind man,' she said softly as she leaned back to ease the pain.

'I wouldn't dream of it. You know that, my darling,' Guillini said, a joyless smile across his face. He looked towards her bag.

'What will you do to him?'

'I'll have a talk with him, a conversation, that's all.' As he said the words Anna remembered Sam's description of the conversation on the top of the building with the agent who'd lost the medallion.

'Just talking, nothing more. You wont harm him in any way. You promise?'

'Sure, my darling and what about *your* promise of some Black Rose? I know you found the original Hellebore genus used by the Ancient Greeks, or so you told me in your last report.'

'I was in a hurry to get here, I'm *not* sure I brought it with me,' she said, rubbing her mouth.

Guillini looked at her, picked up her bag, and turned it upside down. Out fell a plastic bag containing six fresh roots.

'Oh, I forgot, they were already in my bag. Just have it, take it all. It was for you anyway.'

'You'd better go now, Anna. You've been good, better than I remember, but you must be more honest with me in future.'

She ran barefoot up the stone stairway into the warmth of the afternoon sunshine, and found herself in the heart of the Villa Pia gardens.

There was a reviving smell of roses in the warm air, blowing across from the formal displays of flowers by the Fontana della Conchiglia. Anna ran past the security police towards the entrance gate, out of the gardens.

When she reached Via Del Governatorato she saw the familiar squat shape of the Pantheon against the Roman skyline and decided to walk for a few moments to catch her breath.

Her arm was still aching. As she pressed her fingers gently against the chafed skin, she twisted it around and saw a large purple bruise.

7

Anna could hear the shower pelting down in the bathroom as she crept back into the hotel room.

Moses was already back, his clothes strewn on the bed.

She was exhausted and stared blankly out of the window, biting her nails, as she waited for him to appear from the shower.

He emerged from the bathroom dripping, a large white towel around his waist. It fell off his body and onto the floor as he went to hug Anna with open wet arms.

She recoiled, moving backwards as he embraced her.

'What is it?' Moses said. She looked down and coughed.

'Nothing's wrong, it's just you're still wet from the shower,' Anna said, unconvincingly,

Moses' face looked strained, and his voice lost its warm pitch. 'I wondered where'd you'd got to, after the annoying meeting with Guillini. I was worried, I had a feeling something was wrong. I was expecting to find you here asleep.' he said.

'Oh, look, I'm OK' she began hesitantly. 'I just went for a walk, I needed some … air.'

'I see,' said Moses, as he dried his back.

'When I got back to the hotel my head was buzzing. I couldn't sleep so I went for a stroll. I found myself in the Vatican gardens. It was nice just walking around, smelling the flowers, watching insects. I needed to revive my spirit after that meeting with Guillini,' she said, and began to move towards the bathroom.

'Look, I need to take a shower too. Can I see you downstairs in the restaurant in five?'

They were both tired and didn't talk much over the meal. Moses spent some time lecturing her about the difficulty of getting good Italian wine in Vienna.

Sam came into the restaurant to tell them that the car was ready for the long drive to Paris, the double bed available at the flick of a switch. As he showed them the route on a large unfolded map he explained the journey would take sixteen hours and they would not be arriving until two in the afternoon the following day.

They drove out on the Corso Vittorio Emanuele and headed for the autostrada in the direction of Florence and Bologna. Filled with food and a little too much wine, Anna and Moses fell asleep as Sam pushed on. It was 11.30 pm as they cruised onto the three-lane highway illuminated by a full moon, the oilseed rape fields a bright yellow canvas on the edge of the autostrada.

Seven hours later, they woke up on the shores of Lake Annecy. Sam was pulling in for coffee and breakfast at the L'Abbaye de Talloires, a stately four-star hotel.

By 2.20 that afternoon they were driving down avenue George V in the centre of Paris, heading into the underground car park of the hotel.

As Moses checked in and ordered some food, Anna went to the room for a shower. Ten minutes later, Moses joined her.

As he entered the room, she emerged naked from the bathroom with a large smile on her face. She grabbed him around the waist and began to kiss him on the lips.

'How do you like my new haircut?' she said, taking his hand and guiding his fingers downwards.

8

There was a knock at the door.

'One minute,' Moses shouted. Anna grabbed her dressing gown and held it against her body.

'Oh *merde*, I forgot to tell you I ordered a late lunch from room service,' said Moses.

He went to the door and found a purple-faced waiter, balancing a heavy metal tray loaded with plates of food.

'This has arrived much faster than I thought it would,' Moses said, and watched as the waiter placed it on a round table, stepped three paces backwards and waited. Moses was embarrassed.

'Sorry, I can't right now, but I'll come and find you later,' he told the waiter, who marched out, closing the door a little heavily.

'Should've given him a tip,' said Moses, salivating over the salmon and scrambled eggs. They ate the food around the table and downed it with black coffee from a cafetiere. Afterwards,

Moses sat on the edge of the bed watching as Anna squeezed herself into frayed shorts and green luminescent socks.

'You can't go round like that in Paris. They'll think you're a hippy. We need to buy you some clothes from a couturier,' he said as he put down his empty cup of coffee.

As she turned around he noticed marks on her arm.

'Looks like someone's beaten you up. How did you get those bruises?' he asked.

'Oh my God, it's so large, it was nothing at all when it happened.'

'When what happened?'

'I didn't tell you. I fell over in the hotel room yesterday when I got back. I was so tired I just collapsed and caught my arm on the chair. It's amazing how a small fall can make such a large bruise. I'll put some arnica on it,' she said, her face turning pink.

He looked back at her uncertainly, his lips downturned. 'We'll have to get you something long-sleeved,' he said, picking up the phone.

'Who are you calling, Moses?' she asked, biting her lower lip.

'Anyone with the name Delacroix! Relax, it's ok Anna. Come over here and help me choose a number.'

He held her fingers over the list of numbers. The skin behind her wrist looked red. He had a suspicion someone had tried to harm her, but let it go for now.

'Shut your eyes and point to a number on Sam's list of phone numbers.' Her fingernail hovered over a name – it was Mme Celine Delacroix. Moses put a cross against it and began to dial.

It rang for over a minute before an elderly female voice answered hesitantly. '*Oui?*' she said quietly, as if she didn't get many calls from the outside world.

Moses cleared his throat. He knew how to charm people and was extra careful to always be polite and friendly.

'I hope you don't mind me calling, *Madame*, but I'm trying to make contact with the family of Dr Niko Delacroix, the French archaeologist.' He paused – there was no response, and he decided it would be best to expand on his theme. 'You may have heard of him, he was a leading figure in the excavation of Delphi in Greece in the 1930s. I wondered if you were related to him, by any chance?'

'Who are you?' came the sharp response down the line.

'My name is Moses Frank, I'm a dealer in rare antiquities based in Vienna and I believe I have information of great interest to the Delacroix family.' Anna leaned over to listen to the voice at the other end.

'Monsieur Frank, I am not related to the person you want, but I believe you should try a Mme Maria Delacroix in rue Raynouard, in the 16th arrondissement. Her number's ex-directory. I can't give it to you, I'm sorry.'

'And what number on rue Raynouard, please?'

'You'll find it. Goodbye, and good luck!' The phone went dead. Moses uttered a 'Tzzt' as he wrote down the street name and picked up his map of Paris.

'Looks a pretty long street, for Christ's sake. That's ridiculous. I'll call her back,' said Moses, picking up the phone again.

'No, don't do that,' Anna said, adding with a smile, 'I'll find it for you. Maybe I can use my famous powers of intuition.'

Moses shook his head. He wondered if she was joking with him. On the other hand, if she meant it, he didn't want to put her off.

'And why not indeed? Get dressed, we're going,' he said, and watched her as she walked around the room naked, searching for her underwear.

'Did you hear what the Delacroix woman said to me on the phone?'

'What did she say?' asked Anna, squeezing herself into a pair of skintight briefs and a clinging skirt.

'She said "you'll find it." An interesting choice of words, don't you think?'

They went to the front of the hotel and found Sam opening a map of Paris over the leather seats. He'd located a couturiers and they set off from avenue George V, turning into avenue Montaigne for the Yves St Laurent shop.

As Moses led her inside, the staff stared at Anna, as if she were an unemployed waitress. After twenty-five minutes she emerged onto avenue Montaigne resembling the young mistress of Baron Rothschild. Gone were the blue jeans and the Escher print t-shirt, packed away in a discrete cardboard box. In their place, tall Anna looked elegant in a navy blue suit, black stockings and modest high-heels, her Mohican hidden under a small matching hat.

'Anna's never been to Paris before. Take us the tourist route please, Sam,' said Moses.

They made their way along avenue President Wilson, where Anna craned her neck upwards to take a look at the lattice ironwork of the Eiffel Tower.

'The first time, eh?' said Moses. 'Experiencing the greatest phallic symbol in France,' he added, laughing.

'I'm sure the women here love to see it,' she said as the car turned sharply into avenue Paul Doumer, then right into rue Passy, with a final sharp right into Raynouard. The one-way system had forced them into a crazy zig-zag route across town.

The Merc drove down Raynouard and past a succession of opulent apartment buildings, many with granite and marble entrances. Moses jumped out in front of number 92 and walked up the street, looking into several doorways before walking back to get Anna.

'This is where the expensive Paris doctors ply their trade,' he said, pointing at the polished brass plates naming every ailment known to man.

'It's so unhealthy,' said Anna. 'This is for stupid people with too much money. They ought to try herbalism.'

Looking to the other side of the street, the rooftop sculptures caught her eye. There was a façade with statues of Greek gods. 'I've a strong feeling you're looking at Mme Delacroix's apartment right now,' Anna said, pointing up at the seventh floor.

'So you think I should throw away all those other Paris phone numbers?"

'No doubt at all.'

They crossed the street and peered through the panels of the revolving door. Staring into the luxurious lobby entrance they could see an ornate cut-glass chandelier and Louis XVI furniture. In the middle, water cascaded from a small fountain into a ceramic bowl. At the far end, behind a walnut desk, a hall porter sat in his silver grey uniform reading *Le Figaro*.

'The signs are looking good, Anna. If this Delacroix woman is rich enough to live here, she may have been attracted to the Greek sculptures on the rooftop because of her father's work in Delphi,' he said.

'So what do we do?' Anna asked, as they stood arm-in-arm outside the building.

'We'll go inside and ask for her. I've a feeling that within one hour we'll be talking to a Mme Delacroix.'

9

Moses leaned into the doorway and pressed the metal buzzer on the entry phone. The dozing hall porter sprang to life and rose from his chair with a yawn.

'Bonjour monsieur,' Moses said confidently. 'We have come to see Mme Delacroix.' He waited for a response, his hand carefully placed on Anna's shoulder to indicate they were a couple.

'Do you have an appointment Monsieur?' said the distorted voice through the entry phone.

Moses smiled. 'I know she will be very interested in meeting us—'

'No appointment, sorry – no visit,' the porter cut him off tersely, before switching off the intercom and going back to his newspaper.

'Yes!' shouted Moses, hugging Anna.

'Why are you pleased?' she asked, looking confused.

'We've found her. He's confirmed Mme Delacroix lives here. The rest is easy.'

Moses buzzed again. '*Oui*,' the hall porter answered, a little bored. Moses bent down to the intercom.

'I've important information about Mme Delacroix's father, Niko.' He paused. 'Tell her we are happy to wait.'

'A moment.' The porter's voice echoed through the intercom. Moses watched as he got up from his desk, walked over towards them, and made a rectangular shape with his fingers. Moses knew what he meant and pushed his business card through the slot in the letter box.

Printed on the first line of his card was the name 'MOSES FRANK,' on the second line 'Antiquities Dealer,' and underneath that a phone number with the international dialling code. There was no address.

Anna removed her hat and her green Mohican was suddenly on full view. Moses shook his head at her.

'It's not me, Moses. I can't wear a hat. But look, it doesn't matter – he's opening the door for us anyway.'

The hall porter pressed a button to release the outer door. They walked in and Moses checked his watch. 'Anna, we've entered the first level and we have over twenty minutes left to play.'

'It's very pleasant in here,' she said, sitting on a deep leather sofa and looking around at the fresh orchids. 'I'm looking forward to the next level.' She paused. 'You know ... my life seems to be an endless series of games, with different rules for each.'

'Do you feel you're playing a game now, Anna?' Moses said.

She was silent for a moment.

'Why not? It's human to play, isn't it?'

10

Moses put down *Paris Match* and picked up a copy of *Le Nouvel Observateur* from the lobby table. He began to rifle through the pages, but couldn't concentrate on any of the articles.

There was a noise and he looked up.

From inside the elevator shaft he could hear the high-pitched whine of wheels spinning, followed by a heavy clunk. The elevator had arrived.

A few moments later the door split open, revealing an elegantly dressed woman. She stepped out and walked towards him with a determined stride.

Moses wondered if this was her. What a prize if she had really come all the way down to meet him in person. His plans were progressing way beyond his wildest imaginings.

She stopped in front of him and held out her hand. Moses felt the blood rushing through his body.

'Monsieur Frank?' she said softly. 'Maria Delacroix.' Moses was startled by the distinguished-looking woman standing in front of him, his body began to sweat and he managed only a stuttered greeting. He recovered quickly, switched on the charm and warm smile, fairly sure she hadn't noticed his temporary lapse.

'Mme Delacroix – well, how wonderful. I thought I'd have to search for you all over Paris,' he said, noticing the sparkle in her grey eyes.

'This is Anna Nemcova, my assistant. She's an archaeo-botanist – have I said that right, Anna?' said Moses, putting his arm on Anna's shoulder, whilst watching Maria look disapprovingly at Anna's fluorescent green hair before ushering them into the mirrored elevator.

They were transported seven floors up, directly into a spacious hall inside Maria's apartment.

As they entered it all felt strangely familiar. Maria was an art collector with an impressive collection. Moses immediately recognised a sketch by a young Dali, a Matisse, and an early Picasso of a half-dressed model with tousled hair, from the time Picasso was still living in a small studio in Barcelona.

He could have chosen the same pieces of art himself for his apartment in Vienna.

Maria ordered coffee as they sat down on a hard Swedish sofa.

'Tell me, Monsieur Frank, what's your business exactly?'

'I run the WAR Corporation, based in Vienna.'

She stiffened. 'You do something involving *war*?'

'No, WAR stands for World Antiquities Rescue. It's my personal crusade against bad art. I tell my clients to only invest in antiquities and the twentieth-century masters. But, you know something? The ancients have it all.'

'And how did your rescue business come about?'

'I began with a single desk at the back of a coffee shop in Vienna and built it into an international company.' He paused, suddenly aware he was doing most of the talking.

'And the secret of your success, Mr Frank?'

'People trust me,' he paused. 'I think. They bring me their secret treasures in confidence and I try to find them a buyer.'

'Is that all you have to do?' Maria said with some irritation.

'It can be difficult work. Look at it this way – I'm the guy who has to get hold of the unobtainable and the non-existent … on behalf of the invisible. They often want you to perform miracles.'

She laughed and moved closer to him. 'Sounds like you do a lot of your work behind closed doors.'

'Sure, it's highly confidential work.' He hesitated. 'Look, can I call you Maria? I hate to be too formal, I feel like I know you already, we share the same taste, it seems,' he said, looking around at the art on the walls.' She didn't respond.

'Look, Maria, let me assure you, I don't work with the mafia – as far as I know,' he said with a momentary smile. Maria didn't laugh. 'And I work to a strict code of ethics,' Moses added quickly, his eyes drifting uncontrollably in the direction of the pretty young maid as she came in with coffee.

'And where do you think you picked up your values, Mr Frank?'

'From my father,' Moses began, sipping the coffee. 'He was a survivor. He survived Auschwitz. When he stepped off the transport, the guard looked at him and told him to turn to the right. He was given the chance to live, one of the lucky ones. Most were sent straight to their deaths.'

Maria's eyes flickered. Anna put a hand on Moses' back.

'Something suggested you had that kind of background,' she said, gazing into his eyes. 'Your father would have possessed a very special sense to stay alive in that situation. I can see you also have an acute awareness of things around you.'

'It can be helpful, knowing things I didn't even know I knew.'

Maria face twitched with a cursory smile. She looked frustrated, sighing as she poured out more coffee. 'It seems we do share one or two things, but my father was not as lucky as yours.' Moses sensed he needed to go in for the kill soon.

'I gather Niko Delacroix was a man before his time. He was never given credit for finding a major antiquity in Delphi.'

Maria stood up and looked down on Moses, who stayed seated. 'May I speak my mind, Mr Frank?'

He looked up at her wide-eyed, unsure what she was about to say.

'I've enjoyed this interesting conversation. You seem well-practised in the gentle art of charming people. Just tell me honestly now – what do you want from me today?'

Moses looked at Anna uncertainly before focusing back on Maria.

'I understand you,' he said, clearing his throat. 'A few days ago, I was invited to inspect a new discovery, a biblical antiquity, found in Delphi. I was not expecting to see anything exceptional, you see, I get called to check on many such claims, quite a few – and most are a disappointment. But this was different.'

Maria leaned forward, her face brightened. 'Tell me what you saw,' she said.

'I will, but can I ask *you* one thing first? Just a simple question.'

Her mouth quivered. 'What do you want to know?'

'Would you mind telling me your father's middle name?'

'But why?'

'I'll explain in a moment, but please, tell me first.'

'It's Francois, as it happens. Niko Francois Delacroix.'

'And that makes his initials?'

'NFD.'

Moses reached into his breast pocket and pulled out a piece of white paper folded into two.

'Open this please, Maria.'

She hesitated. A small smile formed across her face as she read out the three letters. 'NFD!'

'But how did you know that?'

'Those three letters were scratched onto the side of the biblical relic in Delphi. I have a photograph I can show you.' From his inside jacket pocket he took out a glossy print rolled up in a sheet of newspaper.

'My god, Moses,' she gasped. Her speech changed instantly, she became enthusiastic to the point of being breathless. It was the first time she'd used his first name. 'But you know it all makes sense, because my father wrote to me shortly before he died, mentioning the discovery of a biblical relic.'

'And then what happened?'

'I never heard from him again. All I know is that he was found dead a few days later. I was only fifteen at the time. But tell me – what does it look like?'

'It's a stunningly beautiful relic. The museum director, Dr Green, calls it the Delphic Anomaly and ...' Moses was unable to continue. He was struggling to find a gentle way of saying something.

'What is it Moses? What else do you know?'

Moses looked up at the ceiling and bit his lip. 'I'm not sure about telling you something that may upset you, Maria.'

'I am prepared to hear anything,' she said.

He put two hands together into a triangle and looked into her watery eyes. 'I think you need to know why your father died so young. I believe he was killed *because* he discovered that relic,' said Moses.

Maria reacted with no outward emotion, as if she'd known all along. 'Excuse me a moment.'

Maria went over to the Chagall sketch hanging on the wall, lifted it off its hook and revealed a safe. She tapped in the code and the lock disengaged with a click. The metal door squeaked and rolled open on its hinges. Sitting in the safe was a small wooden box under a pile of envelopes.

'In this box are my Delphi papers' she said, placing it on the glass coffee table. They will confirm what you've been saying, Moses,' she said.

She pushed open the lid and took a short inward breath.

It was empty, apart from a single key sitting on a small sheet of grey cardboard.

'I'm sorry, it seems there's nothing here,' she said hesitantly, shaking her head. 'It's coming back to me now. The papers are in my safe deposit box, in Blvd Hausssman, in the main branch of Societe Generale.

11

The wind was ripping branches off the chestnut trees along Quai D'Orsay, and small waves were rippling across the river.

As the Citroen taxi crossed the Seine at Pont de La Concorde, a small flotilla of tourist pleasure boats rocked sideways.

Maria watched a tall woman who looked like a nightclub dancer stop on the bridge to open her umbrella. A sudden gust of wind blew her dress above over her waist revealing all, leaving little to the imagination.

For a fleeting moment a man on a bicycle enjoyed an intimate view of her legs in black stockings and tiny briefs, before falling off. The taxi driver braked sharply so he could also enjoy the sight.

Maria had seen it all before. It was the usual high winds and high fashion in Paris, she thought to herself, as she wiped the condensation off the taxi window to get a better view.

A rainbow appeared across the sky and she felt the warmth of the sun on her face. But nothing could stop her playing with the key inside her leather bag. Touching the cold metal brought back faded memories of the time when her father used to write letters from Delphi.

The rainbow was still visible when the taxi stopped outside the ornate entrance to the national headquarters of Société Générale, situated at 29 boulevard Haussman.

Corinthian statues looked down on Maria from the mezzanine gallery as she made her way across a Roman style mosaic floor, above her a domed glass roof towered seventy feet into the sky. For Maria, it was reassuring to discover that her old bank had not gone modern, or lost its nineteenth-century splendour.

A uniformed commissionaire approached her.

'Are the safe deposit boxes still down here?' Maria asked.

'We have over eight-thousand safe deposit boxes down there, that is the way,' the commissionaire said, pointing her towards a khaki-coloured elevator. Inside, another attendant pressed the button for Level B. The doors closed and they headed down towards the armour-plated strong rooms.

'I haven't been here for almost thirty-five years. Do you think my box will still open?' Maria asked.

The old attendant raised his hands and shrugged. 'Madame, the locks are serviced once a year, so it should be no problem, as long as you still have the six digit code number,' he said. Maria bit her lower lip and began to worry about whether she could remember it. 'Don't worry. Even if you've forgotten it I think they can still open it for you, if you have your passport and you pass a fingerprint test.'

The guard swung the door open and showed her into a hall full of deposit boxes and a central area of desks. She looked around at the gloomy décor. It was different down here and looked like it had been redesigned in the 1950s under the direction of Joseph Stalin. As Maria looked around in despair, a bright and cheery woman in a blue uniform approached, a plastic badge giving her name as Carole Lagarde, private banking assistant.

'Do you know when you last came here, Mme Delacroix?'

'More than thirty-five years, it must be.'

'That's fine.' She looked down at her paperwork to check Maria's name again. 'Mme Delacroix, don't worry at all, it shouldn't be a problem. The same is true for many of our clients. They don't come for many years and then one day it is busy again, followed by no activity again for five years.'

She led Maria to a fingerprint table. Holding her right hand firmly, Maria pressed her fingers, one at a time, onto the black ink pad. 'Tell me something, I've always wondered – do you simply *look* at my fingerprints with a magnifying glass to check them?'

Lagarde laughed. 'Nowadays it's all done by a pattern recognition computer. And there is Monsieur Claude, as well. Sometimes, if the computer fails to come up with an answer, we ask Claude for an opinion.'

Maria could see a round-faced, balding man with a bushy moustache sitting by a desk at the back of the hall.

'Come and meet him,' said Lagarde with a smile, beckoning Maria to follow her. They walked past two tired-looking security men at the central desk, both yawning as they watched a row of screens with constantly changing black-and-white images from the security cameras. They came to a desk separated from the rest and Maria was introduced to Claude Henri Bovet, a 62-year-old man who was flicking through the pages of a Marseilles phone directory.

He sprang to life as soon as Maria approached. He stood up and came close to her face, his eyes following the line of her cheeks. He focussed on her nose, her chin, and her mouth, studying every feature, but avoided direct eye contact. Maria pulled back at first – she wasn't used to someone standing so near to her – but then decided to let him continue.

'Mme Delacroix, I know your face from August 15th 1955, the date when you last visited us, at 3.25 in the afternoon. Your fingerprint had a rather unusual set of arches and whorls,' he said, taking a pencil and drawing on a scrap of paper. Lagarde opened the folder she was carrying under her arm.

'That was indeed the date,' Lagarde said, and smiled at Maria.

'What? But how did you know that?' Maria stuttered in amazement

'I can remember everything,' he said, smiling at her. 'The curved ridges with no bifurcations are unusual, as well. That helps.'

'But it was over thirty years ago. Can I check if your drawing is correct?' Maria asked.

He handed the paper to her.

'Claude is never wrong. They'll be correct, I've no doubt,' Lagarde said with total assurance, nodding at Maria. 'Only one person in a million can do what Claude has just done,' she said as the fingerprints were displayed on a screen. 'Look, you can see the arches and whorls Claude remembered.'

Maria stared at the screen with her mouth half open. 'This man is unbelievable.'

'Fingerprints don't change over time,' Lagarde said, 'and Claude can also do ten-digit calculations and square roots in his head instantly.'

'But I don't understand how he can do any of this.'

'Tell him your birthday,' Lagarde said. Maria told him it was October 10th 1925.

'You were born on a Wednesday,' he replied immediately.

Legarde explained. 'Claude is a human mystery. No one understands his mind. He's been diagnosed as an autistic savant, but psychologists cannot explain it. All they know is that he may use the parts of his brain that other people use for social purposes. The cortex at the front of the head is a large and a mysterious area, but no one really knows what is happening inside.'

'Will Claude also be checking my fingerprints?' Maria asked.

'He's not needed any longer. With computers he has become redundant.'

Maria sighed and shook her head. 'He should be studied by science,' she said to Lagarde, following her into the main safe deposit hall.

'Try your key,' said Lagarde. Maria inserted it and turned it anti-clockwise. The door was stiff after years of disuse and creaked noisily as she pulled it open.

'We'll be replacing the lock this year,' Lagarde said, as Maria took out a large brown cardboard box, 12 by 18 inches and about six inches deep, held together with white string. It was heavier than she'd remembered. After untying the simple knot she lifted up the top layer of papers – a sheaf of old letters and postcards. Underneath was a collection of black-and-white photographs, and at the very bottom were three thin, round metal cans. She shook the cans and, hearing nothing inside, put them back in the box.

The decomposing letters smelled sweet as Maria held them close to her face. They still retained the innocent scent of childhood. The memories of her father began to flood back as she held them in her shaking fingers. She read them slowly and placed them, one by one, back inside the box.

She set aside four items: a newspaper clipping from the *Athens Daily Post*, a pencil drawing of Mount Parnassus, and two postcards written by her father before he died.

She'd had enough, it was too emotional. She could only go back in time in small doses. She called over the assistant and was escorted back to the upper hall of the bank.

'Do I have to sign anything before taking these out?'

The assistant smiled at her. 'Not at all, they are your property, you can take what you like, whenever you want. We do not own it, it is yours to take.'

'But they are so precious, do you have something to …' she said, her voice trailing away.

The assistant gave her a large brown envelope and showed Maria back to the elevator.

The doors opened and she walked wearily up the staircase into the main banking hall. She'd decided to take the opportunity to make a cash withdrawal. The cashier counted out sixty five-hundred franc notes, and placed the thirty-thousand Francs in a white envelope and sealed it as flat as it could go. Maria pushed the bulging envelope into her bag, closed the zip, and walked down the staircase into the street.

After two hours in the bank's subterranean vaults, Maria had a headache. She squinted in the bright sunlight. Fresh drops of rain sat on the edge of the marble buildings in rue Halevy. A stroll through the Tuileries Garden might clear her head, she thought, and she continued walking until she reached Opera, crossing onto rue de la Paix, past the state buildings in place Vendome. She knew the gardens were five minutes away and she walked to the end of rue de Castiglione, crossed rue de Rivoli with traffic pouring along it, finally finding some calm on the other side.

She walked past the formal beds of roses, found an empty park bench, and took out one of the postcards written by her father. It looked like he'd written it the day before he died. She placed the card next to the yellowing newspaper cutting. As she read the description of his fatal accident, she saw the problem. She looked at the dates again.

The newspaper report of his death was dated June 1st, 1937, yet her father's last postcard, dated June 4th 1937, was sent to her three days *after* he'd supposedly died.

How could he have sent her a postcard three days after he died?

She returned the postcards and the cutting to the envelope and took out her father's pencil sketch of Mount Parnassus. After a few minutes she realised what she was looking at. There was more to the sketch than she'd originally seen – it was marked with tunnel entrances.

A few spots of rain began to fall and Maria put the documents back into the envelope.

She was feeling disorientated and began walking in the wrong direction. Her head was spinning and she looked around for a taxi, put her arm in the air, and waved at a cab on the opposite side of the road.

'Take me to rue Raynouard, No. 70,' she said to the driver's blank face through the window.

12

Maria limped back into her apartment and poured herself a large brandy. She swallowed it in one throw, walked into the drawing room, and placed the postcard from her father on the marble mantelpiece.

Her throat began to feel warm as she gulped down her favourite painkiller. The seventy percent proof liquid gave her the strength she needed as she picked up the phone receiver.

She inhaled deeply, held her breath for ten seconds, and tried to work out what she going to say.

It was impossible to rehearse. Better to just do it, the words will come, she thought.

Maria dialled the number from memory. She hadn't slept well since the row had taken place. It was time to move on, she'd decided. Their week-old argument still echoed in her head. She'd regretted their full-throttle shouting match. It had been pointless. No one had gained anything.

The phone rang for several minutes before it was answered.

'Hello Helena, are you there?' said Maria.

'Hello *maman*. Can I call you back? I'm just having a meeting with my professor,' said Helena in a tired but agitated voice. Maria realised she'd interrupted her daughter at a bad moment. Helena was breathing noisily. Maria could hear that there was someone moving around in the background. She knew these sounds well – she'd often encountered such respiratory noises on Helena's phone.

'I need to speak to you, Helena. I'll hang on until you are ready,' she said. She waited patiently until Helena came back on the line.

'I can speak now,' Helena said, slowly and deliberately.

'I want to apologise for what I said to you last week,' Maria began, gripping the phone. 'I didn't mean it, Helena. Please forgive me,' she said playing with the brandy glass between her fingers.

'OK, *maman*,' Helena said lifelessly, but with the sincerity of brevity.

'Will you come over? There's something I want to show you.'

'Now?'

'Yes, now. If you can,' said Maria.

She put down the phone and took the envelope of cash, locking it in her safe.

Maria was sitting at her walnut desk in her study when Helena arrived smelling of her familiar blend of cigarettes and Chanel. Despite the clash of scents, Maria gave her polite kisses on her cheeks and placed a hand on her shoulder. It was her simple gesture of renewed friendship, clear and unambiguous, telling her she wanted to say sorry and make amends.

Neither of them were able to talk at first.

From the large brown envelope she'd been given at the bank, Maria took out the last two postcards she'd received from her father and held them up. The stamps showed the head of King

George II of Greece and both bore thickly-inked postmarks with the imprint DELPHI in Greek.

'Do these mean anything to you? They were sent to me by your grandfather when I was just 15 years old, some 35 years ago,' Maria said. Helena turned them ninety degrees to read the dates of the postmarks. Etched in italic letters in shiny black Indian ink was Niko's handwritten messages.

'No. I've never seen them before,' she whispered almost breathlessly, and handed the cards back to her mother.

Maria held up the first postcard.

'It's written to make us think the biblical relic he'd discovered was a worthless mistake. I don't believe it for a minute. This is a fake, written by someone who wanted Niko out of the way, and didn't want anyone to believe he'd discovered a major antiquity.' She let the postcard fall onto the desk. It flipped over, revealing the picture on the front – a black-and-white photograph of the village of Kastri. It was a rare photograph of the small Christian village that had been built over Delphi by early Christians to hide the pagan city.

'Oh, look at that. It's Kastri. They moved everyone out and bulldozed the entire community,' Maria told her daughter, her voice strained.

'It was very sad, *maman*, but archaeologists had no option but to sacrifice the village of Kastri to be able to dig up the ancient city of Delphi lying beneath it. It was necessary. Delphi could never have been excavated without it going. Niko would never have been able to work there. Kastri had to go.'

'Do you think so?' said Maria, tears welling in her eyes. 'Do you think your grandfather Niko also had to go, as you put it, because he'd found something embarrassing for the authorities? Something the Catholic Church didn't want people to know about?' asked Maria. Helena shifted uneasily on the leather chair and reached for the brandy bottle.

'*Maman*, I don't believe you invited me here only to show me these old postcards.'

'I want to say something to you Helena,' Maria said, turning to face her, 'which may shock you after what happened between us last week.'

'You can say anything you like, *maman*,' Helena said.

'I've decided I want to sponsor you to go to go to Delphi. I want you to do your PhD, do your orgasm research, do it all. Do the sex research, exactly as you wish. But I also want you to discover what really happened to Niko. Find out if he was murdered because of this discovery. I want you to look for the biblical relic, now that we actually know it is still sitting there. We must stake our claim. We must restore Niko's reputation as an archaeologist. His character was stained, we need to restore the good name of the family.'

Helena looked at her mother with a mixture of surprise and exhaustion. She'd never believed her mother's fantasy that Niko's biblical antiquity was still hidden there, waiting to be excavated, somewhere under Mt Parnussus.

'What do you mean "now that we actually know it is still there"?' she said, shaking her head. 'How do you know it *is* still there? What's happened?'

'I've received some new information,' Maria said in an unexcited, flat monotone.

'What new information?'

'I had an unexpected visit.' She paused to choose her words carefully. 'From an international antiquities dealer.'

'Really? Who was it?' Helena asked.

Maria hesitated. 'OK, I'll tell you, but keep this confidential, especially when you get to Delphi. His name is Frank, Moses Frank, from Vienna.'

'He's not after your art collection, is he?'

'No, I feel confident he's trustworthy. I was visited two days ago by this charming Moses gentleman. He's a Jewish refugee who lost his grandparents at Auschwitz. He's now a respected antiquities dealer. I believed him. I'm quite a good judge of character.'

'What makes you so convinced?'

'He's seen it. I have no reason to doubt him, he proved it to me,' Maria said. 'He has nothing to gain and everything to lose by telling me what he saw.'

'What has he seen exactly?' Helena demanded.

'He's found Niko's biblical relic buried under the Temple of Apollo at Delphi, the one mentioned in this postcard,' she said, waving it in her hand. 'It does exist. It isn't a fantasy. It even has Niko's initials scratched on it – 'NFD.' He took a photo of it. Wait a minute, I'll show you, he brought it round last night.'

Maria went into her bedroom and returned with a large envelope and handed it to Helena. 'See for yourself.'

Helena removed a large black-and-white photograph showing a detail of a relic. She blinked several times as she held it up in front of her eyes.

'*Merde*, it's true. I would never have believed it,' she said as she saw her grandfather's initials scratched onto the bottom of the relic.

'You can see why I believe this man. He actually wants to help us, and told me what we have to do.'

'Are you sure he isn't using you for his own ends?'

'He may have an agenda of his own, but it's a good one. He wants to excavate the relic and put it on public display, show it the world. I see nothing wrong in that. It's one of the most important pieces of the world's heritage.'

'So what must I do if I accept your offer of sponsorship?' said

Helena.

'I want you to go to Delphi and make our claim to the relic to the director of the Temple site. His name is Dr Andreas Green, and he is trying to claim it is *his* discovery.'

Maria was expecting her daughter to shout with joy. Instead, Helena looked back at her with a pained expression.

'Even if everything you've said is correct there is one problem. I'm still waiting for the university to approve the doctorate. They may never support it, it seems. It's too controversial for them.'

'I may have a solution to that problem as well,' said Maria.

'But how? What can *you* do?'

'Not me – this dealer fellow, Moses Frank.' Helena looked at her mother sceptically.

'He's a powerful man, someone of influence. He has a major reputation. I beg you Helena, just talk to him, persuade Moses to help you. He can do it, he knows everyone.'

'But I'm not sure about asking a man to help me, it's too compromising.'

'Trust me, Helena, you will like him. He is a true gentleman and with great influence. You have nothing to lose by talking to him.'

'I dislike begging powerful men for favours. They love it though, it massages their egos, doesn't it?'

'Just do it Helena, swallow your pride and try.' Maria paused for a moment. 'Do it for the sake of the family, to give back your grandfather the reputation that is owed to him.'

Maria went over to the small Chagall painting, removed it from the wall and opened the safe. She took out a bulging white envelope stuffed with cash.

'Here are thirty-thousand Francs. They will pay for your entire trip.' She took out the bank notes and flicked through them with the tips of her fingers. 'But there is one condition to having this cash – the Sorbonne must approve your PhD research first. It will be waiting for you until that time,' Maria said, replacing the cash in the safe.

Helena stood in silence, shaking her head and licking her parched lips. She was craving some stimulation, and rolled a cigarette.

'So what made you change your mind, if you don't mind me asking?'

'I thought about what the act of physical sex means to you. I look at you and your marriage, which still survives, despite everything. I see that you *can* separate your marital love from the purely physical act of sex.

'I can see that it means nothing to you when it is not emotional love, as if it is just a brief moment of physical pleasure, like a shot of brandy or a mouthful of oysters. It does not seem to affect your relationship. I admire you for that, Helena. I salute it.'

'Thank you for taking such an enlightened attitude, *maman*.' Helena took out her diary, her pen ready in her mouth.

'Give me the number for this Mr Frank.'

13

It was late afternoon by the time they drove through the first toll at Champigny-sur-Marne, 20 km out of Paris.

The yellow fields sped past the window but Anna's eyes were focussed on the distance, looking towards a line of elms swaying on the horizon.

Moses had chosen a route through the champagne city of Reims in eastern France before heading out eastwards via Heilbronn and Nuremburg, entering Vienna along the banks of the Danube.

Anna opened the refrigerated mini-bar in the back seat and took out two plastic bags containing her specimens. The laurel leaves still looked glossy and healthy, shining in the sunshine coming through the car window. She replaced a second plastic bag containing a few roots of Black Hellebore and leaned forward to speak to Sam.

'I need to stop at the next village to buy some fruit,' she said abruptly. Five minutes later, Sam stopped in Château-Thierry, a small champagne-growing town, situated on an elbow bend in the River Marne. He parked in the main square just outside a museum.

A plaque in the square declared the town the birthplace of poet Jean de la Fontaine. Anna went into a small grocer's shop and came back with a paper bag containing two pears, a banana, and a bottle of Evian water.

She took her purchases and joined Moses in the café next door. Moses ordered a coffee whilst Anna disappeared into the bathroom. After ten minutes and no sign of Anna, Moses went to look for her. He found the door of the bathroom locked but could hear grinding sounds coming from inside.

'Are you OK?' he asked.

It was a few seconds before Anna's strained voice replied. 'I'm alright. Really Moses, I'm ok. Go back into the café.'

'What's wrong, Anna? You're not behaving normally. I can tell something's troubling you,' Moses said. He heard Anna sobbing.

'Please open the door, I want to help you,' said Moses.

'I'm OK, really. I'll be a couple of minutes,' she said, and he went back to the table and counted the seconds tick by on his watch. After 180 of them he went back to the bathroom and stood outside the door.

'Come out now, you'll feel better, I'm sure,' he said. There was no response. Then he heard footsteps and the door opened. Standing in the doorway, in a daze, her eyes half shut, Anna fell towards him. He caught her and held her in his arms as he scanned the small room.

Peering over her shoulder he saw a glass of thick green liquid at the sink with two spoons inside it. A few shiny green leaves were scattered on the floor. He could see Anna had made a herbal concoction by grinding leaves between the spoons.

'What were you doing in there?' he asked. Anna smiled back at him, but it wasn't a happy smile.

'I'm making a natural contraceptive from laurel leaves,' she said. 'It's what us herbalists do.'

'But why?' said Moses, shocked by her revelation.

'Do you want me to have a little Moses?' she said softly. Moses smiled briefly, looked embarrassed, and stared down at the floor.

'But I thought you were on the—'

Anna interrupted. 'Most people don't know this, but the pill is not safe. Too many young women have been dying from thrombosis. It makes the blood clot. The drug giants don't like to advertise their little pill problem. They haven't got the dose right yet. I'm not going to be one of their guinea pigs. It's safer if I use a herbal remedy.'

'But is that mixture any safer? Plants contain toxins, they could also kill you,' Moses said, looking at the murky green liquid.

'The women of Delphi used this for thousands of years. The Oracles took it to avoid becoming pregnant, after performing their sex rites with the priests,' she said.

'You know about the Elena Text?' he asked.

'Of course I know about it. It's a famous ancient text from Delphi. I did my research before coming along with you. It's a source of written information on herbal medicines used by the Greeks, it's not just a sex ritual.'

'So you're saying the Oracles took laurel leaves to prevent pregnancy?' he asked Anna.

'Sure, and other things too. The seeds of lettuce are pretty good. And there was a herb they used called silphium. It was prized so highly they even minted a coin in its honour. The Romans used it as a contraceptive – it kept the birth rate way down in Ancient Rome,' she said, sniffing and accepting a tissue from Moses.

'I understand what you're saying, Anna, but that green liquid you've just made – is it safe to drink? How on earth do you know the right dose?' he said.

'Trust me, Moses, I know what I'm doing. Everyone thinks you're unscientific if you say you're a herbalist. It's so annoying,' Anna said, twisting her fingers in the palm of her hand.

'I'm sorry, Anna, I didn't mean to imply that,' said Moses.

They went back into the café. Moses looked across into her tired eyes. They had lost their brightness and were bloodshot, with red flecks floating in them, as if she had a virus. The green stripe across her hair had almost faded to a dull straw colour.

She downed the liquid in a series of small gulps and broke off small chunks of a banana to go with it.

Moses took out a pocket knife, peeled a pear, and fed the slices to Anna with his fingers. It made her laugh as the slippery segments slid between her lips. It brought back memories of the crumpled sheets of hotel bedrooms in Paris and Rome.

They walked back to the Mercedes and Sam drove on

towards Rheims. Everyone was quiet for twenty minutes until Anna made her announcement.

'I need to phone Prague. I'm worried about my father, I want to check he's OK,' she said.

'We're quite near Château Petrie, on the Taittinger estate. I have an interest in it – let's stop there,' said Moses.

As they drove down the eighteenth-century driveway Anna recognised a line of gingko biloba trees and pointed them out to Moses.

'What's so special about the trees?' asked Moses.

'One of the oldest trees in the world. I love it, it's an ancient wonder drug, great for the memory and a healthy circulation. It has so many uses, mostly forgotten now,' she said.

They arrived at Château Petrie and were given a room with a phone.

Whilst Anna called her family, Moses went off to inspect the Pinot Noir vines. When he walked back into the room, a bottle of Taittinger champagne in his hand, she was staring blankly out of the window.

'So what's the news?' Moses said.

'I need to go back to Prague,' she said, 'to see my father.'

They returned to the car and took the E50 towards Metz, cruising past the towering gothic cathedral, visible for miles on the skyline long before they reached the fortress town.

From here they stayed on the same road and drove into the evocatively named city of Heilbronn for fuel, beer, and sandwiches. It was their first taste of Germany.

Five and a half hours after leaving Reims, they drove into Nuremburg and went straight to the Hauptbahnhof. It was the first town with a direct train connection to Prague. Moses bought Anna a first-class ticket, and stuffed a bundle of notes into her hand.

'What's this for?' she asked, looking at all the clean, unused bank notes.

'It's your fee as an assistant antiquities consultant – eighteen days at one hundred dollars a day.' She looked back at Moses. He couldn't decide if she was insulted or flattered.

'No, it's not for all the great sex.' Moses was quick to reassure her with a laugh. 'I couldn't afford to pay for that,' he added. Anna managed half a smile.

'Anyway, my daily rate is much higher than a hundred a day,' she said, putting her arms round Moses' waist and gripping him with a bear-hug for several long minutes.

'I want to stay in touch with you, Moses,' she said, and turned towards Sam.

'You're a good driver. Most of the time, anyway,' Anna told him, and kissed him on the lips. She whispered into his ear, 'come and see me in Prague.' Sam smiled but stayed silent. She walked onto the platform and waved the two men goodbye.

'Come and see me again in Vienna,' Moses shouted. 'It's only three hours by railway.'

'I'm definitely coming back,' she said. Her train was sitting on platform eight and she climbed onboard.

'Is it time to go and find your seat now?' Moses asked.

Anna nodded and he watched her move down the carriage. She sat by the window, waved, and wiped a few tears with her sleeve.

The train started to move out of the station. Moses blew a kiss with his fingers. Over the deafening sound of the guard's whistle he turned and shouted to Sam.

'You know, I don't even have her number or address. How will I find her again?'

'I could find her for you anytime. But she'll be back on her own accord,' Sam said confidently.

'Really? Don't you think she might just disappear into the Prague undergrowth?'

'I don't think so, unless you want her to disappear. Then she might take the hint,' Sam said, licking his lips as if he was still enjoying her sweet taste.

'Eighteen days was all she could take of me,' said Moses. 'I suppose it's been a strange experience for her.'

They returned to the Merc and Moses slid back into the comfort of its leather cocoon. He took a sip of spring water.

The midday sun made a rectangle of light on the wall of the therapist's office as it shone through the nineteenth-century window.

'Did you suspect Anna's betrayal at that time?'

Moses swivelled in his chair and tried to answer, but the sun was too dazzling and he had to re-position himself.

It gave him a few more seconds to think about the pain of the discovery of Anna's double life.

'I was infatuated with her. She could do no wrong. At first I couldn't see it. She seemed so innocent and unsophisticated. But I was so naïve.'

'Do you have regrets?'

'Not at all, because once I knew the truth, I didn't let Anna know it.'

14

When the Merc hit 150 km an hour on the autobahn, Moses decided to try his new car phone.

It was a large device weighing 1 kg, made by the Finnish company Nokia. His eyes lit up as he heard the reassuring purr of the dial tone.

He keyed in the number of the Delphi Museum in mainland Greece. It rang for at least two minutes with a distant-sounding and irregular tone until a male voice answered tersely in Greek.

'*Kalispera.*'

'Dr Green? This is Moses, Moses Frank,' he began, uncertain it was Green, who was normally less brusque.

'Ah Moses,' said Green, reverting to his warm voice, with a friendly Greek-American accent. 'Wonderful, it's your old friend Andreas Green here!' he shouted in delight. 'Good afternoon to you, Moses.'

'What's new, Andreas?'

There was a long pause. 'Give me a moment, let me gather all of my many thoughts.'

Moses could hear Green humming as he stalled for time.

'The excavation of the anomaly. I can tell you it's all going extremely … well, very well, my friend.' He swallowed audibly. 'Excellent, actually, Moses.'

'Listen, Andreas. I've an important antiquities sale coming up and want to show some images of the Delphic Anomaly to potential buyers.'

Dr Green went silent for a few seconds before bursting out laughing.

'Who needs photographs when you can have the real thing in a matter of …' Green didn't finish the sentence. Moses wondered if he was going to say weeks or months.

'I would like to tell my clients when the Anomaly will be available for sale.'

'Why? Listen, my good friend, your clients won't be able to resist the Anomaly *anytime* it comes up for sale,' said Green.

Moses laughed. 'If only this were true. Unfortunately, my wealthy international buyers are a highly unpredictable bunch. They have millions of dollars to spend, and a few days later they have nothing. Huge chunks of cash dissolve into thin air, especially in the spring and summer, when they like to buy new yachts or villas in the Mediterranean.'

'So when's the best time?' asked Green.

'The winter and the autumn are the best times to sell major antiquities,' Moses said.

'I see,' said Green, sounding despondent.

'Timing is crucial, and it's best to whet their appetite in advance. I like to send them titbits of news about the latest secret excavations. They like that. They love to hear about all the dramatic new discoveries, otherwise they lose interest. They're like children with new toys.'

There was another long silence. All Moses could hear was an echo of a humming down the scratchy Greek phoneline. He heard a distant click as Green started to speak again.

'Moses, I am delighted to inform you that I am going back into the chamber … the day after tomorrow, if everything works out to plan. I will then have it in my hands, finally liberated from the limestone, by the end of this week,' he said, with a rising crescendo.

'No bullshit, Andreas? Is that really happening?'

'I swear in front of God, this is the truth Moses. I would never talk bullshit, you know that.'

'Great, let me know how it goes as soon as you've done the

excavation. Good luck.' Moses switched off the phone and leaned over to Sam who'd been able to hear both sides of the conversation.

'Green is really stalling, isn't he? I wonder what's delaying him,' said Sam.

'He's a law to himself, but I'm delighted by the call quality of this new phone, even though it takes up the space of a shoebox.'

Moses looked into his small black address book and found the number for EuroMetStat, a weather forecasting service based in Geneva, used by governments and militaries. They supplied the most accurate forecasts of weather patterns in the world, based on analysis of sunspot activity.

He dialled the Swiss number, gave his password, and a polite English-speaking woman answered.

'Can you give me an idea about the precipitation around Mount Parnassus in Greece for the next few days?'

'There will be strong winds and storms for the next three days, followed by high temperatures and humidity,' she said.

'How much rain?' Moses asked.

'15–20 cm is expected. This is unseasonably heavy rain, far more than is normally expected in Greece at this time of the year.'

'Any reason?' Moses said.

'There is a high level of solar radiation associated with the summer solstice, Mr Frank.'

Moses thanked her and replaced his handset.

PART SEVEN

Helena and Moses

1

Helena waited in the foyer of the Karl Jung Institute for her taxi to Zurich railway station.

The weekend had not lived up to its billing. 'The Unconscious and the Orgasm' had been an underwhelming experience, and she needed some fresh air.

Some of the male participants, sex counsellors from California and Germany, came up to her, wanting hugs, her phone number, and an invitation to Paris. But she could see from their leering stares, as they pushed themselves against her, that these elderly men wanted to exchange more than just numbers.

Their leathery skin reminded her of the barbecued wrinklies she'd encountered on nudist beaches on the Greek islands.

Sitting in a lecture theatre discussing sex was a frustrating experience. She had to remind herself she was in a public place.

Her impatient fingers would have to wait a few minutes until she was alone in the back of a cab.

She remembered a private balcony, facing the Indian ocean, a turquoise blue sea surrounded by palm trees, warm sea air blowing gently over her body as she made love on a king-sized bed.

Her fantasy lasted only a few seconds, but it was long enough to reduce the anxiety she could feel rising in her body.

She opened her eyes and was back in the Karl Jung Institute, surrounded by the over-eager course participants brandishing pens and address books. Smiling at them, she obliged, writing down quickly invented phone numbers and a fictitious address in a non-existent suburb of Paris, telling them all how much she would enjoy seeing them again one day, whilst repeating 'never again' under her breath.

She walked to the panoramic windows overlooking Lake Zurich and watched the sailing dinghies skimming over the silver water like pond insects. For a confident woman with a strong exhibitionist bent, the prospect of meeting Moses Frank was filling her with unusual anxiety.

She wrestled with a small chunk of her thumbnail and wondered what role to play when she met the man. She wondered if he would have heard about her PhD research in Delphi and if he would expect her to have a special interest in sex. It was too late to check.

Lifting the payphone, she focused for a few seconds on which way to mould her character. Tightening her core muscles around her slim waist, she stood tall, shook her head to make her crimson hair fall seductively over her shoulders, and dialled his number. As the ringing tone purred, she felt a few drops of cold sweat slide down her arms.

A mellow male voice answered. 'God, he sounds so fucking relaxed,' she thought.

'Hello, it's Helena Delacroix here,' she said confidently.

'I've been waiting for you to call. Where are you now?' Moses said.

She was relieved he had no time for small talk. She hated inconsequential exchanges, she always wanted to get going.

'On my way out of the Karl Jung Institute in Zurich. I'm taking the sleeper to Vienna. It was the only option. Sorry I'm arriving a day later than planned, is that OK?' she said. 'I should get there about 8.30 tomorrow morning.'

'You're in Switzerland, the trains run on time. I've booked you a suite at the Intercontinental, two minutes from my place,' Moses said. 'It's on the house. I'm a good client of theirs.'

'Thank you Mr Frank,' she said appreciatively. 'I hope you don't mind, but I want to visit the Sigmund Freud Museum on the way, before we meet. It's the only time I have to go there. I'd like to rest a little too, before our meeting, so I thought I'd come over to you about six tomorrow evening. Is that OK?' she said, her voice trailing off.

'Fine. It means you can get both of the fathers of psychoanalysis out of way in less than 24 hours. Sounds like a good plan.'

'I didn't want to bother you in working hours.'

'It's no problem. You have my address, 221 Johannesgasse. I'm at the top of the Leopold Tower. You *could* walk from the Intercontinental …' He paused. 'No, don't do that – take a cab.'

She was shaking as she replaced the phone. Moses' calm voice sounded so organised and controlled. He was on home territory, he knew every square inch, why shouldn't he sound confident? She stared out to the lake and saw a dingy make a decisive turn. How could she come over as equally in control? Or better still, how could she dominate him, yet remain physically attractive? Tight and sexy whilst being a hard bargain?

She was craving a cigarette and gestured her need to one of her fellow delegates, tapping two fingers, slightly apart, on her lips. She gladly accepted a Marlborough, lit up, and sat down on a sofa by the entrance, her knees folded, plenty of leg on show, blowing trails of smoke across the foyer. She felt calm again, enjoying the glances from all the male delegates milling around her. It was fine, as long as they weren't groping and pressing themselves against her.

Her taxi arrived and took her to the central station. As she sat in the cab travelling through Zurich Altstadt, the old town, she realised she knew nothing about Moses.

She was directed to platform 6 for the overnight sleeper to Vienna. A spotless train was sitting there, doors wide open, waiting for passengers to board. She found her compartment, threw down her bag, and went for a drink in the bar. She wasn't looking for company, but felt like a glass of wine to help her gaze blankly out of the compartment window.

As the train gathered speed through the suburbs of Zurich she realised why she felt so uncomfortable in the land of the Swiss. The spotless country had pure white mountains and glistening snow sitting on perfect peaks, but no soul. It looked dead and artificial compared to Paris, and she couldn't erase the images of Nazi loot sitting in secret bank vaults, powerful but corrupt drug companies, and the expressionless Swiss, saying nothing about it all.

After two days of socialising at the orgasm conference she was tired and didn't want to talk to any other passengers. She went back to the privacy of her compartment for an early night. Locking the door and taking off her clothes, she did a few yoga poses, deliberately appearing naked for a few seconds to a crowd of people standing on the platform at Munich. As people began to notice her, the train pulled out of the station, but she continued to allow herself to be seen as the train accelerated out of the city, passing through a series of commuter stations without stopping.

Resting on the starched sheets, she felt she was going to need all her energy and vitality for her encounter with Moses. The future of her entire research project rested on her ability to charm him the right way – to seduce him, perhaps, whether she liked him or not. As she switched off the carriage light, her head swirling with erotic thoughts, the motion of the train carriage thumping and grinding over the sleepers, she felt wet and aroused, but she was too tired to do anything about it before she fell asleep.

She woke the following morning at 7.00 am with a knock on the door and a cup of hot coffee from the sleeper attendant. At 8.20 am the train snaked its way into Vienna's Westbahnhof, and she took a taxi into town. She checked into the Intercontinental, took a shower, changed her clothes and began walking to the Freud Museum. She wanted to experience the true grandeur of the capital of the Austro-Hungarian empire, to feel the opulence of the Hapsburgs, to see the birthplace of the waltz. She'd always been amused that a such a sexually-charged dance had somehow sneaked its way into the ballrooms of polite Viennese society.

After a twenty-five minute walk she arrived outside Bergasse 19, a five-storey nineteenth-century apartment building. Upstairs, she wandered into Freud's waiting room. It looked untouched since the middle-class women of Vienna had sat here and waited to see their brilliant doctor. There was no couch, only a few black-and-white photographs of the cigar-chewing psychoanalyst surrounded by his respectful colleagues.

She wondered how these female patients felt after being told that their hysterical illnesses were caused by sexual frustration.

She walked back, disappointed by the museum, determined not to become one of Freud's women.

In a long, steamy shower, she washed away the grime of her train journey and prepared for the meeting with Moses Frank.

Standing in front of a mirror, Helena tested the flight characteristics of her silk dress. She was able to reach the zip at the back and make it fall off her shoulders, onto the floor, leaving her semi-naked. It could work well on Moses, but she knew she'd have to engineer the right moment.

An unopened bottle of cognac, bought at Zurich station, was still using up precious space in her suitcase. She sat on the bed, twisted the cork, and poured herself a glass. There was half an hour to go, and she called reception for a taxi.

Her mouth still warm with brandy, Helena walked up the steps of the New York-style 1930s' skyscraper into an empty marble reception area and saw the brass plate bearing the initials WAR Inc. The commissionaire gave her a suspicious look, as if she was a high-class escort looking for work.

'It's OK, I'm waiting for Mr Frank,' she shouted across with a large smile. He nodded and went back to his security screens.

'It's Helena Delacroix,' she breathed into the entry phone. There was a click and Moses' voice resonated through the speaker.

'Wait by the elevators, I'll be down very soon,' he said, and there was another soft click.

She walked over to the bank of elevators and waited for him to appear, wetting her lips a few times with the tip of her tongue. Moses emerged from elevator 4. She watched his eyes linger on her body for a few seconds, looking her up and down with obvious pleasure. Nothing aroused her more than a man appreciating her body. He held out his arms and gave her a gentle embrace, kissing her on both cheeks, as if they knew each other.

The signals were good as he put his hand onto her bare back and led her towards the open elevator.

'And how was the Freud Museum?' he asked, making polite, inoffensive conversation. His deep voice resonated as he spoke, like a firm embrace.

'You'd never guess the sexual revolution started here,' she said, enjoying the feel of his long fingers on her skin.

Moses was younger and more lively than she'd imagined. She liked the way he stood next to her, his hand now almost touching her, restrained but tactile.

'I'm afraid it's a bit of a journey up to my apartment, but the new elevator is fast,' he said. 'Maybe too fast.'

'How high up are you exactly?' she said.

'I'm on the 52nd floor. As you can imagine, there's a good view of the city.'

'OK,' she said very slowly. 'But where are your auction rooms, Mr Frank?' she asked, looking at him through the mirrors covering the walls.

'It's a subterranean theatre. Our 50-seat auction room is on the lower ground floor. I'll take you down there afterwards.'

'After what?' Helena said, taking his arm to steady herself, as the elevator shot upwards.

Moses didn't answer but leaned towards her and breathed in her perfume.

2

As the elevator doors snapped open Helena fell forwards, her crimson locks flowing behind her like Botticelli's Venus on speed.

She staggered into the vast open-plan penthouse, collapsing like a rag doll onto an L-shaped sofa by the panoramic windows.

Moses ran over to her, and pushed a finger between her dry lips. 'I'm doing this to make sure you can breathe,' he said.

He looked at her lying there semi-conscious. She was undoubtedly alluring – the sleek designer clothes, the flowing red hair, the svelte body drenched in Chanel. It was all there on show in front of him, beautifully set out to feast his eyes on. She was half-goddess, half-butterfly with a broken wing.

Kneeling to wipe her brow he noticed the stress lines around her mouth, and the smell of brandy rising from her lips. It was an unsettling combination.

As he prodded the back of her wrist for a pulse, she came round and pulled herself forward on the cushions, her silk dress slipping away from her body as it fell off her shoulders.

'What happened?' Moses said.

'It went up so quickly,' she said breathlessly. 'Like a rocket.'

'I agree. Unless you're a test pilot, fifty-two floors in twenty-two seconds is too fast, you're right,' he said, and she smiled back at him.

'And maybe drinking two glasses of cognac before coming to see you didn't help either.'

It was 6.00 pm. A larger-than-usual full moon was due to rise over the Danube in the next five minutes. It would make a spectacular sight through the panoramic windows, but Moses wondered if it might frighten her in her present state.

She sat up and looked at the huge canvases on the whitewashed walls. All the big names of modern art jostled for position here.

A colourful Mondrian of blue and yellow rectangles filled one entire side of the apartment, next to it two Klimt nudes painted in gold. On the adjacent wall was a Jeff Koons depicting his wife, La Cicciolina, an Italian pornstar, kneeling in high heeled boots, wearing a short, tight red dress.

Around the corner was a Modigliani of a bare-breasted young girl with alabaster skin, admiring herself in the mirror. Three feet away was a Manet of a dark-haired model reclining naked on a chaise longue; beside it a small Picasso sketch of a young Spanish model undressing, her black hair flowing over bare shoulders.

Helena's eyes moved around the room to take it all in. It was like being in a private art gallery. She walked back to the leather sofa, and stared straight into Moses' eyes.

'I get the picture, Mr Frank. You like to collect art depicting beautiful, naked women.'

Moses bristled defensively. He was deeply proud of his collection.

'Come on, Helena. This is a celebration of the female form by the world's greatest artists. The nude is an artistic tradition going back to ancient times. How about a drink?'

'I've had too much cognac already. Just some sparkling water,' she said. Moses poured half a bottle of San Pellegrino and gave himself a double measure of Scotch. He swirled the pale whisky around his tongue and gave Helena a warm smile.

'I know, Helena – go and see my Dali, you may be happier with that.'

Salvador Dali's portrait of Abraham Lincoln was hanging in an alcove off the main room. She wandered through an archway and came before the familiar square jaw that personified American self-righteousness, the face made up from a series of squares and rectangles.

'It's a portrait of an American President, what's so special about that?' she said.

Moses shook his head and began to laugh. 'Is that all you can see there, Helena? Keep looking,' he said, trying to hold back a smile.

'For Christ's sake!' She'd seen the voluptuous nude hidden inside Lincoln's face. Moses burst out laughing. 'You're really quite obsessed aren't you?' she said.

He couldn't stop grinning at her. 'I bought it from Dali himself. He put my name on the back. It's clever isn't it?' said Moses, but he could see Helena clenching her fist.

'Don't be angry with me, the devil is in Dali, not me. And the shapely rear belongs to Dali's own wife, Gala.' Moses began to shake his head. You see, Helena,' he began opening his arms towards Helena, 'Once you know the story behind a painting, you realise it's a romance painted in oils. It's nothing to do with pornography. The same for the Jeff Koons – it's an expression of love and affection between a man and his wife.'

'Look Mr Frank,' she began. 'I don't buy that, I can see what I can see, I really thought you were a serious dealer. I didn't expect to see all this naked flesh plastered over your walls,' she said, pointing to the Koons, the Dali, and the Modigliani hung all around her.

'What are you saying to me, Helena? Are you really upset by a few classic nudes?' He waited for her response, he knew she'd few personal inhibitions and thought he was on safe ground bringing her up to see his private gallery. She didn't answer.

'And I gather you wanted to carry out research into ancient *sex* rituals. Well, for God's sake Helena, this doesn't make any sense ...'

Her eyes flickered, she looked upset and looked away from Moses. 'I'm leaving,' she said, turning around and looking for the handle of the door near her. Moses knew there was nothing there – it was a visual illusion painted on the wall, a *trompe l'oeil*, a fake archway, complete with an imaginary door and handle.

Moses could see she was angry, but was beginning to think it was all an elaborate act.

'OK, wait a second, Helena,' Moses said, crouching down and clasping his hands in the prayer position. 'I want to work with you, don't go yet. You don't really know what I believe in. We don't know each other at all, let's rewind a few minutes and try again.'

She walked a few steps towards him and shrugged her shoulders. 'Are you happy you've humiliated me now?' she said.

'Not at all, but thank you for staying a little longer,' he said, and breathed out a long sigh. 'Let me tell you one thing – I've never exploited women.' He touched her shoulder. 'Look, Helena. I'm sure we could help each other and I feel we might get on rather well, once we get to know each other better.'

Helena smiled back at him and looked down at the floor. She

started to laugh, and Moses looked at her uncertainly.

'OK I agree we don't know each other at all, so tell me – who is the real Mr Frank?' she said. 'I'd like to know.'

'First, I don't want you to call me Mr Frank. Call me Moses, for God's sake.'

'Alright, my dear Moses,' she drawled. 'The problem is that what I see on the walls is such a contrast to the gentleman in front of me.' She walked along the wall of paintings and turned to face him.

'OK, tell me – are all these paintings *fakes*? I've seen most of them in public galleries around Europe. Isn't that from the Picasso museum in Barcelona?'

Moses nodded with a faint smile on his lips.

'And what about the Klimts over there? I'm sure I've seen them in Amsterdam,' she said, relaxing onto the sofa again. Her silk dress slid up her thighs, revealing black stockings and tight briefs. The outline of her sex was quite visible through a triangle of black lace. He thought he was beginning to understand her game plan and tried to look away.

'So are they for real, Moses?' she asked with a shrug of her shoulders, but keeping still otherwise.

'These are the genuine paintings,' he said. 'It's the public museums and major art galleries who now have the fakes. What you saw in Amsterdam was my copy of the original. A few years ago they needed money, so I helped them out and made them a good copy. It's what I was trained to do as a young man in Florence. I was taught by the best copyist in the world, and I've passed my skills to a few artists who are keen to work for me, from time to time.'

'So you practise forgery?'

'No, no, no, it's called fine copying – and we're doing it with the full cooperation of the national galleries.'

Helena put her hand to her cheek. He could see she was taken aback by his revelation.

'It's been going on for years. All the major galleries do it now, it's not such a bad thing, you know.'

'But aren't people being taken for a ride?'

'The public have absolutely no idea,' he said, swiping the air with his hand. 'It's what people believe that really counts. It's like a placebo pill – if you believe in it, it works. Belief is all important. There's nothing wrong with a well-executed fake, if it still moves people. The colours they see with their eyes are the same, their emotions are the same, and it's helping the major art galleries survive in a tough climate.'

Moses moved closer. 'And I must tell you, it's the only way the galleries can continue to buy new work by young artists. It's my way of helping them out. That's good, isn't it?' he said, draining his glass of whisky and smiling at her

'And it means I can keep the originals here, for you to enjoy.'

3

A helicopter droned overhead, making a sound like muted gunfire. As it landed on the penthouse roof Moses' phone rang.

'I ordered some food in,' he shouted, waving to the pilot. 'Sorry about the racket. It's ridiculous, they always call me on the phone to say it has arrived, as if I won't hear a helicopter landing on my own roof.'

Helena laughed and twisted round to watch the rotors

spinning above her. Her dress rode up her leg again, revealing more of the delicate black lace, pulling tightly at her crotch.

'Venetian lace suits you, Helena,' Moses said, admiring the way it followed her most intimate curves.

She smiled back at Moses in approval at his observation, pushing her forefinger gently under the lace. Without warning, she rose from the sofa. Moses tried to help her stand up with an outstretched arm, but she wrestled him away and placed her hands on his shoulders, stopping him from moving.

'I don't understand you. For a man who deals in ancient artefacts and antiquities, you've a very contemporary taste in art.'

Moses quivered. He wasn't expecting such a weird question. He paused for a few seconds to conjure up an answer.

'You're right Helena,' he said, his breathing relaxing as she let him go. 'You see, when I come back home, after a day of dealing in antiquities, I need to separate from the ancient world.' He began to look around the penthouse walls. 'All this modern art around here brings me back to a kind of reality.'

He pushed open a door disguised as a bookshelf and walked into his office. There was a presidential-sized desk on which sat a row of miniatures of Egyptian gods and goddesses next to an Apple Macintosh computer. On the wall opposite was another semi-naked Klimt woman, sheathed in gold leaf. On a glass shelf was a stunningly beautiful Egyptian bust.

'And here's a very modern-looking statue of Nefertiti, over three-thousand years old. A natural beauty, the wife of the revolutionary Pharaoh Akhenaten.' He paused and looked round at Helena, but she wasn't there.

He rushed back to the lounge and found her standing in front of the panoramic windows, hands behind her neck, eyes wide open. Her gaze was focussed beyond him, a half-formed smile on her face, as if in a trance.

'What are you doing, Helena?'

As she turned around she pulled the zip of her dress all the way down her back in one flowing movement.

'What the hell are you ...' he started to say, as she shimmied from side to side and let the dress fall off her shoulders.

She stepped over it and walked across the hardwood floor in her stiletto heels until she was standing only a few centimetres away from Moses' startled face. He tried to avert his eyes.

'Don't you like what you see?' she asked, spinning round in front of him. She bent down and put her hands flat on the floor, arching her back like the Koons painting of La Cicciolina.

'I was wondering if I would qualify for your private collection, Moses? Am I sexy enough to be included?'

Moses shook his head and began to blink at her uncontrollably. He was feeling totally out-manoeuvered. 'I'm confused, Helena. What are you trying to prove?'

'I thought I'd fit in better here without my clothes – like all your *other* women. That's all.'

4

Moses stood there shielding his eyes from Helena's semi-naked body as she knelt in front of him.

'You don't have to do this Helena, I don't know what idea you have ...' he stuttered, unable to stay focused on his thoughts.

Kneeling on the floor she looked up at him. 'Tell me seriously, Moses, what do you think of me now?'

'I'm not going to look at you,' he said, turning away.

'Why waste it, Moses? Enjoy me, you obviously love the sight of a beautiful woman,' she said, stroking her breast.

'I can't think with you undressed like this. We don't know each other at all. I don't expect women to … strip off naked in front of me. It doesn't normally happen this fast. You don't need to do this, we were having a business meeting. Please get dressed again.' He looked down at her scraps of clothing on the floor and realised she didn't have much to take off.

'Why should I, Moses? You clearly like seeing the unclothed bodies of *other* women, displayed all over the walls of your penthouse,' she said, standing and turning around a couple of times to show him her body. 'So I thought this would be fine and I'd fit well into … the land of Moses.' She laughed at her own joke, and Moses couldn't resist smiling himself.

'That's different,' he said.

'Not, really. Imagine I'm an artist's model. You studied art, didn't you? I heard you went to life classes for several years at the Uffizi School in Florence, so a woman's body isn't at all shocking for you, is it?' she said, twisting her hips.

'Real life is always more exciting than a canvas stretched over a frame. But why are you doing this?' he said. She smiled back at him and placed a finger under his chin.

'I thought I'd lubricate our relationship by, how can I put it? By fast-forwarding,' she said, sitting down and crossing one leg over the other. 'I like pressing down on the fast forward button and saving time.'

'Fast-forwarding, I like the idea. If only I could fast forward through all the dull meetings in my life,' he said. She smiled back at him, pulling her fingers through strands of her red hair.

'But look, Helena. I had the impression from your mother you didn't trust me, or were sceptical at least,' he said. She nodded vigorously, put a finger over his lips and held it there a few seconds.

'I'm not sure I do trust you – *yet*. But that's another kind of trust, isn't it? This is just about enjoying each other. It's not about finances or money.'

'You've a good point there,' Moses said, rubbing his mouth.

'I must confess, I was worried you were after my mother's fortune,' she said.

Moses, the self-made multi-millionaire, looked hurt by the suggestion. 'That's unkind. Look around you – what do you see?'

'I can see all the glorious trappings of wealth. Priceless art, a luxury penthouse. I don't know this city, but you probably own one of the most expensive apartments in Vienna. OK – you don't need my family's money.'

'Precisely. I'm a rich man. I don't need more wealth.'

'So what's this all about, Moses? What do you want from me? Why did you invite me here?' she asked, stretching her legs across the sofa. 'Come on Moses, tell me the truth now, I need to know,' she said, sliding seductively down the cushions.

'It's a simple matter. I have a project I'd like you to help me with and I understood you needed some help from me as well,' he said, and put his hands over his eyes. 'Hang on, Helena. This is getting difficult for me, you know. I need to stop now, or perhaps I can ask you a small favour?'

He walked to his bedroom and returned with a silk kimono. 'Can you put on this robe? Please do it for me, I think you'll like it against your skin. It's sensuous and will cover you up. You understand, I can't sit here looking at you like that. I can't simply stop reacting to a woman's nakedness.'

'OK, I'm sorry.' Helena took it from his hands. 'I wonder which Japanese ladyfriend of yours left this behind?' she said, tying the belt tightly around her waist. 'Is that better? Are you sure you don't want me to put some dust sheets over your paintings as well?' she added, smiling.

He laughed. 'I hardly notice them at all'

But Helena still looked undressed. Her figure hugged the silk, the shape of her body showing through the material. She sat down with her hands clasped together.

'Thanks. I appreciate the small gesture,' he said, and sat down opposite her. 'I'll answer your question now. For me, Helena, this is about taking a new direction. I'm on a personal mission. It's not about money anymore …' he looked to the ceiling for inspiration. 'It's about doing something for posterity.

'After I left the refugee camp I was determined to never go hungry again. I'd known what it was like fighting for scraps of food, wearing the same worn-out clothes for months. It was highly motivating, so I spent my younger years trying to avoid the cold realities. And it worked. I found I had a gift for making money. I succeeded, big time. For some years now I've lived in a rich man's dreamworld. I've profited from the relics of the ancient world. It was a good direction to take, but you know …' he leaned closer to her, 'money has no soul. That only comes from inside.'

'I get it Moses, you want to get your soul back,' she said. 'Maybe that's where I come in.'

Moses described the life-changing moment when he first saw the Delphic Anomaly in the chamber under the Temple of Apollo.

'It mustn't end up in a private museum in Moscow, somewhere under the Vatican, or in the basement of a Chinese billionaire's ridiculous mansion. It needs to be seen by the world. Everyone should see it. I know it will change perceptions for the better.'

Helena looked puzzled. 'Why do you want to engage in such

generous acts of altruism now?'

'I accept it seems out of character. But after years and years of screwing the rich, I want to give something back,' he said, nodding solemnly at her.

'I was hoping you'd finally mention screwing at some point,' she said, standing up and loosening the belt of the kimono.

'Hey,' he mumbled. 'Hang on a minute, Helena …'

5

'For fuck's sake Moses,' Helena said, throwing her arms in the air. 'Life's too short to be boring. OK, maybe I'm a little shocking, but I like to help men discover their sensuous side, especially interesting and attractive men like you,' she said.

'It must be your Delacroix genes,' said Moses. 'I've heard about your grandfather's discoveries, and colourful private life.'

'OK, yes, I confess, I'm an exhibitionist. I can't escape it, it's in my genes. You're going to have to accept me for what I am.'

'You'd have to be an exhibitionist, considering the research you plan to do for your PhD.'

'And do you approve of my research project?' she asked.

'It's a little risqué, but I like it. Very original and quite brave,' he said, and she nodded in appreciation.

'You're a good, liberal man, Moses. I like you,' she said, touching his hair.

'I like the way you combine the ancient with a liberating twist of the modern. I can see it's completely provocative – a perfect way to annoy the self-satisfied bastards at the Sorbonne,' said Moses.

'I love you for saying that, Moses,' she said moving closer to him and placing her arms around his neck. 'They're so stuck in the fifties, they need a liberated woman to wake them up from their long sleep.' She ran her hands down his back, feeling the ripples of his spine with her thumb. His back muscles were stiff, but they softened under her warm fingers. 'And tell me, why do you have such bloodshot eyes?'

'I was working late last night, making international calls, in different time zones. You know the kind of thing.'

'I hope you're not too tired for me,' she said, with a knowing smile.

'But we don't know each other. Doesn't this embarrass you?' he asked.

'Not at all. You know what *really* embarrasses me?' she said, looking into his eyes.

'I've no idea. Maybe nothing?' he said.

She shook her head. 'What embarrasses me is asking you to do me a favour.'

'You can ask me for *anything*. I want to help you in any way I can,' he said, noticing a tear falling down her cheek.

Moses was surprised to see the woman who had been acting like a goddess show her weaker, vulnerable side. She tried to stop the tears rolling down her face with her hands. He gave her a tissue.

'I'm sorry,' she said, dabbing her face. Moses put his arm around her shoulder. 'It embarrasses me to ask you. Look, I'm sorry, Moses, I'm desperate,' she said, sniffing.

'Just ask me, I would like to help you.'

'OK. You have some sway at the Sorbonne, I understand?'

Moses nodded.

'I need your influence to persuade them to accept my PhD project.' She stopped and gently blew her nose. 'I really hate to beg, Moses.'

'Look, asking for a favour is not begging. It's the way of the world, always has been. It will help us both if your PhD research goes ahead, and it costs me nothing to try and help you.' Moses raised his hands. 'I can't stand those cosy, self-satisfied academic hypocrites any more than you.'

'Thank you, Moses. You're a kind man, and you have kind eyes,' she said, kissing him on the lips. The kiss lingered and Moses responded. Almost without realising it he found himself putting his hands around her waist and pulling her towards his excited body. It had been a long time coming.

Everything went black for a moment. He put his hands to his forehead, his eyes flickered open and Moses looked over to the therapist.

'You know know something? Thirty minutes after she entered the apartment, *I* entered *her*. Maybe I shouldn't have given in to her charms. I was seduced. I think it was all part of her plan. But there was another factor in all this. She equated sex with my approval of her as a human being.'

'So you consummated the meeting?' the therapist asked.

'Yes. In retrospect maybe it was wrong, I admit it. We were strangers. We'd never met before that afternoon, although I'd met her mother, but only on one occasion. I should never have ignored my intuition.'

'What particular intuition was that?'

'It was after she collapsed, when she first came up in the elevator. Whilst I stood over her, I first noticed the slight unevenness in the outline of her mouth. I'd seen this pattern before in a number of young women.

'I think Helena was more needy than her glossy exterior suggested. Years of childhood trauma had forged a series of creases around her mouth, culminating in a small twist in the contours of her face. I know it sounds strange, but these things eventually show up. As a one-time portrait painter I know only too well that the face is our primary means of expression and I could read those lines, like a familiar language. No one studies the meaning of these lines on the human face, but they should be investigated.'

'I've never heard about any studies, but I agree it makes sense. It's true that young women who are disinhibited in this way often turn out to have been abused in their childhood.'

'Whatever the reason,' Moses continued, 'I knew there was some problem in her background that made her act like that. Maybe she felt she needed to pay me in advance, with the reward of sex, but it didn't feel like that at the time. She was undressing long before I'd offered to talk to her professor at the Sorbonne. OK, I was physically attracted to her, she's a very beautiful woman. I think she liked me too. Excuse the cliché, but it takes two to tango.

'And that was how it started. I never intended to make it go that way, but I felt I didn't have any choice. Helena was a very forward person, a sexually charged woman. Sex was her oxygen, her modus operandi.'

'But you had a choice, didn't you? You're a rational adult human being who is able to make decisions,' said the therapist.

'OK. One, I'm not a monk. Two, I needed her on my side. I had no choice if I wanted to pursue the Anomaly,' he said, raking his hands through his hair.

'And her sexual appetite was, shall we say, well-developed? In every way. She was the hungriest woman I'd ever met.'

6

The phone rang – Monique Forniere ran into the office and picked up the receiver.

She listened for a moment.

'I'll see if Professor Lenoire is available. Sorry, tell me again – who is it calling?'

'Dr Moses Frank.'

'Which university?'

'The University of Life,' he said, and she laughed. 'Look, he knows me well, we're old friends.'

'No problem, I'll check if he's free, Dr Frank.'

The phone rang in the office of Professor Jules Lenoire three times before he picked up.

'Moses! What a surprise to hear from you,' said Lenoire.

'Yes Jules, it's good to hear your voice. How is the Sorbonne archaeology department?'

'I'm in pretty good health, considering the stress of running this department. It's always a struggle to win funding, but I am still the big cheese, so it's good for me here. We are doing research at some fantastic sites in the Middle East, and I always keep you in mind when we find any extraordinary relics.'

'Excellent. Did my last payment to your Swiss account go through without delay?' Moses asked, pointedly. 'Sorry, I can't hear you anymore Jules, what's happened to the line?'

'Yes,' Lenoire whispered. 'Thank you Moses, it came through, but maybe it's best not to discuss this subject right now.'

'Are you with someone?'

'Not exactly, but you know these lines are not one-hundred percent private.'

'What's your direct line? I'll call you back straight away.'

'Paris 901 2434. Talk soon.'

Moses pressed the buttons on his phone on the top floor of the Leopold Tower. There was a good connection to Paris from Vienna.

'Hello again,' said Moses, picking up the Egyptian dagger he'd been using to open his post. 'I'll get to the point of my call, Jules. Look, we've known each other for many years now and you've done very well from the sale of the relics you've discovered on various Sorbonne digs around the world. Is that right?'

'Yes. It's changed my life. I'm very grateful to your auction house. It's been a highly fruitful relationship.'

'Good, good. I'm pleased for you. You've told me in the past that it's enabled you to buy a summer house in St Raphael. You've moved into the 16th arrondissement in Paris. You've done well out of it all, haven't you?'

'I cannot deny, it's worked out well.'

'And everything has remained truly confidential hasn't it?'

'Yes. Why? Is there a problem now?'

'No, not at all. There shouldn't be. My clients and buyers know the situation. Everything remains confidential. But I have to keep up my guard and make sure everyone plays along. It's a continuous effort on my part to keep everybody sweet, as you can imagine,' said Moses.

'I understand, we have to be discrete.'

'OK, so you're happy with everything I've done for you?'

'Absolutely. I live a lifestyle I could only have dreamed of before I started selling the relics through you, Moses.'

'I appreciate that Jules, and that's why I'm phoning you now. In return for improving the quality of your life so much I'd like to ask you for one small favour.'

'What kind of favour?'

'I understand you have a student whose family I know well.

Her name is Helena Delacroix.' Moses thought he heard a sigh down the phone line.

'Yes, I know her. A clever student, but she has some … how can I say? … unorthodox ideas.'

'I was really disappointed to learn that her PhD proposal concerning the Elena Text manuscript had been rejected.'

'It has little academic merit. We have to be careful not to abuse the good name of the university to sponsor questionable research.'

'That's bullshit Jules, you know it. It's no less scientific than most of the obscure, and frankly irrelevant research you've been doing for years. Let's face it, your department's opposition to Helena's plans stems from an historical prejudice against her grandfather, Niko Delacroix.'

'Hey, wait a minute,' said Lenoire.

'No, Jules, I want to finish. You just don't want to give him any legitimacy because he irritated so many members of the archaeology department, many years ago, by going to the world's press about his discoveries. That's right, isn't it Jules?' Moses said. There was silence for a moment.

'He made too many wild claims, saying he'd found biblical relics in Delphi. It was absurd. He was a fantasist. He simply didn't know when to stop.'

'And you, Jules, are a one-hundred percent moral man who has never committed adultery? Do me a favour. It's common knowledge you select the prettiest girl students at the start of the academic year, in return for a first-class grade. Do you want me to read out a list of their names?' Moses said, his breathing increasing as he spoke.

'Oh really, but Delacroix was far worse than me,' began a rankled Lenoire. 'Listen to me Moses, without authority he published the news of the Elena Text in a newspaper instead of waiting for publication in an academic journal. You may not know this, but Delacroix caused great offence to many of his academic peers.'

'But he did this because his work was repeatedly sidelined by the expedition leader.'

'Where is this going Moses?' said Lenoire, sounding tired.

'I'm glad you appreciate the damage that can be done by publishing things in newspapers. But why are you tarring young Helena with her grandfather's brush? Maybe you need to look at her proposal on its own merits? You don't even need to give her a scholarship. Her funding is taken care of – you just need to accept her project for a PhD.'

'Listen, Moses. If we supported Helena's sexual research it would cause an outrage here. I just don't know if I could get it through my postgraduate research committee. They are a very old, conservative bunch.'

'You don't need to. You run the place. As you told me, you're the head of department. It's up to you. Decision made. Finished.'

'And what happens if I can't do this?'

'That would be very unfortunate for you, Jules. I really can't guarantee that details of the relics you have obtained, removed, and stolen whilst on university excavations will remain confidential any longer,' Moses said. 'Much as I would like to keep you out of prison.'

'I see, Moses. Helena Delacroix means that much to you? It's that serious, is it?'

Moses slammed his fist on the desk in front of him, breaking a pencil into two pieces. 'Now be very careful Jules. Do not presume anything about my relationship with Helena. Is that clear?'

'OK, Moses.'

'I think French newspapers would find your story a

compelling one. I can see the headlines now. 'The rise and fall of a leading Sorbonne academic. How a university professor stole priceless antiquities and sold them at private auctions to finance his villa on the Cote d'Azur. I think the press would lap it up, don't you, Jules?'

There was silence again.

'Are you still there?' Moses heard the line click. He could tell Lenoir was talking to someone in his office and had pressed a button to keep his conversation private. After half a minute the line came back to life.

'Can you hear me Moses? I think, on reflection, that Helena Delacroix has put forward a very important proposal which the Sorbonne archaeology department would be pleased to support.'

'Good man. I knew I could rely on you to see it that way, Jules. When will you inform Helena of the good news? By tomorrow?'

'Yes, it could be tomorrow. I'll call her myself.'

'It's good to talk to you again. Keep in touch Jules, especially if you come across any valuable new relics on future digs.'

'I will. It's been interesting to talk this through with you.'

Moses put down the phone and rang the Intercontinental Hotel.

'Room 3446 please.' The line rang for a long time until it was answered.

'Hello Moses darling,' said a sleepy voice.

'Good morning Helena, I've just spoken to Lenoir. It's all sorted. He's decided your research in Delphi deserves to be supported.'

'What did you say to him?'

'I pointed out the merits of your work and how short-sighted his original decision had been. And he agreed with me.'

'Is that all you said to him?' she asked, anxiously.

'There were one or two other points I also made, but rest

assured he is now fully behind you,' Moses said, with a smile in his voice.

'How can I thank you?'

'What are you doing before you return to Paris?' Moses asked, trying to piece together his broken pencil.

'I've a few hours to kill.'

7

They lay still on the Persian carpet.

Helena was still on top of Moses, her head resting on his shoulder, one hand in the hollow of her back.

He touched her mouth with his fingers to bring her round.

'Now I understand you, Helena,' said a relaxed and mellow Moses.

'What do you mean? she said, woozily.

'I can see why you're so into testing the sex ritual described in the Elena Text.'

'Why?'

'Sex is more than a great passion for you, isn't it?' Moses said, as he stroked her hair. Her limbs were now soft, all the earlier physical aggression and the unspent energy dissipated.

'Oh yes, it's what every human being feels compelled to do. It's not just a passion, it's a personal campaign. Too many people in the world are denied their right to have a sex life.'

'Who are you thinking of?' said Moses

'Priests must be celibate. It turns them into paedophiles and nuns into shrivelled old spinsters. It's wrong and I blame the church for denying people the chance to express their sexuality.'

'It wasn't always like that. Let me show you something,' Moses said, holding her shoulders. She clambered off him, and he stood up and walked into his office through the *trompe l'oeil* wall. His eyes scanned the bookshelves until he found an encyclopaedic book entitled 'Renaissance Art' and began flicking through the pages.

'Look at these,' he said, propping himself up next to Helena. 'This is for you,' he said, turning the pages and stopping at a picture of Bernini's sixteenth-century sculpture of 'The Ecstasy of St Teresa.' She took the volume from Moses to look for herself.

'I love it. You can see Saint Teresa is clearly having an orgasm. Look at the angel standing over her. He's the messenger of God, right? He's thrusting at her with his long pointed arrow. It's so sexual. She's showing all the signs of reaching a climax – her mouth is open, her eyes are closed, her body has gone limp.'

'I thought you might find the books in my library useful for your research,' said Moses, smiling.

'This supports the central claim in my PhD. When a woman has an orgasm she experiences the sweetness and power of God. You know, Moses, this is the truth at the core of all religions, the belief that God is the embodiment of sexual ecstasy. And it existed long before Christianity. It's as ancient as humanity itself.'

Moses put his hands on her bare shoulders, pulled her body close to his, and kissed her on the lips. Their tongues met inside her mouth, and after a few swirls he pulled himself reluctantly away.

'Sorry, you taste good, but I'd like to ask you a few things. Firstly, tell me what you did in Zurich before coming here to Vienna,' he asked.

'Oh, it was so disappointing. I went to visit Jung's birthplace and attended a course at his institute. I'm interested in the Jungian interpretations of the Elena Text. And Freud's, for that matter.'

'Did the two great psychoanalysts have any views on the Text?'

'It all fits like a glove into their psychoanalytical theories. It's obvious the High Priests acted as father figures for the young Oracles.'

Moses looked at her uncertainly, screwing up his face. He didn't like to admit his ignorance of the ideas of Vienna's greatest mind.

'Oh, and according to Freud, young women have an unconscious desire to have sex with their fathers, so they look for sexual partners who look like them, to put it very crudely,' Helena said.

'And do boys look for women who look like their mothers?'

'Exactly. Is that true for you, Moses? Do I look like your mother when she was younger?'

'I don't know. I never really knew my mother. She died when I was a very young boy, so I don't know the answer. And what would Jung have to say about the Elena Text?' Moses asked.

'Let me think a moment' she began, and put her hands over her face for a few seconds. 'OK. Jung believed we all share universal truths which we all know to be true without ever having to learn them,' she said, sitting on the bed and shaking her hair down her back. 'The Elena Text contains a few universal truths, so it's a good fit.'

Moses thought about this for a few moments. 'You know, I think that's why I want to save the Delphic Anomaly for the world. I know everyone will automatically recognise it as a force for good. It has universal value,' he said, making a pyramid shape with his fingers.

She began kissing his neck and stopped to look up at him.

'You see, Moses!'

'See what?' 'It was a great idea to have sex first. It's released all our thinking juices, and a few other juices as well,' she said smiling. Moses laughed and got up, leaving the bedroom and re-emerging a few minutes later with a bottle of Taittinger champagne and two fluted glasses.

'Shall we celebrate the start of … something … interesting?' he said, easing open the cork. There was a muted pop and it bubbled upwards as he poured it into the glasses.

'I know,' he said looking into her green eyes. 'To the pleasures of working together.'

Helena repeated his words, adding, 'and to ecstasy, sensual pleasure … oh, shall we just say to the pleasure of sex?'

'To sex. You were amazing, a woman on fire,' he said, and they clinked their glasses together.

As she took a sip of the fizzing blonde liquid, she leaned forward and kissed him again. 'You see, Moses, my strategy has worked. We've lubricated our relationship very successfully. But you still haven't explained why you're doing all this for me,' she said, adding, 'apart from enjoying the fucking, of course.'

Moses smiled and stretched out his arms.. 'I have a gut feeling about your PhD project. Something tells me it will also be for the good,' he said.

'But *what* do you actually want from me, Moses?' she said, running her fingers around her breasts.

'A promise that you'll try to help me bring back the Delphic Anomaly.'

She pondered this in silence for a few moments.

'I'm not sure what I can do for you, but I can be your loyal supporter,' she said, and clinked her glass against his for the second time.

'Look, I appreciate your priority is to carry out the PhD research,' he said.

'Yes, I want to do that as soon as possible.'

'It may sound strange but I have a feeling it will deliver us the Delphic Anomaly,' said Moses.

Her mouth trembled and she looked back at him with a confused smile. 'I don't understand, Moses. What has the Text got to do with the excavation of the Delphic Anomaly?'

'Don't you realise, Helena? Your research at Delphi will change your life.'

8

It was dark in the underground theatre as he led her through the soundproofed door into the control room. Moses eased up gently on the lights.

Mount Parnassus appeared out of the darkness, complete with the five columns of the Temple of Apollo, underneath it a subterranean chamber with two tunnels.

'This is an extraordinarily detailed model,' Helena said, and pointed to the temple mount. 'That's where I'll perform my experiment.' Moses' face lit up.

'But please explain why've you made such an intricate model of the mountain,' Helena asked, bending down to peer through the tunnels.

'We need to know where the tunnels go in order to get the

Delphic Anomaly out of the chamber. I doubt this tunnel,' said Moses, using a pencil to show her, 'is wide enough. There must be another entrance somewhere,' he said, and put his hands on Helena's waist so he was facing her.

'When you go to Delphi I want you find out where the other tunnel may be located. We can then build it into this model and plan a route for excavating the Anomaly.'

Helena screwed up her face as if he was asking her to do an impossible task.

'But how can I possibly do that?' she asked.

'You'll need to make some headway with the museum director, Andreas Green.'

'What's the guy like?'

'You'll have no problem with him, he's not too complicated to read,' said Moses. 'Green enjoys being told what a wonderful human being he is. Tell him how brilliant he is, he'll lap it up like a child. He likes a pretty lady, so there's plenty of scope in that direction too.'

'I'll try my best,' she said. 'But tell me something – does he realise that my grandfather scratched his initials onto the Anomaly?'

Moses sighed. He realised he may have revealed too much to Maria in his effort to ingratiate himself with the Delacroix family.

'Look, Helena. I need to warn you about those pictures. Please, please don't mention them. I took them secretly. I'm sure Green knows about the initials – it's why he stopped me using my camera in the chamber. He'll deny all knowledge of their existence. But make it clear to him that the Delacroix family will pursue their claim for a share of the Anomaly.'

'I'll fight for it,' she said, clenching the fist of her slender arm.

Moses led her back to the elevator and they went up to the

52nd floor of the Leopold tower. As the elevator accelerated upwards, she eyed him anxiously, holding onto his arm. He could see something was troubling her.

'What is it? Isn't everything agreed now?' he asked.

'No. Not exactly. Earlier on, you said my research would change my life. What did you mean?'

Moses drew breath and looked into her eyes.

He didn't want to create any new anxieties where none existed.

'It's just a gut feeling, that's all, nothing more. I can't explain it.'

'Come on, Moses, you sounded more certain than that. It's my life you're talking about. I've a right to know.'

Moses knew there was a fine line between intuition and being irrational.

He stayed quiet for a few moments before answering.

'If you trust me Helena, I think it will be perfectly OK. But if I talk about it anymore, it may not happen.'

PART EIGHT

Levy

1

Moses turned to 'M' in his address book.

One name sprang out from the rest – Mayerson. Dr Avi Mayerson was director of the National Museum in Jerusalem.

They were two hours ahead of Vienna and Moses decided it was a good time to call his old friend before he went home.

He dialled the thirteen-digit number and the line connected after several seconds of silence. A faint ringing tone purred from inside Mayerson's office, some eighteen-hundred miles away, on the edge of the Judean desert.

The sound triggered a memory of a white marble building set against a constant blue sky, the parched hills and walled city of Jerusalem in the background. It was surrounded by immaculate gardens, trickling with fountains and bursting with prickly pears, cactuses and giant yuccas.

This place had always shone brightly in the Mediterranean sunshine, acting as a bridge between the old city and the charmless box-like settlements across the valley.

The ringing tone ended abruptly and an Israeli-accented voice came on the line.

'Is that Avi? This is Moses Frank,' said Moses.

'What a pleasant surprise to hear your voice,' said Mayerson.

'It's good to hear yours, too,' he hesitated. 'Look, my old friend, I'll be brief. I need to speak to you discretely.'

'It's OK, this is an encrypted line.'

Moses heard a click and Mayerson's voice became softer.

'So what's new with you, Moses?'

'We live through interesting times,' said Moses softly.

'I agree, but tell me something I don't already know.' Mayerson paused. 'You don't normally call unless you have a reason.'

'You're always empathic, Avi. All I'll say now is there's been an unexpected discovery. This is new, not on the grapevine.'

'Where?'

Moses hesitated to answer, there was a few seconds before he uttered a reply.

'It's in Delphi.'

'Doesn't sound like our territory, Moses.'

'Normally I'd agree with you, but this will be of some interest to the Israel museum.' Moses took a breath. 'I can guarantee that.'

'Can you tell me any more?'

'I'm not sure about that now, on a phone line, but I feel confident in saying that it will be of some significance to your museum and the population of Israel.' Moses heard a distinct gasp down the line.

'My God, Moses, what can you be talking about?'

'Look, Avi, don't go wild but this is a bit of an anomaly. It was found where no one expected it to be found,' said Moses.

'I've always felt there were anomalies everywhere, but that people are too afraid to accept them. I keep saying we historians need to keep an open mind,' said Mayerson enthusiastically.

'What I need is some kind of assurance from you. I'm really committed to this thing, it's no ordinary antiquity,' Moses said, coiling the phone cable tightly around his fingers. 'It will need a lot of work to excavate.'

'What do you mean, exactly?'

'This goes beyond a normal business transaction. It means a lot to me personally. But it will mean a lot more to everyone who sees it.'

'Can you give me some idea what's been found?' said Mayerson. There was another brief silence as Moses tried to think of a way of referring to the Anomaly in a coded way that would make sense to Mayerson – and only him.

'OK my friend, let your imagination run wild, think about the seed of Vespasian,' said Moses.

'What did you say?'

Moses repeated the words slowly. 'The seed of Vespasian.' For a few seconds Moses heard nothing down the line.

'OK, very clever, Moses, I think I've worked out what you're suggesting,' said Mayerson. 'If it's what I believe you're saying, this is a serious matter for the State of Israel. Can you come over here for a short visit, so we can talk it over? Have you got any photos?'

'No comment, but I don't think you'll be in any doubt. I'll check the flights and let you know.'

'I'll make myself available anytime. I can arrange for you to be met by my driver. Try and come tomorrow, if you can. Have a safe journey.'

Moses put the phone down and went to 'E' in his address book.

2

LY 366 flew low over the Mediterranean coastline and seemed to hover over the twinkling lights of Tel Aviv as it came into land. As he watched two old men with white beards praying at their seats, Moses heard a group of teenagers at the back of the plane singing loudly in Hebrew.

The huge 747 touched down on the tarmac gently and there

was applause, followed by a sudden rush to the lockers.

Once inside the attractive arrivals building, Moses joined the queue for visitors. A melee of new leather mixed with hot pitta, roasted coffee and expensive French perfume hit his nostrils, all at once.

'Have a nice stay in Israel, Dr Frank,' the young immigration officer said with a reticent smile as she stamped a white card with a visa and placed it inside his Austrian passport.

'Shalom,' said Moses, happy to be back in the country of one half of his heritage. He had no hold luggage and was relieved to not have to wait at the end of the carousel. He walked past a group of four young female soldiers in fawn-coloured military uniforms, their Uzi machine guns hanging loosely off their shoulders like fashion accessories, ready for a photo shoot or a terror attack.

Amidst the throng of relatives waiting for families were dozens of drivers bearing signs with names. At the far end was one that said: 'Dr Moshe Frank.' For a moment Moses didn't recognise his name, but soon realised they were using the Hebrew version of 'Moses.' It was held aloft by a dark-skinned Israeli security man in a white shirt, armed with a small silver handgun on his belt. He was accompanied by a young blonde-haired woman in military uniform, also carrying a small gun around her slim waist.

'Pleased to meet you, Dr Frank. This is Nomi, my name is Ilan. We'll take you to your meeting. Did you have a pleasant flight with El Al?'

'Apart from the loud singing and cheering as the jet approached Tel Aviv, it was all very relaxed, and also the best airline food I've ever had.'

'That would probably have been Havenu Shalom Aleichem. I must tell you something it's very common for this to happen. It means, "Come, hello, be welcome." Many people get emotional when they arrive in their ancient homeland for the first time,' said Ilan.

They walked over to a dark blue Toyota estate that had a metal grill for police dogs. Moses sat in the back seat without question – it was Israel, he expected the tighter security. Nomi sat next to him. She was lean and toned, and looked as if she had been trained in martial arts.

Moses was enjoying the almost perfect symmetry of her lips when, almost unnoticeably, she produced a pair of steel handcuffs from her leather shoulder bag. There was a clunk as she locked one handcuff in a rapid movement around Moses' right hand and the second around her own left wrist. At first he didn't even question what was happening. It was all done so automatically, with no fuss. He knew from previous visits to Israel that the security people took few chances. Then he realised it was ridiculous. He woke up from his travel daze and began to feel the sweat pouring from under his arms.

Both of them were armed and equipped to deal with awkward passengers. He was locked inside their vehicle, and he knew there was no point in struggling.

'What's going on?' he blurted out. 'Is it really necessary to handcuff me?' he asked.

'Relax, Dr Frank, it's OK. We just don't want to take any chances.'

'What do you mean? Aren't you taking me to the Israel National Museum to see my old friend Dr Avi Mayerson?'

'Sorry, Dr Frank, but Dr Mayerson is unwell and will not be able to see you today.'

'Is he really? He seemed perfectly fine when I spoke to him yesterday.'

'Yes. I'm sorry, but he is not well now.'

'So where are you taking me?'

'We thought you'd appreciate an interview with Colonel Menahem Levy instead.'

'What's this all about? Where are you taking me?'

'Only an insignificant government office in Tel Aviv.'

'Not to Jerusalem? Tell me the truth, are you the Shin Bet or Mossad? I never know the difference.'

They laughed and spoke quickly in Hebrew. Moses didn't understand anything they said and was feeling trapped.

'Actually, we don't know who we work for, they won't tell us, it's too secret. We are government employees. You are safe with us Dr Frank.'

'You can't do this to me, I am legally entitled to be here at my own free will.'

'You'll be free to discuss everything with Colonel Levy. Just stay calm, Dr Frank.'

'What about my hotel booking in Jerusalem?'

'It's no problem, don't worry. New arrangements have been made for you. You don't need a Jerusalem hotel any more, you don't need to waste the money.'

'This is madness. Surely you can't hold me against my will. I'll be contacting my embassy.'

'That won't be necessary, we're arriving now. Just wait and it will all be fine, Dr Frank. Don't worry at all.'

Moses noticed that his shirt had become soaked with sweat.

The Toyota was driven into an underground car park and surrounded by armed guards. A dark green shutter slid down behind the car meaning that Moses couldn't run off anywhere, which was impossible anyway as he was still handcuffed to Nomi.

Led by her, he climbed out of the car and was taken through a series of grey doors and into a waiting room. She undid the handcuff and Moses rubbed his chafed wrist.

She took off her military cap and Moses watched with growing excitement as she shook her long blonde hair over her khaki uniform. 'Would you like coffee, tea or a cold drink, Dr Frank?' she asked.

'A black coffee would be nice, but look, I need to go the bathroom, where is it?'

'Oh sure, the door is up there,' she said, pointing to the end of the room.

'It's a private bathroom. Feel free to brush up,' she said, and smiled at him.

'Colonel Levy will be coming down to meet to you very soon.'

3

The doors at the end of the room sprang open and Colonel Emanuel Levy walked in briskly.

He was a wiry but distinguished-looking, grey-haired man in his fifties, dressed in civilian clothes – a white shirt and navy blue shorts.

Moses was already sitting at a table and Levy went to sit opposite him. On seeing his clean-shaven face Moses felt slightly less stressed.

Taking a large gulp of his coffee he looked up at his jailer. 'What's this all about? I've no idea what's going on.' Moses said with an angry voice.

'Dr Frank, I'm so sorry you've been put to all this trouble.

As you know, Professor Avi Mayerson fell ill yesterday, and we felt we had a duty to look after you. We don't want you to come to any harm,' he said. Levy was polite but his repeated head movements suggested to Moses he was embarrassed by what he was doing.

'If I've ever heard pure bullshit, that was it,' said Moses.

Levy said nothing but smiled.

'And who are "we" exactly?' added Moses.

'OK, Dr Frank, I've nothing to hide from you. We work for the government. We do intelligence gathering. We try to prevent acts of terrorist violence against the state of Israel and its citizens, both at home and abroad. I'm sure you understand we cannot afford to sit still and wait for things to explode in front of us. We must be pro-active and strategic in what we do. The reduction in terrorist incidents in Israel has not happened by sheer chance, Dr Frank.'

'OK, sure, Colonel. But what has that got to do with my perfectly innocent visit to the museum? I'm no terrorist. I deal in antiquities. I've always been a friend of your country,' Moses said, his arms outstretched, like a man pleading for justice.

'I'll try to explain the problem to you. By the way, can I call you Moses? Please call me Manny, it's what everyone calls me. Would you like a cold beer?'

'Sure Manny, I'd love a beer.'

Levy walked over to the small white fridge in the corner of the room. Every shelf was stacked with bottles of water, and there was a container of Jaffa juice and a pack of Goldstar lagers in the door. He took two bottles of beer, opened one by hitting the top with his hand against the side of the table, and gave it to Moses.

'Let's establish your situation first. Our intelligence-gathering unit has evidence that you have seen a major biblical relic at the

Greek archaeological site of Delphi, and you have been making plans to excavate this relic with a view to putting it on display to the public. We understand this biblical relic is no ordinary antiquity but is in fact the missing treasure captured by the Romans from the temple of Jerusalem in AD 70, and then taken to Rome. Have I summarised the situation correctly?'

Moses shook his head and looked up to the soundproofed ceiling. 'How do you know all this? It's staggering.'

'Is that a yes?'

'Can I possibly have a cigarette to go with the beer?'

'It's not good for your health, we don't allow smoking.'

'Being locked up here is bad for my health, Colonel.'

'I can see you need one, we'll make an exception. I don't smoke myself, but I'll ask one of the guards if they have any. Just wait a minute.' He soon came back with a single cigarette and a stick lighter.

Moses lit up and inhaled deeply. It was the first time in five years he'd smoked. The tobacco was dark and flaky and smelt like smouldering grass. After a few moments the nicotine travelled to his head and gave Moses an immediate headache. With another drag the aching sensation was replaced by a more pleasant, drifting feeling.

'That's very good, thanks,' Moses said, beginning to enjoy it, inhaling again and shooting smoke from his nostrils. 'OK, let's suppose what you described is true. So what?'

'I need to tell you about certain extreme elements we have here in Israel. What I am going to say now is not a state secret, but it's not very well known outside of our country,' Levy said in a calm and deliberate voice. 'Tell me if you've heard of the Temple Mount Faithful?'

'No, I don't think so,' he said, shaking his head.

'These people are a group of religious zealots who are

determined to rebuild the 2,500-year-old Jewish temple in place of the Al-Aqsa mosque which stands there today. I must tell you that this mosque is considered the third most important in the Muslim world.'

'But the Muslims *did* build their mosque on the site of the Temple. Maybe these Temple Mount guys have a fair point,' said Moses.

Levy got up from his chair and went closer to Moses, so he was just inches away from his face. 'That was over a thousand years ago, Moses. Can you imagine what would happen if the Temple Mount fanatics started demolishing the Mosque today?' said Levy, pointing his finger at Moses.

'I suppose there would be trouble. Riots and bloodshed. Things could blow up,' said Moses.

'Exactly. The seeds of another intifada. There might be hostage taking. Beheadings. Madmen *and* mad women in suicide vests. You name it. There would be explosions across the Muslim world and even in Europe. It would be an act of major provocation.'

'Why haven't they done it already?'

'Good question, Moses. They are waiting for a sign from God. You see, before the Temple Faithful can perform this act of madness they have to receive a sign from Almighty God, to let them know it is time to rebuild the temple. Do you know what the first sign they are looking for is? I'll tell you. It is the birth of a perfect red heifer,' Levy said, rolling his eyes.

Moses looked at him and scratched his head. 'Did I hear you right?'

'Yes, a red heifer. A cow. Religious people in Israel believe in this strange sign because it is written in the bible. According to the ancient law, a perfect red heifer has to be sacrificed as a burnt offering, on the Mount of Olives, before the temple can be rebuilt.'

'Religion is madness, isn't it? But I've heard the need to believe in God is programmed into our genes,' said Moses. 'But surely a perfect red heifer doesn't exist? So why is the Israeli government worried?'

'You are totally wrong, my friend. A red heifer has already been specially bred on a ranch in Texas, owned by a Christian fundamentalist, and a rabbi has declared it as kosher for the sacrifice to be enacted on the Mount of Olives.'

'Is this really true?'

'I don't deal in fairy tales, Moses. The Israeli government has already been forced to ban the importation of all red heifers. You understand we cannot let this happen. Can you imagine the bloodshed when the Temple Mount Faithful start digging into the foundations of the Al-Aqsa Mosque?'

'Is this the same place as the Dome of the Rock, where the bible says Abraham was about to sacrifice his son Isaac?'

'Indeed it is, you know your bible stories. It's holy to both Muslims and Jews.'

'I understand what you're saying,' said Moses, as Colonel Levy opened a folder on the desk and held up a black-and-white photograph.

'Do you recognise the picture?' said Levy.

'How'd you get hold of that?' said Moses. There was no response from Levy.

'You know what this is, don't you?'

Moses was shocked to see a copy of his own photo of the Delphic Anomaly. 'How did you get hold of it?' he asked again, irritated.

'That's not your problem, Moses. Tell me, can you confirm that this is the relic you were planning to excavate?'

'It looks like the same object, yes.'

'OK. Let me tell you some more about the beliefs of the Temple Mount Faithful and their followers. They have the red heifer waiting in the farm in Texas, but they are also waiting for another sign. Do you know what it is?' Levy inched closer to Moses and his cheeks hardened.

'They are waiting for the Temple Treasures to be found, and to be brought back to Israel. They are waiting for them to be returned to their home in Jerusalem. They have long believed they were being kept hidden by the Vatican Church, under St Peter's in Rome. The Popes over the ages have always denied it, but now we know the truth. The main temple treasure, the golden menorah, was actually taken to Delphi.'

'How do you think it reached Delphi?' Moses asked.

'My historian friends have told me that there is some evidence that it was taken to Delphi from Rome by the Emperor Hadrian as a gift. Hadrian was a big believer in the wisdom of the Oracle,' said Levy.

'I congratulate you, Manny, you've certainly done your homework. That's exactly what I've been told. It seems to be the only explanation that fits all the known facts.'

Levy stood up, looked down at Moses, and began to speak in a soft voice. 'You can appreciate, Moses that we cannot allow the discovery of the Temple treasures to become known here in Israel. You must abandon your grand plans to excavate the relic and put it in a museum. I'm sorry.'

'But I was hoping to—' Moses began to say, but was swiftly interrupted by Levy, whose voice rose in volume.

'No. It isn't going to happen. You cannot show it to the world, unless you want the blood of tens of thousands of people on your hands. Unless you want to provoke another war in the Middle East.' Levy reached a piercing crescendo, the veins on his neck swelling through his skin. 'Israel will not let it happen. Do you understand me clearly, Dr Frank?'

The spray of Levy's spittle landed on Moses' face. He leaned backwards, intimidated by the barrage of shouting.

'There's no need to become angry with me, I came here in good faith. Avi Mayerson invited me here,' he said, trying to disarm Levy who had worked himself into a sweat.

A brusque 'Ach' came from Levy's lips, revealing the origin of his forbears with only one short syllable. 'I know you have certain ambitions, but be under no illusions, the Israeli security services will go to *any lengths necessary* to stop this relic being excavated.'

Moses decided he was not going to take these orders without putting up a fight. He stood up, rising several inches over the diminutive Levy.

'Please allow me to say something, Colonel. One of the world's greatest missing treasures has been uncovered. People thought it had been lost forever, but it has now been found. You're trying to deny the whole world its cultural heritage.'

'No, Moses.' Levy began to get angry again. 'It's best you think it does not exist. It shall never be brought into this country. It shall remain underground. It must stay a secret to the world. As far as we are concerned it is another red heifer. It is banned from entry into Israel. Is that understood?'

'Perfectly clear, but I have one question.' He could see that Levy had now calmed down. 'Do you think your policy will ever change?'

'Maybe in twenty or thirty years. Perhaps, sometime in the future, if there was a lasting peace between the Arabs and the Israelis, in an era of mutual understanding, then it could be brought here and shown to the public. Maybe the temple could be rebuilt in a slightly different location. Who knows? But for now it is forbidden.'

'Your answer gives me a slender thread of hope, Colonel.'

'Look, Moses, please don't add to the wars we've fought over this tiny triangle of land by doing something stupid. Don't give these crazy people the ammunition they need to start a new war against the Arabs.'

'I'll bear it in mind.'

'Our driver and assistant will be taking you back to the airport in a few minutes, Dr Frank. You will be put on the next El Al flight to Vienna tonight.'

'But what about—' Moses was silenced by Levy's voice.

'Thank you for coming to see us. Our security services will be keeping an eye on you. And don't worry, you're still free to return to Israel anytime in the future, but do remember everything I've told you.'

Levy held his hand out. They shook hands and Moses walked to the door.

At the last moment he turned around. 'Can I ask you a question, Colonel, before I leave?'

4

The armed guard looked on uncertainly as Moses stood in the doorway.

Levy looked at his watch and nodded at the guard. 'We don't have much time, your flight is leaving quite soon, but I will answer one final question, if you must,' he said curtly.

'If you – I mean the Israeli government, are so convinced

that this temple treasure will be a force for evil and destruction, and not for good, which is bizarre, considering it is the greatest symbol in Jewish history, why don't you simply destroy it? Blow it up?' said Moses. Levy listened and bit his fingernail.

'You know exactly where it is, you have the resources and the manpower to do anything you want. A missile strike from one of your Phantom jets and the relic will be gone forever. Why don't you do it, Colonel?' Levy smiled at Moses and walked back to the desk.

'You ask a reasonable question, Moses,' said Levy. 'I'm not a religious man but there is widely-held belief that God would not like us destroying it. Israel cannot destroy its greatest treasure, it is the symbol of its covenant with the Almighty. He will not be happy with that.'

'Nor would any of your Rabbis, I suppose,' added Moses.

'They wouldn't find out.' Levy chuckled again, clearly enjoying the exchange with Moses. 'Let me show you one last thing before you go,' he said, opening a blank page in his folder. 'You know what the treasure actually looks like, don't you?'

'Yes, of course,' said Moses.

Levy began to draw a sketch of a palm tree. Six inches away he drew the relic itself.

'You see, it is actually a tree – the tree of life.'

'That's beautiful, I like that. You're a good artist!' said Moses.

'If you destroy the tree of life, you destroy all life. That is why Israel will never destroy it. It shall stay in exile, underground in Delphi. That is a good place for it to stay hidden. It has survived under the Temple of Apollo for nearly two-thousand years, and there it must stay, for the sake of peace in our troubled land.' Levy looked at his watch. 'Now I must say shalom, Moses.'

'Shalom, Colonel.'

'It was a real pleasure to meet you.'

Moses was led into the same Toyota in which he had arrived. He held out his arm so that Nomi could handcuff him again. The engine started as the shutters inside the underground garage rose upwards, revealing daylight.

The car drove at full speed towards the airport, the siren blaring, red lights flashing. Moses was hurried by armed guards through passport control and security in seconds.

An El Al 737 to Vienna was standing on the runway, waiting for him, the engines roaring in readiness for an immediate take-off.

Moses ran up the gangway and walked past rows of irritated passengers until he reached 24D, the aisle seat, just above the wing. As he did up his safety belt, the doors of the aircraft were locked by a stewardess.

The engines shrieked and a truck began to pull the jet towards the runway. It was running 22 minutes late, but the captain promised to make up the time.

5

It was 6.00 am when he reached his office.

Unshaven, he sat at his desk in his crumpled clothes and dialled a French number.

'Ah, it's you, Moses. I was just waiting for a taxi to take me to the airport,' Helena said.

'I wanted to thank you for speaking to Lenoir. I can't believe it, he's awarded me a small scholarship for my research in

Delphi. Nothing much, but it's a symbolic victory. It's all OK now. I cannot thank you enough.'

'It's nothing. You've already shown your appreciation, in ways I cannot compare.' He paused. 'Look, Helena, I need to tell you something urgently. I've just had a difficult visit to Tel Aviv. There is, unfortunately, no interest in the Anomaly over there, contrary to my expectations. Actually, it's far worse than that, they are totally against my whole project. I've been warned against it in no uncertain terms by their security people.'

'But I don't understand. It's the greatest Jewish antiquity ever found. Surely they want it?'

'No, quite the reverse.'

'But why?'

'It's all political, but serious stuff.' Moses breathed a sigh and held back a yawn. He was feeling tired from two flights in 24 hours.

'The Israelis are not a disinterested party. They will go to any lengths to stop it ever becoming known to the public. You need to be careful about whom you talk in Delphi. Words can kill, as they used to say during the last war.'

'How did they find out?'

'I really don't know. Israeli security seems to know many things. I was quite taken aback, they must have informers everywhere. Be careful. Don't trust anyone.'

'But I will have to trust the men I'll be working with. I must go now Moses, I'll be late for my flight.'

PART NINE

Helena and The Dane

1

Trails of lightning jumped across the purple and yellow sky.

From her window seat, Helena watched the wing tips of Olympic Airways flight 645 from Paris to Athens shake up and down for a few seconds.

She gripped the armrest as the pilot announced there would be, 'a spot of turbulence due to electric storms over the Mediterranean.'

The safety belt sign flashed on above her seat.

She found it reassuring to watch the forty-foot wing bounce up and down with the air currents and somehow carry on supporting the three-hundred tons of metal along with 126 other passengers.

Within a minute the aircraft shook sideways again and three overhead lockers sprung open, spilling a few bags of hand luggage. It lasted for 45 seconds.

Two minutes later the whole aircraft rattled and shook again for twenty seconds, but less violently. It was over. The flight attendants undid their safety belts, replaced the spilt luggage, and shut the lockers.

Helena wondered if the turbulence was a metaphor for the last three months of her life or, even worse, a sign of things to come.

The plane landed without any further incident on a wet and windy runway at Athens airport. After a 45-minute transfer from the airport to a grimy bus station in downtown Athens she took the three-hour coach ride to Delphi. It was a sticky journey as there was no air conditioning apart from the open windows. As the rasping diesel engine churned noisily along the highway, Helena stared out at the gnarled olive trees in the scrubland lining the road.

The bus swung into the central square of Delphi, and from there Helena walked in the moist air towards her hotel, dragging her suitcase on its plastic wheels. There'd been heavy rain in Delphi and the streets were still glistening. Water flowed along the surface drains, carrying discarded cigarette packets the entire length of the street.

She checked into the three-star Hotel Paramour and collected her room key from a yawning male receptionist. Smells of lamb kleftiko cooking in the kitchen drifted into the lobby.

Helena's face lit up as she heard a Scandinavian man's voice down in the hotel bar. By the sound of his accent he was Danish. Even though she was shattered by the flight and the bus journey from Athens, she rushed to her room to make herself more presentable.

She emerged in a short clinging skirt and went in search of the unseen Dane. Halfway down the stairs, she sniffed herself and returned to the hotel room where she stripped off her clothing and sprayed every inch of her body with Chanel perfume.

Emerging in high heels, she went looking for the Dane in the bar, but he was nowhere to be seen and she limped back disappointed. The shutters had been left open, filling the room with warm humid air and the aroma of lamb. She lay on the bed and fell asleep.

Two hours later she awoke to the noise of shouting voices, the smashing of plates, and clanging of saucepans. She looked out of her window into the central courtyard. A chef appeared, lit a cigarette and leaned against the wall. Another came out and they began to shout again, the argument moving from the kitchen.

Helena rang down to reception to ask for the number of the Delphi Museum. The phone at the museum rang for five minutes until it was answered by a secretary who spoke slowly, as if on sleeping pills.

'I'm sorry,' she said, 'Dr Green is not available most of the day. He is busy preparing for an excavation.'

'Can you tell Dr Green that I'm a visiting archaeologist from Paris, from the Sorbonne University?' Helena said.

There was a long silence followed by random clicking, and eventually Dr Green came on the line. 'Yes?' said Green abruptly, as if he'd been interrupted.

'Ah, good afternoon Dr Green. You are the director of the Delphi Museum?' she asked.

'Yes, it is Dr Green here. How can I help you?' he said warmly, as if he'd become energised by hearing the young woman's voice.

'My name is Helena Delacroix.'

'Did you say Delacroix?' said Green. 'Any relation to the archaeologist?'

'Yes, I'm the granddaughter of Dr Niko Delacroix. In fact, I am also a French archaeologist. I'm staying in Delphi for a few weeks and I'd really like to meet you.'

'Did you say your name is Ellen?' asked Green.

'No, it's Helena. With an "H" for harlot.'

'Excuse me please, young Helena, may I call you back in five minutes after I've checked my diary?'

'Fine, I am at the Hotel Paradore. I'll be waiting for you, Dr Green.'

She lay back on the bed and became aware of the trickle of sweat from under her arms. The call to Dr Green had made her nervous. She dozed for a few minutes until the phone next to her buzzed and woke her.

'Hello Helena, it's Dr Green here again from the Delphi museum. I have my diary here, now let's make a date to meet. How about on Thursday, in three days' time? It's difficult after that as I'm very busy on a new excavation.'

Helena was not keen on this day as it was the summer solstice, a day she hoped to perform the first trial of the experiment, but she realised it could work later in the day if she was well organised.

'OK, but I'll be busy until five in the afternoon. Is that alright for you Dr Green?'

'Perfect.'

'Great, it gives me a few days to find my bearings in Delphi,' she said, hoping she might have made some real progress.

'You know, your grandfather was a brilliant archaeologist. So what brings you here now?' Green asked, clearly wanting to start a longer chat.

But Helena didn't want to talk as she wanted to take another shower. 'My family just want to know what happened to him, that's all,' she said.

'No one really knows, Helena, it's all a bit of a mystery,' said Green. 'We can talk about it all when we meet in three days.'

After taking her second shower of the afternoon she slithered back into her skirt, and strapped herself into cork espadrilles, making herself four inches taller and instantly accentuating her curves. Taking a pack of cigarettes from her box of duty frees, a special treat to herself, she walked back down into the bar, her long wet hair leaving a trail of water droplets on the stone tiles.

The man she hoped was the Dane was sitting there on a bar stool. The situation reminded her of the demonstration in Palousey's Paris flat two months earlier.

She approached him from behind, stepping on the marble floor as lightly as she could. She was helped by the fact that there was bouzouki music playing in the background and no one was manning the bar. He looked as if he was staring at the row of whisky bottles.

There was something about a Greek resort in hot humid weather that made Helena feel predatory. The climate was making her feel aroused. She began to do something she would never have done in Paris. When she was six inches away she brushed her fingernails against his back in a slow meandering touch that lasted several seconds.

'Hi there,' she said softly, swishing her long red hair so it fell over her shoulders.

He took no notice of her tactile assault and ignored her greeting. He was either too drunk or too cool to turn around.

Helena dug her fingertips into his open-necked cotton shirt. There was still no reaction. She walked round to face him and made the universal gesture for someone needing a light. When she saw him face-to-face she laughed self-consciously at her unsubtle attempt to gain his attention.

He attempted a smile, pulled out a lighter from his breast pocket, and lit Helena's cigarette without saying a word.

She smiled back appreciatively, craned her neck back and exhaled a cloud of blue smoke in the direction of the ceiling fan. Smiling at him again, she wondered – was he the man?

Her gut reaction was that he had all the required attributes. He was slim to the point of being gaunt, with no extraneous fat on his body. He was tall, maybe six foot two. He was the right age, around thirty. His clothes suggested he had a sense of style. He was wearing blue jeans, a white t-shirt, and running shoes. He had intelligent eyes.

Helena noticed there was no ring on his hand, but she didn't really care. He looked like he enjoyed the physical side of things and had been running on the beach. His unshaven cheeks looked virile and swarthy.

His slim build, combined with strong-looking arms and legs, suggested he probably had the energy to be an active and passionate lover for her experiment.

Their naked bodies would fit well together, she thought.

She imagined pressing her breasts against his body quite happily. She saw him stroking her back and could feel the lightness of his touch on her skin. She could see herself sitting astride him as he gripped onto her waist, reaching over to suck on her nipples, his tongue playing with them.

'You like to run?' she said, looking down at his Nikes.

'I like to keep fit,' he said, without elaborating. She liked his modest quietness.

He picked up his whisky, shook the ice around in the glass, and gave her a tentative smile. Next to him, on the bar, was an unopened book on the story of the Delphi excavations, written in English.

'I'm sorry for this intrusion, the heat gets to me sometimes. I just needed to talk to someone – this place is so quiet,' Helena said, inching steadily towards him.

'I don't mind. I'm enjoying it,' he said and gave her an awkward smile.

'Business or pleasure?' he asked.

'Both,' she said.

'What do you mean exactly?' he asked, his eyes firmly fixed on her neckline.

'If you get me a drink, I'll happily explain,' she said, dragging on her cigarette and leaning back.

2

She slid her legs over her sleeping companion but couldn't fall back asleep.

As she heard the clatter in the hotel restaurant, she went to the window and peered down into the brightly-lit dining room. It was midnight and the last dinner guests were still eating.

A pair of waiters, smoking in the garden, stubbed out their cigarettes, walked into the kitchen, and returned to the dining room, carrying bowls of cinnamon-topped rice pudding and baklavas drenched in honey.

Helena fell back into the bed and looked enviously at her Danish lover still asleep amidst all the banging down below.

The clock radio crackled into life and began to play 'Leila.' She knew every note like an old friend and lay listening to Eric Clapton with a knowing smile. She reset the alarm and placed her head back on the pillow.

There were too many thoughts swirling around in her mind to fall asleep. She found herself listening to every word shouted by the drunken dinner guests as they staggered to their rooms, slamming doors behind them.

Within minutes the hotel's plumbing system gurgled to life, a chorus of flushing cisterns and banging pipes rattled all around her, followed by an encore of juddering taps and, finally, silence. All was quiet again apart from the buzz of the cicadas in the hotel garden.

Helena slipped out from the cotton sheets, stretched herself in front of the open window, and inhaled the velvet air. She couldn't stop thinking through every step of the moonlit walk they would soon be making to reach the Temple of Apollo, five-hundred metres from the hotel.

A warm breeze rippled around her bare body as she sat down at the small desk and wrote 'pick laurel leaves' onto her list of things to do.

Realising she was still dripping with the Dane's juices after making love earlier in the evening she went into the bathroom to mop herself up.

As she crouched down on the bidet only a small trickle of tepid water flowed out of the tap. It was the second night this had happened – the water pressure in the hotel seemed to disappear at night.

Clutching a towel between her legs she leaned over her male companion asleep in her bed, climbed on top of him, and pressed her breasts against his mouth. As he come round she stroked his hair and kissed him.

All she knew was his first name. All further personal details were not permitted within the rules of the protocol she'd drafted herself. She was bending over backwards to ensure the PhD research was objective, so it was not invalidated by any personal knowledge about her partners.

She slid her hands across his chest. His eyes remained firmly shut, his body still and heavy – she was unlikely to revive him now, and reset the alarm for 4.45 am.

She fell asleep immediately. It seemed only minutes later when the alarm went off.

It was still dark outside when she climbed out of the bed and washed her face. As she stood naked in front of the mirror and slipped on her black silk briefs, she began to feel aroused – but there wasn't time to have any more sex now.

Anyway, she needed to keep their energies for later. He was still lying asleep on the bed as she crouched down and knelt by his side. Moistening one of her fingers with saliva, she ran it slowly over his lips.

Within a few seconds she'd brought him round and kissed him awake.

'How long have you been up?' he said.

'Not long at all, but I'm sorry, we must leave in fifteen minutes, the timing is critical, we have to catch the sunrise.'

She rubbed some body lotion between her legs before squeezing herself into a pair of tight-fitting frayed shorts, a red bikini top and a t-shirt. In her hand she carried her sandals and a small bag containing her personal oils.

To avoid walking past the front reception, they climbed out of the bedroom window and made their way barefoot up a winding path at the back of the hotel.

Their silent progress was broken only by a gasp from Helena as a pair of giant horseshoe bats fluttered past the concrete electricity pylons. Seeing a laurel bush she removed a handful of leaves and stuffed them into her pocket before walking on.

They came to a white-brick security hut. The lights were on and they could hear a radio or TV. As they crept past a small window, they saw a flickering TV screen and two security guards dozing in their chairs, oblivious to everything around them. In front of them on a messy table, coffee cups and empty beer bottles lay scattered about.

They moved quickly past the sleeping guards and clambered over the five-foot high perimeter fence without difficulty. The marble stones felt cold on their bare feet as they continued upwards towards the Temple Mount.

On arriving at the five ruined pillars they leaned against the remains of a thick wall and gazed out towards the horizon in the east, from where the sun would emerge. It was hard to see anything in the darkness, and only an indistinct dark-blue line separated the sky from the ocean.

Helena untied the clip of her red bikini top and let it fall onto the marble floor. She told the Dane to take off his clothes. Once he was naked he began to pull at her shorts. They slipped down her legs, over her knees, and came to rest around her feet. She kicked them into the air and they landed a few yards away, at the base of a four-thousand-year-old pillar.

'Hold me, I'm feeling cold,' she said, and he gave her a bear hug, rubbing his hands over her bare body whilst pressing her close to his chest.

They sat on the marble floor. Helena checked her watch and remembered to swallow the laurel leaves in the pocket of her shorts. As she chewed on the leathery leaves she checked her watch again, pressing a side button to light up the numbers.

In nine minutes the sun would rise over the horizon, bringing with it the warmth of the day and the first shafts of light.

'We must watch the time,' she said, biting through the leaves.

There were signs that the sun was waiting in the wings. The black sky around Mount Parnassus shimmered with a mottling of light and began to turn a lighter shade of mauve. Helena placed her arm around her companion and gave him a small bottle.

'Here. Take this and rub it into me,' she said.

'Where?'

'Everywhere. I want to be well-oiled.'

He pushed her red hair off her shoulders and began to rub the oil into her breasts. They both froze suddenly as they heard voices.

'Security guards. Get down,' she whispered, crouching low on the marble floor and pulling him close to her.

Helena found herself rehearsing the words of a statement in Greek she'd learnt by heart.

'I'm a doctoral student, attached to the Sorbonne University in Paris, carrying out research here in Delphi at the Temple of

Apollo to verify the text of an ancient manuscript, discovered by my grandfather, the archaeologist Niko Delacroix, eighty years ago.'

But it wasn't necessary. The voices faded into the distance.

'I think it's safe to finish massaging you with the oil now.' He shook the bottle and poured it over her body as she lay on her back. 'You're nervous aren't you? Are you feeling safer now?' he said, sliding his hands up and down her legs, gently pushing his finger inside her. 'You feel ready for me, now.'

'Yes I am,' she said, and he began to climb on top of her. 'No, not yet. We must wait a few more minutes. The sun must rise – then you can rise.'

'Oh damn, I forgot. Remind me, why we are waiting for the sun to rise before having sex?'

'I didn't think you paid much attention when I ran through it yesterday,' she said.

'It's a lot to take in – and I was distracted by someone,' he said with a smile.

She sat up and checked her watch again. 'Not long now, your pain will be over soon. I'll do a recap, but hold onto me again, it's still cold out here.' She looked him straight in the eye.

'OK, so an ancient Greek manuscript was found here in Delphi called the Elena Text. My grandfather discovered it. It says that from amongst the young women of ancient Delphi there would be chosen an Oracle, a woman of great sensitivity.'

He stared into her green eyes and placed a finger over her lips. 'That's enough, Helena. I remember it now.'

She stood up, opened her arms towards the ever-changing sky, and saw that the sunrise was quickly approaching.

'So here we are today, making history, re-enacting the ritual of prophecy, for the first time in three-thousand years,' she said, waving her hands in the air, trying to elicit a more excited reaction from him.

'Do you realise this is the first attempt by anyone to repeat these findings? Don't you think that's special?'

'Naturally,' he said. She looked disappointed by his lack of enthusiasm.

'Actually, I believe I'm very privileged to be able to re-enact this ancient ritual today,' she said.

He stood up, encircling her waist with both of his hands.

She shivered in response to his light touch as he ran his fingers down her back.

'I agree. It's truly a historic moment, and I didn't realise that you could have so much fun doing a PhD,' he said, laughing.

'It wasn't easy getting this research project approved by the Sorbonne,' Helena said, her eyes watching the sky as it changed from purple to deep orange. 'Look at the colour of the sky. It's coming now. It must be only moments away,' she said. 'A little more oil, please, where my body likes your fingers to go the most.'

'And your Venus is glowing brightly as ever,' he said, rubbing the oil into her silky mound.

3

The heavy glass doors of the museum swung open and Green edged out.

He sniffed the air – he was happy the weather would stay dry as he walked towards the steps leading down to the museum basement and unlocked the door. The underground storage area was littered with pieces of broken statues and hundreds of exhibits too small to be worth showing in the museum.

Today the musty-smelling room resembled a storeroom of a café – with dozens of cans of *7 Up* piled on every surface.

From an envelope in his trouser pocket, Green produced a small chunk of limestone, which he'd hammered off the wall of the chamber. He placed it in a wine glass, picked up a can of *7 Up*, pulled the ring, and poured the fizzing lemonade into the glass.

Within a few seconds tiny bubbles were forming on the surface. After five minutes there was only a brown liquid left in the glass and nothing remained of the limestone.

Grabbing a pencil he did his calculations on the back of a copy of *Scroll*, an old archaeology magazine, and estimated that he would need to keep the relic immersed in the acidic drink for eight hours to completely dissolve all the limestone. His challenge was to do this for such a lengthy period.

He tried to picture the orientation of the Delphic Anomaly in his head. He knew it was positioned at a thirty-degree angle and presented a technically difficult practical challenge.

But he had worked out a complex plan. He had drawn a sketch of a custom-built bladder to be constructed from banana-shaped sections of plastic, fused together with an electric iron, which would completely surround the limestone.

To prevent the liquid escaping across the floor of the chamber, it would be sealed to the ground with gaffer tape, and as an extra precaution, stones would be used to hold down the plastic.

Green was convinced it was the 'design of a genius,' and would finally make the excavation of the Delphic Anomaly possible.

There was enough room in his metal-framed rucksack for forty cans of *7 Up*. He packed it to the brim, tightened the straps, and placed it at the foot of the staircase leading to the museum.

All that remained, before his ascent to the secret entrance on Mount Parnassus, was the construction of the bladder. He went to fetch the electric iron and plugged it into a wall socket.

After five minutes he tested the temperature on the palm of his hand, and let out a painful cry. It had warmed up faster than he'd thought and was already extremely hot, so he began his unusual task. The plastic pieces fused together easily and they did not split when he tried pulling them apart. He repeated this process eighteen times until the bladder had been constructed, piece by piece.

He allowed himself a final cigarette, as he hadn't smoked for over a half an hour. He hit the end of his pack of Marlboro, and a cigarette fell into his hand. Clicking his lighter into life he sat down to enjoy a smoke.

Wiping his eyes as he wandered outside into the pre-dawn light, he was surprised to be overcome with emotion. His body felt light. He was in a trance-like state, almost floating as he waited for the sun to appear behind the pencil pines. There were still stars and planets visible in the sky, and Venus shone brightly.

A tear ran down his cheek as he saw the first sliver of sun appear on the horizon. The power of this natural event, combined with his personal mission to dissolve two-thousand years of limestone, moved him to tears.

Unlocking the Anomaly, for the first time since Emperor Hadrian had brought it from Rome, filled Green with a sense of supreme power. For a few moments he believed he possessed a kind of supernatural influence over humanity.

Certain he was about to change the course of history, Green marched up the hill, his rucksack clinking with the sound of forty cans.

On reaching the workman's hut he pushed aside the drain

covers and lowered himself down the steps of the cave. As he reached the lowest point, he heard the sound of rushing water. The underground streams were in full flow all around him.

He slithered along the tunnel, dragging the rucksack behind him, until he reached the chamber where the Delphic Anomaly sat incarcerated. He stood upright and felt his heart racing.

Using his cigarette lighter, Green lit four candles and placed them in a semi-circle around the relic. They flickered with a shadowy glow as he stepped backwards to take a photograph.

'We'll get you out of here. Everything will soon be taken care of,' Green said.

His hand shaking, he took the plastic bladder out of his rucksack and suspended it meticulously around the limestone mound holding the relic. After twisting the last wire into place, he sealed the plastic onto the ground using builder's gaffer tape. Finally, to make doubly sure it would not leak, he placed heavy stones all around the edge.

'It will be easy now,' he said, as he lit up and contemplated the final stage of the rescue mission. Within a few hours he knew he would be changing the course of history, and the relic would be liberated from the rock. Over five feet high and weighing around 45 kilogrammes, the solid gold antiquity would be too heavy for him to carry down to the museum on his own, but he had a plan to pay a member of the museum staff to help him.

Green pulled opened the first can of *7 Up* and breathed in the bubbles as if it were champagne, pouring it into the top of the plastic bladder. There was an immediate fizzing sound as the carbonic acid began to attack the limestone.

Half an hour later, as he was emptying the twenty-fourth can into the bladder, Green noticed a small drip coming from the bottom of the plastic bag. It was so small he decided it was unimportant and ignored it, but in less than a minute it grew from a pinhead into a small globule several millimetres across.

It fell onto the ground and soon another began to grow.

'Shit!' Green shouted.

The cave echoed with his frustration. He leaned over the ever-growing drip, pinched the plastic with his fingers, carefully twisting it around itself five times and sealing it with a new piece of wire. His repair was holding. It was as if he was an expert plumber, he told himself.

He breathed easily again and felt in his pockets in search of his cigarettes. He lit up as a reward for his ingenuity and listened to the gentle fizzing action on the limestone. He calculated that it would now take about five hours to completely dissolve the rock.

Placing his rucksack on a patch of raised ground, he inflated his air bed, set his alarm for 8.00 am, took a deep drag before stubbing the cigarette into the ground and collapsed onto his mattress.

Within seconds, Green was asleep.

4

The TV flickered inside the security hut.

The fast-talking voice of an American sports commentator filled the quiet night air.

The two guards were asleep on their armchairs.

'It's a no hitter!' the commentator shouted through the speaker in the small black-and-white TV. There was a loud roar from the crowd in the faraway Chicago stadium and the guards woke up.

Both men staggered to their feet, tottered towards the urinal behind the hut, and filled up the stained porcelain basins, their full bladders producing a long, slow fountain of piss.

They shook themselves dry, dribbled some water from the tap over their fingers, dawdled back to the hut, grabbed baklavas off the table, stuffed large chunks into their mouths, and poured tepid coffee down their throats.

It was still dark, but the sky was filling with a warm glow and Georgios, a short round man with a bushy moustache, decided to walk up towards the top of the site to stretch his legs and watch the sun rise.

He clambered up the marble steps towards the altar buildings, lit up a Karelia, and wheezed as he exhaled.

After a good cough, he looked down towards the temple mount thirty feet below him. Not expecting to see anything out of the ordinary, he began to turn back towards the hut, but stopped abruptly.

He thought he'd seen something move. He was unsure what he was looking at in the semi-darkness. Illuminated only by the orange glow in the dawn sky, a man and a woman seemed to be moving around on the marble floor, their shadowy bodies slowly becoming visible as the sun began to rise.

Georgios began to signal wildly with both arms to his colleague.

'Nikos! We have some early morning visitors,' he whispered, unable to contain himself. 'Where are the binoculars?'

Both men tried to run, but they were too fat and ended up shambling out of the hut and walking up the hill, panting with excitement.

When they reached the low wall, the only barrier separating

them from the Temple of Apollo and the couple, they managed to squat down low.

Georgios turned to his colleague, his eyes rolling.

A knowing smile billowed from his cheeks – his face went wild with excitement.

'I think they're naked, for Christ's sake. But, hey, what's going on now? Oh shit, they've stopped moving.'

'Let me see,' said Nikos, pulling away the binoculars. 'There's nothing happening, they've stopped again.'

'No wait, look, the sun's coming up, something's bound to start now,' Georgios began to say, but paused, unable to speak as he watched the couple stroking each other.

'Oh my God, is this really happening right in front of our eyes? I cant believe it, they're making love as the sun rises.'

He couldn't contain himself and began to jump up and down with excitement.

'Mother of Christ, you can see everything now – they're touching their most private parts.'

5

The orange fireball climbed into the sky and Helena felt the warmth of sunlight on her cheeks.

A pair of seabirds screeched overhead in recognition.

She'd fantasised about this moment for months and had brought with her various incantations to recite before they carried out the ritual.

Looking straight into the eyes of her anonymous lover, she began to hum whilst stroking his body.

When she'd first met him, three days earlier in the bar of the Hotel Paramour, she'd persuaded him to prolong his stay in Delphi by an extra night so they could do the first orgasm experiment on the morning of the summer solstice.

She'd told him she was a keen follower of a new, liberated sexual philosophy which required that she, 'experience as much sex as possible in ancient holy places, preferably before the age of thirty.'

She'd actually told him that their sexual union had been decided by unknown forces beyond their control, and had been willed to take place by a higher being. 'It has to happen,' she said, without a hint of a smile.

As they stood on the temple mount, Helena began to chant the prayer-like verses she'd specially collected for the occasion.

'Our bodies will be linked in time and space,' she began in a monotone, raising her arms upwards.

'An orgasm experienced in this holy place will be magnified by the echoes of orgasms experienced by the historic goddesses of sex themselves, Aphrodite, Astarte, Ishtar, and Venus.'

The Dane nodded respectfully, as if she were reciting some kind of ancient holy prayer, but when he tried to place his hands around her naked waist, she pulled away, preventing their bodies from touching.

'Hey Helena, you're driving me nuts, look at what are you doing to me. What is all this sacred mumbo jumbo? Let's just do it,' he said whilst pointing at his excited organ. Helena smiled at him and took hold of his rock-like erection in her fingers, stroking it gently.

'I can see you're aching for me, but there is a good reason to delay. The longer you have to wait for me, the greater the orgasm will be, which is what we want,' she said, squeezing him tightly between her fingers.

'This is harder for me than for you, I assure you,' she said. He laughed at her joke and grimaced as she pushed a fingernail into his skin.

'Look,' he said, glancing at the horizon, 'the sun has risen. What are we waiting for?'

'Don't touch me yet, not until I've read the passage from the manuscript,' she said, pushing him away and taking a roll of parchment from her leather bag.

His hands fell reluctantly away from her body as she unwound the crumpled paper.

'At the height of ecstasy, it is written,' she said, 'the Oracle will see directly into the soul of Apollo and share his infinite knowledge.' She moved closer to him, holding his face in her hands and putting her tongue into his mouth.

'The moment has arrived,' she began to whisper. 'I am ready to test the prophecy.' He looked back at her uncertainly.

"Now!' she shouted. 'It means you can fuck me now,' she said, placing her arms around his neck and pushing her excited nipples against him.

'OK Sure,' he said. 'I'm ready to fuck you to high heaven, to meet all those goddesses up there, still enjoying their orgasms, after thousands of years,' he said, pressing himself against her.

'Don't wait any longer, come into me right now,' she whispered, pulling him onto the marble.

He climbed over her body and she guided him inwards, placing her arms across his back and pulling him closer so they became a single mass of writhing, slippery skin. She wrapped her legs around his for more sensation, and with every slither, as he rammed himself deeper inside her, slamming against her crotch, she tightened her hold over him. They were locked together.

'Do you like that?' he asked. She didn't answer, but her moans became louder and more desperate with every push until he was exhausted. He stopped still, but remained deep inside her body.

'Have you come already?' she said, her mouth gaping open.

'No, I need a rest. You've tired me out already,' he said, and she looked at him in shock. 'Don't worry, I'm joking. I'm only just beginning.'

His head fell sideways on her shoulder. Their eyes met and she looked at him through her huge, black pupils.

'I want to ride *you*, now,' she said breathlessly. He began to pull out of her,

'No, stop,' she cried, pulling him back inside her again and locking her legs around him.

In one swift manoeuvre, Helena turned him over, changing places on the marble floor so that she was sitting on top of him.

Astride him, she rocked backwards, curving her back so her crimson hair dangled onto his toes.

She could feel he was going to come inside her now. She knew she had to do something to delay matters and leaned forward, digging her red nails into his back.

As she pressed them into his skin, she could feel him shooting off inside her, maybe a dozen times, his body shuddering until she was overflowing with his slippery juice. As he came she ran her nails down both sides of his spine, making a six inch scratch on his skin.

'I think I've given you a lasting souvenir of your trip to Delphi,' she said, licking his blood off her fingernails. 'I hope your girlfriend doesn't see that scratch.' She collapsed onto the ground. His body vibrated with two aftershocks, and then he lay still, drained and finished.

But it was too soon for Helena. He was ahead of her. She shook his exhausted body, and tried to bite him. She didn't know what to do to save the experiment.

'Please – keep going, don't stop now,' she shouted, 'I'm almost there with you. Don't you remember? I MUST have an orgasm. You must understand, it's all pointless otherwise,' she added.

His eyes flickered open. He took a deep breath and pushed himself back inside her. She was pleased to feel that he was still firm as he moved around her tightening pussy.

'That's great, you're such a wonderful lover, I won't forget this. I'm really not far behind you,' she told him and he pressed his fingers into her soft cheeks.

'Yes, do that, press your fingers into me as I come,' she said. Seconds later she came with a series of increasingly loud, shocking gasps, and fell exhausted on top of him. She was silent and still at last, her breathing rapid but slowing fast.

Her cries had echoed through the ruins and she was sure the four-thousand-year-old pillars had shaken on their foundations at the moment of her orgasm.

She felt like warm melting wax as her muscles went soft and moulded themselves around him. When she'd caught her breath, she began to speak.

'I have a confession. I had a vision of Apollo as I came,' she said, her cheeks alight with a rosy glow.

'That's really great. Isn't that what you wanted?' he said, looking pleased for her.

'It was, but I want to see the face of Apollo *again*, just to make sure,' she said, unaware she was shouting. He tried placing his hands over her mouth, but she didn't like it and pushed her head away.

'I want to have another orgasm. Can you help me do it?' His eyes rolled backwards.

'Please. Can we try just once more?' He nodded at her with a slight smile and began to kiss her lips. As his tongue went inside her mouth, she felt him quickly becoming aroused again.

Sliding easily back inside her, he grabbed her by the waist and rolled their two bodies over so she was now lying on her back. As she reached a climax for a second time, a breathless, gasping smile crept over her face.

'That didn't take too much effort, did it?' she said, adding, 'you know, I always come faster the second time around.'

'I'd say we had a good warm up, first time around,' he said, and laughed as he lifted her crimson hair away from her eyes.

It was tousled and wet with fresh sweat, and spread out across her shoulders, in complete disarray.

She couldn't move anymore. Every ounce of her energy had been sapped, but her senses seemed to be heightened – it was not lost on her that this increased awareness was exactly as predicted in the Elena Text.

As the warmth of the sun played on her skin she could hear voices coming from beyond the wall.

6

'You don't see that every day, my friend,' Georgios said, putting the binoculars down and rubbing his eyes. He was feeling exhausted after watching the couple finish their marathon. 'Do you think we should give them a round of applause?' he whispered to Takis.

'Aaah, don't spoil it by giving the game away – isn't she the same woman with the long red hair who arrived at the hotel a couple of days ago? I think I served her breakfast. She's a real beauty. What a lucky bastard to have sex with her.'

'And I've seen him around the hotel too. But why d'you think they're screwing here, so early in the morning? What's wrong with the bedrooms in the hotel, anyway?' Niko asked.

'The mattresses aren't too great, but I don't think that would bother them. No, I think they came here to catch the sunrise, it's a hippy kind of thing to do,' Georgios said, looking at the date on his watch. 'And I think it's the longest day of the year today.'

The two guards yawned and wandered back to their hut, chuckling to each other over their stroke of luck. They brewed up a pot of thick coffee, sweetened with several large spoons of sugar, flicked off a few flies from the remaining baklavas, rubbed them clean on their shorts, and began to argue as they chewed away, spitting lumps of sugar into the air.

'We should arrest them,' said Georgios, his mouth full of honey-drenched cake. He was a balding man with a face as round as a dinner plate, decorated in the middle with a long moustache that crept over his cheeks.

'They've broken the law by having sex in a public place,' he said, dipping another baklava into his milky coffee.

'I'm not so sure we should do that. They're guests at the hotel,' said Nikos.

Both men moonlighted at the Hotel Paramour as waiters. It was a convenient arrangement which enabled them to get paid whilst they slept at the archaeological site, and the only way to survive on the low wages.

'We have a duty to make them feel welcome. They may want to come back,' Georgios said, said draining the coffee from his mug. 'Just think, we could take pictures next time. Could be worth something.'

'OK. I suppose it would be unfair to arrest such a beautiful couple who've given us so much pleasure.'

They stepped outside the security hut and wiped the sugar off their faces, straightened out the creases in their uniforms and, using their fingernails, combed their hair. This took time and patience, and they had both of these.

They still had one more hour of guard duty before they went back to the hotel to serve breakfast.

7

Green woke up to the sound of water lapping around the edge of his rucksack.

It was too dark to see anything. He stretched out his hand and felt cold water on the ground, one finger deep.

For a few seconds he lay there confused – he'd forgotten where he was. He knew he was not in his normal bed and thought he'd dozed off sitting at his desk in the museum.

Gradually, he realised he was under Mount Parnassus, inside the chamber housing the Delphic Anomaly.

He looked towards the relic but couldn't see it. Nor could he see his plastic bladder containing the contents of forty cans of *7 Up*.

'What's happening? Where's my treasure?' Green shouted in the darkness, unable to see anything but shadows. He felt for his torch and switched it on, but it only made a dim circle of light.

When he looked down to the floor of the chamber, he didn't like what he saw. The entire plastic bladder had collapsed. He pressed it inwards and felt a sticky, empty bag.

It had relieved itself of most of the lemonade.

A tangled knot of wires lay on the ground. He shook the torch in the hope it would become brighter. The weight of the dissolved rock, which had fallen into it, had become too heavy – and the whole contraption had collapsed onto the floor.

He gave his head torch a knock and for a few seconds the light was brighter, but soon died again. The relic was safe and sound – but still trapped in its limestone straightjacket.

He became aware that his toes were wet. Looking down at his boots, he realised he was standing in several inches of water. The sound of a running stream was closer than ever, and there was a gushing noise coming from behind the chamber wall.

He looked at his watch. It was 7.05 am on June 21st and he was puzzled – it didn't normally flood so early in the morning.

The date began to trigger alarm bells, it was, he remembered, the day of the summer solstice – he'd read that the sun could increase the moon's tidal effect by nearly fifty percent. 'Shit,' he hissed between his teeth, kicking his foot into a puddle.

He felt his heart begin to race – his body was telling him to leave. With some difficulty, he stretched down and picked up his sodden rucksack, leaving everything else lying on the cave floor.

There wasn't time for a salvage operation, he could come back on another day.

He watched in frustration as a few empty cans and his tube of toothpaste floated past.

As he waded to the far end of the chamber, it pained him to abandon all his unopened packs of cigarettes.

He tried walking faster but, in the darkness, he stumbled over a hollow in the ground, falling head first into the water. He tried fumbling for his torch but was soon distracted by a trickling sensation from his face.

A warm liquid was seeping from the side of his head.

Blood, water or *7 Up* – he wasn't sure. It tasted as if it was probably his own blood.

He felt a surge of adrenalin shoot through his veins. Something told him not to worry about the injury to his head or the loss of his belongings but to make his way as quickly as he could towards the tunnel exit.

There was now a fast-flowing stream running beside him where none had existed a few hours earlier. The desolate thought of being trapped where no one could hear him shouting for help frightened him.

He tried to run but he couldn't move any faster over the slippery surface.

In his desperation to get out he lost his footing and stumbled against the wall of the chamber, ripping his shirt on a sharp corner of rock.

Tears ran down his face. Convinced he would drown, all alone, in this dark, wet hole he began to hallucinate. A carousel of images from his life flashed past his eyes – he saw Isabella running into his arms, and his ex-wife staring down, laughing at him.

He feared this was the end – it's what he'd heard people experienced shortly before they died.

A sliver of light appeared in the distance.

He was sure he was no longer hallucinating and began sobbing in the certainty that he would survive to live another day.

Beneath his feet were the steps to safety. He staggered up to the surface, pulled himself onto the path, and collapsed onto the ground outside the hut, staring at the blue sky above him.

After two minutes he dragged the heavy covers over the entrance, and the chamber below disappeared from view.

In the gentle warmth of the early morning sunlight, Green sat under the warm turquoise sky, wheezing and coughing. His efforts to climb out of the chamber had exhausted his abused body.

Longing for a cigarette, he searched his pockets for a pack. In the breast pocket of his soaking shirt he found a sodden mash of wet tobacco and several unravelling filter tips. His wallet, keys, and inhaler were missing, floating somewhere in the waters of the cave.

A small red droplet of blood fell onto the dusty track by his feet. The gash to his forehead would not steep bleeding, but he thought only of finding a dry cigarette and a lighter. Green was sure that smoking would help stop the blood, as his doctor had told him that smoking made it more likely to clot.

He could hear a tour guide and a group of Japanese tourists only yards away from him. Scuttling back into the workman's hut, he zipped up the canvas entrance. He was now hidden from the outside world. Only his asthmatic panting would give him away.

As he tried to stay totally still, pressing his hand against his bleeding head wound, he was conscious he resembled a man on the run rather than a museum director.

With his other hand he carefully undid the buttons of his shirt, took it off, and tied up the sleeve to make a bandage.

Peering through the narrow gap in the wall of the hut, he saw the Japanese group approaching.

'Such ridiculous tourists, for Christ's sake,' he cursed under his breath. 'What the hell are they doing all the way up here?' he said to himself, as they posed for endless photographs in front of the sign of his hut.

8

'What's happened?' the Dane asked, looking at her anxiously.

Still naked and drizzling between her legs from the after effects of two orgasms, Helena sat down over a fissure in the rocks, resting her drained body, her crimson hair falling all around her.

'Oh my God. How can I be so stupid? I've forgotten something crucial. We can't waste a moment now,' she said breathlessly. 'You must ask me a question – any reasonable question will do – so I can divine the answer. Do it quickly, please, I beg of you.'

He was exhausted and looked back at her blankly. 'What's this about?' he mumbled.

Helena was sure she'd talked about it at some point. 'Surely you remember?' she said in desperation. 'Now,' she screamed at the Dane, 'ask me a question before the orgasmic sensations fade away. Please,' she said, clasping her hands in a prayer position and kneeling at his feet. 'You only have to come up with a question for me to answer.'

There was silence whilst he looked at her for inspiration, his brow furrowed, as if he was throwing out every idea that entered his head.

'Quickly! The energy is draining out of me.'

Helena noticed the smell of ripe bananas. She inhaled deeply and wondered if she could sense the sweet-smelling vapours of ethylene gas, rising up from the cleft in the rocks. It was a new scientific discovery she'd read about in the *Journal of Archaeology*. It was believed that the sweet gas could have caused the hallucinations experienced by the Oracles.

The Dane came close to her face and kissed her lips.

'It's OK, relax. I have a question for you,' he said.

'I'm ready.'

'Tell me, Helena, will we meet again, after today has ended?' he asked with a soulful look, both cheeks of his face revealing a slight tremor.

She was taken aback by the question. The protocol she'd set up required that she did not get to know her sexual partners. She was not expecting the question to be so unfathomable, and she looked away in embarrassment. She smiled briefly before lowering her head to breathe in more of the gas. After a few seconds she started to mumble. A string of incoherent sounds flew out of her mouth.

The Dane grimaced, and looked back at Helena, puzzled by her meaningless utterances. 'I think that means "No," but I'm not sure,' he said.

She made an unnatural rasping sound and nodded in agreement with his interpretation.

Bolstered by the success of his first question he couldn't wait to ask a second. 'I have another one for you,' he said, and she leaned forward eagerly. 'If we do not meet again, will our children ever do so?'

Helena bent down over the cracks in the rock and inhaled more gas. As her head rose up, another string of sounds came out of her mouth. He shook his head in confusion. A stream of tears started to run her down her cheeks, as if she was experiencing a strong emotional reaction to the question.

'Don't cry. I think I know what it might mean,' he said, and she nodded. 'It means ... there will probably always be some kind of a connection between us,' he said.

She slumped over, resting her head on the ancient marble shelf next to her. The Dane left her lying there to take a stroll. After staring blankly out to sea for a while, he returned to Helena and took her by the arm.

She struggled to walk the short distance. After the long bout of highly physical sex, several powerful orgasms shaking her body like electro-convulsive shocks, and the final panic, she was numb with exhaustion. They collected their clothes, but she was still feeling too shaken to cover her body.

'Please put these on, in case we meet someone,' he said, and she slipped on her briefs and red bikini top.

She remained in a trance-like state as they continued towards the village. By the time they got closer to the perimeter fence, some eighty metres before the security hut, she seemed to have returned to a state of normal consciousness. Before they reached the hut Helena began speaking again, but not in her normal voice.

'This momentary spectacle of my flesh will not be sufficiently long-lasting to bring charges against me of indecency in a public place,' she said in robotic-style monotone. A few feet from the security hut they heard the voices of the guards.

'Do as I say,' she said, speaking normally again. 'Smile and keep walking,' she added as she lifted her top away to give them a close-up view of her naked breasts. 'This will distract them. They'll be unable to think straight,' she whispered as the guards watched in shocked silence.

'They won't arrest us now. Don't look back,' she said, as they walked down to the village towards the Hotel Paramore.

The smell of freshly brewed Greek coffee and red melon filled the air. As they swept past the breakfast tables, they saw bowls filled with ripe figs and thick white yogurt being brought onto the terrace by a chef. Helena began to salivate. She'd worked up a major hunger, but knew she needed to return to her room to wash the sex from her body.

She and the Dane parted and agreed to meet downstairs for breakfast in half an hour.

After a long, pensive shower, she walked slowly downstairs in some loose clothing and waited on the veranda for the Dane to appear. She was early. When he came down, ten minutes later, he was pulling a suitcase bag behind him. Sitting down together, they sucked out the flesh of the ripe figs and washed them down with sweet hot coffee. They asked for scrambled eggs and tomatoes, and they came swimming in olive oil and basil leaves.

'I hate goodbyes,' the Dane said, and Helena nodded.

'I agree. The act of goodbye is artificial, and it's too abrupt. I don't want to interrupt the flow of our journey together with some fake farewell greeting. Life isn't like that, is it?' she said.

'Yes, I think I know what you mean,' he said, looking at his watch. 'I'm sorry, I must go now,' he said, and a tear rolled down his face. They stood up and looked out over the veranda.

'We did what we agreed to do and now it is over. I'm booked on the 9.30 bus. I need to start going on my way.'

'Thank you for staying on the extra day. It was a good … decision,' she began, 'no, it was very good …' Her voice trailed off.

'I'd say it was unforgettable, actually.' He looked around at the other diners and took hold of her hand to kiss it. Helena pushed it aside, opened her arms, and held him in a tight embrace.

'I don't care what anyone here thinks, I want to hold you one more time.' They clung to each other tightly for a minute. 'When's the flight?' she said, burying her face in his chest.

'I'm taking the 2.15 to Copenhagen, scheduled to arrive at 4.50,' he said, trying to pull himself away from her.

'Don't worry, we won't exchange names, addresses, or phone numbers, OK? That's the deal and I will not break it,' she said as they walked outside.

'Am I permitted to take back a memory?' he said.

'Don't bother, you'll have forgotten me in a few weeks, with all those beautiful blonde women over there in Scandinavia,' she said, deliberately swinging her red hair over her shoulders.

'Goodbye, and thank you for a very interesting few days. It was a truly great experience,' he said.

With those words echoing in her head, Helena watched him walk towards the bus stop in the town centre.

She went back into the hotel and her room. The chambermaid was cleaning it so Helena went into the lounge with her notebook to write up the events of the day. Taking her pencil from between her teeth she began to write.

'Many things have been learnt from the first experimental trial of the protocol ...' She stopped and wrote down the numeral 1 on a new line. Then she gazed into the distance, and after a while fell asleep in the soft leather armchair.

At 4.45 pm, as the SAS plane was approaching Copenhagen Airport, Helena changed into new clothes – a tight bra, a clinging white mini skirt and a low-cut top. It was the standard formula.

It had been a very long day. Her body felt spent in every way. Her crotch was aching and sore.

She tried to revive herself with a spritz of perfume, sprayed over her face, arms and breasts. Her skin began to tingle from the alcohol as she left her room.

Balancing in her stiletto shoes, she stepped precariously out of the hotel entrance and climbed straight into the back of a waiting taxi.

9

It was hot and sultry as Helena arrived outside Delphi's Antiquities Museum.

She managed to ease her slim body through the narrow gap, separating the glass doors without opening them, making her way to the desk at the far end of the white marble foyer.

The receptionist looked at Helena's revealing outfit with suspicion and pointed her towards a long, shaded corridor. It was lined with glass cabinets containing pottery from the 2nd and 3rd centuries BC, excavated from the archaeological site between 1902 and 1912.

A huge, grainy black-and-white photograph, blown up to cover the entire wall, hung behind the display cabinets. It showed the ancient site as it looked before the original excavation in 1891.

Helena recognised it as the same picture of Kastri she'd seen on the postcard sent to her mother by Niko. Now enlarged, she saw in full graphic detail the pained expression on the face of an old man pushing a wheelbarrow up the zig-zag path of the ill-fated village.

Green ambled out of his office to greet her, bearing a large smile. As he sidled up towards her, she watched his eyes wander down to below her neckline and stay fixed on her breasts, aware that her bra made them look larger with every inhalation.

She gazed quizzically at the white bandage on his forehead, held in place with brown parcel tape. It smelt of disinfectant, but this was soon masked by a cloud of cigarette smoke as he lit up.

'That's my grandfather pushing the wheelbarrow. He helped to uncover the site,' Green said proudly. Helena looked back at Green's cratered face and struggled to see any family resemblance.

'Looks like back-breaking work,' she said.

'They had no vehicles, no mechanical tools, maybe they used a few donkeys and carts to carry the heavier loads, but you know something?' he placed his hand on her shoulder. 'Everything was dug out with their bare hands.'

'So archaeology is the old family business, Dr Green?' Helena said jokingly, but Green's pock-marked face stayed rigid.

'No, not really He was an amateur, a humble fisherman, he had a small boat, he worked every day of the year, all through the night, out at sea. He thought his grandson deserved better, so I became the archaeologist he'd wanted my father to become,' said Green, blowing cigarette smoke out of his nostrils in short bursts.

Helena wanted to get down to matters affecting the Delacroix family, but felt she should make an effort to engage in polite conversation before interrogating Green about her own grandfather.

'It's a reminder that Delphi was kept hidden from the world for fifteen-hundred years. That's the village which the Church built on top of the ancient pagan city,' she said, pointing at the photograph, 'deliberately used to airbrush pagan Delphi out of history.'

'This place is haunted with the secrets of the past. It's all that exists of Kastri now. Only this photograph and a few tasteless Christian relics,' Green said. 'Come, let's go into my office.'

There was a large fan whirring on his desk. His white cotton shirt inflated with gusts of air every thirty seconds as it rotated. Helena looked around. The desk was littered with archaeology journals, drink cans, and empty packs of Marlboro. On the floor, a duty-free carton was sticking out of his leather briefcase, ripped open at the top.

'Excuse the mess everywhere. I've just come back from the hospital after a small work accident,' he said in a deep monotone.

'Sorry to see you've been injured, Dr Green. What happened?'

'I was excavating a new area of the site and I walked into a piece of scaffolding by the temple, it was stupid of me,' he said, holding his hand over his mouth as he spoke.

Green stubbed the cigarette onto a yellow plastic ashtray, opened a small tin on his desk, and placed a white mint on his tongue. Helena watched as he cracked it into smaller pieces between his molars. She leaned forward and breathed inwards.

'I am searching for information about the discoveries made by my grandfather, Niko Delacroix,' she said, reaching over the desk. Green leered at her breasts and she smiled back.

'Do you think you can help me, Dr Green? I've heard my grandfather discovered a major biblical relic, buried somewhere underground at Delphi. A temple treasure from Jerusalem, I believe,' she said.

After a few seconds, Green leaned back in his chair and coughed.

'So you want to find out about Niko Delacroix's discoveries?' he said, and shook his head.

'Whatever he discovered here my family have a moral right to claim as their property,' she said.

Green laughed out loud like a drunken hyena. 'If only that was possible, my dear. Niko was a highly colourful character, by all accounts,' said Green, his eyes still fixed on Helena's chest. 'I'm afraid I know nothing more.'

'But don't you think the relics he found are still buried there?' she asked, leaning forward again.

'You know something, my dear Helena, anything is possible on an ancient site where fifty percent of the treasure remains unexcavated,' said Green, crunching another mint between his teeth. Helena smelt the cool peppermint vapours drifting from his breath.

'Did you realise that, my dear? Half of the archaeological site at Delphi remains unexcavated, anything could be buried here.'

'Look, Dr Green. Perhaps I haven't explained myself,' she said, coming closer to him. 'My grandfather actually saw the temple treasure. He wrote about it to my mother. It's definitely been found – it's not still buried.'

'You know, I'm so sorry to disappoint you,' he said. 'No one has ever found anything under the mountain in all the years I can remember.'

Helena looked upwards and breathed in deeply. She was beginning to feel that she would not get any morsels from Green.

'OK, let me ask you about something else, Dr Green. Did you ever hear the rumour that Niko may have been killed? Deliberately thrown off the mountain because of this discovery?'

Green pushed back his leather chair and looked at the ceiling, avoiding eye contact with Helena.

'Murdered? But why would anyone do that? I've never come across such a claim, sounds very extreme,' he said, and began to clean his fingernails with a jumbo-sized paper clip.

'The church would have liked him dead.'

'Look, my dear Helena, it all happened such a long time ago,' he said, taking a pottery lamp from his desk. He lit the blackened wick with his cigarette lighter and the lamp flickered to life.

'This is over two-thousand years old and still works perfectly well. It uses olive oil, the same oil they would have used in Roman times,' he said, pushing it towards her. She leaned closer to touch it. A large smile appeared on his face, revealing a gold filling. 'I'm so sorry, Helena my dear. I don't believe I can help you,' he said, rising from his chair.

'Thank you for talking to me. I must be leaving now,' Helena said, and she stood up to go.

Green lit another cigarette and blew a smoke ring towards her, as if he was showing off his skills. As the ring hovered in the air a young child ran into the office.

'Papa, Papa, I found you, at last,' she said, and sat on his knee. She stared at Helena.

Helena breathed inwards. She was not expecting to meet a child and put her arm over her top to cover her partially-exposed breasts.

'Isn't my Isabella beautiful?' said Green.

'Like a Greek doll,' said Helena, turning to leave. 'I'm sorry I have to go now, but if you find out anything about my grandfather do let me know. I'm here until the end of the month.'

'If you give me your address I'll be in touch,' he said. Helena wrote it quickly on a page in her notebook and tore it off. Green took it in his fingers and placed it under a coffee cup on his desk.

Helena left the smoke-filled room and walked through the haze of the early afternoon heat back to the hotel, filling her lungs with fresh, clean air.

As she collected her room key she heard an American accent in reception.

She went back to her room and took another shower to wash off the smell of Green's smoke rings. Feeling refreshed, she told herself that she had to keep going – for the sake of the research project.

If her orgasm research was to have scientific credibility she needed to gather at least ten subjects.

Forcing herself to stay awake, wearing a whole new outfit – a black uplift bra, a low cut top, a black short skirt and stilettos – she walked down to the bar in the name of science.

10

Looking down at the jagged white peaks of the Italian Alps from inside the Boeing jet, Helena chewed hungrily at her crimson-lacquered fingernails.

In her hands she was clutching an unopened miniature bottle of Beaujolais.

The decision to leave Delphi earlier than planned had not been hard to make. She felt sure she could fudge the number of subjects with whom she'd had sex and turn her PhD into a narrative study rather than a traditional scientific investigation.

Pressing four small white tablets of *Loestrin* out of the blister packet, she swallowed a high dose of the pill. She knew it was rather simplistic and crude biological thinking, but she'd heard from her doctor friend that a large dose of oestrogen could work as a morning-after pill if she'd forgotten to take her tablets for a few days.

Sitting in the cramped aircraft seat, Helena's mind travelled back to the day when her life had changed, two months earlier, in her mother's elegant Parisian apartment.

Now on the way back from her mission to Delphi she was feeling tormented by her distinct lack of success.

She'd failed to find any tunnel entrances in the mountainside. Moses would not be happy.

And her meeting with Dr Green had been a waste of time. It had only convinced her that Green was a compulsive, chain-smoking liar, with disgusting personal habits. Remembering the smell of his tobacco breath, only partially masked by the mint in his mouth, made her feel nauseous.

She took a sip from a bottle of water on her folding tray. The only thing she'd discovered was that Green was covering up the discovery of the Delphic Anomaly by her grandfather. His body language had said it all. He was a man with no conscience.

Helena decided that this is what she would tell her mother, but feared she'd be disappointed. Maria was a determined woman. She would fight to resurrect the Delacroix name until she took her last breath.

And what of Moses? What would she tell him? He was a more reasonable proposition, a pragmatic fellow who understood the vagaries of hunting down antiquities. Conveniently for Helena, she had sweetened their relationship with sensual pleasures, and she felt confident he would remain firmly under her spell.

She knew she could easily seduce Moses, on the floor of his apartment, in a hotel bedroom or wherever he felt like having her. He was a relaxed, patient man, and would accept her lack of progress. He understood that some things can take a lifetime to achieve – and he had time on his side.

But what of his belief that the experiment would change her life. His certainty of this result continued to gnaw at her anxiety levels. It made her laugh. If only it were true. She knew she would soon be heading back to a predictable pattern of Parisian existence. University–doctorate–liaisons–family tensions–love affairs–eat–sleep–movies.

The blonde Olympic Airways stewardess roused Helena from her doze and asked if she wanted the chicken or the tuna for lunch. The foil pack arrived and Helena pulled open the lid revealing the steaming food inside, and pushed the plastic fork into the warm chicken. It tasted like tuna. She gave up on the food, drank the rest of the wine, and shut her eyes.

Inside the cabin of the Boeing 727 the engine hum changed to a higher pitch and the wing flaps extended outwards to slow the aircraft for the final approach.

The safety belt signs lit up as Helena rehearsed what she

would say to her mother. It was a good distraction from the disturbing clunking noises made by the landing gear as the jet approached the runway three-thousand feet below.

Helena looked out of the window, gripping the armrest of her seat as the plane slid onto the tarmac.

She took a gulp of air, unfolded herself from the cramped seat, and wriggled around the armrests. As she walked down the gangway Helena realised she was re-entering the zone of real life.

After two weeks of sunshine, sea, and sex, it was a frightening thought.

Warm rain drizzled onto her shoulders as she walked down the gangplank of the plane and made her way to the arrivals lounge at Orly. She queued with the other French passengers at immigration control, and within minutes was waved through. She took a taxi back to her apartment in the 16th arrondissement.

On opening the double locks on the front door, her home looked like a rented apartment that had not been lived in for a few months. There was a smell of plaster and Persian rugs, but none of the comforting smells of recent habitation by another human being. No fresh baguettes, no bolognese sauce, no red wine or coffee aromas wafted into her nostrils. No sweat, no soap, and no deodorant had been used here for some time. It could have been an untouched hotel bedroom. She felt alone and empty as she walked slowly around the high-ceilinged rooms.

Her bedroom, its untouched bed, the double pillows placed centrally for a single occupant, looked sterile. It was not a place of warmth or passion. Her husband Michel was still away after two weeks in Geneva but would be back around 7.00 pm. She took her second shower of the day, trying to wash away the sweat of the journey and any lingering male smells from the last sexual encounter in Delphi.

She would like to have had more subjects for the experiment but felt drained by the whole process. Initiating the contact took longer than she'd planned. The security guards at the temple had also prevented further research being carried out, with their nightly patrols. She was sure they'd been taking pictures.

Helena's main hope was that she could make use of the first experiment with the Dane. She looked at her notes and believed that there was enough material for analytical purposes, if it was treated as a narrative case history, with supplementary data from the American and the Japanese.

She was dozing on the bed when she heard the front door click open and Michel stepped into the room. They embraced politely. There was no lingering kiss. She always found it difficult to show much affection after a separation.

He was expensively dressed and wore a blue suit and a white shirt. A mathematician, he used his analytical skills in the international markets for a Swiss hedge fund.

He had it all – a salary with a bonus in the higher six-figures range, and a stunning wife in Helena. When she accompanied him on official functions, he liked to brag that she was, 'the only archaeologist in Paris who looked like a movie actress.' Why she'd married him so young was a mystery to her family. They'd had a glamorous wedding. It boosted her ego.

How could such a wild and provocative woman want to be under the thumb of one man? The truth was that they led separate lives much of the time, but she enjoyed their sexually satisfying reunions. And his money. Money was a powerful aphrodisiac for her, but she insisted on staying independent, preferring to use her charm and sexuality than go begging to Michel. His job whisked him from Paris to Geneva every month so he could have private time with his mistresses.

It also left her time to play.

At first he worshipped her or, more to the point, her tight svelte body. And she was happy with that. She enjoyed wielding her erotic power over him.

When they touched and their eyes met she could see he found her painfully attractive. Her body responded to him in a most enjoyable way.

He bought her erotic underwear and she liked to dress up for him and make him wild with uninhibited desire.

He made it clear that he could never have too much of her. It was the rampant physicality of their relationship she revelled in most of all.

But today was different. At 7.30 pm, when she heard the door of the apartment open, she sprang up and ran over to put her arms around him, but within seconds Michel was bristling with irritation.

'You smell different,' they both said to each other, at the same time.

'It's not an accusation,' Helena said, trying to mollify him.

Michel turned away. Out of sight, he unbuckled his Italian leather briefcase and took out a small cardboard box, gift-wrapped with a satin ribbon. He turned round to face her and placed it in the palm of her hand. Opening the box, she found a heavy object, swaddled in tissue paper. She teased it open and discovered an antique silver necklace, encrusted with dazzling clusters of green gemstones, each the size of a small grape.

'I love it. It looks Middle Eastern and very old.'

'It's more than old, it's ancient,' he said. Helena unfolded the accompanying note and read it aloud.

'To the sexiest woman in Paris. I will always stay with you. M x.'

Helena was moved by the dedication and hugged him again. She knew this was no tourist memento, and would have required serious bidding at an auction house.

Michel held her waist for a minute, kissed her face, and slid his fingers down to her crotch.

'And you know, there is an extraordinary story about its provenance,' he said fingering her wet lips.

'What do you know about it?' she said, smothering his hand with kisses.

'You'll like the story. It's extraordinary. It was part of Freud's personal collection. He was a collector of Egyptian art, and sold this necklace to a private collector, to help pay for a house in London after he was forced out of Vienna by the Nazis in 1939.'

'And I've just been there – to Vienna, I mean,' she said, as Moses' face came to mind. 'It's so extraordinary to think that this was owned by the father of psychoanalysis,' she said, sniffing whilst trying to wipe away her tears with the back of her hand.

Michel smiled and tried to dry her tears with his fingers.

'I love everything that Freud wrote. He was a rare genius,' she said, as Michel began to unbutton her blouse.

'It would look good against your bare skin, on your new Greek tan,' he said as his fingers felt for her breasts. Helena could sense that after three weeks of his Swiss mistress he now wanted to see his own wife in the nude.

Offering no resistance, she wriggled out of her blouse, untied the front clip of her silk bra and let it fall onto the floor. She sat on their bed, naked to the waist, as Michel carefully tied the chain around her neck.

'I'd like to appreciate it on its own,' he said.

Helena obliged and removed the rest of her clothes and lay down. They shared only a few brief moments of sex. He came quickly and Helena stared blankly at the ceiling all through their half-hearted reunion.

Lying on their bed she felt she could have been any woman

he'd just picked up in a hotel lobby.

It didn't compare with Delphi or Vienna. But it got them physically closer and triggered a conversation.

'What happened with your investigation of Niko's hidden treasure, the so-called Delphic Anomaly? Did you make any progress?' Michel asked. 'Your mother will want to know what she got for her thirty-thousand francs,' he laughed.

'I found out nothing, or nothing I didn't know,' she said, explaining that she'd gone to some trouble to see the slimy Dr Green. She lit a Gauloises and exhaled quickly. The high dose of nicotine flowing through her lungs made her feel light-headed for a few seconds.

As she held it smouldering in her fingers, she looked towards the floor and realised there was more energy in the way she smoked than in the way she'd just made love.

'He lied to me through his disgusting brown teeth,' she said.

'Even with your charm offensive, which I'm sure you tried on him?'

'He claimed he knew nothing. But he was such a transparent liar. I suppose I'll have to tell my mother that the whole Greek adventure was a waste of time, apart from my PhD research into the Elena Text.'

'So what did Green actually say?' Michel said as he put on his shirt.

'That he knew nothing, but whenever I asked him a question he displayed the body language of a man telling lies,' she said, pulling up her stockings.

Michel screwed up his face, as if he didn't follow her train of thought.

'People cover their mouths when they lie. It's not rocket science, it's simple psychology,' she said, attaching her stocking to her black suspender belt.

'That's sexy. I should have asked you to keep it on as we made love.'

'Sure. Next time I won't get undressed. It'll be more fun.'

'But you were sceptical anyway, weren't you?' he said. 'And you didn't really care about your mother's obsession.'

Helena shrugged. 'I was happy to play along with her. It made us talk, but I admit I always thought that my grandfather Niko was a wildcard. He must have been a pretty crazy guy.'

'That didn't stop you buying into the ancient text he found,' Michel said, smiling at her.

'Niko was either crazy or a genius, they are that close,' she said, holding up her thumb and forefinger a quarter of an inch apart. 'And the Elena Text has been proved genuine anyway.' Helena's tone of voice changed. She didn't like anyone criticising the subject of her doctoral thesis.

'Leave it Michel. It's been verified by carbon dating. It's in the French National Library for Christ's sake. It's an acclaimed ancient Greek text which has been studied by scholars for many years. Its cultural significance has been the subject of dozens of academic papers. What more do you want from me? A copy written in my own blood?'

She looked up at him. 'And you know, Michel, I think I've now got the evidence to prove the authenticity of the most sensational claim in the Elena Text.'

Michel had not been told the exact purpose and details of her latest trip to Delphi. She'd told him that she was going over to do preliminary research, to take a closer look at the Temple of Apollo, to study the archaeology and take measurements and photographs. In her state of anxiety about the whole project she'd been happy to let him think that was it.

He took her in his arms and kissed her neck.

'So tell me, when shall we go to Delphi and test it out?' he asked.

Helena was silent for a minute and started to shake her head. 'I don't think we'll need to do that,' she said, looking away and avoiding his gaze. He stood back from her and watched her bury her face in her hands.

'What do you mean?' he asked abruptly.

'It's OK, we don't have to anymore.'

'You've already tested it, haven't you? You've been testing the orgasm theory with other men. Admit the truth, I can see it in your eyes,' he said softly, but with anger in his strained voice.

Helena bit her lip and felt a tear slide down her cheek.

'Now I understand why you didn't come to me for the money,' said Michel bitterly.

'My research is a Delecroix matter. It's nothing to do with you,' spat Helena. 'And I'm sure you were living the life of a monk in Geneva.'

Michel went silent and walked off and poured himself a beer.

Helena switched on the TV and flicked through the channels.

As she came to the shopping channel selling jewellery, she began to feel queasy and ran to the bathroom.

PART TEN

Peter

1

The psychologist's office was a sunny room on the first floor of a nineteenth-century house in the Marais quarter. Helena sat on a comfortable single sofa, her back to a large window overlooking the garden.

'Please continue, in your own time. You told me that you had returned from Delphi and had a reunion with your husband Michel. What was the next event in your life?'

Helena half smiled and looked at the polished wooden floor. 'I eventually realised I was pregnant. I was in denial about it. I had very mixed feelings. I wasn't ready to have kids.' She hesitated. 'And I wasn't sure who the father was, either – if I'm honest with myself.'

Helena sighed and put her hands over her face. 'Nevertheless, I gave birth to my son Peter eight and half months after returning from the research trip to Delphi.'

Helena stopped for some kind of a reaction from the therapist, but there was no response.

'I'm sorry, I thought you'd want to say something about the birth of my son.'

'No, no, it's fine, we'll talk later, go on. You're doing well, Helena.'

'He was christened Peter Charles Nicholas Delacroix. My husband, Michel, was listed on the birth certificate as the father, but I wanted my son to have the Delacroix name. Why not? I'm a feminist.

'What was good was that the birth of our first child brought Michel and I closer together. We became a family, rather than two individuals leading almost separate lives.

'Peter is the great-grandson of the archaeologist Dr Niko

Delacroix. He was the first grandson of Maria Delacroix, a milestone for her. The Delacroix line would continue for another generation. As she saw it, the birth of Peter was a real chance to clear the family name and she rewarded him with unconditional love.

'From the start Maria felt very warmly towards Peter. It was the first time in many years that she felt uninhibitedly affectionate towards another person, something she was never able to express for me. Peter was easy to love, he carried no baggage – at first. It was an adoring relationship between Maria and a grandchild, and nothing held her back.

'He seemed a normal and healthy child, unaffected by the cocktail of drugs and hormones I had consumed earlier in the pregnancy. I had been worried about this, but he was fine.

'That was until he turned three and we decided to go on a family holiday to Greece. He must have heard me say "Delphi" at some point. From that day on kept saying he wanted to go there.

'We arrived in mid-June, one day before the summer solstice, staying at the Hotel Miramar near the centre of town.

'When we arrived we walked through the village and it triggered something in him, it seemed. He stormed off uncontrollably, running all the way through the main street and into the archaeological site, finding his own way to the temple. He seemed to know the exact route. It was uncanny.

'I chased after him but Peter ran past the ticket barrier at the entrance, up the hill, and towards the Temple Mount. The security people were amused at first by such a young child and I was told I needed to control him, as he might cause an accident or hurt himself if he didn't look where he was going.

'But the strange fact is that little Peter seemed to know exactly where he was going.

"'Is this your little boy?" the security man asked me. He was a balding man with a round face and a thick black moustache – it was an unforgettable face. As he spoke to me, the hairs on the back of my neck tingled. I didn't recognise him at first, but unconsciously I had not forgotten this man.

"'Don't I know you from somewhere?" he said to me rather loudly. "I'm sure we've met here before." I pretended to not hear him, and tried to avoid an encounter. I just carried on as if he had said nothing. I was praying he would not ask me again.

'Then I remembered who he was. I remembered his face from the morning I began the research. It was the same man I'd smiled at when I walked half-naked past the security hut, on the morning of the summer solstice four years earlier.

'He looked at me and shouted again. He wasn't going to let it go. My face had been haunting him, it seemed.

"'Hey, I'm really sure I know you from somewhere," he said to me.

'I asked him to leave me alone, but he persisted. It seemed he wanted confirmation.

"'I'm *sure* we've met before" he said, yet again.

"'I don't think so, really," I said, lying through my teeth. I could feel my body flush bright red with embarrassment. I was also anxious that Michel would soon catch up with me.'

'Was that the end of the episode?'

'Not at all, it was only the beginning.'

'I had caught Peter but he started to scream. He was twisting and pulling at my hand, so I let him run to the top of the hill at the Temple Mount, and caught up with him a few moments later. When I reached the inner sanctum of the Temple everything become quiet. Peter had fallen asleep on the temple mount, or maybe he was unconscious, I don't know, I was petrified, I didn't know what was happening to him. His head was on the marble floor, and he was curled up. I shook him, but he wouldn't wake up.

'Michel arrived a moment later, and said, "Has he had a seizure? My younger brother suffered from them as a child. We need to keep an eye on him."

'It was at this point I began to wonder if the drugs I'd taken early in the pregnancy had affected Peter's brain and given him epilepsy. We shook him and he woke up.

'"I was having a funny dream," he said. "I was in the dark, it was cold, but then rays of sunlight warmed me up and brought me back to life."

'I'm not a child psychologist, but his language was not like that of a three year old. His understanding of concepts and his vocabulary seemed far beyond that of such a young child.

'It's strange to say this, but I felt that Peter's dream was an exact description of the sunrise on that morning of the summer solstice four years earlier. I remembered feeling cold on that momentous morning and later feeling the warmth on my skin as the sun rose into the sky. I'm only saying this because I remembered this was the spot where I made love to the anonymous Dane, years earlier.'

'And what happened after that?'

'Oh, we just made our way back to the village from the archaeological site and that was that. Apart from one strange thing. After this, every morning, Peter would wake us at dawn in the hotel bedroom. He would ask to visit the Temple of Apollo, saying he wanted to go back to the "warm" place.

'I would ask him if he'd had that bad dream again, and he would say he had. This daily ritual began to unsettle me. I decided we had to leave Delphi as I could not bear going back to the temple again and again. Peter had become obsessed with the place.

'So we decided to do some island-hopping and visited Zante.

'We drove 120 km to the port of Piraeus and waited in the ferry queue. Peter did not suffer from any further incidents. His nightmares disappeared. He loved swimming in the warm crystal-clear waters. He played on the beach, just like a normal kid with his parents. He made friends with other children. It was blissful – finally.

'On our last evening on Zante, at around 10.30, we drove the short distance to Laganas for a meal at a beach taverna. After the meal, shortly before midnight, we were walking along the promenade when we saw a crowd gathering on the sands.

'I asked a local fisherman what was happening. He told us that the turtles were returning to the beach to lay their eggs. We stood and watched the once-a-year arrival of nearly two-thousand loggerhead turtles at this particular beach.

'Peter was completely mesmerised by the sight of dozens of turtles crawling out of the sea under the light of the moon, onto the sandy beach. The turtles waddled onto the sand, dug shallow holes with their flippers and, in a moment of triumph, laid their eggs inside. Finally, with a flick of their flippers, the turtles covered the eggs with sand. A few minutes later they disappeared into the depths of the Mediterranean sea. It was so enthralling to see with our own eyes.

'But then, Peter made a most remarkable comment for a three year old. He said, "isn't it clever that the turtles know where to come each year?"

'I thought about it and it reminded me that people, like turtles, do things they do not fully understand. The turtles, you see, return to the same beach many years after being hatched there. Of all the possible beaches in the Mediterranean, those turtles somehow retain the knowledge to return to that beach on Zante.

'The parallels between Peter's strange behaviour in Delphi

and the turtles' arrival on the beach were too obvious to avoid.

'I know it may sound fanciful, but I seriously wondered if Peter had been somehow compelled to return to the Temple Mount in Delphi because he knew he had been conceived there.

'It was as if he had some unconscious knowledge of where he was conceived. Is that possible? It sounds strange, but after seeing the turtles crawling out of the sea onto the beach at Zante it no longer seemed such a crazy idea. I wondered – if a turtle can retain knowledge of where it was hatched and conceived to return years later, then perhaps it is not a huge leap to think that human beings can do the same thing.

'Maybe all creatures are programmed to return to the place of their conception.

'Perhaps this is our human destiny – to make the one essential journey every human being has to make, back to the place where they were created. The more I think about it the more it seems to make some kind of sense. Why not?'

'It's an interesting idea. Thank you very much Mme Delacroix. We will continue next week at the same time.'

2

Helena downed a final mouthful of black coffee as Peter played with a toy tractor at the breakfast table.

'Can we return to Delphi on the summer solstice, next year?' he said, whilst pushing the boat across the table. She looked surprised at her three-year-old's use of the word 'solstice.'

'Do you actually know what the solstice is?' Helena asked, convinced she'd never used the word around him, realising she could never be sure what he might have overheard.

'I love that Solstice day,' he said.

'Why do you like the solstice so much?' Helena asked, expecting to get a child-like reply.

'It's my birthday present from the god Apollo,' said Peter confidently. She smiled at him, wondering where he'd heard about the sun god.

'But it's not your birthday on the solstice,' she said.

'Don't you know, *maman*? I have *two* birthdays every year,' he said with all the certainty of a bright child.

'Oh, I see,' said Helena, trembling. 'So you think you have *two* birthdays? Clever boy. I see, you want to have double the number of birthday presents, is that it?'

'Oh, I didn't think of that,' he told his mother, and looked back at her as if he was hurt.

'So tell me, when are your *two* birthdays?' she asked in a soft, kindly voice.

'Well, my first birthday is on the day of the summer solstice and the other one is, let me see,' he said, and began to count using his small fingers. 'Yes, I know it. It's on April 2nd,' Peter replied.

Helena went to the calendar hanging on the wall of the kitchen and did some quick sums to check the date. She saw there was a forty-week difference between the date of the summer solstice June 21st and Peter's birthday on April 2nd the following year.

She could not understand how he had calculated the length of a full-term pregnancy so accurately.

'Everyone has *two* birthdays, not just me,' he said. Helena needed more coffee but there was none left in her cup. The cafetiere was drained. She went to the fridge for a carton of orange juice and poured herself a glass.

As she sat down again, she gripped her hands to reduce the tension she could feel rising through her body.

'Look, my darling. You can only have *one* birthday, I'm afraid. It's all everyone is given,' Helena told him emphatically.

'No!' he shouted at her. 'You're wrong, *maman*. First, everyone has to be created, that's when their soul is made – that is your *first* birthday. And when you come out of the mother's tummy, that's your *second* birthday, I told you that before,' he said, twisting his fingers with irritation.

'I see what you're saying now,' said Helena, who was shaking. 'Tell me, who told you about having two birthdays?' she asked him, not expecting an answer of any great insight.

'I know it. It's there in my thoughts. Like I know when I'm hungry. No one told me. No one tells me I'm hungry, I know it myself,' he told Helena.

She could not decide if Peter had a profound understanding of something beyond his years, or whether his ideas where simply the imaginative thoughts of a curious child.

Helena picked up the phone and was about to dial when she stopped herself. After a few moments she pressed Maria's name on the auto dial.

Helena could not speak for several seconds as she tried to unknot her fingers from the telephone cord.

'Are you alright?' her mother asked.

'No, not really. Can I come and see you later tonight?'

3

Helena poured a second glass of wine as she waited for her neighbour's daughter to arrive.

There was a knock at the door as she gulped down the remains of a bottle of Cabernet Sauvignon and Julie, a mature fourteen-year-old girl, who looked more like sixteen or seventeen, walked confidently into the house with her own set of keys.

'Peter's watching a video, he may have fallen asleep. I think I'll leave without saying goodbye, it's easier that way – back by eleven, I promise,' Helena said, grabbing her bag in a hurry and leaving the house.

She drove herself to Maria's elegant penthouse in rue Raynouard, shooting through two sets of red lights. Arriving fifteen minutes later she stepped out of the car unsteadily, realising she should've taken a taxi.

The elevator took her up to the apartment and Maria welcomed her with a cursory embrace, casting her eyes away from Helena and looking at the new Chagall canvas hanging in the hall.

'Isn't it wonderful?' There was no response from Helena. She looked up and her eyes glazed over at the sight of another expressionist painting in her mother's apartment.

'It's beautiful, but I need to talk to you about Peter,' she said, turning away from the painting.

They went into the main salon and Maria poured her a glass of cognac.

'I'm sure Peter is fine. He's an intelligent young child, he's so aware of everything,' said Maria.

'But he knows things he shouldn't know, for a child of only three,' Helena said.

She clutched the warm brandy glass in both hands, her fingers stretched round the onion shape.

'What is it Helena? I've never seen you look so tense.'

Helena looked at mother and slid her tongue over her dry lips. The alcohol was making her feel dehydrated. 'Don't laugh at me when I say this, but Peter remembers where he was conceived,' she said. Maria stepped back in surprise and laughed.

'Are you crazy, Helena? You don't believe in all that nonsense? It's anti-science,' Maria said, cupping her daughter's hands in her own. 'Look at me,' she said. Helena twisted around to face her. 'You really don't need to screw yourself up with all that mumbo jumbo.'

'You're wrong, *maman*. It's not incompatible with science. It's all possible, look at what Einstein discovered.'

Maria rolled her eyes and put her hand on her cheek. 'Children say strange things—'

'—and Michel may not be his father,' Helena said in a low voice, running her fingers through her hair.

'That's what happens when you perform sex rituals at the Temple of Apollo. The Gods give you an extraordinary child in return! Look, this will sound shocking, but it doesn't matter who the biological father is. It's the father in the home that counts,' said Maria, as she looked into the fireplace and watched the flames flicker. 'You do realise I had a critical part to play in these events? You could say it's all my fault.'

Helena shook her head and looked back at her with a puzzled expression.

'Yes, you can blame me. I made the Delphi research possible. I remember handing you a brown envelope, stuffed with thirty thousand francs. Peter wouldn't have been conceived there if you hadn't done your PhD research in Delphi.'

Helena turned away abruptly as she felt the blood rushing

into her cheeks. Her face felt like it was on fire. 'Peter's not an accident of my research, he's a human being,' she began to shout at her mother.

'Calm down and be quiet, Helena. The neighbours will hear everything. Just be grateful you have a child, a son and heir, to carry through the Delacroix line.'

Helena closed her eyes to block out the light in the room and pressed her fingers into her ears. She saw Peter playing on the beach at Zante. Turtles were dragging themselves out of the sea and digging holes for their eggs.

'Peter will come good, he's a special child,' Maria said.

'I want an ordinary boy, I don't want him to be special.' said Helena, slowly and precisely, still red with anger. She drained the last drops of brandy into her mouth and stood up to leave.

As she opened the door to the hallway she paused and gave her mother a guilty look. She knew she hadn't behaved very well.

Maria put her arms around her daughter.

'He will surprise us all. I know it.'

4

Peter Delacroix parked badly and hurried out of his car towards his grandmother's penthouse apartment in rue Raynouard, Paris 16.

He was late and didn't care if he got a ticket.

'She's been waiting for you all morning,' said Louis, as Peter swung through the revolving entrance of the luxury apartment block.

He was out of breath as the mirrored doors of the elevator closed around him. The motors silently defied gravity and took him up to the seventh floor. Stepping out of the elevator, he stood in front of the door to brush down his jacket and tuck in his shirt.

Juliet, the Corsican maid, opened the heavy teak door and they kissed on both cheeks. He squeezed her waist with one hand, and ran his fingers down her neck with the other, lingering at the top of her heaving breasts.

He kissed them and walked into his grandmother's bedroom.

Maria was lying on her bed and smiled as soon as Peter came into the elegant room.

Her bony fingers, swollen with arthritis, stopped shaking and she began to step down from the bed.

He tried to help her but she pushed him away, walking across the room unaided, stepping lightly around the Louis XVI furniture.

She paused for a moment in front of the Chagall, staring at the starlit sky. A white goat was flying over the moon while a violinist played outside a church.

'Given to me by the artist himself. It represents everything I am not. It's irrational, dreamlike and whimsical,' she said with a sigh. 'I always knew I had to be the hard-headed and business-minded member of the family – unlike the other Delacroixs.'

Peter sensed a criticism of his mother coming down the track and tried to change the subject. It was something he was used to hearing over the years. Helena's risqué activities as a twenty-something had left an indelible mark. And there was the assumption that, as he had her genes, he was also a wild card – impulsive and out of control. Deep down, he knew there was some truth in it, especially in connection with his sexual appetite.

'I'm really sorry, I was delayed … by the traffic,' he said hesitantly, looking down to make sure his shirt was tucked in.

'I've been waiting a long time for you, Peter,' said Maria, in a warm voice devoid of any criticism.

'It's fine, you have your own life to lead. You're an adult,' she said, making it clear that her love for her grandson was unconditional. She opened a drawer on her desk and took out a small white package, sealed with black tape.

'This is for you. Open it later.' He took it in his hand, trying to feel the contents through the bubble wrap liner. Maria's eyes were watering – something was troubling her.

'No, don't ask me about it now, please. I just want to make sure you have it in your hands,' she said, as Peter felt it with his fingers.

'I need to tell you about something important,' she said. He looked up sheepishly, concerned he was about to receive a lecture.

'Don't worry, Peter, this is about me, not you,' she said, walking to the door and shutting it firmly.

'Sorry I had to do that, but Helena has been staying – she's asleep in the spare room,' she said, reducing her voice to a whisper. 'I don't want her to hear our conversation.'

'It's OK, I understand,' he said, nodding. Maria sat down in her armchair and stared out of the window. Without turning to Peter she began to speak in a flat monologue.

'They've succeeded in silencing me for most of my life. They were experts in the psychology of punishment,' she said, pausing to look down at the floor.

'What are you talking about?' he asked. She ignored his question, stood up and started to perform a series of Tai Chi moves.

'This keeps me going. I don't care what they do to me now,' she said, her voice returning to normal. As she turned her head back towards the window, her grey eyes began to flicker in the sunlight.

'I still don't know what this is all about,' Peter said standing opposite her. 'Who are "they"?'

'Come closer to me, Peter,' she said. He looked around the room and pulled over a chair so he could sit opposite her.

'To explain who "they" are I need to tell you about a strange event I witnessed, about thirty years ago. It happened in Delphi – it was totally unexpected,' she said deliberately. He looked towards her, completely puzzled by what she was saying.

'You look so surprised – maybe even shocked,' she said.

'I don't understand. Why are you telling me *now*, so many years after it happened?'

She sighed and took a deep breath. 'Because I was forbidden from saying anything about it – they made serious threats against me and the family,' she said, gesticulating with her hands. Maria was one-quarter Italian, and those Roman genes still showed themselves through her lively hand gestures when she talked.

'Now you're an adult, on the cusp of your own career, I need to explain certain things. You were far too young to understand before,' she said, pausing for breath.

Peter leaned forward, hand on chin, keen and curious but also slightly wary of her.

'Also, I have something I want you to do for the family *now*,' Maria said, moving closer to him. 'I trust you, Peter, above everyone else.' She paused again and put her hands on his shoulders. 'There's an important task I want you to carry out. It won't be easy, but I want you to try.'

He sat back and shook his head, still confused.

'What do you want me to do?' Peter said slowly. A grey pallor began to colour his face.

'I want you to clear our family name.' Maria shook her head in despair. 'It upsets me that our Delacroix name remains blackened by the scandal involving your great-grandfather and that manuscript he discovered.'

'You mean the Elena Text?' Peter said, and she glanced back at him.

'Yes, the Text. He was treated badly. But look, he did what he believed was right at the time. He was a maverick, it's the family trait, but an honest man.' She looked Peter in the eye. 'I can see it in you, too,' she said, and he smiled back at her.

'Be careful Peter, not everyone likes a maverick. They're too threatening, they don't fit easily into a box. They have a mind and a will of their own, unlike most people.'

'No, we Delacroix don't conform much, do we?' he said.

'Never – and that's where the trouble begins.'

'So what happened to you at Delphi?' Peter said, catching sight of his watch and desperate to hear her story before she became too exhausted. He knew half an hour was normally her limit.

'To put it simply, this may sound far-fetched. I was arrested by the Greek police, who were working with the Americans. Their secret service, you know – the CIA.'

'What?' Peter was lost for words.

'Greece was like an American colony in those days. They didn't release me until I'd signed a legal document, an affidavit, assuring them I'd never say anything about what I'd seen take place in Delphi. They said they'd harm my family if I broke my agreement. So this is why you've never heard any of this before.'

'My God, what *did* you see that they were so worried about?' Peter said, scratching his chin.

'I saw something I should've never have seen,' she said.

'Come here,' she said, beckoning to him. 'You know, you're more important to me than my own life,' she said. He knelt beside her and she stroked his face. 'We'll have to continue another day, I'm tired now,' she began, and started to drift, but recovered for a moment.

'I'm old now. It's time you knew the truth,' she said before her eyes closed. Her hand fell away from his cheek and he clasped it as she struggled to stay awake. Her energy drained away as fast as it had appeared. Within a few seconds she was asleep.

Peter placed a pillow under her head and walked unhurriedly into the kitchen, shutting the door behind him.

Juliet was waiting for him, sitting seductively on a kitchen stool, a bird of paradise in her turquoise and crimson silk blouse. She smiled as she undid the top buttons to reveal her tanned cleavage underneath the silk. Next to her, on a wooden board, were cloves of garlic, freshly chopped parsley and coriander, and a lemon in two halves.

Peter took her hand and licked her fingers. 'She's fallen asleep,' he said, looking at his watch. 'But it's later than I thought.' He backed away from her slightly.

'Don't go yet. You can stay a few more minutes. She's asleep, she won't wake up for an hour at least,' said Juliet.

'We'll have to make it another time. I'll text you tomorrow,' he said, but she grabbed his belt, pulled him back, and began to unzip his fly.

He protested as she took hold of his half-excited organ, knelt down, and put it in her mouth. 'Look Juliet, I'm busy at work. There's a new client coming tomorrow from Greece. Waterbury's have called me in, I need to …' His voice trailed off as she alternately licked and kissed him.

'Oh my God, don't, please, I have to go now,' he said breathlessly.

After two minutes of intense sucking, she stopped abruptly and pushed him away. He zipped himself up and tried to kiss her goodbye.

'Looks like you're in the middle of making lunch, anyway,' he said, walking half-bent towards the elevator. 'Sorry Juliet, next time, I promise I'll ...' he tried to shout through the narrowing gap as the doors came together.

PART ELEVEN

Anna and Moses

1

The phone came to life and Moses read the screen.

> I'm in town. Can I come and see you?
> Anna N.

Moses looked twice at the name. Anna who? Could it be Anna Nemcova? After all this time? He put his hand on his head and began to recall moments from the time they'd spent together some twenty-five years earlier. His memories were clear as daylight. He saw her wispy Day-glo green hair, her ethereal and uncertain smile. He saw her turning the pages of the battered *Materia Medica*.

Could she still be the green-haired Anna of years ago? Maybe she had teenage kids by now? Had her figure changed from the thin, lanky look with small but perfect breasts?

He would be happy to find out. He started to tap a reply.

> Hello stranger, sure would love to see you
> again. please call me. Mx. PS how did you
> find my number?

Within a few minutes Anna's reply had bounced back and they'd agreed to lunch near the Leopold Tower on Johannestrasse. They met in Cafe Salonika, a small Greek restaurant on the corner of Schubertring.

Moses stood in a daze as Anna entered. He was overwhelmed. He could not believe how young she still looked despite the years that had passed. The bright green stripe had morphed into long blonde hair down her back, tapering into an arrow head. They embraced with a polite kiss, followed by a long, tight hug which seemed in proportion to the number of years that had passed.

'It's been too long, Moses,' she said, sliding her fingers down the stem of her wine glass.

'You look – well, what can I say? Amazing. Younger than ever. I can't believe it,' Moses said as he sipped a Frizzante Frascati.

'Well, I was passing through Vienna and wondered if you were still based here. I couldn't resist seeing if … you were the same Moses I remembered.'

'So what are you doing tonight?' Moses asked hopefully.

'I've a room at the Metropole, on expenses with Hypericum. Yes, sorry, I still work for them, I know I should have moved on, but I like what I do. I enjoy discovering new herbal-based drugs, sorting out their herbarium. They sent me to the Brazilian rainforest a few times.'

'Married? Any children?'

'Oh yes, that was between having my two daughters,' she said, producing her phone and showing him two teenage girls.

'And you, Moses? Still running the secret antiquities auction house? And are you married with kids?' she asked, touching his hand across the table.

Moses smiled as she played with his fingers. He felt himself become rigid and was reminded that Anna always had a physical effect on him.

'Still at it, I'm afraid, it's what I know best. And yes, I have a daughter. It was unplanned, she was a beautiful surprise. I'm not married, I cherish my freedom, I don't think I could live every day with the same person. It would drive me crazy.'

'And did anything ever happen with the Delphic Anomaly? Was it ever excavated?'

Moses buried his head in his hands for a second and slowly opened his fingers to look at her. 'Poor old Dr Green has been promising me every year that he's going to excavate it. But he's had big logistical problems. Floods, subsidence – you name it, he's had it. He always has a good excuse. Every now and then he'll call me and tell me it's finally about to happen. And then silence. And yet more silence. So it goes on. But I haven't given up all hope,' he said, pouring wine into their glasses.

'I remember it was going to mark a turning point in your life. You always said you wanted to do something for posterity,' Anna said, fingering her hair.

'I haven't given up. Let's say it's still simmering. Certain major organisations, even governments, have tried to scare me off, but I'm not bothered by them. You have to do what you believe in, don't you?'

'What do you mean "tried to scare you off"?' she asked.

'I'm not sure I should tell you.'

'No one will ever hear this, I promise you,' she said, shaking her head and then sealing her lips with a swipe of her finger.

'OK, it's fine. I believe you, Anna. I went to see an influential friend in Jerusalem who runs the National Museum, and intelligence officers from Mossad, I think that's who they were, arrested me at the airport and took me to an interrogation centre and left me with a pretty clear message – don't bring the Delphic Anomaly anywhere near Israel, it will cause a war between Arab and Jewish extremists. So since then I've kept my activities much more under wraps.' He drank his wine.

'So are you still going to excavate it?' Anna said, biting her lip.

'I don't know. I hope it's still possible,' Moses said, looking down. 'But everything has changed in the Middle East with the new treaty.'

'It would be such a great symbol for peace,' she said.

Moses smiled at her and reached across the table to touch her arm. 'I would like to, but you don't mess around with Mossad,' he said.

Anna leaned forward, putting the fingers of both hands together to make a pyramid. 'And how about the church? What about your old jousting partner in Rome, Guillini? Is he still running the Vatican Secret Service? Still doing unspeakable things on behalf of the Pope?' she asked.

Moses shook his head with exasperation. 'You know, I really thought with the abdication of old Rottweiler Ratzinger, and his replacement with the so-called liberal, Pope Francis, that our friend Guillini would be left out in the cold. No way, far from it – the old rat is thriving in his bunker, as if nothing's changed. I'm afraid Pope Francis is not everything he appears to be.'

Anna moved closer to Moses and placed her fingers on his hand. 'And tell me,' she whispered, 'do you still have the bed in the back of the Merc?'

Moses smiled. He looked into her eyes and watched her mouth open slightly and her silky tongue venture over her lips. The sight made him lean across the table and brush his fingers over her cheek. As she drew nearer, he smelt her perfume and felt compelled to kiss the back of her hand. The smell of her scent brought back graphically detailed memories of their journeys in the back of the Mercedes.

'Hey look, Anna, this is stupid,' he said with a touch of embarrassment. She looked at him with open lips and large eyes. 'What I mean, to be honest with you, is that this is somewhat … frustrating. As you can see,' he said, uncrossing his legs. 'You still have a rather powerful effect on me. Why not come back to the apartment?'

She smiled at Moses and looked at her watch. It was only 3.00 pm. 'There's plenty of time for a reunion. I suppose,' she whispered into his ear, 'I could enjoy some … unhurried sex. That would be very nice, if that's what you had in mind.'

'I'm relieved to see you still retain an interest in the sensual side of things.'

'Do you still have the dark, tinted windows in the Merc?'

'I wouldn't drive anything else, but it's a newer model. We could always put down the back seat, make up the bed in the back, and ask Sam to drive us around Vienna in ever-decreasing circles.'

He watched as she crossed her legs. She was a wearing a short skirt, and he could see there was little underneath. It brought back memories of mid-morning sex in the Hotel Minerva after walking down the Roman Forum.

'How about your apartment. Have you still got the water bed?'

'Sorry, it had to go. Caused a small flood in the offices below. I've installed something more pleasurable.'

Moses took out his phone and sent a message to Christina, his PA, to say he had an extended business meeting and could no longer take her out for dinner.

'Who you texting? I hope I'm not causing you any problems.'

'Don't worry, I'm a free man. It's to my PA to say I won't be coming back to the office today.'

Moses stood up and explained that he needed to have a break before continuing any further. The therapist agreed to stop for ten minutes. Moses went downstairs, walked through the door and into the suburban street. There was no traffic. It was calm and quiet. He walked briskly to the end of the tree-lined road, checked his watch, and turned back. The tension was clearing from his head.

He strolled back into the two-storey house, up the carpeted stairs and into the therapist's first-floor office.

'OK, I'm much better now,' he said, looking at his watch.

'Out of interest, Mr Frank, when did this reunion with Anna

take place?'

'Actually, only two days ago.'

'I see. And are you seeing her again before she leaves Vienna?'

'Yes, I will see her later tonight,' said Moses.

'Well, it's good to work with fresh material, but I think it would be best if we stopped now. My next client is due to arrive.'

Outside, Sam was waiting for him at the wheel of the new Mercedes. He drove at speed back to the subterranean auction rooms in downtown Vienna.

Moses crept into the theatre and waved a greeting to the technical crew who had just completed setting up the sound and lighting for the new presentation.

As he cued the signal for the rehearsal to begin his phone began playing Bach's Toccata and Fugue in D minor.

A new call was coming through.

2

Moses didn't want to talk to anyone and looked quizzically at the bright screen.

The words 'Unknown Caller' were superimposed over his home screen image of the sixth-century Santa Caterina monastery in Egypt's Sinai, set against an intensely bright turquoise-blue desert sky.

His hand hovered indecisively over the on-off switch. As the Bach organ piece played on his phone, struggling to be heard above the music playing all around him, he decided to accept the call.

He waved at the technicians and gestured that they should take five. The triumphal notes of Rossini's *Moses in Egypt* playing through the massive sound system died down.

He tried to concentrate on the booming and excited voice from his phone, but his mind was still focussed on the presentation. A mummified Pharaoh, Neferkare II, and assorted tomb relics had come into Moses' possession via an intermediary based in Cairo and were to be sold in two days' time. His head was full of the complexities of the lightshow being created to get the Jupiter group into the state of mind to bid for a morsel of Ancient Egypt.

'Hello again, Moses,' the thickly accented voice said, and Moses laughed out loud. He knew its owner immediately, even though he hadn't heard the husky Greek tones for two years.

'How are you, Andreas?'

'Happy to be recognised by you after such a long time,' Green purred contentedly down the phone.

'Yes, long time no hear, my Greek friend!'

'I'm afraid so, Moses. But tell me, how are your business activities going?' Green asked with an upbeat tone to his voice.

'We've had another strong year,' Moses began.

'Tell me some of the highlights. I love hearing about your secret world of antiquities,' said Green.

'Let me think a moment. The Cross of Jesus was authenticated and sold for a very good sum. But the big event was the sale of the Ark. I suppose that was a major achievement.'

'Oh my god, Moses, do you mean the Ark of the Bible? The Ark of Noah and all his animals? You can't be serious?' said Green, his voice becoming high-pitched.

'Yes, the Ark did very well, as expected. It was bought by a Russian oligarch. He's had a special underground museum built for it in the grounds of his English manor house,' said Moses.

'That would have to be enormous in every way,' said Green, with undiluted enthusiasm.

'It was our largest ever sale.'

'Tell me, where was it uncovered?' said Green, trying to sound like someone in whom Moses could confide his business secrets.

'In a mountainous area of Iraq. But, you'll appreciate this, Andreas, it wasn't easy to transport from its historic resting place, in the middle of a warzone, to the auction house in Vienna. But money talks. Even fanatical fighters will take a bribe if it's large enough. They need money to buy weapons. Everyone has their price, no matter what they're fighting for.'

'But how did you keep such a large relic quiet from the press?'

'There were enormous problems involved in shifting it around the world without anyone knowing. You have to fly low, under the radar. It's a problem we'll have with the Delphic Anomaly. Isn't that right, Andreas?'

'Sooner than you think, Moses. It's wonderful to be still working with the biggest and the best,' said Green.

At this point, Moses put the conversation onto speaker phone as his ear was beginning to ache.

'So Andreas, are you up for it? Will you get the Delphic Anomaly out of the chamber, after all this time?' asked Moses.

'We've had many years of flooding, but I am convinced that the waters inside the chamber have now fully subsided,' Green told Moses, chuckling with an air of confidence. 'I've obtained the biggest pump in mainland Greece, powered by a diesel generator the size of a small house,' he said, sounding as if he was back in control.

'Tell me honestly, Andreas. Is this for real or is it just the normal bullshit?' said Moses, sounding tired.

'I can give you a one-hundred percent – no, make that two-hundred percent guarantee that the Delphic Anomaly will be removed from the chamber by the end of this week. Today is Monday. It will be moved by Friday, Moses, you have my promise. It's my personal guarantee. What more can I say?'

'This is excellent news,' said Moses, shaking his head, almost convinced by the exuberant sound of Green's overflowing confidence. 'You've really got things moving at last.'

'You should pencil in the transport plane for Saturday. Do you still have your private jet?' Andreas asked Moses, who had now gone silent as he listened to Green's over-optimistic schedule.

'Oh yes, I have my wings, but I charter now. It makes more sense financially. It can be booked easily. But look Andreas, I have to pay a fifty percent cancellation fee, so I'll wait for your call to confirm the excavation has taken place before chartering the jet, OK?' Moses said.

'No problem, I understand. We're definitely getting there now. You'll be getting my call soon,' said Green.

Moses had heard it all before and looked at his watch. He was ready to bring the conversation to an end, but something made him think of Green's daughter Isabella.

The anxious little girl he'd met years earlier must have grown into a beautiful young woman and would now be in her early thirties.

'And tell me – how is your daughter Isabella getting on these days?' said Moses, conjuring up a picture of a mature, dark-haired young woman.

'She's doing well. She studied for a Masters in Paris,' said Green proudly. 'And she now has a job with UNESCO, working as an archaeologist in the development office. They decide which sites around the world merit World Heritage listing. I think she knows far more than I do. I'm so proud of her ...' said Green, his voice trailing off with emotion.

'That's wonderful,' said Moses, hoping to set up a meeting

with her.

'I wish I saw more of her, but it's hard to leave Delphi,' said Green, mournfully.

'Maybe I could meet her, take her out to dinner perhaps. I could advise her on aspects of the archaeology trade,' Moses said, hoping for her phone number.

He could hear Green flicking his worry beads. He thought he might see him as a man with a bit of a reputation, someone who might take advantage of his precious daughter. There was a long pause before Green spoke up.

'Yes, yes, please do that for me, Moses. You know something, I would really like you to keep an eye on her, I'd appreciate that. I worry about Isabella. I'm sure she'd enjoy meeting you,' Green insisted.

'It would be my great pleasure. Text me her number and address,' said Moses.

'I must say goodbye now. There's a lot to be done for the excavation tomorrow night,' said Green, haltingly.

'I'm excited by your plans, Andreas. It's all sounding good,' said Moses. 'Goodbye and good luck.' Moses pressed the 'end call' button, putting the phone back in his breast pocket.

Christina brought him coffee and handed Moses a list of hotels across Vienna where the members of the Jupiter group would be staying. There were two days to go before the auction took place.

'OK, fine, let's finish this now. Can you change the Chinese to another hotel. It's better they don't come face-to-face with the Russians in the elevator,' he said as he watched her tie her hair back, revealing her shapely neck. He was tempted to touch her shoulder, but she was holding herself at a distance. He could see she was still irritated by his last-minute cancellation of their dinner date yesterday evening.

'And that reminds me,' said Moses. 'Put the Israelis with the Vatican group. They like to talk about their collections over breakfast.'

He waved to the sound and lighting engineers. The room went black and the state-of-the-art hydraulics under the vast basement began to whir into action.

Out of the darkness, the biggest turntable outside of the Vienna Opera House began to rise silently out of the depths. On the stage a shaft of sunlight appeared as the lamb's horn in the desert echoed across the theatre. A matrix of dazzling spotlights faded up on the stage. Part one of Rossini's *Moses in Egypt* began to play from the twenty-thousand watt sound system.

A mummified body began to rise from the underworld.

Pharaoh Neferkare II had arrived in Vienna.

3

They walked along Johannestrasse until they arrived outside the WAR headquarters. Moses keyed in the six-digit code and they took the elevator up to his penthouse flat.

As Anna took a shower Moses caught a glimpse of her outline through the steamy glass door.

'Still heart-shaped or have you gone Brazilian these days?' he said, looking at her body.

'For you to find out, Moses,' she said, emerging from the shower, one hand discretely placed over her crotch.

She came into the bedroom in a white robe loosely tied around her small waist. He was finding it hard to hide his excitement at having her back.

'I can see you're pleased to see me again,' she said with a smile.

'Try the new bed.'

She sat down and spread her fingers across the silky king-sized sheets. Moses joined her with a remote control in his hand and pressed the button.

'Look up at the ceiling.'

She saw a huge, suspended rectangular mirror. As she waved at herself, the image switched to her profile and she realised it was not a mirror but a giant TV screen, cutting between three different cameras hidden around the room. She looked at Moses with a grin.

'Can I watch the recording afterwards?' she said.

'It's not set up to record, I'm sorry to say. You can't be too careful. I don't want anything falling into the wrong hands or appearing on the internet. It's only for our immediate pleasure,' Moses said.

'Do you think I'm in pretty good shape after two kids?' she said, holding her hands under her breasts.

'Like a goddess. You look sensational, more perfect than I remember,' he said, stroking her breasts and exciting her nipples. He sucked them like small grapes and wondered if she'd had cosmetic surgery to make her look more voluptuous.

'I like to keep my husband interested,' she said, climbing on Moses.

They made love twice, the first time quickly and desperately, both of them coming quickly with a thunderous and exuberant climax, as if they'd been deprived of sex for twenty-five years. After a glass of champagne, they became aroused again and took their time to play and explore their bodies through a series of positions.

'You've definitely become more adventurous, Anna,' Moses said.

'I was young and inexperienced. I've learnt some great new positions as I've grown older.'

Afterwards, they lay on the crumpled sheets, a post-coital shine on Anna's apple-red cheeks. She was more porcelain doll than hot, perspiring woman. They leaned close to each other, against a cluster of pillows, their legs entwined, Anna's head resting on Moses' shoulder.

'That was really the best sex I've had for a long time. These are so delicious I could eat them all day,' he said, kissing her nipples again.

'Stop now, it's too intense for me, you've made my body hyper-stimulated,' she said, biting her lower lip.

He felt that this was a good moment to talk. 'Something has been on my mind.'

'Tell me about it.'

'Can you explain why you left me twenty-odd years ago and didn't get in touch until now? That's a hell of a gap. I'd given you up for good.'

She turned and looked at Moses without saying anything.

'Why didn't you get back to me, Anna?' he asked again.

'It just seemed our time together had run its course,' she said, stroking his face. 'One reason I wanted to come back to you today is because I have a confession.' He looked back at her, raising his eyebrows.

'It's been weighing on my conscience for years. Will you forgive me?' she asked

'How can I know?' he said, opening his arms. 'It depends what you've done, Anna.'

'I had a relationship with your enemy *numero uno.*'

'And which enemy is that?'

'Guillini, of course.'

'The old fox, Guillini. You seem to be attracted to hard bastards.'

'I suppose they turn me on.'

'What kind of relationship was it?'

'Put it this way, we didn't sing hymns together in Mass. It was purely physical, nothing else. Look, I'm sorry.'

'You know the man's a torturer and a sadist. I hope he didn't inflict too much pain on you, Anna,' Moses said, gripping her fragile body with his hands.

'It was nothing like that. Imagine we went running together, it was just the same. At the end of the session you ended up covered in sweat and a little exhausted,' she said. She buried her face in a pillow.

Moses leaned over and began to massage her shoulders. 'It's alright, it's all water under the bridge now. Spare me the details,' he said, kneading her skin and allowing his fingers to drift around her rib cage, up to her breasts.

'Are you angry with me?' she asked.

Moses thought for a moment. He didn't know, he was still sensing his own feelings. 'Tell me what sort of *working* relationship you had with him.'

'He trained me as a Vatican agent. I was supposed to spy on you. He chose me, he said, because he knew your taste in women.'

Moses frowned and scratched his head. 'That's ridiculous. When I met you at that dinner party it happened spontaneously, on the night,' he said.

'Not exactly, Moses. It was all planned by him from the start. Before I came to your party I was trained by Guillini to be an informer. I was taught communications, seduction, how to create a cover story. You name it, they teach it at VISI.'

Moses' eyes bulged. 'The whole pick-up, the invitation and everything? That was all a set-up? You're joking, aren't you?' he asked quietly. 'You mean he decided that you should seduce me into taking you to Delphi?'

'Yes, that as well. I've told you everything now. And I want to apologise. I'm sorry, but I had no choice,' she said, looking up, her hand on her forehead, trying to avoid eye contact.

'For Christ's sake, how could you do that?' he said, throwing his arms in the air.

'It was easy. Every battle is won in the planning. You know that,' she said. 'You were hooked using a classic honey trap. But actually, I really liked you as a person, Moses. I loved your maverick lifestyle, your way of thinking, your art, your charms and also your body. I loved everything about you, please believe me,' she said, rubbing a tear from her eye.

Moses listened in open-mouthed silence.

'I'd fallen for you, but I was working for Guillini at the same time. So I told him everything you were doing. And what Dr Green was doing, or *failing* to do, in Delphi.'

'But why? Why do all this? And for such a bastard too? I can't understand why you'd work for such a nasty piece of humanity, masquerading as a man of God.'

'Easy. I don't care what Guillini does. That's a personal matter for him,' she said softly. Moses listened intently, unable to move.

'This may shock you, but the simple fact is that the Vatican has the world's greatest botanical collection. He promised me access to the ancient herbarium if I became an informer for him. I was perfectly happy to use my body in exchange for a key to the Botanical Library. I'd do it again. It's the greatest plant collection on earth.'

Moses rolled his eyes. 'Is that it? You lied, spied and betrayed just to gain access to some dried-up plants in a library!' he said, smacking his fist against his hand.

'Not just a library, a herbarium – the finest one in the world.'

'Are you crazy, Anna? Surely your principles were worth more than a few seeds and some dead leaves?'

She pulled the sheet around her body and came closer to him. 'But they weren't *any* plant specimens, Moses. They were the rarest plants in the world. They were vanished species you cannot find anywhere else. Let me tell you something, they even had silphium, which the Romans used as a panacea and a contraceptive and has since disappeared off the face of the earth. You cannot imagine what that meant to me. It has changed my life.'

'You must have been brainwashed by Guillini. I know him, he's a cruel bastard, not afraid to use brutal force.'

'No, he wasn't like that with me.'

'Tell me honestly – did he threaten to hurt you unless you had sex with him and spied on me? Tell me the truth Anna.'

'Don't worry, it's history. It was all over many years ago,' she said and began to get dressed.

Watching her as she pulled up her stockings, Moses began to remember the day they'd been in Rome when she'd returned to the Hotel Minerva with a bruised arm.

But as she slipped into her close-fitting dress he was too distracted by the reverse striptease to say any more.

4

Alitalia Flight AZ7573 from Vienna Schwechat touched down at 12.30 pm at Rome's Fiumicino airport.

After the ninety-minute flight, Anna didn't feel like being crammed inside a public bus and took a taxi for the 29 km journey to St Peter's Basilica.

Stepping out at Piazza Angelica she walked 600 metres to the VISI building, passing through a warren of narrow streets, enjoying the warm and sweaty embrace of Rome's chaos.

It seemed to give her new energy.

As she turned into St Peter's the familiar silver exterior caught her eye on the far northern corner of the square.

Walking through the revolving glass doors, she found an elderly nun in a black habit sitting at the reception, tapping a mobile phone. Anna cleared her throat. The nun looked up and, in perfect Italian, Anna announced she had a meeting with Dr Vincenzo Pilotti, the head of Botanical Research.

She was directed to the elevator. The door opened and Anna was asked to follow a second nun. The elevator descended six floors and she was now in the Hypericum Research wing, recognisable by the symbol of an acorn seedling superimposed on a red cross.

Passing several subterranean office entrances she came to a door marked *Direttore*, and Anna was shown inside.

A smiling Guillini stood in front of his desk as if he'd been waiting for her for some time.

'How's my friend Vincenzo Pilotti today?' said Anna, as she embraced him.

'I'm well, thank you Anna – and so is Vincenzo,' he said.

As Guillini held her in his arms she felt his hand slip under her blouse and release her bra. She wriggled as his fingers moved round to feel her breasts. After a few seconds he pushed her body way from his and looked at his watch.

'Let's get the business out of the way first,' he said, sitting down on a Chesterfield sofa, to the right of his large desk. Anna sat down next to him, staying within touching distance.

'The deed is done,' she said, turning to Guillini, holding her head high and pushing back her shoulders.

'So you finally had the long-awaited reunion with Moses?' She nodded in silence, smiling at him discreetly.

'And how is the old double-dealer doing?' said Guillini.

'Oh, you know Moses, full of energy as always,' she said, looking down to avoid eye contact.

'Any idea of the timetable for the new attempt to excavate the Anomaly?' he asked. She nodded in the affirmative.

'It's on again, it's imminent. He's going to attempt it very soon, maybe at the end of this week.'

Guillini pulled his head back in surprise.

'Seriously? So soon? Are you sure?'

'He gave me the impression that it was definite, this time.' Anna said. She took his hand and began to kiss it, but kept her lips away from the heavy gold ring encircling his middle finger.

Guillini brought her fingertips into his mouth. 'Tell me, Anna, does he trust you still? Does he know anything about your work for us?'

'He will tell me whatever I ask of him. He's helpless when he sees me,' she said, undoing his belt.

'OK, good girl, you've done excellent work.' His head fell backwards and his eyes closed as Anna slid her hand between his legs.

Something began to vibrate on his desk. His smartphone was buzzing with a new message. The smile dissolved from Guillin's face as he hauled himself off the leather sofa and searched for his phone amongst the papers spread over his desk.

'It's HH. I must leave you now.'

Anna gave him a quizzical look.

'It's extremely short notice for him, every minute of his diary is normally planned weeks ahead,' he paused, leaned over her and squeezed her waist. 'Something out of the ordinary must have happened.' He stood up and opened the door of his office, glancing back at Anna.

'Stay around, it would be a shame not to make the most of your visit.'

'Just as were getting to know each other again,' she purred.

'I'll be back in half an hour,' he said, leaving the office.

'GG, wait!' she shouted.

Her voice echoed down the corridor as Guillini hurried into the adjoining Papal wing.

5

Guillini's run turned into a walk as he made his way through a door marked 'Uscita di Sicurezza' at the end of the corridor.

From there he took the staircase down into the communications centre one floor below. It was the lowest room under the Vatican, reinforced with steel and concrete, designed to withstand highly explosive crater bombs.

He sat at the computer desk and began to type out a message to his operative in Delphi.

He checked his watch. It was fifteen minutes before his first meeting with the Holy Father. He went up six floors to the private office, knocked twice and waited.

A secretary came to the door and let him into the antechamber. 'The Holy Father has eight minutes to see you,' he said. 'Please stand by this door until he is ready for you.'

Guillini stood there cracking his knuckles. When they had all been cracked he bit his tongue until he could taste blood in his mouth.

'The Holy Father will see you now,' the private secretary announced, and disappeared into the antechamber.

Guillini stretched his fingers and entered through the wide maple doors, walked forward, bowed, and kissed the gloved hand of the Holy Father, keeping his lips tightly pursed.

The two men were alone.

No secretary was allowed to stay to take notes. This was always the rule Guillini insisted upon when security matters were discussed. He didn't like to entertain the risks of informers leaking papal secrets.

They sat across an ornate table inlaid with religious icons made from onyx and lapis lazuli in the Florentine tradition of marquetry.

Pope Francis looked down at his hardbound notebook for a few seconds, raised his head, and looked at Guillini.

'I will come to straight to the point, Giovanni. I know you have served the Vatican loyally for more than thirty years and created a security service for my predecessors which is second to none. And you have continued with this excellent work during the transition period. I'm indebted to you and your staff for this vital work. Thank you Giovanni,' the Pope finished, and wrote some notes in longhand with a fountain pen.

'Thank you, Holy Father. I am indebted to you for your

generous comments,' said Guillini, his smile dissolving almost instantly.

'But as you know, the church is moving on,' the Pope continued in monotone. 'We must adapt to the new reality across the globe. In the spirit of reconciliation, many of the activities in which you and your teams have fearlessly engaged are no longer required in this new climate.' The Pope smiled at Guillini, who was gripping the fingers of both hands with locked fists.

Guillini tried to interrupt but thought better of it. It was against Papal protocol to interrupt His Holiness. He sat listening like a well-behaved subordinate priest.

'I must be honest with you, I want to reform things for the better, Giovanni, so we no longer need to engage in any covert operations. I want to try an alternative course of action. It will involve taking risks, but I believe we must do this now. We will all have to become more accepting of the new reality, especially in our relationships with other faiths.'

Guillini's nose twitched as he listened politely. He knew what the Pope was going to say. He'd read the reports of the planned reforms in *L'Osservatore Romano*, the semi-official Vatican newspaper. He knew what was coming and he'd prepared himself. The Pope paused for a sip of water and Guillini took this as his cue to speak.

'I understand the desire to be more open and make changes,' he began, 'but I must advise your Holiness that there may be serious unforeseen risks with such a new policy—'

The Pope interrupted, smiling and opening his arms.

'Look, Giovanni, progress and reconciliation require a bold step into the unknown. Risks must be taken. I am grateful for your advice and value it, but I have decided that from immediate effect your unit will be dissolved.' He paused, and Giovanni's face fell.

'You will remain in the service of the Vatican in a non-security role in relation to spearheading the promotion of our new prayer book for the developing world. You are a superb ambassador, and the Church should not waste your massive talents, Giovanni.'

'I understand, your Holiness. In some ways it would be a great honour to work on the New Book of Common Prayer,' said Guillini, a taut expression gripping his face. He would not allow his empire to be destroyed without a fight, and had no intention of selling prayer books for the Church. He would rather work in a call centre.

The Pope smiled, showing his fine set of white teeth.

'I would like to offer you a pivotal role in launching our anti-poverty prayer books around the world. This will require the establishment of a team of educational workers, it will mean extensive travel, which you clearly enjoy, and dealing with communities at every level. I know you will make a huge difference to the lives of millions impoverished people.'

Guillini's lips quivered as he stared at the Pope in disbelief. He said nothing but knew he would rather cut off his own testicles than lead a troop of international do-gooders on the Pope's crusade against inequality. Had the Holy Father no idea who he was talking to? It felt as if the boss of the Mafia was being asked to give up organised crime to run a sweet shop. He knew he had nothing to lose by using scare tactics.

'With great respect, your Holiness, I've given my life to protecting the Papacy and I know the many threats facing the security of the church. We live in dangerous times. I am deeply concerned that the dissolution of the Security Office will create even more enemies for the church,' he said, shaking his head. 'It could threaten the entire fabric of the church.'

The Pope looked at Guillini with a taut expression on his lips.

'There are forces out there determined to destroy us, we must never forget that, your Holiness.'

The Pope drew his lower lip inside his mouth and looked surprised by Guillini's claims. He made a cross in the air with his right hand. 'Giovanni, tell me – what is your biggest fear?'

'Holy Father, I must tell you that we have been protecting the church from potentially lethal damage emanating from archaeological discoveries made in Greece for some twenty-five years.'

'What has been going on?' the Pope said, his eyes focused on Guillini.

'The church security service, through my highly trained operatives, has managed to ensure these finds have never been made public. We've had to be vigilant day and night. The risk remains high and a new danger is imminent.'

'And what exactly was discovered twenty-five years ago?' The Pope said, his voice quiet. 'I don't believe I know about this matter.'

'It all started before you were made a Cardinal and has been kept under great secrecy. A complete blackout has been maintained, with some difficulty.' The Pope looked concerned and began fingering his rosary beads.

'What was found that worries you so much?'

'It was a surprising discovery made in a cave in Delphi. The Holiest Jewish Icon, captured by the Romans from Jerusalem in AD 70, was found buried there, but set in stone. After two-thousand years it has become encrusted with limestone,' said Guillini.

The Pope stood up and went to the arched window, looking across at the gathering crowds in St Peter's Square.

'So the greatest symbol of God's covenant with humanity has been found in Greece, of all places. How disturbing.' The Pope paused. 'This is strange because I had always believed this relic was kept in the vaults under the Basilica.'

'I'm afraid not, your Holiness. It was never returned to Rome. I'm sure you can appreciate the damage this icon would do to the church and world peace.'

'Undoubtedly so, Giovanni. I'm sorry, I hadn't realised I was in the dark about this discovery. Look, on reflection, I think perhaps you need to continue your excellent work, if only to keep this relic out of the public eye. I can see it is vital, so you must continue.'

Guillini smiled and rubbed his hands together. 'And you want me to keep the security department running, your Holiness, as before?'

'I do, Giovanni. Ignore my previous orders. I now see they were ill-informed.' The Pope pulled his white cloak over his shoulders. 'Will you kindly excuse me, Cardinal Giovanni. It is time for the Mass in the square. I'm sorry, I must leave you now.' The Pope left the room and headed towards the balcony overlooking St Peter's Square, humming the music of the prayers.

Guillini stood still for a few moments, looking out over the crowds. There was a thunderous roar from the thousands of worshippers as the Pope appeared at the balcony.

Taking a bow in their direction, he stepped energetically out of the room and made his way back to the VISI communications centre. He sat down at his terminal and began to type the orders to the Greek operative.

'Go ahead with planned interruption. Authority for action is given at the highest level. Do not delay, urgent action required. Let me know if you need explo—' He stopped himself and deleted the last four letters, replacing the offending word with the phrase 'essential materials,' and signed off with his usual absolution.

In nome del Santo Padre. GG.

PART TWELVE

Peter and Maria

1

Peter Delacroix received the call from Waterbury's as he was driving along rue Montmartre, on his way to visit his grandmother.

It had been over two weeks since she'd told him about her being arrested in Delphi. There was also the question of the package she'd given to him.

He didn't know what to do with the contents. It was just a key with no tag. No address label, nothing – he had no idea what it might open.

As he made his way down avenue Gabriel, the unmistakable husky voice of Jacqueline Deauville came through on his mobile phone.

His heart skipped a beat.

She was the personal assistant to the new Director of Antiquities at Waterbury's auction house. He'd taken her out for lunch a few months earlier and had been quietly hoping that she'd repay him in some way.

From the enthusiasm in her first few words, he knew something had come up.

She spoke quickly, without pausing for breath. There was a short-term job requiring great diplomacy, a one-week contract to inspect a private collection of Ancient Greek vases from the fifth century BC. It would be well-paid.

'This client is a nervous-sounding woman, an archaeologist, a Miss Isabella Green. I can't tell you very much about her collection, only that it's from Delphi. She's been very secretive and repeated that "discretion was necessary" as the collection was "of a confidential nature".'

'What does that mean?' Peter asked.

'Probably means that the antiquities have no certified provenance. But you never know, it's best to check out every collection. Sometimes we find something important – it's unpredictable,' she said. 'And I've agreed you a great consultancy rate of three-hundred euros per day.'

'Three hundred. Wow! You're a genius,' he said, as a huge smile spread across his face. 'See you next Monday. And thank you Jacqueline, I won't forget this.'

'Don't forget to arrive early,' she said, and hung up.

Relieved to see a red light at place de Concorde, Peter had a few seconds to call his mother and tell her the good news. He thought she'd be impressed by the daily rate. It might mollify her after his last request for a 'temporary' loan of eight-hundred euros to pay his rent. He also mentioned that Melanie was off to Berlin for a fashion shoot, which would also bring in a sizeable cheque next month.

'You'll be valuing antiquities from where?' she said. 'Did I hear you say Delphi, for God's sake?'

'What's wrong with Delphi? I know a lot about the place,' he said, and heard her sigh.

'But where are you now?' she asked, exasperated by his lateness. 'Your grandmother has been waiting to see you all afternoon.'

'I promise to be there very soon. I'm not so far away now, but you know there's been terrible traffic jams. Many streets are closed because of the terrorist incident.'

Peter let his mobile phone drop onto the passenger seat as the lights turned green and accelerated towards avenue de Lamballe. He was trying to prepare himself mentally for a quiet encounter with his dying grandmother.

He was hoping she'd have enough life left in her to finish her story.

He had to park a hundred and fifty metres from the apartment, and after switching off the engine he counted down from thirty to collect his thoughts – and to comb his hair with his fingers in the rear-view mirror.

As he jumped out of his Citroen Picasso a young woman came bounding up to him. He sighed as he set his eyes on her, unsure if he wanted to talk to her.

It was Suzy Cartier, with whom he'd had an on-off relationship at university.

As Peter stood there, she put her arms around him and kissed him on the lips. He could sense she was after something, as her 'hello' kiss soon became a warm tongue thrashing inside his mouth.

It was a far more intimate embrace than the polite peck on the cheek he'd expected from a casual meeting in the street with an ex-girlfriend.

As her uninhibited kiss came to an end, she cupped his face with one hand and stood back on the pavement, smiling at him.

Peter could not help but stare at her short black skirt, bound so tightly around her thighs he could see the pencil-thin outline of her thong.

He remembered she always like to wear skin-tight clothing. It's what had attracted him to her in the first place during a lecture on palaeontology.

He tried to play it cool and make an excuse, but Peter was a prisoner of his erotic memories. Four years on, he was still recollecting the nights they spent screwing in her bed when they should have been working in the archaeology library.

As she rocked back and forth on the pavement in her red stilettos he could feel himself reacting to her. He was losing control and he knew it. And he was also running late.

'Have you got five minutes to spare? I really need to go over something with you?' She paused. 'I mean you and me, now,' she said, looking straight into his eyes. He knew exactly what she meant by this vague request.

From the first time they'd met, she'd always used euphemisms for sex, as if she were a shy and easily-embarrassed girl. He knew it made no sense at all, given her ravenous appetite, but he played along with her game.

'Look, I'm really sorry. I'm going to see my grandmother, I'm already late. But ...' he paused.

'If you're already late, another few minutes won't make much difference, will it?' she said, and placed one of her red fingernails in her open mouth.

His face went into a series of strained contortions as he tried to fend her off. But it was all a pretence to himself – his body had already made the decision.

She glanced at her watch and made a thirty degree turn as if she was about to continue up the street, but instead she looked back over her shoulder.

'Look, Peter, I could really do with talking in your car for a few minutes. There's something very private I need to tell you,' she said breathlessly, tilting her head so her hair fell around her neck. She reached out and touched him on the shoulder like a kitten wanting physical contact.

He twisted his wrist and looked at his watch. It was 3.50 pm. He calculated he had fifteen minutes to spare, maybe twenty. It wouldn't look so bad if he arrived at his grandmother's by around 4.30.

'I can really see you need to ... get something off your chest,' he said, touching her waist, to show he wasn't disinterested.

'I'll only need a few minutes of your time, I'm sure,' she said, looking around. 'But we can't keep standing here in the street.'

'Let me make a quick phone call, I'll be a minute,' he said, and turned away from her whilst she leaned against the side of the car. He walked a few yards up the road and spoke briefly to his mother on his mobile. She was angry and shouted at him, but he stayed cool and firm.

'Look, for Christ's sake. I promise I'll be there by 4.30,' he said, and pressed 'end call' on the screen.

'OK, I'm free to talk to you now,' he said, walking back to Suzy.

He opened the car door and she jumped in. He drove to place Laroche, a dead-end alley off rue Fauberge where municipal refuse vehicles turned around at six in the morning.

It was totally deserted. He parked and switched off the engine.

By the time he'd applied the brakes she'd got into the back seat and had pulled up her skirt around her waist. There was not much of her thong, it was just a fine silk ribbon, so she already looked naked from the waist-down as he climbed over to join her. As soon as he caught a glimpse of her firm, rounded breasts he felt himself losing control.

Her body felt even smoother and firmer than he'd remembered. She'd been working out, he decided, as he pressed his fingers against her warm skin, feeling her every curve and crevice.

As she unzipped his flies, he froze. Someone was walking around outside the car, and Peter stretched over to the front seat to lock the car from inside.

'Don't worry about them, the windows are too steamy to see through,' Suzy said, as she continued playing with Peter.

'It's OK, they've gone now,' he paused. 'Now remind me, what were you saying you needed to talk about?'

'The problem is I need more of this,' she said, holding his stiff organ in her fingers, pulling her satin thong to the side, and guiding him inside her.

He leaned forward and grabbed her by the shoulders to give himself leverage as he pushed himself inside her, riding back and forth, teasing her before ramming it into her. He remembered why they'd stayed together so long. She had the sweetest and tightest pussy in the Sorbonne.

The car rocked gently on its springs. It didn't take long until they both came, pretty much simultaneously, testing the suspension of the old Citroen Picasso to its limits. As she came, he put his hand over her mouth to muffle her screams.

'I'm so sorry for making all the noise,' she said, gasping for breath and kissing him twenty times over.

It was over. Peter looked at his watch as she rolled her skirt back down over the tops of her legs, buttoned her top, and opened the car door.

'I'll drive you back to rue Raynouard,' he said.

'No, this is where I want to be, it's perfect,' she said. He looked back uncertainly at her.

'Smile, Peter! It was great, just as I remember you. Better!' she said, kissing him on the lips and stepping out onto the pavement.

He rubbed away the condensation from the back window with his shirtsleeve and watched her wave goodbye through the wet glass.

As his eyes followed her walking briskly down the street he felt physically relieved. They'd both enjoyed themselves, it did more good than harm and no one ever needed to find out.

He wondered if he would be late for his grandmother. He looked at his watch. It was still only 4.25 pm.

2

Moses put the receiver down and gave up trying to call the Delphi Museum.

Green's words were still echoing in his head. 'I'd like you to keep an eye on Isabella. I'll send you her contact details.'

It was six weeks since their phone conversation, and he'd still not heard a thing.

He tried the number of the Delphi museum one more time. It rang for five minutes with no answer.

He found the number of the phone that Green had used to call him. The line produced a continuous high-pitched sound. It was either dead or out of order.

Moses decided to call the Ministry of Culture in Athens. After a long wait, his call was answered by a disinterested civil servant.

'Delphi is always open,' a woman said in painfully slow English. 'You have to remember it's a very large archaeological site. People may be away from the office.' The official told Moses what he already knew.

'But Dr Green should be there,' said Moses, hitting his desk.

'The director may be on holiday. We do not keep a record of these things. I'm sorry. Goodbye,' the woman said, with customary Greek bluntness, and the line went dead.

Moses put the receiver down calmly and looked through the window. An idea was taking shape.

His mobile buzzed on his desk. He smiled hopefully. It must be Green, he thought, glancing at the screen. It was a text from an unknown number. Moses had worked it out. It was unlikely to be Green himself, but it could well be from Isabella, Green's daughter, who lives in Paris.

He opened the message folder. It was not what he'd been expecting.

> Hello Moses. Maria Delacroix here in Paris.
> Finally tracked down your mobile number.
> Contrary to rumours, I haven't died yet, I'm
> still walking around.
> I heard something today, about my grandson
> Peter, which you may find interesting. He's
> now working for Waterbury's in Paris and
> is meeting someone, a young woman from
> Delphi, at the end of this week with a private
> collection. Thought you should know this
> with our shared interest in antiquities from
> Delphi.
>
> Kind regards,
> Maria Delacroix

Moses laughed, and asked Sam to come into his office.

'Do you remember many years ago we drove all night to Delphi to meet Dr Green, when he showed me the Delphic Anomaly for the first time?'

Sam nodded. 'How could I forget that crazy time? It was the eighteen days of Anna, too,' he said, putting his fingers through his greying hair. 'What about it?'

'Green was supposed to contact me about six weeks ago. When we spoke he sounded so confident he was going to finally excavate the Anomaly. But everything's gone dead since then. He hasn't answered his phone since.'

'I can understand why you feel worried,' said Sam.

'And do you remember his little daughter? She was about nine at that time. She must be about thirty-something now, I suppose. Apparently, she works in Paris assessing sites for World Heritage status. When I spoke to Green he asked me to keep an eye on her,' Moses said, turning a broken pencil between his fingers.

'Is she in some kind of trouble?'

'I don't know, I thought he sounded a little concerned about her safety. I made him an assurance I'd keep an eye on her,' he said, holding the new text message up for Sam. 'And I've just had this text from Maria Delacroix, totally out of the blue, which may be connected.'

'So what do you want to do?' asked Sam.

Moses went over to the map of Europe that hung on his office wall.

'I feel I have a duty to Isabella and her father, even if the old man has driven me crazy in the past,' he said, as he found Vienna and drew a line all the way down to Delphi in southern Greece. 'Could we leave for Greece in two hours?'

Sam looked at the map and reminded himself of the countries they would need to travel through.

'OK, I can see no visa problems. We can buy supplies as we go. The new Mercedes is all ready and insured for the whole of Europe. It could do with a long trip to make sure everything is working properly.'

'We may need to do some discrete eavesdropping, so bring along the new surveillance gear.'

Sam smiled and left the office in a hurry. Moses sat at his desk and pondered whether to call Maria. He hadn't spoken to her for several years and she'd probably given up any hope of retrieving the Delphic Anomaly.

Wondering how much to tell her, he picked up the phone and started to dial the numbers. The maid answered in a quiet voice.

'*'Allo*, Mme Delacroix's residence. Who is calling please?' Moses was reluctant to give his name.

'Tell her I'm an old family friend.'

A few seconds later Maria came on the line. 'Hello Moses, how are you after all this time.'

'But how did you know it was me?'

'I had a feeling you'd call me. Strange, isn't it? I think we have a telepathic gene in the Delacroix family. Or maybe I knew because I sent you a text this morning.'

Moses laughed and launched into his story about Green. 'Can I ask you something, Maria?'

'Feel free to ask me anything.'

'Are you still committed to our agreement?'

'Absolutely. More than ever. Not a day passes without feeling I have to restore my father's reputation. It's all about the family name, I can't let it remain splattered in mud.'

Moses looked down at the tourist boats on the Danube from his office window. 'I know how important this is for you. I want to do something personally. I want to show the Delphic Anomaly to the world. It's too great a symbol to stay hidden underground, in some dark chamber, water dripping over it, slowly being transformed into some kind of golden stalagmite.'

'You must do it, Moses. Go back there and find out what's happened,' she said, as if ordering him.

'But what shall we do about this young woman who is coming from Delphi with a collection of antiquities? I have a bad feeling about her,' he said, digging his nails into the palm of his hand.

'You mean the girl meeting my grandson Peter at Waterbury's?'

'Yes – what's going on there?'

'I don't know, but Peter will soon be finding out.'

3

They cruised out of Vienna, crossing the Brigittenauer Bridge and making their way towards the Hungarian border.

Two and half hours later they arrived in Budapest, stopping for their first cups of kave accompanied by slices of apfelstrudel. After pushing hard on the autobahn for three more hours, they crossed the border into Serbia and headed down into Belgrade. They took a rest stop and filled a flask with black coffee for the remainder of the all-night drive.

Approaching Macedonia, Moses wanted to stop at the reconstructed town of Skopje. At three in the morning they reached its outskirts. There was little evidence of the ruined city and its destruction by a massive earthquake three decades earlier.

As they crossed the old Roman bridge over the River Vardar a cluster of minarets appeared on the skyline, reminding Moses they'd entered a Muslim country.

As dawn broke they came to the Greek border and took the main road south towards Thessaloniki, the 'city of ghosts' when it was plain old Salonika.

Moses looked at the old, neat sandstone buildings. He found it hard to equate them with the city ruled by the Nazis during World War Two. From here, all the city's Jews, half of the population, including two of his own cousins, were shunted onto a one-way train journey to their deaths at Auschwitz.

The roads remained quiet apart from the heavy iron quarry trucks rumbling up and down the single-lane highway. For three long hours, they remained on a bumpy pock-marked concrete road, heading further south towards the ancient city of Delphi.

It was the worst road Moses could remember experiencing in Europe.

Arriving in the village at four in the afternoon, they made their way to the Hotel Amalia in Apollonos Street.

Moses sat on the balcony of his room, enjoying the view of the sparkling blue waters of the Gulf of Corinth. He checked his phone. There were no new texts. Still no word from Dr Green.

He told Sam to get some sleep and drove himself over to the archaeological site. The ticket office was still open but the museum was shut. A typed notice on the glass doors outside said it was closed for two weeks, but no explanation was given.

As the sun began to set, tourists wandered down from the Temple of Apollo towards the main exit. Moses took a fifty euro note from his wallet, rolled it up between his fingers and went to the ticket office.

'I wonder if you can help me, please,' he said, pushing the note into the hand of the young female cashier. 'I'm trying to find Dr Green. We are old friends. I don't suppose you can tell me where he has gone?'

'Sorry sir, the museum is closed,' she said, uncertain about taking the bribe.

'But do you know where Dr Green's villa is located? Here, take this, you can have it.'

The cashier took the note, smiled back at Moses, and pointed towards a modern architect-designed house on the first hill above Delphi.

'You can see it clearly on the top of the hill. Here, take these binoculars,' she said, handing him a pair from behind the desk. Moses focused the lens and saw the unmistakable house on the hill.

'Is it the modern house with the silver scales and purple-red flowers growing on the side? What's the plant called?'

'Yes, the bougainvillea growing up the side. It's the only one like it.'

'And which road do I take to get up there?'

'The Mount Parnassus road – you'll see it as you leave the village.'

Moses drove up to the mountain road and saw the silver-scaled roof behind a clump of trees. There was a track down to the house and he tentatively drove down the uneven stony surface.

The house was shut up and there was no car in the drive. He rang the bell, but all remained quiet. He went round the back and could see no sign of life.

Exhausted after the long drive from Vienna, he decided to go back to the hotel for a rest. It was now 7.30 pm.

Back at the Amalia he asked about getting a meal.

'Dinner is from 9.30 until midnight, sir,' said the receptionist. He knew the Greeks ate late, but this was extraordinary. He set his phone alarm to wake him at eleven and went to sleep.

Moses woke three hours later at 10.30 pm and staggered onto his balcony to look at the stars. It was possible to see Green's villa perched on the hill if he leaned over the wall. He was surprised to see bright lights coming from every window of the house, and went to get his binoculars for a closer view

The windows of the villa were covered by blinds, allowing nothing to be seen inside. He scanned the length of the house and saw a light go out and another come on seconds later.

Steadying the binoculars over the largest window he saw a faint shadow moving around. He rubbed his eyes and looked again, seeing another flicker of movement.

Moses packed his small overnight bag and rang down to reception. 'Can you connect me to Room 208?' The phone rang several times until Sam answered.

'Sorry to wake you, Sam, but you've had five hours sleep. It's going to have to be enough for tonight,' he said, and heard Sam trying to stifle a yawn. 'We need to drive up to Dr Green's villa tonight. There's someone in there now.'

'How much time have I got?' asked Sam.

'Two minutes. Sorry, I need you quickly, and we may need to follow them for a while, so we're leaving the hotel I'm afraid.'

Moses went down to reception and found the night porter watching an old episode of *Dallas* dubbed into Greek.

'Excuse me, I'm sorry to disturb you, but we will have to check out tonight. Very soon in fact. But I may come back after a few hours, I don't know yet. Here's my credit card for the the bill. Also, can you ask the kitchen to make some sandwiches, a picnic, anything they have – I need some food for two people to take away. And some cold drinks please.'

'Very good sir. No problem, the kitchen is still open, I'll call them,' said the porter.

Moses took the takeaway, two aluminium boxes of warm lamb stew with aubergines and tomatoes, complete with plastic spoons, knives, and forks. Wrapped in napkins were two loaves of white bread, along with bags of crisps, two freshly-picked oranges, their leaves still attached, and four cans of Mythos beer.

Sam came down into the hotel lobby carrying his case and placed all the food in the back seat.

It was 11.15 pm. Moses stood in the road, lifted his binoculars to his eyes, and looked towards the villa. It remained lit. A bright segment of moon hung over Mount Parnassus.

'It's the house on the hill with all the lights. The rather ostentatious building with the silver scales on the walls,' Moses said, passing the binoculars to Sam. He climbed into the driver's seat. 'I'll drive. It'll be quicker, I know the way.'

Moses drove down Aggelou street, turned right into Apollonos, and headed out of the village, climbing above the archaeological site until they could see Green's villa ahead of them, slightly set back from the hill, down a short lane.

He took the Merc at walking speed for the last few hundred metres so as to not cause any noise and parked in a layby, hidden from view.

'We'll walk up from here and take a look,' said Moses, grimacing as Sam's shoes crunched noisily against the ground.

'Be very quiet when you step on the gravel.'

4

Guillini held the iron key in his right hand.

It was eight inches long and designed to open a four hundred year old door, some twenty-five feet high.

Anna held onto him as he pushed it into the blackened lock and turned it three times in an anti-clockwise direction.

Leaning his body weight against the mighty oak door it slowly creaked open on its long iron hinges, making a narrow gap, just wide enough for Anna to slip through.

As she entered the hall of the Vatican Botanical Library, shafts of sunlight pierced through the sixteenth-century leaded windows, casting a purplish-blue glow over an entire wall of leather-bound books.

For Anna, this was the holy of holies – the greatest collection of plant specimens in the world, all under a magnificent gold-painted Renaissance roof.

She ran down the aisle in search of two glass cases. The first was a cherry wood drawer, containing the seed heads of the poisonous *Helleborus niger*. Struggling to read the faint letters on the handwritten labels she put on her glasses to see the fading Latin script.

They'd been harvested from all over the Roman Empire, including Delphi. She looked around for Guillini and whilst he wasn't looking she took a few seeds marked *Italia* and *Grecia* and put them in her bag, but he'd seen her.

'I don't mind, take whatever you want, no one will ever notice,' he said.

'I'm looking for sylphium, the Roman drug,' she said to a disinterested Guillini. 'I can't find it anywhere. Do you know where they might keep the *Sylphium*?'

Guillini shrugged his shoulders. 'Just sit down here for a minute,' he said, grabbing her by the wrist. 'You can spend as much time as you like looking for your favourite seeds later, but I need to talk to you.'

'What do you want from me?' she said, trying to pull her hand from Guillini's grasp.

'The date when Moses will take the Anomaly out of the chamber,' he said, tightening his grip on her arm. 'We've taken care of Dr Green, but that won't put Moses off from trying something.'

'Couldn't Green have a miracle?' she asked. Guillini didn't respond, but twisted his mouth.

'Miracles, ugh. The church has enough problems finding miracles for all the saints. Look, Anna, I need you to use your skills of persuasion to find out what your friend Moses is planning to do, that's the deal,' said Guillini, still holding onto her arm.

'Let me go, GG. You know I'll do whatever you want, just help me find the *Sylphium* seeds.'

He released her wrist. 'OK, my sweet. I must tell you I have new authority from the Holy Father to do whatever is necessary to stop the Delphic Anomaly seeing the light of day. You understand me, don't you, Anna?' he said, but she wasn't listening. She was holding a waxy leaf in her fingers and twisting it around in the blue light.

'Are you paying attention to me or that old leaf?'

'OK, it's no problem, I understand,' she said, and ran between the lines of glass display cases.

'I should never have brought you in here,' he shouted, his voice echoed in the vaulted roof.

'But it was our agreement,' she said, as he came marching towards her.

He put his hands on her shoulders, to stop her from moving. 'Do you want to come here again?' he said, pressing his thumbs into her flesh.

'There's no question, I must return. You agreed to it,' she said. 'Let me go.'

'I will, but only if you go back to Moses,' he said and released her arm.

'Alright. I'll arrange something.'

5

'*Merde*,' Helena screamed as the phone began to ring. She was in the middle of pouring strong hot coffee from a cafetiere.

She ran into the kitchen to pick up the phone and heard Peter's hesitant hello.

'You've let me down again, Peter. I don't want to hear your

lame excuses. When will you get here? Your grandmother has been expecting you all day,' Helena shouted down the phone, unable to control her anger.

She pressed the red button to end the call and went back into the bedroom.

Helena looked around the apartment. Even without all the art hanging on the walls she was sure it was worth more than five million euros. But her mother seemed to be in no hurry to leave it all behind.

Half-French, half-Italian, she was a fighter and had reached the age of 90, surviving a year longer than the doctors had predicted. As ever, she liked to confound the so-called experts.

'When will he be coming?' said Maria, sitting up against the pillows.

'He promised very soon, around 4.30. He said he's been caught up in traffic.'

Maria focussed on her daughter with grey, watery eyes, but her weak voice became drowned out by the police sirens in the street below as she attempted to speak. She turned her head.

'I hate those lights. Curse the ISIS terrorists!' she said angrily, pointing at the blue reflections pulsing on the wall of the bedroom. They waited for the wailing of the emergency vehicles to end.

'I know we've had our differences over the years. We don't agree on what is best for Peter, but he's the one I've chosen. I need to tell him the truth about the family history.'

'What exactly is on your mind?'

'I want him to track down Niko's discovery.'

Helena pinched her arm. 'Are you sure he's the right choice? Maybe someone else in the family would be better-suited?' she said.

Maria sat forward. 'You know, whenever I see him, I feel

he has such determination – the smile, the knowing look.' She paused to take a breath. 'And he's empathic too.'

Helena raised her eyes to the ceiling. 'But you don't know him. I don't like to say this, but he's a troubled young man.'

'We mustn't blame him, he had a difficult time as a young child, please don't catalogue his faults. I don't need a perfect human being; I only want someone who cares. He is human, he errs. Maybe he's a little like us?' Marie made a dig at her daughter with her knuckles. 'I know he isn't easy, he's a wild spirit. But he has a rare gift.'

Helena looked puzzled.

'He has intuition. You know what I mean, the philosopher Pascal knew,' Maria said, and quoted his famous line. '*Le coeur a ses raisons que la raison ne connait pas.* Peter follows his instincts. It's healthy to do that, I believe, and what's needed in the family.'

'Have you considered anyone else?' asked Helena.

'No one comes close. We must use Peter's instinctive skills, otherwise Niko's discovery will never be found,' said Maria.

Helena nodded with a frown of acceptance. 'Look *maman*, I have to accept that Peter does have a remarkable knowledge of Delphi. He knows things about the place which cannot be explained.'

Maria held her hands out towards Helena. 'Yes, Peter is the spark of light in the family. Allow me this, Helena. I know he'll find it.'

Helena had a momentary flashback to the meeting with Dr Green years earlier in Delphi. She remembered his irritating words – 'any relics will be safe if they remain buried underground.'

Maria was still speaking to her. 'No, the crime against Niko mustn't be forgotten,' she said, trying to place her hand on Helena's face. 'He's a bright boy. Promise me you'll tell him *everything*, Helena, won't you?'

The words echoed in Helena's head. She felt sweaty with embarrassment. A long-forgotten sensation rippled across her body.

She couldn't stop the graphic memories flooding back. The surroundings were bright and clear but the faces weren't there at all, as if they'd been airbrushed away. She knew from the accent that she was with a Danish man at Delphi, on the morning of the summer solstice, some twenty-five years earlier, the sun warming her skin. She couldn't see what he looked like, but she could feel they were making love in the open air.

'Helena!' a voice called out.

6

'I have an idea, let me take in your tray of patisserie,' Peter said, grabbing it from Juliet.

'OK, why not? It's a good idea,' she said, opening the door.

'At last,' Maria gasped as she saw him enter. He hugged her frail body. The lines and wrinkles of her 90 years disappeared from her face as the blood rushed through her veins. Her pale skin turned a vibrant pink.

Helena stood up to leave. 'I'm making some hot drinks before I go. Do you want a tea or coffee?' she asked Peter, staring at his untidy hair with a flicker of disapproval.

'A coffee would be great,' he said.

As soon as Helena had left the room Maria began whispering. 'Peter, I want to tell you something ...' she said in a low, almost inaudible voice, but she couldn't finish the thought. He wondered if she'd become over-emotional. Her breathing became slow. Placing his fingers under her wrist he felt a weak pulse throbbing gently under her skin.

'Let her sleep,' said Helena, as she came back into the room with coffee and Darjeeling tea.

'But I'm scared she won't wake up and I'll never find out what she wanted to tell me,' he said.

'She's not going to die on you, she'll be fine – now that you've arrived. She's been awake a long time, waiting for you. Let her rest,' Helena said.

'Where are you going?' Peter said, biting a nail on his forefinger.

'It's something private, I don't have to tell you everything Peter. I have a life of my own – I'll be back in two to three hours,' she said, walking briskly out of the door.

7

Helena arrived in Sainte Marguerite, a small suburb on the opposite side of town. She was late and ran up the path of a nineteenth-century house on the tree-lined street.

Upstairs, on the first floor, he was waiting in a large carpeted room with off-white walls. He gave her a warm smile as she sat down on a single armchair. Opposite her, the orange glow of the late afternoon sun was streaming through the window.

As she crossed her legs she watched him looking at her.

The crimson hair, the limpid green eyes and the shallow cheekbones remained striking. Helena still enjoyed having an effect on a man. Her age had not dampened her appetite nor made her any less attractive.

A cut-glass mirror hanging above the fireplace reflected a thin line of purple-blue light onto the wall. It ran like a laser beam across the carpet, climbing up Helena's legs, curving seductively as it made its way up her body.

'Last time we came to the day you left Peter alone for the first time,' he said, stabbing his notebook with his pencil. 'What happened?'

'We'd gone to the cinema. He was twelve years old and we thought it was safe to leave him alone. But when we returned, just before midnight, we couldn't find him. He was not downstairs watching TV, and he was not in his bedroom. Finally, I looked in my study.' Helena stopped and took a sip from the glass of water on the side table.

'And did you find him?'

'Oh yes, he was fast asleep in my study, his head on my desk. He'd taken a ladder from the basement and set it up so he could reach a book at the top of my bookshelf. He'd found the only copy of my PhD. It was lying open and looked like he'd been checking my experiments in Delphi.

'Michel carried him off to his bedroom and I replaced the book. I was a little shocked. What was he doing exactly?

'In the morning he said very little about it, but I got the impression he wanted to check where he was conceived, and exactly when. He's always had this strong feeling he was conceived in Delphi.

'I tried to dissuade him from this, but he was convinced it was true.

'A few weeks later I was sitting alone in my study, staring at the photograph of the Temple of Apollo on the wall. It reminded me that something had to be done. I couldn't leave things as they were. It was too dangerous.

'I took the stepladder back up to the study, leaned it against the wall, next to an Escher print. I looked at the Escher for a moment before I climbed up the ladder. It was an appropriate image for what was happening in my life.'

'Why was that?'

'It was a staircase going nowhere, up and down at the same time, never arriving anywhere.

'My thesis was on the top shelf. I stretched up and took it down. A plastic wrapper, from a packet of crisps I think, was sandwiched between the pages which showed the dates of my experiments. This is what Peter was obsessed with. He must have left the wrapper there when he found it. He was the only one in the house who ate those crisps.

'I sat back at my desk, took a long, deep breath, picked up the volume, placed it in my backpack, walked out of the door, and drove off.'

'Where did you go?'

'Forêt de Saint-Germain-en-Laye. It's about an hour away from Paris, to the northwest. It's a favourite place for picnics, but not on that day. The weather was cold and grey. No one was around. It was perfect for my task.

'After walking in the woods for ten minutes, I came to a large oak tree, growing on a raised mound. It was dry and hidden from footpaths and people. I had to do this alone, out of sight. I didn't want to arouse suspicion.

'I was feeling cold and took a shot of brandy from a hip flask. I needed to make a fire. There were stones on the ground, so I began to make a hearth. From a few pieces of wood I made a pyramid shape, leaving room for the air to get in underneath.

'I took the PhD out my backpack and began to tear up the pages, one-by-one, It felt so liberating to destroy it, once and for all. I screwed up the pages into paper balls, and placed all of them under the twigs.

'I flicked my lighter and set it alight. It began to burn well. The dry wood crackled nicely. Within half an hour I'd watched every page burn away into nothing. I smoked two Gauloises as my PhD thesis turned into a pile of ash.

'It ceased to exist. All that remained were the two thick covers and the spine. With a pair of pliers, I tore them apart so they were small enough to burn as well.

'I poured water over the hot stones and the embers fizzed and died.

'It felt wonderful. I drove home, happy and calm. That was it – gone.'

As Helena finished speaking she collapsed into the armchair and let her body relax.

'You're the only person I've confessed this to,' she said, smiling and opening her arms to the therapist.

'I'm honoured, Helena. May I ask you something?'

'Anything at all.'

'What about the copy of your PhD that remains in the French National Library?'

'I think you'll find it is not available anymore,' she said, interlocking the fingers of both hands. He looked at her sceptically.

'Fortunately, the security is not too good at the university. I just took it away one day, hidden in my jacket, and burnt it as well. Please don't tell the authorities, I know it is a crime, but I had no choice.'

The therapist nodded and placed his fingers across his lips. 'But why destroy every trace of your own work?' he asked, scratching his forehead.

Helena wanted a cigarette but she knew the no-smoking rules in the house. She stood up and went to the window, stretching her arms over her head and bending down to touch the floor.

'Oh, I don't know, it just seemed a sensible precaution at the time. No one can dredge up my old life now, it's gone forever,' she said, head between her legs, upside down. She straightened up and returned to her chair.

'I don't want my life to unravel. I'm a different person now. I was fooling around then, exploring myself, acting on impulse. It was crazy – a fun piece of research, nothing more.' She hesitated. 'Look, I don't want it to define my life.'

'What do you mean?'

'My sex research in Delphi was over in a few weeks and now, many years later, I don't want my life to be undone by such a crazy thing. It's finished. I've moved on,' Helena said, running her fingers through her hair.

'And what did you fear Peter would do?'

'He wants to ruin my life. Not consciously, but he wants to go looking for his biological father.'

Helena looked at her watch and jumped out of the chair. 'I have to go back to see my mother, Peter is there with her on his own. That could be a dangerous combination,' she said, standing by the door.

'Until next week, Helena. And …'

'Yes?'

'Don't rush into anything.'

PART THIRTEEN

Isabella and Moses

1

Isabella pulled up her filmsy t-shirt towards her face and wiped the sweat off her cheeks and from around her tired eyes.

The gossamer-thin cotton was already damp and did little to absorb the mounting wetness dappling her face.

She tried to focus on the screen again. An email alert flashed in the corner – but she only managed to read the word 'meeting' before it dissolved away.

Her fingers slid to a halt on the keyboard.

Something was going on outside. She thought she'd heard the click of a door – but she couldn't tell with all the windows locked.

There was another click – it felt closer this time. She stopped breathing and listened only to the blades of the fan pushing the humid air around above her.

Holding her half-naked body rigid, she felt her nipples harden underneath her top. Now she knew she was scared.

All went silent as she looked towards the door – she was half-expecting it to burst open.

After a few seconds of eventless silence she leaned back and began to breathe again, grateful for the cool breeze spiralling down from the ceiling fan.

'Holy Father, please make the bastards leave me alone,' she mumbled, unsure if she was speaking to herself or aiming her words at some higher force floating around above her, somewhere in the ether.

Tying her long black hair back, she grabbed a tissue and soaked up the slippery film of sweat from her neck.

There was less than an hour to go before she had to leave.

Every light was burning in the house – a white marble

hexagon, with exterior walls made from curved silver gills. Looking like a swarm of fish, perched on a slab of limestone rock above the ruins of the temple, it tended to attract its fair number of cranks.

Grabbing her father's heaviest-looking Murano vase, she crept to the window and lifted a slat of the Venetian blind with a half-eaten thumbnail.

She looked out at the night sky – a sliver of moon hung low over Mount Parnassus. The cosmos was sparkling that night. In six hours, with the arrival of the tourist buses, the moon would have shrunk to a small five cent coin, dwarfed by a hot glowing sun.

She put down the vase, glanced at the bolts on the front door and remembered she didn't have to stay a prisoner inside her father's villa.

She stood on her toes to reach the top bolt, pushing her body weight against the door so it eased open.

It swung out on its wooden frame and the scent of warm honeysuckle and purple bougainvillea filled the air as she stepped out.

Thirty yards up the track, on the mountain road towards Klovinos, she could hear the hum of an idling car engine.

Cupping her hands together into the shape of a loudhailer, she took a deep breath.

'Come out you scum! I know you're up there,' she shouted into the darkness, her lips trembling.

There was a click of a car door, similar to the sound she'd heard earlier. A few seconds later she heard the cracking of eucalyptus bark shattering into small pieces under the wheels of a vehicle.

'Cowards!' she shouted again, her voice trailing off when she realised it was speeding away.

From behind the trees, a pair of headlights snaked into the hillside, re-appearing several times until it was finally snuffed out by the undulating terrain.

The engine noise faded into the night. It was quiet again. Moths fluttered around her, determined to barbecue their wings on the tungsten light hanging in the porch.

She was alone.

2

'How did it go?' said Moses.

'It's stuck firmly onto her wheel hub. It's an Audi TT, a fast little sports number. I don't think she saw anything.'

Sam switched on the tracker screen and could see the vehicle was alive and transmitting, showing up as a red dot on the map. 'How can you be sure she's travelling tonight?' he asked.

'She has to be in Paris in three days with her cargo of antiquities. She'll have to leave tonight,' said Moses. 'Don't look surprised, I have friends at Waterbury's.'

They drove for ten minutes and Sam stopped in a layby, half a kilometre outside the village of Galaxidi, on the E65 highway between Delphi and Patras.

'When she comes I want you to get in there behind her and stay close on her tail. We can't afford to lose her,' Moses said, pausing to rub his chin.

'Actually, I'd really like her to know someone is following her.'

3

Isabella staggered back into the house and slammed the door, locking herself inside using both bolts.

'Fucking freaks,' she said under her breath, knocking over a wine glass stained with last night's Rioja.

She was used to the oddballs who came to stare at the architecture, but it was the second time it'd happened time that day.

In the kitchen the inkjet printer was spewing out details of her overnight hotel in Milan. Eight pages of car-hire deals, cancellation policies, and holiday breaks cascaded onto the floor.

As the printer juddered to a halt she could hear the music playing again. The comforting notes of Glenn Gould's *Bach Preludes* wafted across the room.

Four fragile vases lay on the kitchen table in front of her, cocooned in plastic bubble wrap. She packed the ancient vases gently between her ski clothes and kissed the packages goodbye.

Made from translucent blue glass dating back to the fifth century BC, they were decorated with a palm tree motif and an unidentified script, probably Phoenician, she wasn't sure. She placed the swollen bundles inside a suitcase, adding sweaters and thick woollen socks to cushion the delicate glass

She calculated the drive to Paris would take thirty-six hours. She recited her cover story out loud. 'I'm taking a late skiing holiday in Val d'Isere. I know the village well because I've skied there since I was five years old …'

She looked at her face in the mirror. She felt drained and twenty years older than her thirty-four. She couldn't quite believe what had happened. Appointed overnight as the youngest-ever director of the site, selected in a hurry to succeed her father, it was all a colourful blur. There had been no time for a proper handover.

When she received the call she'd flown the next day for the interview. The all-male board liked the idea of having such an attractive ambassador. Her sultry and melancholic looks, the long black hair and large brown eyes, had come from her Spanish mother, who'd left her father when she was nine.

The whole of the ancient city was now her kingdom.

Every nationality trampled over its marble steps. Every language echoed across the ruins. She wished they would disappear for a day a week, but the hordes never stopped arriving in their air-conditioned buses and 4x4s, clutching their iPhones, UV sunglasses, and tubes of Factor 50.

Mountains of plastic water bottles engulfed the site and she wanted to ban them, but it was the most popular item in the museum shop and the profits paid her salary.

Her body was still shaking with tiredness as she summoned up the mind to finish the export certificates.

She needed more caffeine and downed her third cup of cold, oily coffee, keeping it away from the pile of blanks. It was her last batch, given to her by a short-term lover at the Ministry of Culture in return for some lunchtime sex.

Using a test strip of 200 gm card she wrote out the Greek alphabet to warm up the nib of her favourite fountain pen. With her muscles relaxed, she began practising the spidery signature of Pavlos Geroulanos, the minister of culture, copying his curves and thicknesses from a genuine government certificate.

She waved her completed forgery in front of a fan heater on full power, threw a kiss at the fake document, and slid it into her leather travel case, next to her scuffed passport.

The email sitting in her inbox was from Waterbury's, confirming her meeting with antiquities expert Peter Delacroix on Friday April 24th at 11.00 am. She read it again and copied the address.

She had only ten minutes left before she had to leave the villa if she was going to catch the first ferry out of Patras.

She gathered her scattered items of personal life support – her passport and wallet, a tube of toothpaste, an electric toothbrush and, after a moment's hesitation, a packet of condoms.

With a bottle of water in her left hand, she set the time switch for the houselights and programmed a mix of Balkan music, Swing, and Vivaldi to play every afternoon and evening until twenty past midnight.

Keying four digits into the pad of the alarm, she locked up and swung her Audi down the driveway.

A dazzling Venus was rising above the ruins of the Temple as she headed towards the E65, the single-track mountain road snaking along the rocky coastline of the Corinthian sea.

The sight of the moon rippling on the seawater spooked her as she drove alone on the empty highway.

Terrified she was hallucinating she bit her tongue, tightening her grip on the wheel until she felt a stinging pain.

The taste of her own warm blood was oddly reassuring.

4

Moses and Sam sat in the layby, 15 km out of Delphi, just past the village of Galaxidi.

'Keep the sidelights off Sam, let's not draw attention to ourselves,' said Moses.

Sam switched off the lights but kept the engine running.

'I'm ready to go as soon as she swings by,' he said.

Moses was looking down at a long list of Milan hotels on a booking app on his phone. 'She's taking her time if she wants to catch the first ferry. If she doesn't pass here in the next 15 minutes she won't make it. She'll have to do an overnight stop. Milan is my bet,' he said, dialling the first number. Sam jolted as Moses' voice boomed into his phone.

'*Buongiorno,* I would like to leave a message for a guest who is arriving at your hotel later tonight. Her name is Isabella Green.'

There was a short delay whilst they checked their guest register.

'Sorry, we do not have a guest with this name.'

'OK, I must have mistaken the name of the hotel. Goodbye,' said Moses.

He tried the next hotel with the same request.

'*Buonasera*, Good evening, I'd like to leave a message for Isabella Green.'

When he reached the eighth hotel on the list, the Hotel Michel Angeloin on Milan's Via Marcus Aurelius, the receptionist confirmed there was a Dr Isabella Green due to arrive.

'Can you please leave her the following message? Tell her Moses Frank called and would like to take her out to dinner. And one more thing. I'd like to make a booking for myself and a colleague,' said Moses. 'Can you possibly give me the room next to Ms Green's?'

The hotel booking clerk checked availability on her computer and offered Moses two rooms.

As he switched off his phone Sam called out. 'That's her, the tracker's moving, she's just leaving the villa in Delphi. Look she's winding up the track. My God, look at her move, her speed is extraordinary,' said Sam.

'Are you ready to keep up with her? Looks like she's going to swing past us any second now,' said Moses.

Sam's fingertips became white as he gripped the steering wheel and pressed down on the accelerator.

The 4.2 litre Merc engine roared but remained where it was.

'Remember Sam, stay right in there, close behind her – we can't afford to lose sight of her.'

5

Isabella leaned over the wheel and looked for some gum. After eight hours driving with only short coffee breaks since leaving Brindisi, her body was feeling shattered and numb.

She couldn't believe she'd driven all the way from the heel of Italy in one long drive.

A sign with a giant arrow for Milan flew past her and she realised she was only 12 km from the sprawling city.

She opened the glove compartment and felt for a packet of chewing gum, or a sugary sweet – she was desperate for anything to keep her awake for the next half hour.

All she could feel with the tips of her fingers was a plastic box – the tracking device handed to her earlier that morning by the mechanic.

She'd forgotten the tracker had been sitting there for the last eight hours, transmitting her location to someone, somewhere. Her eyes began to flicker and, for a fleeting moment, they closed.

She remembered she wanted to find out who'd been tracking her, but she was too tired to care now. Her eyes opened again and she saw the sign for the Melegnano service station.

Reducing her speed to 15 kmh she turned into the car park, switched off the ignition, and stretched her arms over the wheel.

It was only a few metres walk to the café entrance and, too exhausted to look for her jacket, Isabella staggered through the revolving doors, bra-less, wearing only her t-shirt and jeans.

In the queue for coffee, a well-dressed man in a light cream suit came up to her. Isabella began to feel that this stranger was hovering too close to her. Had her stalker finally caught up with her? Or was this man a plain-clothes officer with bad news about her father?

'Isn't it Dr Green? We met at the Delphi Museum a couple of years ago. I couldn't help but remember your face as I saw you waiting there,' he said in a slow and tuneful Italian accent whilst staring down at her loose t-shirt.

'I'm a great fan of your father's work. I should introduce myself – Dr Ricardo Haskey. Just call me Ricky, department of geology, Naples University.'

Isabella fidgeted uncomfortably with her watch, conscious he was looking down at her breasts. 'Oh, quite. You've caught me in a bit of rush, I'm afraid,' she said.

'Can I just ask one favour? It won't take long.'

Isabella looked uncomfortable and positioned her arms over

her chest.

'I'm hoping to visit Delphi to look into how the young women oracles, the Pythia,' he said, emphasising the last syllable *-thia* by placing his tongue against his front teeth, 'were induced into an ecstatic trance.' He drew closer and smiled like he was enjoying her company. Isabella tried to step back but was already crammed into the back of the aisle and had nowhere to move.

'We've developed some very sensitive equipment in my department which can detect if the young Pythia inhaled gases seeping out of the rocks.'

'How fascinating, I never knew about that,' she said, with a tired voice, trying to work out her exit strategy as she took her coffee. She'd been looking forward to sitting alone in the cafeteria for ten minutes, staring out of the window and doing nothing.

'I'm afraid I've got to get going. It's very nice to meet you, maybe you can write to me at the museum and I'll get in touch.'

He followed her towards the exit. 'You see, Senorita Green, if we can find evidence of the gases, the mystery of how the Oracles achieved their state of ecstasy and extraordinarily accurate prophecies will be solved,' he said, trying to keep up with her fast walking speed.

She kept nodding every few seconds as if she was listening, but her head was elsewhere. She looked at her watch and turned to face him with a fixed smile. 'As I said, I would like to follow this up, but I have to be in Milan for a meeting quite soon,' she said, putting her coffee down. She opened her suede bag and produced a white business card, placed it in his hand, and disappeared through the revolving doors.

It was only a short distance into Milan as she entered the ring road around the city, sipping from her cardboard coffee cup as she stopped at a set of lights.

Twenty minutes later, Isabella turned into Via Marcus Aurelius for Hotel Michel Angeloin. The orange twelve-storey building was on the left side of the street.

No one could have known she was staying there as she'd only booked it on the night she left Delphi. She'd been in no communication with anyone, so she was somewhat disturbed to be handed two messages when she collected her key card.

She gave the bellboy two euros, dumped her luggage and sat on the bed, slowly opening the two pieces of paper.

The first message said: 'I'm looking after you – MF.'

'Who the hell is MF?' she said out loud. The initials meant nothing to her.

She unfolded the next slip of paper. 'Please join me for dinner, kind regards, Moses Frank,' it said in the hotel clerk's handwriting.

There was no number to call, but the name confirmed her earlier recollection – this was the man from the Patras ferry, whose name she'd remembered as she was driving along on the autostrada, near Brescia. The same man who'd visited her father some twenty five years earlier to inspect the Delphic Anomaly.

She felt her heart racing as she realised that this was the man who had been following her all the way from Greece.

Her body began to sweat. She stripped off her clothes and walked into the shower to cool down.

As she switched off the water and stepped out of the cubicle there was a loud knock at the door. She grabbed a towel and shouted, 'not now, I'm busy, come back later, please.' A second later she heard a female voice call out and realised it was only the maid wanting to turn her bed.

Isabella collapsed onto the mattress and slid between the silky sheets. She was almost comatose with fatigue from the twenty-three hour drive. Within seconds, she was unconscious.

Fifteen minutes later the phone beside the bed started to ring.

'Yes,' she said sleepily. 'Isabella Green.'

'Hello Isabella, it's Moses Frank here,' a deep, loud voice boomed at her through the receiver.

'Remind me please, Mr Frank,' she yawned, 'who you are, exactly? My memory is not so great at the moment. I've been driving a long time.'

'I'm an old friend of your father's. We met many years ago when I paid a visit to Delphi, but you were just a little girl at the time.'

'I've a hazy memory of it. Can you remind me why you came to see him?' she said, although she was in no doubt about the reason.

'Your father wanted me to take a look at something he'd discovered in a chamber under the Temple of Apollo. I deal in antiquities,' Moses said. 'He wanted my opinion on an unusual find he'd made.'

Isabella lay back on the bed, barely able to hold the telephone to her ear.

'Actually, I can still remember that day quite well,' she said, wondering if this really was the same man who'd been tormenting her on the road from Delphi to Patras in a silver Mercedes.

'Look, Mr Frank. I don't wish to sound unfriendly, but *why* are you calling me after all these years? That was a very long time ago,' she said, yawning again as she spoke.

'My dear Isabella, I'm merely fulfilling your father's wishes. He told me that if anything should happen to him I should look after you. I was very concerned when everything went quiet a few weeks ago. Your father has disappeared, so I felt I had to come and check you were OK.' He paused. 'I felt it was my duty. I promised him.'

'Explain one thing first – how did you know I was staying here?'

'Let's meet and I'll tell you everything. Don't worry Isabella, I only have your interests at heart.'

She listened but exhaustion got the better of her, and her head fell forward. The sudden movement revived her momentarily.

'I'm really sorry, I can't even stay awake, I'm too tired to socialise. I've been driving all day and have to set off early tomorrow. I must get some sleep. It's kind of you, but now is not a good time,' she said, and put the phone down.

After thirty seconds it rang again.

'Look, I can come to your room. There are things I need to tell you I don't want the whole world to hear.'

'You're very persistent. Where are you, exactly, Mr Frank?' she said.

'I'm actually staying in the next room. How about just one drink in the bar?'

Isabella didn't say anything. She was confused. Why had this man been tormenting her all day, following her for hundreds of miles? Why was he pushing himself onto her? It was all very unsettling. She decided she needed to stop the harassment now.

But then – maybe this 'MF' character could help her. He'd told her he was an antiquities dealer.

'OK Mr Frank, I can see you're not going to take no for answer. I'll meet you in the bar in fifteen minutes,' she said. 'I'll be in a blue jacket.'

6

Moses was sitting in a leather armchair, drinking a whisky, when a dog-tired Isabella drifted towards him. The skin beneath her eyes had turned a pale grey.

As he saw her approach he stood up and beamed at her, putting his arm around her shoulder.

'Let me get you a drink, my dear Isabella,' he said.

'Just a sparkling water. No alcohol please, I won't sleep,' she said softly, collapsing onto the adjoining seat. He went to the bar and brought back a tall glass of fizzing water packed with ice and lemon.

As he stood there talking to the barman, she could see Moses was a tall and elegantly dressed man with a sense of style, lean and fit for his age, in his early fifties perhaps.

'So how's your father doing?' Moses asked as he gave her the water.

'He's OK,' she said, with no hint of an expression. Moses smiled back as if to say 'that wasn't a good enough answer.'

'But tell me, what's actually happened to him, Isabella?' he said, locking his fingers together. 'I've been trying to call him for weeks. Everything's gone dead.'

'Look, Mr Frank, I know you feel you know my father very well. But it was a long time ago when you came to visit us. Excuse the old cliché, but a lot of water has flowed under the bridge since then. And let's face it, we don't know each other, so why should I tell you details of my personal life?'

Moses took a large sip of whisky and shrugged at her.

'Actually, I feel like I we're old friends. You know, I only spoke to your father a few weeks ago. He was very confident of excavating the Delphic Anomaly within days. So what's happened?'

Isabella looked at the floor and covered her mouth with her tapered fingers. She was an unpractised liar and had sworn not to tell anyone the whole story about her father.

'Rest assured, he is OK, Mr Frank. He's gone away for a while …' She hesitated. 'For some time, actually. I cannot say any more,' she said, leaning forwards, before taking a sip of water.

'But is there anything I can do to help him?' Moses asked, moving closer to her.

'That's kind, but not now. I'll let you know if anything changes,' she said, and pushed her glass away to signal she'd had enough.

Moses leaned forward and whispered across the table.

'I think I can help you sell your father's collection,' he said, nodding. She felt her face going crimson with embarrassment.

She'd been determined to keep the details of her mission to Paris a secret. He didn't need to know about it, she'd decided, and she didn't want a stranger finding out any more.

Moses looked across, waiting for her to respond.

'Look,' she said angrily. 'What makes you think I'm trying to sell his collection, anyway?'

Moses brushed his sleeve. 'It's a small world, I know most people in the world of Greek antiquities. I hear a lot through the old grapevine,' he said, moving closer to her again.

'I should warn you, there are many disreputable people in the field. Keep me in mind. I'll be there to protect you from any unforeseen problems, should anything arise.'

'OK, I'll keep it in mind,' she said, covering her mouth, trying to hold back a tired yawn, her energy fading.

'I think we can trust each other. I have a good feeling about you Isabella, and I have a duty to help you. I promised your father.' She pushed her chair back to get up.

'I'm very tired now. I really must go and get some sleep,' she said.

Moses put his hand on her wrist.

'How about something to eat? Dinner perhaps? I'm sure you'll feel better with some food inside you, and I can help you,' he said, looking into her eyes as she stood over him. 'I can advise you that with the right buyer – you could get yourself an apartment in one of the best arrondissements in Paris, maybe the 16th.'

For the first time she smiled back at him.

'Are you serious?' she said, sitting back down. 'Look, no dinner – I'm not hungry at all, it's too late to eat,' she said. 'But you might as well come up to my room and take a look.'

7

Inside the bedroom, Isabella took out an iPad from her case. As there was only one chair, they sat on the bed next to each other so Moses could see the screen.

A series of large colour pictures of her collection began to appear on the glass display.

'Can you make this vase larger please?' Moses said, pointing at the screen.

Isabella touched it, widening her fingers and made the image double in size.

Moses blinked.

'Christ, this is amazing quality,' he said with a startled tone.

'Is this really fourth century *before* Christ?'

'Fifth century BC, actually,' Isabella said confidently, trying to restrain her own excitement.

'That's odd. No, let me re-phrase that – unusual. I want to know – why is this symbol on this fifth century vase?' he said, pointing at some unfamiliar script. 'Do you have any others like this?'

'Quite a few. Fourteen altogether,' she said, scanning through the remaining images. He looked through all the vases, zooming in on the lettering inscribed on the sides.

'You know, this script may be early Phoenician, or possibly what some archaeologists have called "proto-Hebrew." Very unusual,' he said.

Moses turned towards her, put his hands on her shoulders and looked straight into her eyes.

'And you, young lady, are going to Paris to Waterbury's to see if they will auction them for you?'

She ducked under his arms and looked at him with irritation. 'What makes you think that?' she said.

Moses smiled back, lifting his head. 'And I understand you're meeting a young Greek expert named Peter Delacroix?'

'My God, how the hell do you know all this?' she said, glaring at Moses.

'Just take it for granted that I know a lot of people in the international trade, my lovely Isabella.'

'I'm not *your* lovely Isabella,' she shouted. 'Just tell me what they're worth.'

'Unseen, without looking at them all, apart from the one fine specimen you have with you, I'd give you ten thousand Euros for the complete collection. I'm probably being too generous, but I want to help you,' he said, weaving his fingers together as if it might seal the deal.

Isabella spat into his face.

'That's half the value of one vase alone. I know they're worth much more,' she screeched, as Moses calmly wiped her spit off his cheek.

He put his hand on her arm, but she twisted herself away. 'Look, I must be honest with you. These vases might as well be stolen goods. They only have a black market value, I'm afraid.'

'But why'd you say that? she said.

'The problem is that these beautiful pieces have no provenance. Coming from your father's private collection, they have no certifiable history. I think you understand what I am saying without me going into any sordid details.'

'So what?'

'They will be unsellable at any public auction. No reputable auction house will touch them.'

'But I need a much better price than what you're saying. I'll get it in Paris, I'm sure. Peter Delacroix will appreciate their worth. He's a real expert,' she said, and sat back on the bed.

Moses put his hand on her shoulder again and tried to smile at her.

She grimaced. 'Fuck off, don't try that on me. Don't think you can negotiate yourself some easy sex. I'm not available for that kind of transaction.'

'For God's sake, Isabella, I am just trying to console you as a family friend.'

She lay back on the bed and laughed.

8

'You're a rogue, aren't you, Mr Frank?' she said, staring him in the face, her anger written over her down-turned lips.

'A total bastard, actually, if you want to get technical,' he said with a smile.

Isabella laughed. 'But there is something about you,' she said, as she began unbuttoning her blouse. He took a sudden deep breath and began to shake his head.

'I must warn you, Moses. I'm very tired. I've no energy left for anything.'

'Look, I'm just going to keep you company. Keep an eye on you. Nothing will happen Isabella, I promise you.'

'But on the other hand, why waste it? she said, smiling at him. 'Can you pull these off me? I'm too tired to do it,' she added, stretching her legs out in front of him. He removed her high-heeled shoes and placed them carefully by the bed.

'And the rest, please,' she yawned, revealing her legs to him. He carefully pulled her stockings down the length of her legs and let them drift onto the floor.

'And these?' he said tugging at her satin briefs.

'Sure,' she said. 'It's easier without them.'

She wandered naked into the bathroom. When she returned to the bedroom, she crawled into the king-sized bed and felt Moses slide in beside her. A few minutes later she felt his hands cupping her breasts, his mouth over her lips.

Her eyes slowly closed and everything lost focus, quickly going black.

An hour later, she woke up and discovered that Moses had climbed out of the bed. She heard him opening the minibar and unscrewing the top of a small brandy bottle.

A half-moon shone through the open window, casting a blue shadow over the room. Moments later she could smell the alcohol on his breath as he came back and lay next to her. She quickly lost consciousness again.

Five hours later Isabella's eyes opened as the sun was rising over Milan.

A pale azure dawn had replaced the moonlit sky.

She lay half-awake for several minutes, thinking about her exit.

Slithering out of the bed she washed in the sink so as not to wake Moses, repacked her overnight bag, and crept out of the room. As she shut the door firmly behind her, she blew a kiss in his direction.

Inside the elevator she caught the smells of fresh croissant and coffee rising from the restaurant.

She realised she was hungry. Having missed dinner, she went to the buffet and took several slices of watermelon, a chunk of pineapple doused with lime, and two pieces of brown toast spread thickly with dolcelatte.

As she left she scooped four patisseries into a paper napkin and handed in her key.

From the hotel's underground garage she turned right onto a deserted Via Santa Margherita until she reached Piazza della Scala, which was also empty of traffic.

At Viale Certosa there was a sign for the autostrada. Soon she was cruising along at 140, biting into a pain au chocolat, one hand on the wheel, happy to be on the road again, heading north out of Milan in the direction of Geneva.

One hour later, as she heard the bells ringing from the basilica of Novara, a message arrived on her phone. Moving into the slow lane, she dropped down to fifty and read the text.

> Pity we didn't get better acquainted. call me
> if u need help in Paris. Until we meet again.
> Take care. Your faithful friend Moses xx

It was seven in the evening when she arrived at the Paris apartment. She was jittery from all the caffeine she'd been drinking en route and stumbled as she got out of the car.

As she heard the familiar sound of another text message arriving on her phone, she dropped her bag and looked at the screen.

> Welcome to Paris. I look forward to meeting
> you tomorrow morning at eleven am.
> Yours, Peter Delacroix, Greek Antiquities
> Dept. Waterbury's International Antiquity
> House.

9

Moses picked up the phone in his hotel room and dialled the seven-digit local number.

'Hello Maria, it's Moses Frank here,' he said, doodling a sketch of Tintoretto's Venus on the back of a copy of *Time* magazine.

It was a painting he always enjoyed re-creating, especially the peach-like breasts, which he knew well.

Maria came on the line and he abandonned his unfinished sketch.

'I know it's you, Moses – I haven't forgotten your voice,' she said.

Moses laughed. 'And how are you?'

'Since Peter came to see me I've felt rejuvenated. It's quite extraordinary, seeing him makes me feel so much younger,' she paused. 'He gives me some hope for the future.'

'Look, thanks for the information about his meeting with Isabella Green. It was very timely, as things worked out. There's more to Peter than meets the eye. I need to talk to you about his role in all this,' he said. 'When can I come over?'

Maria thought for a moment.

'Do you like eating?' she asked, laughing down the phone. 'Why don't you come for lunch? I've a talented cook from Corsica, Juliet. She's a pretty girl too, I'm sure you won't mind that, Moses.'

Moses arrived two hours later with a bunch of roses. Like all male visitors he enjoyed an exchange with Juliet, who showed him into the salon.

He hugged Maria warmly and they sat opposite each other on elegant nineteenth-century armchairs.

'You know, it's good to see you again. We've survived another quarter of a century whilst the world has been going nuts,' he said. Maria smiled.

'I remember the day you came to see me. I can see it clearly. You helped Helena get approval from the Sorbonne for her doctorate at the Temple of Apollo. And you did it. And then what happened?' She paused for a few seconds. 'Nothing, for all these years. We've had complete silence from the extraordinarily well-connected Moses Frank.'

Maria sighed as if the intervening time had been wasted. Her hollow face spoke of lost chances. Moses was beginning to feel guilty and played with his fingers in embarrassment.

'I could blame others. I won't. But maybe we *had* to wait for something to happen. Have you thought of that possibility?'

She twisted in her chair, puzzled by his comment. 'I don't know what you mean, but tell me, why has it been so difficult to get the Delphic Anomaly excavated from Delphi, Moses? I don't understand it.'

'I've a confession to make,' he said.

'You mean you've done it?' she asked.

'No, not quite. But I've been waiting a long time for something to happen, and now it has we can move on.'

'You speak in riddles, Moses. What do you mean?' she said, taking the bottle of whisky and pouring herself a double measure.

'I've been waiting for someone to be born and to become an adult. And you can't make these things happen.'

'Who exactly?' she said.

'Your grandson, Peter,' said Moses with a large smile. She beamed back at him as she heard his name.

'He's a shrewd and promising antiquities expert, I understand from friends at Waterbury's. I had a feeling he may be the man to save the Delphic Anomaly for us,' said Moses.

She moved closer to Moses and began to whisper. 'You do realise, he's almost certainly the love child of Helena – conceived at the Temple of Apollo, just a few metres away from the Delphic Anomaly? I'm a rationalist, but you can't ignore all those coincidences, can you?'

Moses looked up to the ceiling and shook his head. 'I believe you have to keep an open mind on these things. What's he like as a person?'

Maria rocked backwards and forwards in her chair before answering. 'He's bright, but a strangely obsessed young man. I like him, he's empathic and highly popular with women – a true charmer. But I think he struggles with his identity,' she said.

'But do you think he will help us?'

'Yes, I believe we could get him on our side, if we help him,' Maria said, her eyes shifting towards the door as she spoke.

Moses looked up as Juliet entered and asked if they would like to sit down to eat. They went into the dining room and Moses poured two glasses of well-chilled Sauvignon Blanc.

'So are you going to tell me, Maria, exactly what *is* his obsession?' Moses said, putting down his glass.

'He's convinced he's the result of Helena's hippy experiment. He's sure he was conceived at the Temple of Apollo, and not in Paris.'

'I suspected that was it. I suppose everyone has a right to know their father,' said Moses, standing up and inspecting the Chagall painting on the wall opposite.

'Why? It's not some God-given right. And in this particular family it could cause more harm than good,' said Maria.

'Will Helena ever reveal the truth about what actually happened all those years ago?' said Moses.

'No way, she's dead against it. She's convinced it will blow open a hornet's nest,' said Maria, hesitating. 'I don't think she even knows who the father is. And if it was some passing stranger in Delphi, it will be impossible to find him now.'

Moses tapped his fingers on the table. He could feel the clock was against them. 'Maybe you need to talk to Peter – and soon. He could be reminded of his family loyalties before he climbs into bed with Isabella, metaphorically speaking, of course,' said Moses.

'Your metaphor is apt – I wouldn't put it past him. In fact, I'd be surprised if he didn't try to sleep with the girl,' Maria said, nodding at Moses. He could feel the blood rushing to his face, he looked down to eat his food, hoping his embarrassment would quickly fade away. After a few difficult moments he managed to think of a new subject of conversation.

'I'd be happy to provide a sweetener. A few thousand euros, handed over in an envelope, can be quite persuasive,' he said, looking at his watch.

'He'd like that. The boy's always running out of money. Freelance life, you know. I'll call him,' she said. Moses looked at his watch again and signalled that he needed to go.

They kissed cheeks and Moses turned to leave. As he pulled open the door into the hall he found a woman crouching on the other side.

'My God! What a surprise!' said Moses. She looked at him briefly with an awkward smile and began to finger her red hair.

'Sorry, I didn't want to interrupt you,' she said breathlessly, covering her mouth as she spoke. 'Actually, I've only just arrived.'

10

'I need to talk to you, Moses. Can we go for a walk?' Helena said with a taut expression on her face.

'You're looking – how can I say, really wonderful, Helena,' Moses said, feeling slightly overwhelmed, as he eyed her up and down in the elevator, unable to believe how youthful she still was after all this time.

She was twenty-five years older since their last encounter, but after one glance he knew she'd lost none of her erotic power.

Every detail was coming back to him as they stood in the elevator together. The slightly open mouth, the high cheekbones, the discretely revealed neckline, and the close-fitting clothes

– they were the same as he remembered them, and began to trigger a flood of memories.

He smiled at her as he enjoyed having her close again, inside the tight confines of the elevator. She looked back at him suspiciously, trying to hold herself at a distance from him as they descended to the lobby.

They walked down rue de Rivoli and headed towards the Tuileries Garden.

Maybe it was the smell of the musky perfume lingering on her skin which triggered the associations. It didn't matter what caused his reaction – walking with Helena right next to him was both pleasant and uncomfortable for Moses. He struggled with his physical response to her, trying to make his body lose interest by naming the cars going past under his breath. But he couldn't stop himself undressing her inside his head, feeling her body.

The Tuileries Garden was celebrating Bastille Day with waves of white, blue, and red flowers, making up a giant French flag.

'So what do you do with yourself these days, Helena?' Moses asked as they sat on an oak bench overlooking a seventeenth-century fountain. Neither faced each other. Instead, their eyes stayed fixed on the water cascading from the fountain.

Helena didn't look happy, but Moses could see she was trying to put on a good show.

'I'm still at the university … and I continue to do research into the female orgasm,' she said.

Moses laughed and smacked his hands together triumphantly.

'Don't laugh at me, it's serious work, benefitting many women,' she said.

'So in the end the Sorbonne liked your risqué sex experiments at Delphi?' he said with a satisfied smile, remembering the painful conversation he'd had with her professor.

'Oh yes, my findings are now referenced in all the standard

textbooks, and they've been replicated under laboratory conditions. Fortunately, my supervisor kept the only copy of my PhD thesis and realised the potential. I was awarded a post-doctoral research fellowship and now I'm in charge of an international project which looks at the neuroscience of human ecstasy,' she said, as Moses grew increasingly curious.

Her crimson hair was now short, revealing more of her cheekbones and making her eyes look bigger than Moses remembered.

'How do you go about it?'

'Oh, it's all very scientific, but very straightforward really. We invite couples to our lab and measure their responses using MRI scans. We see what parts of the brain light up when women have orgasms and make many comparisons.'

'You've become quite an expert.'

'It's good news for women, and probably for men too. As I expected, the orgasm is accompanied by an increased blood flow to higher cognitive regions. As a consequence, an orgasm improves memory recall, speech, and deductive and mathematical reasoning.'

'So sex makes you smarter?' Moses said.

'Exactly. And you, Moses, must be a pretty clever man, given your sex life.'

'And you must be a very clever woman, considering your enthusiasm for having orgasms.'

'That was history, Moses. Don't assume anything about me now.'

'Well, look, I'm just pleased to find out I played a useful role in your career.' He paused to pick up a stick from the ground. Snapping it into several pieces he tossed each one into the air. 'And tell me – are you still married?'

'That's irrelevant. What gives with you Moses?' she asked

him, taking a cigarette from a packet of Gauloises and lighting it.

'Oh, I'm still doing OK. The world has not lost its appetite for antiquities. But you know, I still want to change the world. Maybe it's a bigger project than I first thought, twenty-five years ago. Perhaps that's why it's taking so long,' he said, laughing at himself.

'And how can you do that?' she said dismissively.

'I still have this stupid idea that I want to do something for posterity.'

'Still chasing the elusive Delphic Anomaly?' she asked, blowing smoke into the nectar-filled air.

'Sadly, yes. It remains as tantalising as ever, but I have new hope. It's the tree of life after all, it will have a meaning for everyone, everywhere. Maybe with the help of your talented son, Peter, it will finally happen,' he said.

She nodded, and there was a long silence before she turned to face Moses. 'So I gather you plan to bribe him?'

'That's ridiculous!' he said, shaking his head.

'Don't play innocent with me, Moses,' she snapped at him. 'I heard the conversation you had with my mother. I was listening to every word through the door.'

Moses put his hands up in protest. 'I think you've misunderstood. I would pay him a fee for his time, that's all,' he stuttered.

She stood up and looked down at him. 'Why do you want to harm me, Moses?' she said, and began walking away, leaving him sitting on his own.

Moses ran after her until they were walking side by side. 'How will it harm you?' he said.

Helena did not answer but stopped in front of a nineteenth-century statue of Marianne, the female symbol of France, the epitome of liberty, reason, and beauty.

'I don't want Peter to drag up my old lovers from the past, that's all. I've spent years working on a good stable relationship. Peter has a loving father who brought him up, why screw all that up?'

Moses began to realise she'd matured into a far more rational and level-headed person than the wild woman he once knew.

'But isn't it everyone's right to know the identity of their biological father?'

'No, Moses. There's no absolute rule. That's some ridiculous mantra floating around in your head,' she hissed. 'Sometimes the truth is best left hidden. Ask any good doctor about telling the whole truth. They know it can kill people. It can take years off lives. I know this knowledge won't do Peter any good. Nor me. I will stop it Moses, I promise you.' She stared straight into his eyes without blinking.

Moses listened without interruption. It was disturbing and eloquent. He'd forgotten how persuasive Helena could be, and how easily she could ignore the feelings of those closest to her.

She walked off and left Moses standing alone in the middle of the gravel path.

He couldn't stop his mind wandering back to the day she'd visited his apartment and took off most of her clothes to 'fast-forward' their relationship, as she put it. He knew there was zero chance of rekindling that relationship and walked back alone, through the Paris rain, past several Metro stations, and finally reached his hotel.

Their meeting had triggered a physical reaction in him. Her anger had made him want her more. An angry woman was a real turn on for him, and all the more satisfying when he'd tamed her.

His stomach was rumbling. Alone in Paris he felt hungry and

lonely. He saw a McDonald's and the gourmand from Vienna bought a double cheeseburger, eating it ravenously on the pavement, but throwing away the fries and half the bun.

Back at his hotel he saw two long-legged, short-skirted young women in the bar, plying their trade to businessmen. He thought of hiring one of these young escorts for the evening. He knew it would cost him the price of a good meal and an expensive bottle of wine, but he didn't care. The idea of a no-arguments, no-complications hour of sex was an attractive proposition after Helena's dismissal.

Night fell quickly as Moses walked into his room and switched on the TV. He was too lonely to feel like doing anything. He wanted his mind to be left blank for an hour. Later he might go down into the hotel bar, have a few drinks, check out the available women. If no one looked too promising, he could take a taxi to a gentleman's club and enjoy the naked dancing. A few ten-euro notes would buy him a personal lap dance. A couple of hundred euros would buy him sex with a young Polish prostitute. Five hundred euros would pay for an entire night. Was this what he really wanted?, he asked himself.

As he lay fantasising on the bed, his phone buzzed. There was a new text message waiting.

11

Moses smiled and read the text one more time.

> In Paris. Are you here too? Would you like to
> see me? AN

He'd had to think for several seconds to decode the initials.

Then he jumped from the bed and shouted at the top of his voice: 'You lucky bastard, Moses.'

Pulling open the door of the minibar, he unscrewed a miniature bottle of Bell's whisky – there was no brandy – and swallowed it in two gulps, each one separated by a brief moment to breathe.

The thought of Anna sent him into an immediate spasm of arousal, fuelled by memories of her long legs and pert breasts pressing against his face. His large fingers tapped out an unintelligible and surreal reply of inappropriate words as he tried to text back immediately. After several attempts, he managed to input his correct address.

> Come to Hotel Sierra, corner of ave Dupres
> and blvd Henri Piquet. Rm 5046. Call me
> from foyer.

He re-read the message and pressed 'send,' but immediately began to have second thoughts. Last time, when she'd visited him in Vienna, she'd admitted to having slept with the Pope's devil himself, Guillini, in exchange for entrance to the Vatican Herbarium. Moses couldn't quite believe she'd given her body in exchange for an old collection of plants.

Sitting by the minibar, flicking his fingers on a Stella Artois beer mat, he waited for her reply.

And what was she doing in Paris? Was she on another fishing trip for Guillini? He knew he'd have to be on his guard. He would limit himself to a couple of drinks and not allow his lust for Anna to overrule his common sense.

His phone alert sounded.

CU in 1 hour, Ax

He went down to the hotel lounge to buy two bottles of wine and waited by the window until her taxi arrived. A Citroen estate drew up after five minutes. The memory of her green Mohican still flashed in his head as she slipped through the swing doors. She was dressed in white and he noticed she had longer hair. As soon as she'd entered his room, he shut the door and locked it.

'You're looking sexy' he said, running his hand across her cheek, in the direction of her mouth. Her skin felt soft and firm, her tongue coming to life as his finger pushed its way between her lips.

She blushed and sat on the edge of the king-sized bed. 'I look after myself. I've been working out at a gym in Prague since I last saw you. I also went to India few months back and took a course in Tantra,' she said.

'Is it true what they say about this tantric yoga thing?' he said with a smile.

'Sure, it really works, it does help you have amazing sex, but you need to practise the techniques,' she said, getting closer to him and putting her fingers through his hair.

'You do need to keep fit for decent sex,' he said, stroking the hollow of her back.

'Oh, I still like to enjoy *indecent sex*,' she said, laughing.

His fingers reached the base of her spine. She shuddered and arched her back. 'I like that,' she said, unzipping the back of her dress. 'Let's talk afterwards, I want you now.'

'But tell me, how is the work with the plants going?' Moses said, his fingers failing to find her bra. 'I like this, there's nothing here to undo.'

'It's quicker to go bare,' she said.

Moses watched her slip easily out of her dress, revealing her bare breasts. She still looked young and vibrant, he thought.

'My work is blossoming, in every way,' she said, catching her breath as he kissed her nipples. 'I've re-discovered several species of plants thought to have become extinct. I'm finally doing the first trials with the Roman drug Sylphium. We're planning to grow half an acre in a field south of Naples next year.'

He looked at her with a puzzled expression.

'It was the miracle drug used by the Romans. The world's first contraceptive pill, anti-depressant and painkiller, all rolled into one. It was lost for two-thousand years until I re-discovered it in the Vatican Herbarium.'

'And which company is doing all this exciting work?'

'Nemcova Health – my own business. I've a few investors who believe in what I'm doing,' she said with a smile.

'Wow, you really have blossomed,' said Moses, his eyes wide, enjoying the sight of her naked breasts.

'A turnover of fifty-thousand euros last year,' she said, kneeling on the bed, fingering herself.

Moses caught sight of the silver chain around her waist. 'I'm glad to see you're not completely undressed yet,' he said.

'You'll like this, I bought it especially for you, Moses. It comes with a secret opening. Here, feel the *ouverte*,' she said, bringing his hand between her legs.

'I love secret openings,' he said. They kicked the covers off the bed and she lay on her back as he slid inside her. She quickly thrust her body upwards so he could push deep inside her. Anna was uncontrollable, squeezing and pushing him in every direction. Trying to keep her still for a moment, Moses pushed her legs together so she held him tightly, enveloping and gripping him as they lay as a single rigid body.

'I always feel you want to devour me,' he said.

'Is that OK? Do you like being eaten alive?' she said.

'It's fine,' he paused. 'No, my God, it's much better than that – it's wonderful. I love it,' Moses said.

'It's the memory of being consumed by you which brought me back to see you,' she said, as they held onto each other.

They turned over. She leaned backwards, rocking back and forth, but soon collapsed onto his shoulder, preferring the all-embracing contact of their two bodies pressed against each other.

The room was filled with a variety of cries, moans, and quiet screams as they arrived together. For a few minutes they lay motionless and quiet until Moses broke the silence.

'So tell me, have you kept to your word and not paid any more visits to the old rogue Guillini? I'd like to know you're not still engaging in that particular form of sado-masochism,' he said. She looked down for a moment.

'As I told you last time, I parted ways with him. It finished its course some time ago,' she said.

'Promise?' said Moses.

'Yes. I'm an independent force, free to roam where I want,' she said, spreading her fingers, one by one, across his chest. 'And you, Moses – are you still after that elusive Anomaly in Delphi?'

'Yes, I confess I am, but I've learnt to take the long view. As I've grown older, I've discovered something called patience,' he said, weaving his fingers through her long, silken hair.

She sat up and kissed his face.

'You know, you must make the Delphic Anomaly known to the world. Rescue it, exhibit it, make it famous,' she paused for a second and grabbed him with both arms. 'I'd be very proud of you, if you did that.'

'The problem is that it may cost me a fortune. And my freedom,' he said.

'Forget about making money for a while. You don't need it, it's become an addiction,' she said, laughing.

He took a deep breath and pondered her brutal verdict.

'But what about your prickly friends in the Vatican? Won't it make them angry? Piss them off, big time?' he asked, suspecting she'd recently been to Rome.

'Forget Guillini – he's all hot air. I think there's a different climate now with the new Pope. The Vatican is changing, the old crusade against the modern world is over. They've accepted the mistakes of the past and want to go forward. It's the only way to go,' she said.

Moses looked at Anna and shook his head. 'Funny you should say that. I take the opposite view. I've a feeling the Catholic Church will never change, even with this new so-called liberal Pope,' he said. 'The place is still riddled with superstition. It'll never shake off the old beliefs. It has to give the people what they want – masses and miracles.'

Anna wasn't listening. She was kissing his neck. 'So tell me, when are you going to start excavating the Anomaly?'

'I've waited twenty-five years. I'm not going to hurry for anyone. I've a plan, but it's too early to say. It involves recruiting a young member of the Delacroix family. He's almost ready. It will demand a great deal of him, but he has the personal skills which will enable him to do it.'

'What makes him so special?' she asked.

'He's driven by an obsession. He's the great-grandson of the archaeologist Niko Delacroix.'

'Is he on board yet?' she asked.

'Not quite. Almost. There are a few technical problems to sort out. I have to finish mapping the whole area so I can see how we can bring it out. We'll need a wider tunnel. The anomaly is quite a large beast to lift out of the mountain.

'When do you think you'll start?'

'Soon. I cant be any more accurate.'

Moses snapped his fingers. He was angry with himself and turned to face the therapist.

'I realised I shouldn't have told her so much. But she was bliss. I felt such a sense of physical release after we'd made love. It'd been building up all day, I had to do something about it. I was about to pay for sex with an escort when I received her message.'

He stood up and walked to the window. The summer flowers were in full bloom in all the gardens.

'How could I stop myself? The afternoon had been very frustrating with Helena. She'd wound me up and tightened me like a spring. Anna just appeared from nowhere at the right moment. She wanted to be with me. She was twice as sexy as I'd remembered her. I couldn't believe it, but she'd learnt to be a better lover. She was bolder and more extroverted in bed than anyone I can remember. Maybe it was the tantric yoga.'

'Did you believe her?' the therapist asked Moses.

'Maybe I'm naive, but how can a woman give herself so freely without being genuine?' Moses paused for a moment and looked down at the floor. 'That was my view anyway,' he said softly.

'Tell me something – do you love her?'

'I don't know. How does a man ever know the answer to that question? I've spent my life running away from any kind of commitment.' He moved from the window and paced the room.

'Put it this way – I believe it's possible to start having casual sex with someone, and for that sexual relationship to grow and evolve into something deeper. Yes, you might call the end result of that process "love".'

'Did you worry she wasn't telling you the truth about Guillini?' the therapist said, writing in her notebook with a pencil.

'She said she was no longer working for him, but I suppose it's possible everything I said was relayed to him. I didn't care in the moment, I was blinded by my impulses. But, yes, it worries me.'

12

As Peter arrived outside the stunning Waterbury's building he saw a throng of selfie sticks waving in the air.

Two large groups of Japanese visitors were jostling around, taking pictures of themselves in front of the curved glass atrium, their backs to the enormous desert palms growing to a height of sixty feet inside the cathedral-like building.

Peter walked across the Italian marble floor towards reception.

He looked around with amazement at the Las Vegas style recreation of the ancient world.

There were miniature models of the Acropolis, the Pyramids and the Colosseum, plus an entire Roman amphitheatre, complete with 3-D holograms of gladiators fighting each other.

A classical Greek fountain trickled into a pool glistening with Roman coins.

The Egyptian Sphinx dominated an entire corner of the reception. Next to it a mummified Pharaoh lay solemnly inside a stone coffin on desert sand, a life-like scorpion by its side.

Looking upwards, a trailing vine of passion fruits cascaded down from the mezzanine level – here were the Hanging Gardens of Babylon, set in an ancient fortress, surrounded by statues of the gods.

Two elegantly dressed receptionists, exuding the subtle scent of expensive perfume, sat at a wide ultramodern desk behind their Apple Macs, behind them the bronze busts of the Roman emperors Julius Caesar and Marcus Aurelius.

Above it all, enormous flat-screen monitors flickered away with a stream of video clips from recent record-breaking sales at the Waterbury's auction house.

To the right of the beautiful young women at the desk, neither of whom would have looked out of place at a French fashion house, was a glass-sided elevator, seemingly in constant motion, going up and down the side of the twenty-one storey building.

Peter introduced himself and the blonde receptionist stepped forward, greeted him enthusiastically, and led him to his new temporary home, located on the ground floor of the building.

She opened the heavy teak door of his office suite. Opposite the enormous desk was a deep leather sofa, wide enough for four people with a large TV monitor on the wall. She switched on the closed-circuit TV and selected the reception area for viewing.

'You can see when your guest arrives on this channel,' she said, checking the cafetiere was full of hot coffee.

From the small fridge she took a selection of fresh fruit and pastries and placed them on the table.

'You're all set Mr Delacroix. Let me know if you need anything. I'm at your service on extension 3535.' She smiled and closed his door.

He sat down to read the memos sitting on his desk and immediately his phone rang.

'Monsieur Delacroix, I have a call for you'

'Who is it?' he said, taken aback he'd been called as soon as he'd sat down.

'It's a Monsieur Moses Frank.'

'Sorry, not now, I'm expecting my guest very soon. Can you take his number so I can call him back this afternoon?'

At precisely 10.30 am Peter saw Isabella arrive. She parked in the guest car park by the front of the building. Through the CCTV he watched her walk through the revolving doors in a short black skirt as she approached the reception.

She was slimmer and taller than he'd imagined, maybe an impression created by her high heels. He watched her long black hair flow over her shoulders as she swept into the building.

On the security camera he could see her lips glistening as shafts of magenta light, streaming from the stained glass windows at the top of the atrium, illuminated her face. He followed her as she sat down to wait on the sprawling leather sofa in reception. A few seconds later his phone rang.

'Your visitor Ms Isabella Green has arrived. Shall I direct her to your office Mr Delacroix?'

'I'll come and meet her.'

She was sitting on the sofa, clutching a grey steel case when he arrived. She glanced in his direction and smiled nervously, as if uncertain who was standing over her.

'Mme Isabella Green, I'm delighted to meet you, I'm Peter Delacroix.'

She smiled and shook his hand quite formally.

'How was your journey from Delphi?'

'It was fine, longer than usual – I normally fly, but I didn't want to risk the safety of the collection getting mixed up with all the baggage at an airport, so I drove all the way from Delphi this time,' she said, breathlessly, as he guided her through reception and down the corridor into his office.

'It's a great pleasure to meet the person behind the name,' he said, showing her through the door.

As she sat down opposite him he tried to maintain direct eye contact, focussing intently on her face, without glancing down too obviously at the heart-shape of white flesh at the top of her legs, made partly visible by her somewhat short skirt.

The tantalising view of her seemingly bare crotch made it difficult to concentrate, no matter how hard he tried to direct his attention onto her collection.

'Can I offer you tea or coffee?' he said, trying to move onwards.

'A black coffee, and a glass of water please,' she said, slowly crossing over her legs, revealing herself again.

He wasn't sure if it was intentional on her part, even if only unconsciously, but she kept doing it and he was unsure how to respond.

Opening the fridge he took out a bottle of Evian water, placing it next to her with a crystal glass.

'So you've brought some items from your collection?' he said, pointing at the silver case.

She didn't answer for a moment.

'Tell me, Monsieur Delacroix,' she said, gripping the handle of her case and leaning forward, until she was sitting on the edge her seat. 'How did you gain your knowledge of Delphi's antiquities?'

'I took a degree in archaeology, specialising in the Hellenistic-Roman period, but long before that I'd made many visits to the ancient city of Delphi as I grew up. It became a passion for me. I was drawn to Delphi by the extraordinary story of the place. I visited again as a student – I even joined a dig led by your father.'

She wasn't expecting this information about her father and

moved guardedly back on the sofa.

'Look, I'd really like to see some examples of the collection you want to sell.'

'Alright Mr Delacroix, but can you assure me that this meeting will remain strictly private and confidential? I don't want any details getting into the press or other auction houses hearing about it,' she said.

'You have my word, not only as a professional antiquarian, but also as a representative of Waterbury's, whose integrity is undisputed worldwide.'

'Everything will stay confidential?' she asked, her face tensing.

Peter nodded vigorously.

'OK, no problem, I will take you on your word.'

She leaned towards him again and pulled open the case. 'Here's a typical piece of blue glass from the collection,' she said, unwrapping the foam packing material and holding up a semi-transparent azure vase, about fourteen inches in height.

'This is fifth century BC,' she said, placing it on the table. Peter gasped and realised that this was no ordinary collection.

One side was decorated with a line drawing of a young girl sitting on tripod, a pillar behind her, holding laurel leaves.

'The clarity of the colours and all the details are of such a high order, I've never seen such quality before. Tell me some more about it,' he said, turning it around.

'Come over to this side so I can show you the details,' she said.

He came to sit next to her and she moved closer to him.

'Judging by other pieces from Delphi,' she began, pointing at the girl, 'this is a representation of the Oracle, the young prophetess, known as the *Pythia*, captured here in a trance state, probably induced by chewing on the laurel leaves.'

She turned to Peter who was nodding and looking at her as

she spoke.

'I believe the laurel leaves are represented here. Look, they are unmistakable. Their shape is accurately portrayed. Some archaeologists have said that this vase was used to show how the Oracles put themselves into a trance by sitting in a certain spot in the temple, inhaling the gases bubbling up from the cracks in the rocks and chewing on the leaves.'

'Superb, absolutely beautiful,' Peter said. 'Everything is so clear, it's extraordinary. I've never seen anything of this quality before.'

'No, nothing like this has *ever* been displayed in public before. And look on this side.' Isabella turned it around to show Peter the engraving. 'Here is the unique palm tree motif,' she said.

Peter looked at its simple lines. 'Very unusual. Again, I've never seen this emblem used before,' he said.

Isabella placed the vase on the glass table in front of the sofa.

'Do you like it, Mr Delacroix?' she said, brushing a finger over his knee. 'Oh, I'm sorry,' she said, apologising for the physical contact.

Peter smiled.

'It's magnificent … I like it very much,' he said, stumbling over his words.

'So how much is it worth?' she asked.

'I haven't seen the whole collection, but if there are other examples as fine as this, they would be worth far more sold together than as singles. Valuers have a saying – there's safety in numbers. It would definitely have intrinsic provenance if there were more like this,' he said, wiping the perspiration from his forehead.

Isabella stretched down and unzipped her leather briefcase.

Peter sat there enjoying the sight of her slim body, her black hair falling off her shoulders. He was wondering what she would show him next.

'Would you like to see more examples? I can show you the rest of the collection on my tablet. Please wait a moment,' she said in a quietly confident voice.

Isabella placed a finger on the screen and summoned up a series of images.

'Look at these,' she said, taking an inward breath as she edged closer to Peter. Within seconds, forty-five pictures of vases and artefacts found at Delphi lit up the screen. Peter was mesmerised by the images and felt the warmth of her thigh next to his, though they were not quite touching.

'So that is the whole collection. They range from fifth century to first century BC. It has never been seen in public – you are the first to see it,' she said with a large smile.

'May I ask how you got hold of such remarkable pieces?'

'They belong to my father. As you may know, he was director of the Delphi Museum before I took over from him. It remains his private collection, but he has asked me to sell it now. He wants it to be appreciated more widely. It's a unique opportunity.'

'And where did he get it?'

'He was often able to buy things the museum could not afford for his own private collection over the course of many years,' she said.

'I see,' said Peter, quietly, a note of alarm in his voice. 'And do any of the individual vases have any known provenance?'

'Not yet. The problem is this is the first time anyone has seen them, so they've never been exhibited or catalogued.' She paused, placing a fingernail into her mouth. 'But does that really matter in this situation?'

'Look Isabella, I like your collection very much. It's one of the most beautiful things I've ever seen. But we may have a slight problem.'

Her mouth fell open and she looked at him with a rigid expression across her face.

'What do you mean?'

'It has no recognised history, no provenance.'

She sighed, leaned forward and crossed her legs again, looking straight into his eyes.

'But look Peter – can't you treat these antiquities as if they are totally new discoveries? They should be accepted by everyone because they come from my father's long-held private collection. Why not?' Her eyes welled up and she looked down at the thickly carpeted floor.

'You only need to catalogue them, surely, and that will create a provenance instantly.'

Peter smiled and stretched a hand to her knee, but at the last moment stopped himself.

'I wish I could do that, Isabella. But Waterbury's has a reputation going back 250 years. We have to work inside the law – they are very cautious about handling anything without a known history. Interpol are very concerned about stolen antiquities these days.'

'But my father has a worldwide reputation. No one would question his integrity.'

'If it was up to me personally I would take them on, but I know there would be many questions asked by the senior partners here.'

'What kind of questions?' she said, her mouth quivering.

'Why aren't they part of the Delphi Museum? How did they come into your father's hands? When did he buy them? Who from? Where are the receipts? Awkward questions like that, I'm afraid,' he said.

She was upset, her face became flushed.

'Look, it's not the end of the road. I may be able to help you,' he said quietly, moving closer to her and looking towards the door. 'I shouldn't really recommend a rival, but this avenue may be another way. There is a private auction house in Vienna, run by a Dr Moses Frank. A good man, I hear. I could get you an introduction.'

Isabella shook her head and put a finger to her eye to stem a small tear.

'It will be fine. You could still get a reasonable price, I'm sure,' said Peter, as she took out a tissue.

'I'm really frightened that unless they're sold at a public auction they'll go for almost nothing. There's no incentive to pay more at a private auction. There's no real bidding. In a real public auction people will be fighting over this collection,' she said, wiping her eyes.

'I must leave now. I don't want to waste any more of your time.'

Isabella carefully wrapped the vase in the foam, eased it inside the case and snapped it closed.

As she stood up, starting to leave Peter's office, she pulled out a card. It was printed with her address and a mobile phone number. She placed it on his desk and went to the door.

'Call me if you change your mind. I'm here in Paris until tomorrow. I leave at midday. I hope we can still do work together,' she said, turning around as she pulled open the door.

Peter felt himself go white. He realised no sale would be forthcoming from the meeting. He'd failed in his first assignment for Waterbury's.

'Hey, wait a moment, Isabella,' he called out. 'What are you doing later tonight? Can I take you out for dinner?'

'Call me in a couple of hours.' she said, and disappeared through the door.

13

Peter watched her through his office window as she drifted slowly into the car park.

Opening the boot of her Audi TT, she placed her case inside, slammed it shut and went to sit inside the car.

Her shoulders slumped, and her face stared blankly at the windscreen. After two minutes in her motionless trance he saw her drive off.

Peter decided it was time to leave the building. He wandered out of his office and through the glitzy reception, oblivious to the smiling receptionists, and strolled out, heading for the tabac on the opposite side of the road.

For the first time in a year he bought himself a packet of cigarettes and a cheap lighter.

He walked back to Waterbury's and stood in the car park. As he lit up and began to cough, he realised he'd totally forgotten the bitterness of tobacco smoke. He'd also forgotten the instant headache he used to get as the nicotine shot through the head. Stubbing it out with the heel of his shoe, he ran back into the building and threw the entire packet into the bin by the elevator.

He was desperate for caffeine. He walked down the corridor into his office, and poured himself a black coffee from the cafetiere. As he sat on the leather sofa his head was beginning to clear and he lifted the phone. In his hand was Isabella's card.

It rang for a long time, maybe a minute and a half, before an out-of-breath Isabella answered.

'It's Peter Delacroix from Waterbury's here. Look, sorry about earlier,' he paused for a moment, 'I've decided I must do something to help you. I've been thinking about your father's collection. I'd like to see more of it.'

There was silence.

'Hello Isabella, can you hear me still?' he said anxiously.

'That sounds good. OK, when can you come over here?' she said.

'It will have to be late tonight, I'm afraid. I've a family duty. Do you mind if I leave it until after 10.30?' he said. She was quiet for a moment.

'But why so late? I might be asleep by then,' she said.

'I have a difficult clash, I'm afraid. I must see my grandmother, she's been unwell.'

'I understand. Don't worry, we all have our family obligations.'

'I'm pleased you understand, I'm sorry it's so late, but I think we should talk before you return to Delphi.'

'I'll stay up for you. Come to my apartment, 9 rue de la Tour, off avenue Paul Doumer, in seizieme, near the Trocadéro.'

14

Peter ran into the elevator and pressed the private code for the penthouse. Twenty seconds later the doors opened on the seventh floor and Juliet was waiting for him, her arms wide open.

'She wants to see you now, she's been waiting a long time for you,' she said, holding his body against hers for several seconds until finally letting him go.

Before pulling himself away, he ran his knuckles down the hollow of her spine, squeezed her waist, and stroked his fingers over her right breast. It was the usual greeting.

'You'd better go in. I'll be here when you come out.'

As he entered the salon Maria gave him a beaming smile, stood up unaided, and steadily walked over to him.

'It's amazing to see you walking so confidently again.'

'I always feel better for seeing you, Peter – but where've you been all this time?' she said, stabbing at his chest with her swollen fingers.

'Oh I'm sorry, I started some new work today at Waterbury's – I couldn't get here earlier. Is my mother … I mean, is Helena also here?' he asked.

'No, she's gone out. We're all private now, we can talk freely.'

She looked up at him with an intense stare.

'I want to finish what I began to tell you a few weeks ago. Where did I get to? Can you remember?' she asked as they sat down on two large leather sofas, arranged opposite each other.

'You told me you'd been arrested in Delphi by the American security people, and you'd been sworn to secrecy for thirty years. I couldn't really grasp what was happening to you. It all sounded strange and unlikely,' he said. She nodded in silent agreement.

'It *was* surreal, Peter. As surreal as anything painted by my friend over there, Monsieur Marc Chagall.'

'You never explained why you were arrested in the first place,' he said.

'You're right, and I've decided it's finally time to reveal everything. I've nothing to lose now.

'In the 1980s there was an American President called Ronald Reagan. He was an old Hollywood actor. Anyway, after some madman tried to shoot him, he decided to consult an astrologer to improve his luck.'

Peter looked back at her, screwing up his nose and momentarily shutting both eyes.

'I can see you don't believe this, but yes, the President of the United States was consulting an astrologer, it was in all the papers. When the story hit the headlines everyone thought it had to be a joke, but it was never denied. And so people began to panic. They were worried that this astrologer woman might have her finger on the nuclear button.'

'And how did the President get to meet this astrologer?' Peter asked.

'I gather it was via his wife Nancy – she was interested in that kind of thing, apparently. And it was Nancy who also told President Reagan about the Delphic Oracle.'

'Really – how did that happen?' he said.

'Nancy had met the wife of the Greek ambassador at one of those Washington embassy parties. Nancy loved the story of the Delphic Oracle advising Emperors, Kings and Queens on major policy decisions thousands of years ago.

'This set her mind thinking. Knowing her husband was making a state visit to Greece, Nancy advised the President he should pay a visit to Delphi to seek answers from the Oracle for the major questions facing the world.'

'As crazy as it all sounds, I can see that if you *do* believe in astrology then the Delphic Oracle isn't really a million miles away,' said Peter.

'Exactly. And so it was all arranged. If the president asks for something, he gets. I understand it was one of the most secret events in modern history—'

'But wait a minute,' Peter interrupted. 'There hadn't been an Oracle for over two-thousand years. How could they recreate such a thing out of thin air? It would have been completely fake, wouldn't it?'

'You'd think so, yes. But the Greek government was bankrupt, as usual. It was desperate to obtain US aid so they decided to play along with it.'

'But it sounds completely crazy.'

'Not at all – the Greeks relished the idea, and they needed the American money. Once it was decided by the Greek Prime Minister that they should bring the Oracle back to life, a huge budget – by Greek standards anyway – was set aside for the event. They figured that if it cost them half a million dollars to recreate the Delphic Oracle for the US President it would be a good investment.'

'But how could Reagan have taken it seriously?' said Peter.

'Now this is where it gets quite interesting. Everyone who saw it happen was convinced that the prophetic powers of the Oracle were actually harnessed on the day the President came. It *was* remarkable, by all accounts.'

Peter scratched his head.

'But how do you know all this?' he said.

'I know because I was there. I saw it happen in front of my eyes.'

'You were there on the day?' Peter asked, tilting his head back in disbelief.

'It's why I was arrested. I was a volunteer on a dig taking place on the site. I'd always wanted to spend some time in Delphi, and noticed that they were looking for people to help on an excavation.

'On the morning of the visit I watched all the stretch limos arriving. The site had been shut early and the Temple of Apollo was covered with a great white tent. We were all ordered off the site and told to take the rest of the day off. I remember we were actually escorted out of the area by security people,' she said.

Peter listened and moved closer. Her recall of every small detail seemed highly convincing.

'We were overseas volunteers and I suppose they'd every right to ask us to leave the site. I'd heard the ceremony was not taking place until the night time. We hung around in the village and decided to go back later to take a look. When we did, we somehow managed to sneak back into the site through a small back gate.

'I knew the geography of the site well and we were hidden by a small underground arch, next to the temple, quite close to the action. It meant we could see and hear everything.

'As it got dark, we saw the lights of a huge helicopter circle over the Temple. It landed in the stadium, the place where the first Olympic games took place about three-thousand years ago.

'A few minutes later the President walked over to the tent, surrounded by the government officials, the Greek Prime Minister and all those kind of people.'

'But how did they keep it so quiet with helicopter landings and limos everywhere?' Peter asked, finding it hard to contain himself.

'There was a cover story. I remember the *Athens Post* had reported that the President was taking a short private holiday at a villa up the coast before returning to Washington.'

'And what about the Oracle herself? What did she look like exactly?' Peter said, keen to picture the young woman.

'She was a really beautiful young Greek girl, about nineteen years old, dressed in a white costume, leather sandals. I can still see her face to this day. she must have been a trained dancer.

'Behind her were the so-called High Priests, swaying in their white robes. She was singing the most lovely aria, accompanied by three young girls playing those small harps – lyres, they call them.

'At their feet I could see smoke or white gases swirling up from the ground. Probably just dry ice, but it looked quite effective.

'When the music stopped the young Oracle sat down on a three-legged stool, a tripod. The president smiled appreciatively and I heard him rather shyly ask her a question about his parents. He had a friendly voice.

'She couldn't have known the answer, I suppose. It didn't matter. She sat on her tripod and looked around for inspiration. I could see her huge dark eyes focussing on the President.

'He clearly liked her – she was pretty and sang like an angel. I saw him lean forwards as she started to sing. A priest came forward and interpreted the song. It was magic, but very Greek magic, with a bit of Hollywood special effects.'

'Did it work?' said Peter, biting his nails.

'The President looked very happy. He gave her a fatherly smile, picked up his notes and got down to the serious business of asking the Oracle some political questions, like what to do about China's nuclear weapons.

'I remember he asked her if the USA should build a missile defence shield around the earth, as if this young girl had any clue. But that wasn't the point I suppose. He must have believed that she was a channel to a higher being.'

'But did the whole charade work?' Peter asked again.

'Oh yes. The Greek government got its millions of dollars in aid from the Americans. Recreating the Oracle at Delphi was the best investment they'd ever made.'

'And what about *you*? What happened to you?'

'The security police found me, right at the end, just as we were leaving and I was arrested for spying,' she sighed. 'It was so stupid, really.'

'Can I ask you something?' Peter said, putting his arm around her shoulder. 'I feel flattered to be trusted with this knowledge of your secret – but why have you told me about this now?'

Maria took hold of his hand.

'Bless you, Peter,' she said, gripping his fingers. 'My life was changed because of Delphi. Every generation of the Delacroix family has become deeply entwined with that place. Your grandfather made his great discovery there, and he died there,' she said mistily. 'I have lived and studied there, I was a volunteer there, your mother researched her PhD there.' She paused and looked at him with a small shake of her head.

'And you, Peter ... you ...' Her voice trailed off into an embarrassed silence. She began to shake her head.

Peter froze, his mouth remaining half-open, waiting for her to finish her thought.

'And what about *me, grandmère?*' he whispered.

'... you have a great, yes, a great ...' she paused for a moment, she was stumbling over her words, 'a great ... fascination, that's it – a great fascination with Delphi. And not surprisingly.'

It was all too obvious to Peter that she was hiding something from him.

15

Although she'd read it several times before, Isabella looked at the text message again. She was alone in her apartment and had three hours to kill before Peter was due. It was her last night in Paris. Tomorrow she'd be driving back to Delphi.

The second and last phrase stood out.

> Call me if u need help in Paris. Until we
> meet, your friend
> Moses

It had been sitting in her phone like a get-out-of-jail card, only to be used if she was desperate.

She dialled the number and Moses answered immediately as if he'd been sitting there, waiting for her to call.

It reminded her of when she'd driven out of Delphi and he was waiting for her in a layby in his silver Mercedes. It was the start of nine-hundred miles of sweaty harassment as he followed her on the road to Patras, up the spine of Italy and across France.

His voice came through as if he was sitting next door.

'How are you, Bella?' Moses purred down the phone.

She was surprised to hear him call her 'Bella,' but accepted it. This was not the moment to make critical comments.

'I've been worried about you. Are you still in Paris?'

'Yes, I'm here in the 16th,' she said, and swallowed before continuing. She'd prepared a short speech in her head, but instantly forgot it as she heard his voice reverberate down the line.

'Look, this is difficult. I want to apologise ...' she paused to choose her words carefully, '... for abandoning you, at the hotel in Milan.' She stopped speaking to work out what she was going to say next.

'I had to get going early. I had no choice. You understand, don't you?' She twisted her hair around her fingers as she heard him laughing at the other end of the line. Looking at the crumpled scrap of paper in her fingers, with her list of 'things to do' scrawled on one side, she saw that no. 1 was 'say sorry to Moses.'

'So I want to say "sorry," Moses. Please forgive my bad manners. I was tired and upset and didn't mean to leave you like that. It was a childish thing to do.'

'Don't worry. I only felt a little hard done by for a few minutes, but I'd a feeling you'd be back in touch.'

Isabella breathed in deeply, relieved to discover she hadn't burnt her boats with Moses. She knew he was too good a contact to lose.

'Life's too short to bear grudges, Bella. All is forgiven, I was only trying to fulfil your father's wishes, you know that. So tell me, how did the long-awaited meeting at Waterbury's go? Was the young Peter Delacroix any help?'

'Not really. He was no good at all, that's why I need to talk to you before I go back home tomorrow.'

'What did he say to you?'

'He insisted that Waterbury's couldn't touch my father's collection because it has no provenance, just like you said. I suppose you're always right, aren't you?'

'I'd rather have been wrong, for your sake.'

Isabella untwisted the hair coiled around her fingers. She was reassured the man had a conscience.

'I want to ask you a favour. Will you reconsider my collection?'

There was a short silence. She gripped the phone and could feel the vibrations of her heart pounding inside her chest.

'I realise you need to raise some cash quickly, so I'm happy to take another look.'

She wanted to explain she didn't need money urgently, but decided not to quibble, it just wasn't worth the effort.

'When can you come over and take a look? I haven't got a lot of time,' she said.

'How about now? I can grab a taxi,' said Moses.

She gave him her address and he promised to be with her in less than half an hour.

16

Peter was blinking, trying to hold back a tear. He feared the worst.

'Was that the whole story you told me just now? Please, be honest with me – I must have the truth.'

'It's alright, you've nothing to fear. Let me reassure you Peter, you're connected to Delphi in far more ways than you think,' she said, trying to comfort him.

'What do you mean "connected"?' he said, sitting on the armchair opposite her.

'I know in my heart that fate has chosen you to do this, Peter. You're a very special member of the Delacroix family. You can't escape your genetic inheritance. I believe you're destined to find your great-grandfather's archaeological discoveries in Delphi and bring them back for the family.'

'But I don't understand. You say I'm connected to Delphi?'

Maria wrung her hands and looked at the ceiling.

'Tell me honestly Peter – how much do you know much about your mother's experiments in Delphi?'

Peter began to sweat and wiped his forehead with his sleeve. He felt his cheek quiver. Maria's question was unsettling him.

'My problem is that she won't talk about what she did in Delphi, or more to the point, what she was doing nine months before I was born.' He paused. He could feel the anger rising up through his body as his blood pulsed through his veins.

'She won't tell me who she slept with … I mean, the name of my real, biological father.'

Maria put her hand on his shoulder. 'It's a very personal matter. Maybe she doesn't know – have you considered that?'

'Are you serious?'

'Perfectly serious. Look, I understand how you feel, but I can see her point of view as well. Why should your mother tell you? It's her own affair, even if she does know who your father is.'

'But I need to find out if I'm the result of some hippy experiment. I want to know where I come from. I have the right to know these things, don't I?'

'No, you don't. Not if it destroys your mother. She's entitled to some privacy. Anyway, you are the person you are. You're an individual, you're Peter Delacroix – whoever your father was. Nothing can change that. If your biological father is intelligent, it won't make you any cleverer. If he's stupid, it won't make you a fool. You'll still be the same Peter Delacroix you were yesterday.'

Peter felt a fine layer of sweat forming on his face. He was shocked his grandmother was siding with his mother. 'Hang on—'

'No, let me finish,' Maria said firmly. 'Why destroy the relationship you have with the man who brought you up as his son?' she asked.

Peter looked at her with a frozen expression, as if she'd no understanding of his personal crisis. 'OK, he's a decent man, he's brought me up with affection, but the truth is he cannot be my father because I know I was conceived on the Temple mount at Delphi.'

'You will never know that for certain,' she said.

Peter leaned back and stared at her. 'But I know it in my heart. It's why I wanted to get back to Delphi as a small child. I can still remember finding my own way to the Temple even though I'd never been there before. I'll never forget that day.'

'And so what, Peter? What does it prove? All it means is that you can remember running away and finding yourself at the Temple. Every child can remember traumatic events like that happening to them.'

Peter bit his lip. He was taken aback she was not taking his side, but felt if he explained his ideas more fully she would side with him.

'We all have an instinct to return to the place where we were conceived. I've researched it across several different species. I've seen salmon fighting their way up rivers to do it. I've watched birds fly across the world to find it.

'It's all been established by biologists, but no one talks about it. They always call it something else, like migration or breeding patterns, because it sounds more scientific.

'But scientists can't explain it away by calling it something else. It's obviously a basic universal urge. I believe it's programmed into our DNA. No one can deny it – everyone spends a major part of their life looking for the place they were conceived. Can't you see that's what I'm trying to do? I can't help myself – I'm programmed to do this.'

Maria listened politely, but Peter could see she didn't agree with his theory. Her facial expression made it all too clear. Her eyes looked downwards, her mouth remained half open.

'What a charming but ridiculous idea,' Maria said, laughing out loud.

Peter slumped to the ground in front of her, his eyes staying fixed on her as he rolled over.

'No, let me rephrase that, Peter,' she said, getting down on the floor with him. 'Actually, I think it's a fascinating but highly provocative theory. Tell me, is there any scientific evidence for it?'

'Yes, there is. But as I said, it gets referenced as something else. No university would associate themselves with doing the kind of research that's needed. It's like telepathy or ESP.

'Normal scientific testing doesn't work with these phenomena. The results can change depending on who is recording the data.

It's the observer effect, it's a well-known problem in this kind of research, as well as particle physics.'

Maria asked him to join her to look down at the garden.

'I have an idea, maybe we can help each other,' she said. 'Whilst we may not agree on everything, I trust your instinct Peter. Go to Delphi. Trace the biblical relic which Niko discovered and bring it back home, for me and the Delacroix family.'

'That's a tall order.'

'It will change your life for the good, Peter.'

He paced up and down the wooden floor, stopping in front of her prized Chagall. After gazing for a few seconds into the blue and silver sky on the canvas, he turned to face Maria.

'If I go back to Delphi it will be to find my true biological father. If I can find the relics for you at the same time, that will be a bonus.'

She nodded.

'Let's keep talking, Peter. I still believe you're the right person to do this,' she said, giving him a kiss on his cheek as if he was about to leave. His lips were trembling as he tried to smile back at her.

Maria was looking tired and drawn. She'd expended a huge amount of energy telling Peter the story of her arrest by the Americans. As he walked around to stretch his legs he found himself looking at the old family photographs, carefully displayed on the walls and bookshelves of the apartment.

Something was bothering him as he studied each photograph. He went back and checked every image again.

17

They touched cheeks quite formally.

Moses wandered in and looked around at the opulent furnishings, the deep sofas, the tasteful décor, the mass-produced art on the wall. It had the soulless aroma of a place in which no-one lived and was occupied only on occasional visits to Paris.

He placed a bottle of chilled Tattinger on the glass table.

'Looks like you're dressed for some serious seduction, Isabella,' said a smiling Moses, enjoying the view as she reached up to look for champagne flutes in the kitchen.

'Oh, yes. I wore this to impress the young Peter Delacroix at Waterbury's, but it was wasted on him.'

'That's a shame,' he said, twisting open the bottle and filling their glasses to the brim. 'Is this your own place?' he asked, taking in the melange of scents rising from Isabella's warm skin as they sat down on the suede sofa. As he leaned forward to imbibe more of her perfume he noticed the red carnations sitting in a vase on the table.

'Quite sensual aren't they?' he murmured pointing at the flowers, to make the reason he was hovering close to her less obvious.

'They were here when I arrived. The cleaner brings them in. I've a friend in Geneva who lets me use this place, but I'd really like my own apartment. It would make sense,' she said.

'Well, maybe you'll have one soon, if we can find a way of selling off your father's collection.' He turned towards her as if he'd just had a brainwave. 'Look Isabella, I've a strong feeling we can help each other,' he said, glancing down at her neckline. 'How's your father since we last talked? I'd really like to know he's alright.'

'I'm not in touch every day, but as far as I know he's doing well,' she said abruptly.

'That sounds good. But why not tell me what's actually happened to the poor man? Why all the mystery?' Moses asked. There was no flicker of response on her face.

'When will he be returning to Delphi?' Moses said.

'Leave it now, Dr Frank. I don't know the answer,' she said sharply, dropping her glass on the carpet. The bubbling champagne ran across the floor and floated on the pile.

Kneeling down, they mopped up the spilt champagne with some tissues. As he faced her on the floor Moses could see she wasn't bothered about shielding her cleavage from his view. He helped her stand up and refilled her glass.

'You don't make it easy for me,' he said.

'Back off, Moses,' she said, pushing her hand out in front of her chest. 'Let's remember why you've paid me a visit. You promised to take another look at my collection, that's all. There's no other offer on the table. Nothing else is included. OK?'

'Alright,' he said slowly. 'Show me what you have.' She led him into the dining room where the fifth-century BC vases stood on an oak table.

Moses whisked out a magnifying lens from his breast pocket and held it up to the blue glass, pausing to focus on the palm-tree motif.

'I know it may sound strange but this symbol reminds me of the Delphic Anomaly. It's the palm tree shape all over again, isn't it?'

'But the Anomaly is shaped like a lamp, not a tree,' said Isabella.

'Precisely,' said Moses, 'and that's the point.'

'I don't get it,' she said.

'Do you have a scrap of paper and a pen?' he asked. She handed him a white envelope and her fountain pen. Moses held it lovingly in his fingers, opening it gently, and studying the eighteen-carat gold nib.

'I'm impressed. I like a classic writing instrument. It's the possession of a truly cultured person,' Moses said, rolling the steel barrel of the Mont Blanc in his fingers.

Pressing it lightly against the paper, he started to sketch a palm tree on the left side of the envelope. 'It writes like fine silk. What a sensuous pen,' he said, as he drew a second sketch – the seven fingers of the Delphic Anomaly.

'The next part is trickier. Maybe *you* can to draw it,' he said, laughing.

'I can't draw,' she protested.

'I think you can do it.'

'No, I can't – I'm useless.'

'Listen to me, I know everyone can draw. I've taught art. It's like music – we're all musical, but teachers often tell us we are not. Art and music are part of the human condition, we can all do it,' he said, handing her the pen. She took it in her right hand, uncertain where to start.

'What do you want me to do?'

'Draw the middle stage between the palm and the lamp. Imagine you're morphing the two images together.'

He watched her slowly draw the outermost branches of the

tree.

'Keep looking at the picture on the left and then look at the picture on right, so you don't stray off.'

Isabella drew eight branches and a thin trunk for her in-between tree. 'I'm done,' she said.

Moses looked at her drawing and smiled at her. 'I think you may be surprised,' he said. 'I think you've drawn the missing link.'

'How?'

'Look through the magnifying lens and tell me what you can see,' he said. She focussed on the tiny emblem etched onto largest blue vase.

'I can see the shape I drew.' She smiled at him. 'But how did you know what I'd draw?'

'You had no choice. I think we may have discovered the origin of the shape of the Delphic Anomaly. The design of the ancient lamp is no accident. It's one of mankind's earliest symbols,' he said, making a circle with his thumb and forefinger.

'I still can't see where you're heading with this,' she said.

Moses beamed at her. 'According to the old Bible, after running away from slavery in Egypt, the Children of Israel wandered through the desert for forty years, looking for a homeland. It's not surprising they chose the palm tree as their symbol,' he said, clapping his hands together in excitement.

'I still don't get it,' she said, repeatedly running her fingers through her hair in frustration.

'You've heard of the tree of life? The tree gives us food and shelter. It's a universal symbol.'

'OK, that was a great diversion Moses. But how does this affect the sale of my collection?'

'It means, my dear Isabella, that your blue vases and the Delphic Anomaly itself may well have a common origin,' he said, glancing at the iPad on the table. 'Can I just check something on your tablet?' She handed it to him. Moses put his finger on the screen and nothing happened.

'It responds best with a lighter touch, just like a woman,' she said smiling at him. 'You should know all about that, Moses.'

Moses rolled his eyes. 'OK, I can get over-excited and be a bit heavy-handed, but look – this could be a sensation.'

He typed Delphi into the search engine and the archaeological site zoomed towards him. He zoomed out to show its location within the Mediterranean world. Jerusalem was now in the centre.

'Look on the map at the distance from Jerusalem to Delphi, travelling across the Med.'

'OK, I see it.'

'Now look over here, in the Nile,' he said, pointing to an island near Aswan in southern Egypt.

'This is a tiny island called Elephantine, in the middle of the River Nile. It's where archaeologists discovered an ancient temple, just like the one in Jerusalem. What is extraordinary is that much of the life of the community that lived there was written down in the Elephantine Papyri.'

'And how old are the Elephantine Papyri?'

'Like your vases from Delphi, they date back to around the fifth century BC. So it seems this was going on at exactly the same time in both places.'

Moses measured the distances involved using his fingers as a tape measure.

'Extraordinary,' he said, quietly.

'What have you discovered?' Isabella asked.

'Look here, this is revealing – you can see it's not a lot further from Delphi to Jerusalem compared to the distance between Elephantine and Jerusalem. The distances are broadly similar.'

Moses smacked his hands together as a smile spread across his face.

'You know what this may mean, Isabella?'

'No, please tell me,' she said.

'We must auction your vases and the Delphic Anomaly at the same time.'

'I don't understand,' she said, screwing up her face.

'We can now propose that they may have been crafted by the same people, in or near Delphi.'

'I'll drink to that,' she said, and gulped down her champagne.

She stood up and swung her glass downwards to show him it was empty. Her speech was beginning to slur as she pointed a finger at him.

'But you're deluded, Moses,' she said, jabbing in the air at him. 'You don't even have the Delphic Anomaly. It's still stuck inside a chamber, under the Temple of Apollo, incarcerated in stone.' She stared into his pupils.

'You know in your heart that it will remain like that forever, don't you?'

Moses looked hurt. He felt a part of himself was being crushed by her words.

'You're wrong, Isabella,' he said, smashing his fist against the palm of his other hand.

'If I decide to do something, it happens, no matter how long it takes.'

18

Maria was watching Peter as he stood by the fireplace, searching amongst the faces in the family photographs.

'What's upsetting you so much?'

His eyes continued to scan the frames neatly arranged on the white marble fireplace.

'Where's Helena's father? Why is my grandfather missing from every picture?'

'You mean – where's my husband?' Maria said.

She was looking down, avoiding eye contact with Peter as she spoke.

'Yes, exactly – I've never seen a picture of him. I assume he died young and you never remarried, so I didn't ask … in case it was too difficult to talk about.'

'So you want to know the identity of your grandfather? Don't you know about him?' she said, biting her upper lip.

'Know what? said Peter, wiping the sweat off his forehead. 'I can't remember anyone ever speaking about him. So what's the truth?'

'I thought your mother would have told you.'

'I don't think she did. Why – was he in some kind of trouble? Did he walk out? Was he an embarrassment to the family for some reason?'

'You really want to know the truth, Peter?'

He looked nervously at her, wondering if he was about to be told a terrible family secret.

'Well, I think so.' He paused to think about it for a moment. 'Why not?' he said slowly.

'The truth can be painful,' said Maria in a soft voice.

'Just tell me, for God's sake,' he said, his voice raised.

She coughed to clear her throat. 'Alright, if I told you that I had no idea who he was when I bought the plastic bag of sperm from a woman in Lyon, would that bother you?'

Peter made a choking sound. 'You're joking, *grandmère*, aren't you?' he said.

She shook her head. 'No, I am not. I'm afraid that's the truth. Your mother's birth was the result of artificial insemination, from an anonymous donor.'

Maria shrank into the corner of the room and began to weep. After a few moments she began to speak again, in a soft and muted voice.

'All I wanted was a child. I didn't have a partner, it was the only solution.' She paused for a second and watched Peter wring his hands in despair.

'Peter, please don't hate me for doing this,' Maria whispered. She stood up, walked across the room to put her hand on his cheek.

'Not *you* as well. It can't be true!'

She shook her head.

'Look at me, Peter.' Their eyes met. 'It's no big deal these days. Society has changed. Thousands of births happen each year using artificial insemination with a donor.'

'You don't understand – it's about knowing who my father is, that's the problem.'

'I understand how you're feeling. But if I hadn't done it you wouldn't be here today. You wouldn't exist at all.'

19

Moses helped Isabella into an armchair and dragged his own chair closer to her. She'd drunk too much but he decided she was still capable of understanding him and placed a hand on her shoulder.

'Look, it's now up to *you*, Isabella. You hold the key to solving this puzzle.'

'But what can I do? I'm just a powerless young woman trapped in this ancient mess,' she said, opening her arms out towards Moses and staring straight into his eyes.

He shook his head.

'No, no, you're not so powerless as you think. You can tell your father to complete his part of the bargain – to excavate the Delphic Anomaly.'

Isabella shrugged. 'It's not possible. The truth is, Moses, he, he ...' she began to say, but she stopped herself.

'Go on, finish what you were saying. Tell me the truth, tell me what's really happened to him,' he said, withdrawing his hands from her shoulders.

There was a long silence as she sat there, tapping her thigh.

'Look, let's get this out of the way, once and for all ...' she said, speaking slowly at first. 'You can't rely on my father to do anything. End of story,' she said, gazing out of the window towards the Trocadéro Gardens.

'Is that because ...' Moses hesitated to say what was on his mind, 'he's actually ... dead?'

Isabella laughed out loud. 'Do I look like I'm in mourning?' she said, pulling her skirt down to cover the tops of her thighs.

'No, you don't actually,' he said with a smile. 'But has he had an accident? Is he paralysed? If so, I'd like to visit him –

take him something, a bunch of grapes, a restorative bottle of champagne,' said Moses with a mischievous grin.

'No, no, no. Don't be so stupid Moses, just accept the situation. My father is not available for visits, he's away. He'll be back at some point, but he wants to remain in his own private space for now,' she said, and sank back into the chair, breathing deeply, her eyes closed.

After staying silent for a few moments, she opened her eyes and leaned forward.

'I feel you're driving me crazy Moses, you're making me go round in endless circles. And I need another drink. Look over there, there may be some whisky or brandy, I think,' she said, lying back in the chair and gesturing at the drinks cabinet.

'Are you sure? You've had quite a few,' he said.

He found a bottle of Napoleon Cognac and filled a small glass, raising it to his nose to enjoy the bouquet. He offered Isabella a bottle of spring water, but she pushed it way.

'Don't make any assumptions about me. I'll have some of my own cognac as well, if you don't mind.'

'But don't you think you've ...' he began, but she didn't let him finish.

'No. I really like the way it dissolves my inhibitions,' she said, grabbing the bottle.

'Can we sit down together for a moment? said Moses. 'I'd like to ask you something which could make all the difference.'

He sat next to her on the sofa and turned to face her.

'I was wondering if you can recall a particular day from your childhood in Delphi? Do you remember the day when your mother went to Athens and you came running up the mountain, looking for your father?'

'Sadly, I can remember that day quite clearly. Why do you ask?'

'Can you remember the path you took up Mount Parnassus to reach the tunnel, the one leading to the chamber with the Delphic Anomaly?'

She rubbed her eyes and shook her head. 'I can't remember anything from that time.'

'But you just said the opposite. You know something Isabella, psychoanalysts say we never forget anything, please try to remember. It would be very helpful to know.'

'Fuck off Moses, stop asking me to remember that time,' she said, and began to sob.

'What's wrong Isabella?'

'You've no idea at all, have you? I don't want to be reminded of anything from my childhood. I've spent my whole life trying to erase all that.'

20

Peter left Maria's apartment and walked down Rayounard to get his car. Sitting in the driver's seat, he looked at his watch. It was 9.25pm, and there were still an hour before he was expected at Isabella's. He rang her number but she didn't answer.

He needed to talk to someone – he was feeling alone after his grandmother's revelations. There was a bar he knew off avenue de Lamballe, *Le Chat*, where he'd once chatted to an intelligent and sympathetic barmaid, an out-of-work actress, who worked there between acting jobs.

As he walked along rue Henri Fornier he saw the neon sign

with the black cat. He ran down into the basement cellar and she was standing there behind the bar, an attractive blonde in her mid-thirties – she had a very sexy mouth, he thought. She seemed to recognise him and gave him a pert smile as he walked towards her.

He ordered a glass of Cabernet Sauvignon, and sat on the barstool opposite her. She had one of those reassuringly happy faces – it's probably why casting directors used her as a young mother for washing powder commercials.

'Peter, isn't it?' she said. He smiled, pleased that she'd remembered his name. 'It's nice to see you again. I'm Adele, I think you may remember?'

He nodded.

'How goes it with you, Peter?' she asked warmly.

'So, so,' he replied, and took a large mouthful of red wine.

'You don't seem such a happy man tonight?' she said, glancing around the bar at the handful of customers. 'Would you like to talk to me? I'm not so busy,' she said with casual directness.

'Yes – I'd like that,' he said, trying hard to smile.

'Looks like you've something on your mind.'

'Oh, just the usual family shit,' he began.

She nodded as if she knew it well. 'So tell me all about it.'

'OK.' He paused to gather his thoughts. 'I've just been to see my grandmother. She's a tolerant woman, I've always liked her.'

'Because she's kind and wants to see you happy.'

'Partly true. She never casts any judgement on me. But today I discovered something about her past which made me think again.'

'What do you mean exactly?'

'Under her gentle surface, she has family secrets she's been hiding away,' he said.

'Bad things?' Adele said, placing a hand on her cheek.

'Possibly, I don't know. All I know is today she told me about something she's hidden all my life, and I was shocked.'

Adele drew closer to him.

'They like to carry around secrets, don't they?' he said.

'Who?'

'Women. My mother and grandmother. Why are whole chunks of their lives off limits? They won't talk about them. But it affects me, personally. They are about *my* life,' Peter said, gulping more of his wine.

Adele saw that the glass was almost empty and took the bottle of Cabernet from the rack behind her to refill it. 'You need this, I can see it's helping,' she said, pouring the wine.

'Tell me something – do most women walk around with secrets hidden inside their bras for their whole lives? Do they go to their graves with their secrets?'

'It's totally true. Women do keep more secrets than men, but that's a fact about society's prejudices, not about women.'

'What do you mean?'

'It's still not acceptable for women to talk about their lovers without shame. We think we are liberated, but we don't do such things. We are frightened of being called whores. We don't want to upset our men, so we pretend chunks of our lives never existed.'

'Yeah, that fits my mother, she's quite repressed nowadays – thirty years ago it was a different story. She was a hippy in those days, free love and all that – she'd have sex with anyone, no relationship was necessary.' Peter quickly swallowed more wine.

'I'm not even sure who my father is. I ask her but she's in denial about it all.'

'And how do you feel towards her about that?' Adele asked.

'I feel like a stranger, cast adrift, with no definite identity. I don't know where I belong. It's unsettling, but what can I do? She won't talk about it,' he said, and wiped his lips.

'My God, I shouldn't have said all that to you,' he added,

finishing the second glass of wine.

'Don't worry, your secrets are safe. I'll carry them around until I die, like women do!' she said and laughed. 'So why are you biting your nails?' she asked, looking at his hand.

He sighed and glanced up at the ceiling to avoid direct eye contact.

'You can talk to me about it.' She took hold of his hand. 'Look, I don't really know you, you don't know me – it gives you a licence, you can say anything,'

'OK, help me with my dilemma. My grandmother is begging me to do something for the family. A big task. It will take months of my time, and it could be risky. I want to help her, but … I feel torn about it after what she's revealed.'

'But why?' Adele asked.

'I'm not sure I trust her anymore,' he said.

Adele poured herself a glass of San Pellegrino.

'Screw your family. Break away – do your own thing. They had no concerns about the children they would bring into the world – you. That's the reason they're so secretive now about their past. They're feeling the guilt – you owe them nothing,' she said, opening a bag of chips and emptying them into a bowl.

'Enjoy life – eat some chips – stop guilt-tripping yourself,' she said.

Peter looked at his watch. It was 10.25 pm – time to leave for Isabella's.

'Thanks for listening. How much do I owe you?'

'The advice is free, the wine is ten euros.'

'See you again some time,' he said, placing two ten euro notes down on the bar and kissing her lightly on both cheeks.

'Don't forget, Peter.'

'What?'

'It's time to break away.'

21

'Can I tell you something?' Moses began to say in a quiet voice. 'Ever since I made the agreement with your father about rescuing the Anomaly, all those years ago, when you were just nine years old, not a day has passed without it taking over my thoughts.'

'You've become obsessed.'

'Maybe I am, but I know it will have a profound effect on everyone on the planet. Don't you see? It's the ultimate human story.' He paused to wipe his brow.

'What do you mean?'

'Look Isabella, I can't ignore a call from the tree of life, so I'm willing to pay any price,' he said, shaking his head.

'That's all very grand, but not everyone can afford to throw endless money at some ancient relic. Some people have bills to pay. My father's …' She stopped herself.

'What were you about to say?'

'Nothing,' she mumbled, pulling at her hair.

'OK, fine, I've made a decision, I'd like to offer you a special deal as an old friend of your father. I want to help you both out, I'll make nothing out of it,' Moses said. 'I'll put your collection up for private sale, in Vienna, at the same time as the Delphic Anomaly,' he said, pausing to refill his glass with brandy.

'Auctioned together, I believe they'll both fetch a very healthy price.'

She looked at him and shook her head. He could see she didn't believe him.

'Believe me, they will, and I will match the highest bid with my own cash – in that way I can keep hold of the Anomaly myself, to show to the world.'

She looked at him with sideways glance.

'But why? It sounds crazy. What if they fetch millions at your auction. You'll be made bankrupt.'

Moses clicked his fingers. 'It's not a problem for me,' he said, rattling off his words at high speed. 'And you'll receive a handsome price for your collection too. And the proceeds of the Anomaly will go to Maria Delacroix and her family, whose father originally found it.'

Isabella turned sharply to Moses, her face rigid.

'Did I hear you right?' Isabella stood up to look down onto him. 'The Anomaly money will go to the Delacroix family?' she asked, her body shaking.

Moses was taken aback by her reaction. He thought she would be pleased by the arrangement.

'Hang on, Isabella—'

'So my father, the man who discovered the Delphic Anomaly, will not receive a penny from its sale? Are you *really* saying this Moses? Really?'

'But why *should* he get anything? He wasn't the *first* to discover it. Niko Delacroix found it *years* before your father stumbled across it. And so his family are claiming it – quite rightly so.'

Isabella lurched closer to Moses, her lips trembling. Without warning, she spat in his face. The saliva slid down his cheek.

Moses stepped backwards and wiped it away with a tissue. He was getting used to her spitting, and in some ways admired her ability.

'That's my family's money,' she hissed at him. 'My father invited you to see it. Your great obsession ... no, your great *passion*, is a result of my father allowing you to see it, all those years ago.'

'That was twenty-five years ago. Everything's changed,' he said, shaking his head.

'But you made an agreement with him. You're trying to screw

us,' she screamed, and lunged at him.

As she tried to punch him in the face, he raised his arm to shield himself.

'Hey, calm down, the truth is he hasn't delivered,' Moses said, shaking his head. 'After all these years the Anomaly is still stuck under the Temple of Apollo. I'd call that a failure to honour his side of the bargain. A breach of contract.'

Isabella sat down again and put her hands to her face.

'I thought you were a man I could trust,' she said, lowering her voice.

Moses tried to put his arm around her shoulder, but she pushed him away. 'Here's a suggestion. Go and tell your father to get in touch with me and we'll talk about it.'

'I can't do that,' she said, pushing him in the chest.

'Easy now,' he said, holding down her arms so she couldn't move.

'No, I won't take it easy,' she said, her top hanging loosely off her shoulders as she pulled herself away from him. He could see she was no longer in control.

'Are you OK, Isabella?' he asked, knowing she wasn't at all OK. He realised it had been a bad idea to let her have the brandy.

'Just leave me alone and fuck off out of here,' she mumbled, almost inaudibly.

He went into the kitchen, filled a glass with water and gave it to her. 'I think you're quite dehydrated, you need to drink some fluids.'

She looked surprised by his gesture and gave him an uncertain smile. 'Come back Moses, I'm sorry I lost my temper,' she said softly, and he sat down next to her.

'I'm sure there are a few things we can agree on,' she said, undoing the button at the top of her blouse.

Half an hour later a weary Moses opened the front door to

leave. He was shaking his head and uttered a long sigh.

Gathering his thoughts, he decided to repeat his offer, now she was in a more receptive mood.

'As I said, I'm available anytime to talk through the details with you,' he said in a measured voice.

As he shut the door, Isabella's phone pinged with a new text message.

It was 10.25 pm.

PART FOURTEEN

Isabella and Peter

1

Isabella grabbed her phone. At the top of the screen a new message appeared.

> On my way, see you in five, Px

Isabella sniffed the air whilst looking around at the debris of her discarded shoes and clothes.

The room smelt of sex and cognac.

She went into her bedroom, found a bottle of Chanel, and sprayed as she walked through the rooms. A musky smell began to drift around the whole apartment. It was so intense that she had to open all the windows. It would take an hour or two to settle. As she walked into the bathroom she worked out a solution. She began to text.

> Ravenous. Let's go 2 eat. See you in 5 in lobby
> x

Her phone started ringing as soon as it was sent. Peter was already downstairs, waiting in the lobby.

There wasn't time to shower.

She looked at herself in the mirror, brushed her tousled hair and put on a clean bra. More perfume and cold water thrown on her face would have to mask the signs of her recent hook-up with Moses.

Peter was also hungry and she soon realised that, like her, he was also fairly drunk. They began walking down rue de la Tour in search of somewhere to eat. A few minutes later they were standing outside an expensive restaurant on avenue d'Iéna.

Over glasses of Pinot Noir, Peter explained his mother's earlier revelations.

'So tell me, why does it bother you so much that your father may not be your biological father? Must be quite common, no?' Isabella said, tearing apart a white roll.

'Can I trust you? Will you never repeat what I am going to say to anyone?' Peter said to her, anxiously staring into her large brown eyes.

'Sure, of course, Peter, I can promise that,' she said without too much thought. She could see something was making him edgy as he tapped his fingers on the table.

'I heard rumours that my mother did some strange sex experiments in Delphi in the year before I was born. She was a bit of a free spirit, I always had the suspicion she got pregnant with some random guy she met on the Greek mountains.'

Isabella looked at him with a smirk.

'Actually, I think I heard something about that, but go on. What makes you believe all this?' she said, picking up crumbs of bread from the tablecloth and putting them in her mouth.

'Since I was three I've always had the idea that I was conceived in Delphi. When I was twelve I found the evidence on my mother's bookshelf.'

'What do you mean?'

'It was weird and unexpected. My parents had gone out to the cinema. I was watching TV. It was the first time I'd been left in the house alone. I'd been waiting for it to happen for weeks.

'I walked up two flights of stairs and opened the door to my mother's study.'

'What did your mother's study look like?' Isabella said.

'Why do you want to know that?' Peter asked, surprised by her question.

'I've heard about her from my father. She once visited him. He met her when she first came to Delphi to do her PhD research. I got the impression that she was very passionate about her work. A strong-minded woman,' Isabella said, savouring the taste of the red wine on her lips.

'It's a relief to hear such things said about her. We don't get on that well, I've always found her difficult, as if I was an embarrassment – which only makes me more convinced I was the product of an experiment she did in Delphi.'

'But what about her study? I want to know what it was like.'

'OK It had two walls filled entirely with books – sociology, history of art and archaeology, the usual academic mishmash of soft science and social theory – and another wall filled with valuable paintings, including a beautiful Modigliani, a Dali print, and a few paintings she'd bought at galleries. In pride of a place was a terrible child's painting, some rubbish I daubed when I was at a nursery school, aged only three or four. It was complete shit, but she was attached to it.'

'She valued your work above the Modigliani,' Isabella asked.

'That's what mothers do.'

'Some do, not mine,' she said mournfully.

'What is she like?' asked Peter.

'A bitch. Left my father when I was nine years old to live with a younger man. I don't want to talk about her. So tell me how you made the discovery about your mother's sex life.'

'I stood looking at all the books and noticed, on the top shelf, a single volume without a title on the spine. It always struck me as suspicious. I sensed it might contain something bad, or sexy. I didn't know. I couldn't reach it, so I ran down into the basement to fetch a ladder.'

'So you took it down?'

'Yes, sure. I had this big book in my hands at last. I didn't know what I was opening. I saw the remains of the gold lettering on the spine had been rubbed off. She'd done it deliberately, of course.'

'I held it in my hands. I had a feeling it was going to be full of secrets. I began to feel hot and sweaty as I sat at the desk and opened the first page. On the inside cover were the words: "Doctoral Thesis, University of the Sorbonne, Paris. Helena Delacroix (copyright)." And there it all was – a scientific description of how she'd had sex by the temple of Apollo.'

'Did you really want to read this stuff about your own mother?'

'But it was a line-by-line description of my own conception. Wouldn't you?'

'But how did you know for sure you were conceived there?'

'She'd written down all the dates of the sex. I could work backwards from my date of birth, it was simple maths.'

'So how did you feel about it?'

'I liked it. I actually wanted to have been conceived on the marble floor of the Temple, especially during the re-enactment of an ancient sex ritual. It would explain everything – my need to keep going to Delphi, my unexplained knowledge of the ancient city.'

Isabella began to shake her head. 'I suppose it sounds more exciting than being conceived on a foam mattress in a suburb of Paris.'

'Absolutely, far more exotic.'

'But no, it all ridiculous, you can't be serious,' she said, as their soup arrived.

'Everything makes sense if I was conceived there.'

'But if that's the case, Peter, what's your problem?'

2

Moses sat down in a leather armchair in the hotel reception, searched for 'D' in his contacts, and pressed down on the phone symbol next to Maria's number.

It rang away for thirty seconds until a recorded announcement clicked in. It was the voice of her Corsican maid, Juliet. 'I am sorry that Madame Delacroix is unavailable to take your call,' it began, and rolled out the options to call back later or leave a message.

He had only a few seconds to decide on whether to leave a message before he started his drive back to Vienna.

After all the hours he'd invested in following Isabella across Europe, it was hard for him not to paint a rosy picture of the latest developments.

A Japanese businessman sat next to him. Moses stood up and walked over to a corner of the lobby to give himself more privacy. He heard the electronic beep at the end of Juliet's announcement and took a deep breath.

He hated talking to machines – he knew he was better talking to a live human being. He began to speak into the phone, covering his mouth with his hand so his message was not heard across the lobby.

'Hello Maria. I've some news about our mutual problem.' He paused.

'I believe everything is now fixed. She will stay on side. I believe Isabella will come to an understanding with us. I think she understands now that she should work *with* us, not *against* us, to recover the Anomaly. OK, that's all. I'm about to drive back to Vienna. Let's talk when I'm back in a few days and we can discuss the best way to keep Peter on side too.'

Moses pressed 'end' and the small picture of Maria's smiling face disappeared from his screen. He tapped his fingers against the phone case and wondered if he'd overstated his position with Isabella. It was too late now – his words were etched onto a piece of digital stone.

He walked through the revolving doors to find Sam standing outside by the Mercedes, parked in front of the hotel entrance.

'All cases packed?' he asked, and Sam nodded with a polite smile. 'Any thoughts on where we should make our stops?'

Sam opened a map of Northern Europe and laid it across the front of the car. In the bright sunshine Moses could see every detail without his glasses.

'I was thinking about Chalons en Champagne for a meal in about four hours and an early breakfast in Passau, on the banks of the Danube. How does that sound?' Sam said, pointing to the route with the tip of his pencil.

'You know me too well,' Moses said, and slid into the back seat.

3

Peter buried his face in his hands. Isabella looked on, unsure what to say.

'So what? I don't understand why it matters to you so much.'

'The problem is that the man who's always said he's my father is a fraud. He can't be my father. The dates in my mother's PhD thesis prove it. I want to know the identity of my real, biological father. Why not, for fuck's sake? Why can't I do that?'

'But what difference will it make to your life?'

'I just want to know, that's all. It might be important one day.'

'Relax Peter, it will never happen.'

'I'm sorry about this. I fear I've confused you, I've talked too much about myself. Let's change the subject. Tell me what's happened to you since we met at Waterbury's this morning,' he said.

She looked back at him, curling her lower lip.

'I'm exhausted. I've been fighting to get somewhere with the sale of the collection. It deserves more than your knee-jerk rejection, Peter.'

He held up his empty wine glass, twisting it round, as if he was about to make an announcement.

'OK, Look. I'm sorry for what I said this morning – have you tried calling Moses Frank, the guy with the private auction house in Vienna?

He can sell anything. He doesn't care so much about provenance, as long as it's an interesting item. Everything's sold in secret, so it's less of an issue. I'm sure he could help you.'

Isabella began to stir her coffee.

'Actually, I've ...' she began, and stopped to think how to describe her meeting with Moses. 'Been ... in touch with him,' she said, choosing her words carefully.

'Have you seen him?' Peter asked politely, holding his wine glass at an angle.

'Oh yes, I saw Moses quite recently. He's actually been in Paris,' she said.

'Did he come and visit you?' Peter asked. 'I'd like to know what he thought of your father's collection.'

'He was quite excited by it, pointing out a similarity between the collection and the Delphic Anomaly.'

'Any connection sounds most unlikely,' said Peter. 'The Delphic Anomaly was brought to Delphi by the Emperor Hadrian, it was a gift for the Oracle – how on earth does Moses link it to your father's collection?'

'He spotted an ancient symbol, etched onto my glass vases – the same shape as the Anomaly itself. He told me it represents the tree of life.'

She took out a crumpled page of paper from her purse and unfolded it.

'Sorry about my artistic talents, but can you see the connection?' she said, pointing to what she'd drawn earlier.

Peter studied her crude sketch and shrugged.

'I suppose it's plausible. It's a powerful universal symbol, it's been used in many cultures,' he said.

Isabella smiled, her cheeks softening with a sense of relief. She drank some water to soften her lips, reached over the table, gripped his hand, and pulled it towards her.

'I need your help, Peter. The Anomaly still needs to be excavated. Moses believes if we can put my collection on sale at the same time, it will be worth a fortune. Will you help me?' she said, focusing on his eyes.

'You're a Greek expert, you know the area of Delphi well,' she said, running a finger over his lips.

'I want to help you, but I'm not sure I can do that.'

'What's your problem?' she said sharply, letting go of his hand.

'I'm being pulled by my family in the opposite direction. I have a duty to them. They want me to help them find the Anomaly for themselves, to restore the Delacroix family name. They say my great-grandfather, Niko Delacroix, was crucified by his colleagues, and never recognised for his archaeological work. Finding the Anomaly under the Temple of Apollo will prove he was right all along.'

Isabella moved closer towards him again.

'Do you really believe in all that family shit?' she said, leaning over the table, sliding her fingers around his. 'Families fuck up lives. Sometimes, you need to stand back and see how they are destroying you. Say "no" to them, for Christ sake.'

'I suppose I'm quite involved with the family. Maybe I need to break away, you may be right.'

'Breaking away sounds like a good move,' she said, placing her fingers over his hands. 'Maybe it's time to be yourself, Peter.' She noticed a flicker of doubt in his eyes.

After glancing around the restaurant, she kissed his fingers and pushed three of them inside her mouth, biting them gently. He breathed in deeply, shutting his eyes for a moment.

'I think we should go back to my apartment now,' she whispered.

4

A clap of thunder sounded as they walked out of the restaurant, down a deserted avenue d'Léna, back to the apartment via the Trocadéro Gardens.

The charcoal grey sky flashed with white light as they reached the entrance to the gardens – a few seconds later a heavy downpour began.

'We're in the centre of a storm,' Isabella said, gasping as they ran through the warm rain.

After two or three minutes the rain stopped.

'I like the sweet smell in the air after it rains, it reminds me of the fresh sweat on a lover's skin after some really hot sex,' she said, running her fingers through his wet hair as they walked through the deserted gardens towards the fountains.

'Look,' she shouted at Peter as she climbed onto the low wall of the central fountain and lifted her dress to show the absence of any underwear. He smiled.

A faint wisp of her pubic hair dripped with fountain water from between her legs.

As he reached over to stroke her dripping pussy, she pulled him into the cascading waters. They both began to laugh uncontrollably as they stood waist-high in the falling waters, splashing around like drunken teenagers.

'Now we're baptised, we're ready for our final initiation,' she said, climbing out of the fountain. Peter looked back at her with a twist of his head, but said nothing more. Arm-in-arm they walked down avenue Paul Doumer towards the apartment on rue de la Tour.

The commissionaire begrudgingly let them into the lobby and they made their way to the elevator, water leaking out of their shoes onto the thick red carpet.

One floor up, Isabella unlocked the front door and walked into the bedroom. She sniffed the air, the scent of the perfume she'd sprayed earlier had disappeared, but rain had entered through all the open windows and the floors were soaking wet.

'You can take your clothes off in the bathroom, there's a spare robe in there,' she shouted, soaking up the rain with a towel.

He walked into the bedroom and found her sitting on the bed.

'We can continue our conversation now,' she said, placing her hand over his fingers and looking into his eyes.

'If I'm going to trust you, and work with you, I want to see you naked, nothing more. You understand me?' she said, untying her towel. She sensed him scanning her body as he leaned towards her. As his fingers tried to touch her, she jumped back.

'No, don't touch me, you've got the wrong idea, this is not about sex – it's about honesty, showing yourself for who you really are,' she said. Hesitantly, Peter began to untie his robe.

'What do you want from me, Isabella?' he said, folding his arms over his bare chest. 'You know, I don't really need to play your strange games.' He re-tightened his robe.

'I want to see the true Peter Delacroix. In the long term, I think I want the same as you, and I can see what you want now. That's not … hard to ignore at the moment,' she said, smiling at him.

'But look, I don't feel that's right for us now, we must keep it for later, when you've proved yourself to me,' she said, laughing, extending a hand and loosening his robe. 'Maybe we can work towards it.'

'And how do I prove myself to you?' he said, his body quivering.

'You go to Delphi and you bring back the Anomaly – that's all.'

'That's crazy. But OK, let's imagine I do it – what do I get, in return?

'I'll give you what you crave most of all,' she began, raising her head to look him in the eyes.

'And what you think I crave most of all, Isabella?'

'Look at me and I'll tell you.'

Their eyes met. He blinked and looked away. She could see it was too intense for him.

'That's better, I can see you properly now. This means I can say it and mean it. Here goes – I will give you the impossible.

Yes, the impossible.' His eyes began to flicker again.

'Keep looking at me. I can see it's hard for you to actually look a woman straight in the eye, but this is very important for me. The eyes are the gateway to the soul. Please don't look away from me again.'

'I *am* still looking at you.' He bit his lower lip. 'So what did you mean when you said you'd give me what I crave the most?'

'But don't you know? Surely, you know it yourself?'

'No, actually, I don't think I do. How can anyone ever know that kind of thing for certain? Just tell me, Isabella, for fuck's sake, and stop giving me such a hard time.'

She laughed, and stroked his hardened cock with her fingertips.

'But I thought you liked this. All men do, don't they?'

'Just tell me, it's no joke any more.'

'Alright,' she said, and placed her hands on his shoulders, sitting down on top of him, their faces inches apart.

'What you crave most, Peter, is your own father. So I will find your biological father for you.'

'Of course. And if I crave something else too? What most men crave?'

'And that. I will give you that as well. But you must deliver your side of the bargain first.'

She pulled him closer, pressing her breasts against his chest.

Kissing him, she pushed her tongue inside his mouth and began tapping her forefinger against his back. When she'd tapped ten times she pushed him away. He moaned and fell onto the bed.

'That's all you're getting for now.'

He lay there as she slowly put on her clothes, his eyes following her every move.

'Goodnight Peter. I think you should go home now.'

The story continues in books 2 and 3 of
The Moses Frank Trilogy, available from 2017.

Book 2: *The Delphic Anomaly*
Book 3: *The Astra Switch*

For full details see the Freewheel Books website
www.freewheelbooks.com

If you have enjoyed reading *The Elena Text* and would like a
half-price copy of *The Delphic Anomaly*, the next book in the Moses
Frank trilogy, sign up to the Freewheel Books newsletter on www.
freewheelbooks.com, or visit
www.theelenatext.net

Thank you!

Over the years that I've been researching and writing *The Elena Text* I've become indebted to many people who helped me, cajoled me and encouraged me to complete this book. What started as an idea inspired by a visit to the archaeological site at Delphi has grown into a complex and twisting thriller, now spanning three books – The Moses Frank Trilogy.

First and foremost, I must first thank my beautiful wife and lifelong partner Dr Lynn Maddern, psychologist and author, who I can remember encouraging me to start making notes in our Delphi hotel. Later on she read my early drafts, and despite that still encouraged me to continue writing. My son Joe and his partner Laura also gave me very useful feedback on my early drafts. At the same time I received some keen support and positive interest from Sam and Jasmine, plus large doses of cool advice from young Rob. Thanks to all of the above also for their advice on digital media and website production.

I feel I learnt a great deal from professional literary critic and author, Ashley Stokes, to whom I remain highly indebted. I must also thank my friend and mentor Bob Richards from Boston, USA – an avid and discerning reader of thrillers, who has been exceptionally supportive and given me a better understanding of the American way of thinking. Thanks also to my kind friends Robert Feather and Jeremy Josephs, both successful published authors who have been very generous with their advice, and my niece Katy Weitz, a bestselling author who has also helped answer questions on book promotion – a field in which she excels.

On the historical research side I must thank Professor Knut Kleve of Oslo, Norway, who expertly answered my naive questions on Greek mythology and the Delphic Oracle.

Above all, I must thank my copy editor Graham Clarke, who has an exceptional ability to assimilate and evaluate great quantities of detailed text, and Camilla Umar, who designed and typeset the book. They have both shown infinite patience with my revisions and corrections.

I am very grateful to many dear friends who have shown not only a polite but also an enthusiastic interest in my writing progress. They include Pete and Bron, my publisher friend John Adler of Pomegranate Press, my trainer Claire, and my favourite laughter-makers Roger and Liv.

Finally, I must make special mention of James Willis, the creative director of Spiffing Covers, who has not only designed an eye-catching cover for this book, but has also demonstrated the patience of Job in his ability to make a seemingly-infinite number of changes and amendments and still keep smiling.

Health warning: none of the above-mentioned, kind, and talented people are in any way responsible for any mistakes, omissions, or anything else considered to be wrong contained in this volume – these things are, I must confess, all my fault.

Martin Weitz, Bristol, UK
December 2016

www.ingramcontent.com/pod-product-compliance
Lightning Source LLC
Chambersburg PA
CBHW031051260626
47172CB00001B/18